The Mandate of Heaven

天命

Tim Murgatroyd

Myrmidon
Rotterdam House
116 Quayside
Newcastle upon Tyne
NE1 3DY

www.myrmidonbooks.com

Published by Myrmidon 2013

A catalogue record for this book is available from the British Library.

ISBN (Hardback) 978-1-905802-78-4
ISBN (Export Paperback) 978-1-905802-82-1

Set in 11.5/14.5pt Sabon by
Falcon Oast Graphic Art Limited,
East Hoathly, East Sussex

Printed in the UK by CPI Group (UK) Ltd, Croydon, CRO 4YY

1 3 5 7 9 10 8 6 4 2

INVERCLYDE LIBRARIES

Also by Tim Murgatroyd:

Taming Poison Dragons
Breaking Bamboo

For my honoured parents, Jim and Dori Murgatroyd

Part One

Pine, Bamboo and Plum

Hou-ming City, Central China. Spring 1304

one

天命

Hard ground loomed below the high boundary wall. Yun Shu dangled in mid-air, her legs tensed for a fall. Giggling made her wobble. It was like being a fly in a spider's web, except the threads holding her were friendly: Teng gripping one wrist, Hsiung the other.

'Faster!' she cried, swinging back and forth. Trees and ponds and walls in the ancient garden blurred.

'Jump!' urged Teng, his almond eyes wide and earnest.

'Can't hear you!'

'You're too heavy,' said Teng, 'you'll hurt yourself!'

'I like it!'

'We'll drop you,' grunted Hsiung, though he was strong enough to swing her by himself. Then he let go. See-sawing wildly, Yun Shu clutched Teng's hand until he, too, released his hold. She landed with an outraged shriek. The boys hooted as she rose, brushing twigs from her skirt. Two tousled heads vanished over the wall and their laughter faded into the trees.

Yun Shu took a moment to adjust to the silent garden. Earlier she had stalked crickets in dusty lanes, free to exclaim or sing or caper whenever she chose. At home different rules applied, like stepping from sunlight into a cold, bare room.

She glanced around for spies, aware she had been careless to make such noise. Golden Lotus hated noise, and while it might be tolerated from Yun Shu's older brothers, a girl should never draw attention to herself.

Wandering up the path, shoulders hunched, she did not notice the very object of her fears swaying towards her on exquisite, tiny feet – every step displaying the elegance and power of a lotus gait.

'Yun Shu!'

The willowy creature's make-up was a flawless white mask. Silver and jade hairpieces drew the eye to shiny coils of silken black hair and a figure as neat and pleasing as any fine lady's. The girl became conscious of her plump legs and unshapely body, her ridiculously long eyelashes and puppy eyes; most of all, her black hair that never combed obediently or stayed in its bun.

'Why are you scowling?' demanded Golden Lotus, in a high, singsong voice. 'How many times must I tell you? Smile and glide! Smile and glide as I do.'

Yun Shu bowed very low – she knew what happened otherwise.

'Youngest Daughter,' continued Golden Lotus, 'Honoured Father wishes to converse with you.'

A flicker of fear. Golden Lotus didn't use cultured words like converse, it must have come from Father himself. But the Provincial High Minister of Salt seldom noticed his daughter, let alone spoke to her.

She followed the swaying young man into the ancient mansion they occupied on Monkey Hat Hill. The area had a reputation as a haunt of scholars and other potential rebels. They passed tiny courtyards with neat gardens and closed doors; venerable corridors gleaming with wax and polish. Golden Lotus's four inch slippers squeaked slightly as he shuffled along.

He led the girl to Father's bureau, propelling her into the long room. At once Yun Shu started bowing. She knelt on the floor before Father's writing table. Salt Minister Gui, a pale, gloomy man with a wispy beard, somehow managed to both notice and ignore his daughter. An abacus clicked in his meaty hands, beads flying from side to side.

'Five thousand and sixty-three taels,' he muttered to himself. 'Twenty one thousand b-blocks at s-seventy-two cash.'

Golden Lotus remained by the door, cooling himself with a fan.

It was the first time Yun Shu had been invited into the bureau, though far from her first visit. She sometimes stole there when Father was away on official business – which was often – to read old books and scrolls.

'Ah,' he said, at last. 'Good!'

His eye crept down to a letter he had been reading when she entered. Yun Shu pressed her forehead to the varnished floor.

'Yes,' he said, clearing his throat. He peered at her as one might at a dubious underling. 'She's g-grown, hasn't she?'

Golden Lotus's white mask offered no encouragement. It had frozen around a demure smile.

'Quite right. Straight to b-business,' said the Salt Minister, awkwardly. 'Youngest Daughter, you're getting older. High time to b-be useful! You may have noticed ladies calling here over the past few months?'

Yun Shu nodded seriously, proud of her grown-up knowledge. 'They were matchmakers,' she replied. 'I think they came for Eldest Brother.' She hesitated then added recklessly, 'When I saw him last month there was fluff on his chin!'

The Salt Minister blinked in surprise to hear her speak fluently.

'Of course, you're quite wrong,' he said. 'It was you they wished to discuss.'

Again the abacus clicked. Yun Shu's long eyelashes fluttered rapidly. 'But Honoured Father,' she said, 'my ceremony of hair-pins will not take place for *years*.'

Five or six to be exact. So long she could hardly conceive becoming a woman.

'Never mind,' said Gui, 'the contract's signed and sealed. Now we must deliver!'

He looked to Golden Lotus for appreciation. The young man laughed, his painted red mouth open but making no sound.

While Yun Shu knelt dutifully, Father explained the contract in a dull, precise voice. A family of very respectable merchants in Chenglingji with extensive dealings in the salt trade were keen to secure his co-operation. They had even agreed to waive the dowry, a prospect of real advantage to the family.

'You see,' he concluded, 'everyone profits. Especially your b-brothers.'

Yun Shu screwed up her eyes to hide tears. 'Honoured Father, you have not mentioned who is to be my husband!'

He waved aside this question with clumsy fingers. 'A son . . .' He checked the letter. 'Ahem, not specified. It is the connection that matters. Do you understand?'

She nodded. Yet it was too sudden a change. To be ignored all her life then learn – years before she might reasonably expect it – Honoured Father had already arranged to get rid of her!

'There's something else,' he said. 'G-golden Lotus has agreed to ensure your feet are, as specified in the contract, no longer than four inches.'

Yun Shu glanced down. Her feet were already over six inches long!

'Do you mean to bind my feet, Father?'

'How else will they shrink?' He seemed genuinely puzzled.

'Grandmother's feet were not bound!' protested Yun Shu. 'Mother's were not bound!'

'It would have been better if they had been,' muttered Golden Lotus, fluttering his fan.

'Father, I'm too old! I don't want tiny feet! I don't want . . .'

Pain silenced her as Golden Lotus tugged her hair. 'It shows how much your Father loves you!' he whispered.

'Please, Father!'

The Minister of Salt's eyes narrowed. He clicked away at his abacus. Golden Lotus tapped Yun Shu on the shoulder with his fan to indicate she should leave.

天命

A hot wind made the bamboo groves on Monkey Hat Hill whisper and slur. That night a wave of monsoon rolled in from the east, black clouds billowing inland, connecting Six-hundred-*li* Lake to the dark sky with rods of rain. A million tapping nails on roof tiles, scratching, trickling, trying to find gaps.

Yun Shu slept badly, her dreams invaded by Golden Lotus bending her feet until bones snapped like twigs.

At dawn, she twitched and curled into a ball. Some animal instinct deep within noted the night rain had slowed. Rosy light glowed through the soft skin of her closed eyelids, stirring fear and urgency.

Yun Shu sat up in bed and cried out. Any day, perhaps today, Golden Lotus would begin the binding. After that? A lifetime of wretched hobbling. Compelled by a sudden hope, Yun Shu dressed swiftly and crept out into gathering light, birdsong, scented flowers and wet, impressionable soil. Soon she reached a secret hole in the boundary wall of the splendid house and gardens occupied by Salt Minister Gui. Her hope lay somewhere far less respectable: Deng Mansions.

Deng Mansions adjoined Yun Shu's home. It consisted of a large compound of courtyards and shabby wooden buildings surrounded by gardens wild as grass seed. Built on the same grand scale as the Salt Minister's house, it was topped by similar ornate, upward-curving red tiles. However, its wooden walls and doors sagged and several ceilings had fallen in on themselves.

Positioned two-thirds up Monkey Hat Hill, Deng Mansions

was one of a dozen houses formerly occupied by absurdly rich officials and merchants. That was before the Mongols put the entire city to the sword. Now, all the other great houses on the Hill were burned or abandoned. Only the Deng clan clung to their ancestral home. Monkey Hat Hill had gained a reputation for being cursed and few risked the taint of misfortune. As for Salt Minister Gui, he only lived there because no one was alive to charge him rent.

She found Hsiung and Teng in the weed-choked central courtyard. They stood side by side, emptying their bladders into a thorn bush, competing to see who could spray highest.

'I win again!' crowed Hsiung. He was tall and muscular for his age, whereas Teng's thin limbs suggested delicacy. Both had shaved heads topped with small tufts of black hair.

'I could eat a banquet,' said Teng, yawning. 'I bet we get millet for breakfast.'

Then they noticed her. Neither was embarrassed as they pulled up their breeches. They hardly considered her a girl at all.

'Why are you here so early?' asked Hsiung. Despite being a servant, he often spoke up before Teng, his master's son.

Breathlessly, Yun Shu told her tale of betrothal and bound feet. They sat on a decaying wooden step like a huddle of geese.

'My mother didn't have bound feet,' she concluded. 'She was a doctor's daughter from Nancheng. Mother told me my Grandfather called bound feet unnatural. If only she was still alive!'

'How old were you when she died?' asked Teng.

'Five.'

'My mother died seven years ago,' he said, tonelessly. 'Sometimes I see her ghost. Especially at night. But when I look again it's just shadows. She's never there.'

The children fell silent. Hsiung began to whack the earth with a stick.

'I wouldn't let any one crush *my* feet,' he declared. 'I want to be free to run wherever I like.'

14

Teng stirred. 'We must all obey our Honoured Fathers. Confucius wrote . . .'

'What if her father's got it wrong?' broke in Hsiung.

'We should obey our parents especially if they are wrong,' countered Teng. 'Otherwise you're wicked.'

'I don't want to hobble like a cripple all my life!' cried Yun Shu.

The boys fell silent.

'Will you help me?' she asked. 'You're my only friends.'

Teng grew suddenly enthusiastic, as he often did when inspired by noble notions. 'I know, let's be Yun Shu's *xia!* Her heroes! Hsiung, it's just like that book I told you about. The hero saves the lady and she stabs herself because he won't marry her!'

Hsiung liked the sound of that. They were interrupted by a voice inside the house: Teng's father, Deng Nan-shi, wishing good morning to Lady Lu Si. Perpetually forlorn and annoying, Lady Lu Si was the Deng clan's only other retainer, aside from Hsiung. Her position in the household was ambiguous, half honoured guest, half servant.

'Golden Lotus and Father will be at Prince Arslan's palace all day,' said Yun Shu.

'Meet us at the usual place in an hour,' offered Teng. 'Hsiung, we must remember to take our bamboo swords.'

Yun Shu escaped from the overgrown courtyard moments before Deng Nan-shi emerged into the sunlight with Lady Lu Si to receive his tiny household's morning bows.

天命

The two boys pushed through gardens choked with common shrubs where once rare orchids and dwarf trees bloomed. They reached the lofty brick wall dividing Salt Minister Gui's compound from Deng Mansions and scrambled nimbly to the top. Yun Shu waited on a stone bench beside a pool of anaemic carp. She glanced anxiously back at her home as the boys' faces bobbed over the wall.

'Yun Shu!' called Teng, softly.

With a final backward glance, she grabbed their outstretched hands and was hauled over the wall.

Monkey Hat Hill formed a wooded headland jutting out into Six-hundred-*li* Lake. High cliffs lined the headland so the lake waters lapped against boulders and sheer, vine-clad limestone precipices, home to nesting birds and troupes of silver-backed apes. It was here, amidst grassy lanes and ruined mansions, that the three friends usually played. Today, however, they had a new place.

Deep in the woods crowning Monkey Hat Hill, Teng had discovered the remains of a stone watchtower. He led them past Cloud Abode Monastery into the bamboo groves; they climbed steep paths until they caught sight of shattered stone defences poking through thickets. A family of apes shrieked and leapt at the children's approach.

The tower teetered on the cliff as though it might crumble over any moment. Dense bushes with glossy leaves and tight fists of pink blossom partially concealed the walls.

Much prodding with Hsiung's bamboo sword revealed an opening through the thick, ancient wall. Without hesitating, he wriggled into the narrow gap. Yun Shu went next, eager to prove she was brave as any boy. Teng adjusted his ragged scholar's robes and followed, warning everyone to be careful. Inside the children found an abandoned world.

The square interior was littered with scattered bones, mottled and cracked. Teng counted nineteen skulls. He picked up a shinbone, squeezing speculatively. Its softness reminded him of other bones he knew dated back to the Great Sacrifice. Perhaps these people had hidden in the tower, praying the Mongols would not find them . . . A sudden noise startled the children. Bird wings clattered.

'What do you think?' asked Teng. 'We could make it our Prefect's Residence.'

Hsiung stirred uneasily. 'Too many *bones*,' he declared, stamping on a rib cage. It cracked loudly like old twigs.

'Don't!' whispered Teng, fearfully. 'We must treat them with honour.'

Hsiung's sandal hovered over a skull. Reluctantly, he lowered it to the ground.

'Let's throw them over the cliff into the lake,' he said, 'otherwise it's their place, not ours. Anyway, something's been gnawing this one. And the walls stink of foxes or wild dogs.'

Foxes! Yun Shu glanced from face to face. Her own flushed with exhilaration to be out on an adventure.

'We should lay their souls to rest properly. With a rite,' said Teng, using a favourite word of his father's.

'You'll never bury them all,' said Hsiung, referring to Teng's crazy vow to make Monkey Hat Hill safe from hungry ghosts by burying decently all who had perished in the Great Sacrifice, nearly thirty years earlier. Otherwise, Teng argued, their spirits would roam forever, causing mischief to the living and – though he never mentioned it – especially to the Deng clan. Or what little remained of it. After all, his own grandfather, Prefect Deng, had issued the insane order that condemned the city to death.

'What do you know about *rites*?' jeered Hsiung.

'My father is a scholar of high purpose,' replied Teng, loftily. 'We Dengs know all about things like that.'

Hsiung fell silent, abashed by his friend's confidence. Teng's forehead furrowed. Yun Shu wondered what he would do. Then Teng chanted an ancient poem composed by Emperor Wu – one of a great many taught to him by his father – and scattered leaves and pink blossom over the bones:

Autumn wind rises,
Plump clouds burn,
Pine, bamboo, plum tree wither,
Geese fly south and north.

Yun Shu picked up the words. Her high, solemn voice joined Teng's while Hsiung watched, grinning. Wind made the bamboo groves on Monkey Hat Hill whisper and nod as though in approval. In the distance, snow-capped mountains glimmered.

天命

Everything was quickening on Monkey Hat Hill that day: sprays of bamboo, the feathers of young birds, water bubbling and trickling over stony streambeds. Yun Shu's fate, too, rushed towards her.

Late in the afternoon she returned from the watchtower to find a slender figure in the doorway of her bedchamber.

'Golden Lotus!' she gasped, breathless from running. 'You're back early.'

Whether by accident or design she did not kneel or even bow. His plucked, crescent-moon eyebrows rose a little.

'Where have you been?'

Gripped by sudden defiance, Yun Shu replied: 'I ran to the cliff and looked out across the lake and over the rooftops of the city. I saw mountains where the holy men live and I looked right across the lake, right across!'

They regarded one another.

'A lady never runs,' said Golden Lotus, suspiciously. 'That's what servants are for. Come with me.'

Salt Minister Gui's mansion had many unused rooms and corridors. Golden Lotus led her to a part of the house rarely visited except by rats and beetles. Here the chambers were thick with cobwebs and dust, lacking furniture or purpose.

One room in the centre of this maze had been transformed, its floor swept and walls washed. Two chairs had been set up, as well as a footstool and low table. On the latter sat a plain wooden box. A large bowl of clean water stood against one wall. On the opposite side was another bowl. Yun Shu detected a liverish, metallic odour in the room.

'Sit down,' commanded Golden Lotus, indicating the taller of the two chairs. 'Take off your shoes.'

'Please!' she cried. 'I promise not to tell Father if you pretend it didn't work!'

Golden Lotus shuffled over so his painted mouth was inches from her face. She trembled before his unflinching stare.

'I shall not pretend,' he said, forcing her onto the chair. When she tried to rise he slapped her face. 'And it will work!' he added.

Yun Shu hugged herself, tears running down her cheeks.

'I'll run away!' she cried.

'If you do I'll have you beaten and starved. And I'll make your lotus feet *three* inches long, not *four*!'

She subsided at this prospect.

'That's better,' he said, 'now sit still.'

Golden Lotus carried over the basin. The girl recoiled from its shiny, crimson surface. It was full of blood and herbs.

'Lift your feet. Lower them in gently.'

'But it's *blood*!'

'Of course, stupid girl! It will protect you from sickness. See how I take care of you.'

He knelt and forced her feet to soak in the concoction. Meanwhile, he fussed over an endless bandage. The liquid tickled at first but, after a while, the girl's heartbeat slowed: this was not so bad. He bent over the box and produced a tiny razor. Her terror returned. Did he mean to cut off her toes?

'Your left foot,' he commanded, 'then your right.'

Once the nails had been pared to the quick, he instructed Yun Shu to soak her feet again. They sat in silence. All the words never spoken or shared between them filled the bare room with loss. Her heart beat so fast she found it hard to breathe.

'Do you know how old I was when my feet were bound?' asked Golden Lotus.

Yun Shu did, though she knew little else about Father's flawless male-concubine. He often boasted that he had never cried or complained when his own feet were bound by the brothel keeper who bought him from his parents.

'You were seven,' whispered the girl.

'Yes, and that is a good age. Bones are soft then. There's less pain. But you are ten years old.'

Yun Shu waited. Surely some awful conclusion was coming.

'So, Youngest Daughter,' said Golden Lotus, 'don't curse me if it hurts. It will and it must. It *should* hurt. That way, on your wedding day, your new family will measure your four inch lotuses with a ruler and know you are a strong, obedient girl.'

'No!' cried Yun Shu, upsetting the bowl of pig's blood. Some spilt over the floor, spreading out thick, glistening red fingers.

She was silenced by another slap across the cheek.

'Stupid girl!' hissed Golden Lotus.

First the bandage, wide as her wrist and twenty feet long. Golden Lotus placed the end on Yun Shu's instep, still sticky with pig's blood, and ran it forwards, wrapping it round her toes. Then more tightly round the big toe. Only when the bandage was wrapped round her heel and the toes yanked down did Yun Shu cry out. Golden Lotus frowned at this early sign of weakness.

Now tighter round the ankle, tighter, pulling the toes down and back.

'Stop it! Please!' Yun Shu tried to rise. Struggle off the high chair. 'Please!'

Slap. Slap. 'You are ungrateful,' said Golden Lotus in his cold, singsong voice, all the while winding the bandage tighter.

'I am showing you a true mother's love. Unlike that ugly creature who gave birth to you. Her feet were as nasty as yours.'

Yun Shu shrieked in reply.

Slap. Slap.

Golden Lotus wrapped all the way around once, twice, then three times. A hot burning pain shot up from Yun Shu's foot, scalding every nerve in her body. Her backbone ached as though her entire self had lost its stem.

The pain became a haze. For a moment she no longer suffered in this deserted chamber, her leg pinned to the footstool by Golden Lotus's weight. She was skipping down the lanes of Monkey Hat Hill, bright birds singing and trilling all around, pink flowers turning towards her as she danced like a fragment of sun . . .

Then Yun Shu was floating up the Hundred Stairs that wound through the bamboo woods to Cloud Abode Monastery. Up there, the Nuns of Serene Perfection were chanting and Yun Shu longed to join them, melting into the woods and lake and distant mountains and music of birds . . . And she recognised a fearful truth, that her vision was a farewell, a dying, like being carried from this world to the Jade Emperor's Cloud Terrace where Immortals live forever and ever . . .

Agony split the vision open and she was back in the hated room, staring at pig's blood soaking into the floor while Golden Lotus's needle and thread worked busily, ensuring she could not loosen the bandages. Then it was time for her right foot. After that would come a stern command to walk, walk until the bones of her feet strained and bent like masts in a terrible storm, by some miracle not yet breaking.

two

天命

Hsiung lay awake on his blanket winnowing angry thoughts.

Yesterday he and Teng had returned to the watchtower after roaming Monkey Hat Hill, free as shadows, swishing bamboo swords like *xia* of old. Hsiung had gone in first and called out an all clear. When Teng followed he found the ground disturbed. Some of the bones they had buried so carefully dug up. 'Foxes or wild dogs,' muttered Hsiung, 'told you so.'

The boys had lounged on thrones of fallen masonry, chewing liquorice roots, pretending not to be afraid that the animals would return.

'I discovered this place on the anniversary of Mother's death,' Teng announced, suddenly.

'Do you remember her?' asked Hsiung, sullenly tapping a skull with his thick, bamboo sword.

'Not much. Father says she was beautiful and noble.' He sighed. 'Truly, we Dengs are the most tragic family in Hou-ming Province. At least, that's what Lady Lu Si says. Father is compiling a history of our ancestors, you know.'

Hsiung threw a stone over the cliff edge.

'I know nothing about my parents,' he said, 'not even my family name.' The servant boy leaned forward. 'I bet my ancestors were as good as yours!'

Teng smiled at such an outlandish notion. 'Unlikely.'

'Is it?' pressed Hsiung. 'People take out lucky charms when-ever you or your father pass by. They say you Dengs are cursed.'

'Common rabble! Traitors!'

'My ancestors *are* as good as yours,' maintained Hsiung, less certainly.

'You mean *were* as good. Well, I know better!'

Possessed by some demon that lived in the old watchtower, Hsiung leaned over and grabbed Teng's throat. 'What do you know about my parents? What do you know?'

'I . . . Let go!'

'Your father told you something, didn't he?'

'Y-you're choking m-me!'

Abruptly Hsiung had relaxed his grip. Stalking from the watchtower, he left Teng rubbing his bruised throat, gasping for air.

In the hour before daybreak birds sang in ones or twos. Hsiung dozed on his blanket, digesting grievances. Only the sound of mice in the eaves and his soft breathing disturbed the room.

Perhaps the birds were noisy that summer dawn. Perhaps that was why he rose earlier than usual. The fact he did, Hsiung later realised, changed the course of his life.

Soon he was blowing on wood chips until embers glowed and the kindling took flame. Hsiung took pride in his work, he was good at fires. Then he wandered out to the well where the winch creaked as he hauled up a bucket of cloudy water. After a while it would clear, the fine mud and sand settling. Yet if he shook or agitated the bucket it became cloudy again.

Hsiung remembered yesterday's quarrel with a pang of guilt. It was all Teng's fault. Anyone would have got angry after hear-ing his ancestors insulted.

He watched the bucket clear then kicked it, reviving the white clouds of swirling sediment. Was Teng a friend anyway?

True, he rarely put on airs, but he was still his master's son. Sometimes, when Hsiung bullied Teng into helping with the chores, he knew it was to punish him for being of higher birth.

Yet after their quarrel in the watchtower, Teng had tried to make peace, explaining excitedly that a hungry ghost had temporarily seized control of Hsiung's two souls, his *hun* and *po*, and that the ruin was a dangerous, cursed place.

Hsiung still suspected Teng knew more than he was saying. Once, Deng Nan-shi had dropped a hint about a soldier – and an uncommonly valiant one – being his father. When pressed the thin-faced scholar's reply had only deepened the mystery. 'You'll get your inheritance,' he said. 'In the meantime, see if Lady Lu Si needs help in the kitchen.'

Hsiung shook the bucket less violently. Again clouds swirled. He wished Teng's throat hadn't been the one he'd grabbed. It occurred to him that once mud is poured into pure, bright water it can never be quite filtered out. If nothing else, a bitter taste remains.

As he returned to the kitchen, Hsiung heard dragging feet, gasps of pain.

'Yun Shu?'

Her former bustle had gone. She dragged her plump body across the uneven ground of the courtyard with the aid of a fallen branch, wincing over each step.

'What's happened? Who did this?'

Before she could answer, he understood. Her bare feet were stained with dried blood and purple-blue bruises. Shreds of grimy bandage hung loosely from her toes. A hot, baffled feeling took him. 'Sit down! Here!'

He helped her to the brick wall round the well. She was clutching a bag of clothes. Tears stained her cheeks, yet she did not cry as she told him about the room with the bandages. How she had used a knife to saw through the bindings. A troupe of monkeys arrived, scurrying across the rooftops. Their watchful, bobbing faces formed an audience. When

Yun Shu finished, Hsiung frowned, unsure whether to wake Teng.

'You must hide,' he announced, more confidently than he felt.

'But where?' she asked. 'Here?'

Hsiung looked round. There was no shortage of empty rooms in Deng Mansions. She seemed to read his thought.

'This is the first place they'll look,' she said.

Hsiung nodded. 'We must go somewhere they don't know about. If you have the strength.'

The Hundred Stairs leading up to Cloud Abode Monastery were steep. Especially burdened by a hollowed gourd of water and Yun Shu's bundle, as well as her weight on his shoulder. Each step made her gasp and cling to his arm. Halfway up, he examined her.

'Do you want to go back?'

'No! Not until . . . No!'

'You're sure?'

'It will be easier in the woods,' she said. 'I want to go on.'

Dawn had hardened into day when they entered the bamboo groves round Cloud Abode Monastery, following a barely discernible path. Yun Shu sobbed as she stumbled. The glinting waters of the lake showed through the trees and the ruined watchtower came into view.

'Nearly there,' urged Hsiung.

She had no strength to reply. They reached the crawl-way into the tower and Hsiung peered at the sun. Old Deng Nan-shi and Lady Lu Si would be wondering where he was. Most likely the fire for Master's tea would have gone out.

'Yun Shu, I must go back. They'll be suspicious.'

'Don't leave me!'

'I'll come back. You're safe here. Your feet can mend here. When your father realises you'll never surrender, he'll . . .' But Hsiung did not know what Salt Minister Gui would do. He felt the girl's large brown eyes upon his back as he hurried away. When he turned to wave, she had vanished into the crawl-way.

A little way further into the wood he paused. Was that Yun Shu's voice calling? The cry sounded urgent. He could not tell whether it belonged to human or bird. Meanwhile the sun would not stop climbing. He descended the Hundred Stairs two at a time, for Hsiung knew Yun Shu's father would find his way to Deng Mansions all too quickly.

天命

Morning passed in its usual way. Lady Lu Si pretended to sweep the entrance, occasionally staring into space and clutching the broom so tightly her knuckles whitened.

Lady Lu Si had been the favourite concubine of Teng's grandfather, Prefect Deng, when Hou-ming fell. Her survival that terrible day could be blamed on her exceptional beauty – or disloyal refusal to leap off the cliff with the other concubines. After the Mongols finished with her she was too broken in spirit to do more than curl into a ball. It said much about Deng Nan-shi's forbearance that he allowed cowardly Lady Lu Si to stay in Deng Mansions as an honoured servant.

The two boys were busy ignoring each other when she approached with her twig broom. Still graceful, she bowed respectfully to Teng.

'You must help scrape the vegetables,' she told Hsiung.

An ugly flush crossed his sullen face. 'Horses in the lanes!' he cried. 'Riders! They must be Mongols!'

Lady Lu Si shrank back. Picked at her bony hands. The broom clattered to the floor. Her careworn mouth trembled. 'I . . . I really must . . . I really must!'

'Don't be afraid, it's all right,' said Teng. 'Hsiung's just joking!'

She had already fled into the house where she would hide all day, weeping and sighing, her only comfort an amulet given to her by the Nuns of Serene Perfection from the monastery up the hill.

Hsiung pretended to whoop with delight. Before Teng could utter a reproach, he ran whooping and jeering into the lanes that led down Monkey Hat Hill to the old Ward Gate, and thence into the city.

Deng Nan-shi ate his usual lunch: a small bowl of rice and vegetables. Today the hunchbacked scholar did not leave the house to teach the basics of writing and reading. His pupils were the sons of men who, before the Mongols, would have grovelled to a Deng.

Instead he searched through chests and boxes in the library for family documents. What he sought was apparently a great secret, for when Hsiung poked his head in upon his return from the city, the scholar hurriedly hid the scroll he was reading. This interested the boy, though he had never bothered to learn his characters and found the entire inky business tiresome.

Moving down the corridor, Hsiung located Teng in an abandoned bedchamber he called his 'study', diligently copying poems from an old woodcut book. Hsiung watched, deciding whether to mention Yun Shu. She would need something to eat soon, which was partly why he had risked sneaking into Hou-ming. Noticing him, Teng smiled. 'Lady Lu Si has left her room,' he said. 'She told me to tell you that she is very grateful for the steamed buns you gave her. And the peonies.'

Hsiung decided not to mention he had stolen both gifts. The penalty for theft was a hundred strokes of the bamboo.

'Don't you get bored of writing?' he asked, to change the subject. 'They say the new Emperor can't read or write yet he rules the world.'

'He's not a real Emperor. He's a barbarian.'

Hsiung had no clever reply to such assurance. 'Yet the Mongols rule everywhere,' he said, doggedly, 'far beyond the Middle Kingdom.'

'One day they won't,' said Teng. 'Father says their rule is . . .' He struggled to remember the right words. 'Inept and unjust.

He says the Mandate of Heaven will be taken from them.'

Hsiung's reply was a harsh braying laugh: 'If the Mongols came here you'd hide behind your chair and wet your trousers! Waving brushes at them is no good. Me? I'd wave a sword!'

'You're always bragging,' said Teng. 'You'd hide like everyone else.'

'No, I wouldn't. I'm not afraid. Not of them or even Salt Minister Gui!'

'Why do you mention him?' said Teng. 'He's no Mongol, just their servant.'

'Wouldn't you like to know?'

Teng returned to the poem he was copying.

'Well listen to this!' said Hsiung. 'I've hidden Yun Shu in the watchtower so they can't crush her feet. *That's* how afraid of him I am!'

Teng's brush hovered above the paper.

'Hidden her?'

'You said we should be her *xia*, her heroes!'

Teng wiped the excess ink off his brush onto the mixing slate. Holding it delicately between finger and thumb, he swirled it in a small bowl of water that turned grey. Hsiung remembered the bucket he had filled with cloudy water that morning. His friend's hands were shaking.

'You've hidden her in *our* watchtower?'

'I'll show you,' offered Hsiung.

He was prevented by the arrival of strangers.

'Through here!' called a gruff voice.

Teng rose and stepped behind his chair, dragging it towards the corner. But Hsiung maintained his stance near the doorway. A burly man appeared. He wore his robes loose in the heat, revealing a bare, hairless chest covered with tattoos. A sword hung from his belt and he carried a short two-pronged spear. Hsiung recognised him as one of the Salt Minister's hired bodyguards. It was unwise for an official in the Salt Bureau to travel without protection. Salt provoked endless thirsts and grudges. He examined the boys impassively. Only Hsiung returned his gaze.

'Something here!' called out the man. He was joined by another mercenary with a halberd.

'Take them to Master,' ordered this second soldier.

Aware that running away would excite suspicion, Hsiung followed.

They found Deng Nan-shi still in his library. Except that now their neighbour, Salt Minister Gui, occupied the scholar's high-backed chair while its owner knelt before him with a bowed head. Hsiung glanced swiftly at Teng, who had flushed with shame.

'Your Honour can be sure we know nothing of your daughter's disappearance,' Deng Nan-shi was saying. 'We live quietly here, in strict obedience to the Great Khan's laws.'

Salt Minister Gui reached for an abacus hanging from his belt. He frowned and gripped it tightly.

'Let us hope so,' he said. He leaned forward and waved a pointing finger. 'I have heard about you!'

The hunchbacked scholar smiled modestly.

'I have heard,' continued the Salt Minister, 'all about your father. B-because of his pride and vanity this city is like a g-graveyard. Is it true?'

The kneeling scholar lifted his head and met the Salt Minister's eye.

'I fear you may be right,' said Deng Nan-shi.

'I've also heard,' continued the Salt Minister, 'one of your ancestors was no less than the illustrious General Yueh Fei. A name loved by rebels!'

'He was indeed my revered ancestor,' said Deng Nan-shi, quietly.

'How strange! Look at his g-great household now! A spine-less scholar, two scrawny b-boys and, oh yes, a madwoman.'

Lady Lu Si had begun keening and moaning in the next

room, having curled herself into a tight ball that refused to open, however hard the Salt Minister's men prodded her with halberd butts.

'Your Excellency is well-informed,' said the grey-haired scholar.

'I am. I am. So, as I say, let us hope my daughter is *not* here.'

Deng Nan-shi sighed regretfully. 'Your Honour has already searched . . .'

'Just remember,' interrupted Gui, 'inform me. At once, I say!'

With that he rose. Deng Nan-shi remained on his knees. When the official had gone he met the boys' frightened gaze and raised his eyebrows.

'See if you can discover his daughter,' he said. 'It seems she's disobedient in the matter of binding her feet. Because she shames him, he feels compelled to shame us.' Deng Nan-shi chuckled scornfully then went off to comfort Lady Lu Si.

'We're done for now!' moaned Teng. 'You heard what Yun Shu's father said. They'll slave us and ship us across the lake to the Salt Pans.'

'I thought we were her *xia*,' replied Hsiung.

'She has put us all in danger! Can't you see? Everyone hates us Dengs!'

The panic and distress in Teng's voice could not be ignored. 'I don't hate you,' said Hsiung, 'and neither does Yun Shu.' He struggled to think of another, and then his face brightened. 'Neither does Lady Lu Si! So that's three people!'

They sat at the foot of the Hundred Stairs, afraid to venture further in case Gui extended his search to the bamboo groves.

'I shall visit her at dusk with water and food,' said Hsiung. 'You can come, too.'

Teng's eyes flickered. 'Oh, I'll come,' he muttered, 'I'll come.'

The sun crawled from east to west. For reasons neither could explain the boys kept within each other's sight. Teng even helped to prepare the family dinner of millet and steamed greens. As was his custom, Deng Nan-shi ate in solitude and contemplative silence. Lady Lu Si had recovered sufficiently to dine behind a painted screen, lest she make an indecorous noise with her chopsticks. All the while crickets chirruped excitedly and dusk drained the passing day.

The boys stole to their secret hole in the garden wall. Glancing back, Hsiung saw the faint glimmer of his master's lamp in the library as he sifted through the family archives.

'Have you filled the water gourd?'

Teng nodded.

'Then let's go.'

They crept up a steep path running parallel to the Hundred Stairs. It was gloomy in the bamboo groves at this hour. Even the monkeys had fallen silent. A deep, ancient calm lay across the Hill, but as they approached the watchtower both boys halted, straining to hear.

'What is it?' asked Teng.

Cries for help were drifting from the direction of the cliff. Hsiung surged forward, leaping through the twilight, slashing aside plants with his bamboo sword. Nearer the watchtower they heard the snarl and growl of a wild animal. Unmistakeable now, Yun Shu's cries for help. She sounded desperate, as though she had been calling in vain for a long time. Birds circled, disturbed from their roosts. Further down the hill a troupe of apes began to shriek.

Hsiung sensed what was happening within the ruined walls – walls that no longer protected but trapped. There had been signs: scraped earth, fox scents, gnawed bones . . .

He hesitated, looked for Teng. The scholar's son hung back fearfully. Easy to melt into the shadowy groves, join his friend and run back down the hill. Then Yun Shu screamed out Teng's name and Hsiung's own. The snarling animal answered furiously, yapping and growling.

The boy gripped his bamboo sword with both hands and dived

into the crawl-way through the bushes. A moment later he was on the other side of the ruined wall. There could be no retreat.

The fading light confirmed his guess. A nest in the earth was occupied by yelping puppies; and standing over them, a frightened mother, a large red wild dog, leaping up at the ruined staircase where Yun Shu cowered, just beyond the reach of its snapping, yellow fangs.

For a long moment boy and dog surveyed one another. Hsiung saw the mother would never abandon her pups or allow Yun Shu to leave without a savage attack. They were trapped. Just as the people had been trapped in this stone square when the Mongols came.

'Aiee!' he bellowed, leaping at the wild dog, bamboo sword raised above his head.

Perhaps the creature did not expect so sudden an attack from so small a human. It shrank back. Bamboo smashed onto its skull. At once it rolled away, twisting to leap at the boy.

'Hsiung!' wailed Yun Shu from above.

He did not hear. The creature had fixed its jaws round his calf, worrying, biting. In fury he stabbed down with the end of the bamboo onto the top of its head. Again, again. Abruptly the slavering jaws, foaming pink with his blood, loosened. The wild dog's head fell back. Hsiung wobbled and almost collapsed. Blood was trickling from his leg.

He lurched back onto a pile of masonry, still gripping the bamboo sword. Glancing round, he realised Teng and Yun Shu were on either side of him. As adrenalin left his body waves of pain followed. The girl wept hysterically, telling a story he could barely comprehend, 'When I came here this morning I found the puppies! I tried to warn you but you'd gone. Then the mother returned from hunting. For a long time she wouldn't enter. Then she grew desperate to feed her puppies. That's how . . .'

Ignoring her, he turned in wonder to Teng. 'I killed it!' he whispered. A deep exultation opened in Hsiung's soul like a clenched fist unflexing strong fingers. A hand discovering its force, power. 'I killed it!'

天命

Teng splashed Hsiung's leg with water from the gourd. A bandage torn from Yun Shu's spare clothes staunched the wound. Once the bleeding had slowed, Teng put an arm round his friend's shoulders.

'Yun Shu,' he said, 'see what trouble you have caused! Go home! And do not mention our names.'

The two boys watched her. She was kneeling by the dead mother and the mewling pups.

'Did you not hear me?' demanded Teng.

'No,' she whispered, tears still wet on her cheeks.

'What do you mean, *no*?'

Hsiung had never seen Teng so angry. It made him want to laugh in a dizzy, exulted way.

'All you think about is yourself!' cried Teng. 'Do you intend to live here forever? Where will your food come from?'

Yun Shu sat back on her heels, one hand resting on the dead dog's warm body. 'There must be a reason.'

Teng examined her in disgust. 'You're mad! Go back to your father. He scares me! Just make sure he leaves us in peace.'

'There must be a reason, Teng,' she repeated, tears welling again. 'It is fate! It is the Dao!'

At that word of power they became aware the wind was rising. Bamboo groves swayed and muttered. Sighs like mournful ghosts swept the cliffs.

'It is the Dao,' she repeated. 'Can't you hear it?'

Teng stepped back, alarmed by the restless wind.

'You are mad and selfish,' he declared. 'I found this place, not you! I forbid you to live here and I am no longer your *xia*.' He turned to Hsiung. 'Let's get home before they catch us. We must hurry.'

In the shock of his injury and triumphant pride, Hsiung felt no desire to argue. Leaving Yun Shu bent over the wild dog's corpse, they struggled into the thickening darkness. Hsiung's blood-stained bamboo sword turned from weapon to crutch. He leaned on Teng's shoulder for the slow, painful walk home. Half way down the Hill it was necessary to hide. A dozen men with burning torches were climbing the Hundred Stairs, prodding the undergrowth with spears, calling out Yun Shu's name.

three

天命

The pups whined and crawled around the dark interior of the tower as Yun Shu knelt beside the dead mother. Warmth left its body. All she could do was wait until morning.

Yun Shu took a deep drink from the gourd-bottle: the water tasted earthy. Hsiung had also bought some steamed buns which she ate hungrily. Then she froze. Voices out in the bamboo groves, calling and whistling to the rhythm of sticks threshing the undergrowth. She winced her way to the crawl-way and peered out through leafy branches. Lights in the wood, flickering red demon eyes moving methodically towards her. Yun Shu pulled the concealing foliage tight and wiggled back, stifling a cry when she stubbed a tender, bruised toe.

In the dark ruin she felt the panic of all trapped creatures. Was it best to flee before they reached the tower? Or remain hidden? Her feet were too damaged for a swift escape.

Yun Shu gingerly ascended the round stairway and crawled into a corner. Too late she realised the water-gourd and pile of clothes remained in full view: anyone peering into the tower would spy them immediately. By now voices surrounded her; she even picked out words.

'Here's the cliff. If she's gone further she has wings.'

'Hey, P'ao! What's that hole?'

Yun Shu tried to merge with stone.

'Some animal's been digging,' came the reply.

'What about this tower? Perhaps the little bitch is in there listening.'

'Hush! Master might hear.'

'How? He's dining at Jebe Khoja's while we search for his precious daughter. That's how much he cares about her.'

'I've heard Jebe Khoja likes to invite Golden Lotus to dinner along with Master.'

'Ha! Ha! You're bad!'

'Who's this Jebe Khoja?' asked a new voice with a strange accent.

'Only Prince Arslan's favourite nephew. *And* Deputy Governor of the Province. You can be sure Master will rise alongside him.'

'I didn't agree to this kind of work,' said the new voice, crossly. 'What kind of man can't protect his own daughter?'

'It's not his fault she was taken by rebels.'

'*If* she was taken. Maybe she ran away. The maids say she isn't afraid of anything and disappears for hours at a time. I've heard she even reads her father's books when he's not around.'

'What about this tower?'

Their torches flickered beyond the walls and she sensed them staring up at the ruins.

'Nothing here,' called P'ao. 'Let's tell Master.'

'Not yet,' suggested another. 'Wait for a while on the Hundred Stairs. That way it looks like we searched longer.'

So saying, they left. Yun Shu listened until their noise faded into the sounds of a wood at night.

The puppies had instinctively gone silent at the sound of human voices. Now, in their hunger, they mewled once more. Yun Shu descended to the lowest step and arranged her spare clothes as bedding.

What use was it to stay here? Teng was right, sooner or later she would be forced home. The longer she hid, the deeper her disgrace and Father's anger. Yet as Yun Shu hugged herself on the step, gazing up at the clear night sky, she thought of Immortals floating through patterns of stars. Then she remembered another occasion she had slept out beneath stars, in an open river junk bound for Hou-ming and Father's wonderful new appointment as Salt Minister. She'd been just four. Her mother was already thin and pale with the nameless disease that killed her not long after Golden Lotus became Father's concubine.

Yun Shu stared up at the constellations, longing to hop across them like stepping stones. She had read in Father's books that invisible threads connect night to day, river to land, moon to stars, earth to water. For the first time she understood properly. The Eternal Dao joined all things.

This odd thought comforted her until she fell asleep.

天命

Doves were perching on the tower's jagged walls when Yun Shu woke. She stretched and winced. Yet her feet no longer felt aflame. Though purple and blue, they were already mending. She massaged her toes in the dull light of an overcast morning. The pale sun was higher than she had expected. In her exhaustion she had slept late. Yun Shu heard boots tramping in her direction.

'Is this the place, boy?'

Sergeant P'ao's voice! Yun Shu ducked fearfully before accepting the futility of further concealment. No, she would not be found cowering or dragged out. Instead she crawled out into the sunlight and tottered upright.

At that moment Salt Minister Gui turned the corner of the tower, carried in a sedan chair by two sweating porters. Behind him, escorted like criminals by Father's soldiers, came Teng and Hsiung. Last of all, the hunchbacked scholar, Deng Nan-shi.

Yun Shu tried to find Teng's eye but he evaded her. She

became aware Father was gripping his abacus with white knuckles.

'Cover your feet!'

She struggled to her knees and bowed, trembling.

'Is this where you hid her?' he demanded, turning to Hsiung.

Hsiung said nothing, his face blank.

'Sergeant P'ao, if he does not answer, hit him!' commanded the Minister of Salt.

'Your Excellency,' broke in Deng Nan-shi, 'my son has already explained. A stupid child's game, that is all! They could not imagine the upset they were causing.'

'A g-game?' snorted Gui. 'Then I hold *you* responsible.'

Hopping from foot to foot, Teng cried, 'Father didn't know! It's our servant's fault. I warned Hsiung . . . Oh, he never listens to me! But I found the tower and showed it to her. I should take the punishment, not Father!'

Gui's glassy, slightly bulging eyes flicked from child to child, one defiant, the other tearful. He turned to Sergeant P'ao. 'Search the tower, as you should have done yesterday.'

No one spoke until he returned. In his arms were diverse things: Yun Shu's clothes, the empty gourd and the mother *dhole*'s corpse. A second soldier retrieved the puppies, blinking and wriggling.

'Otherwise, Master,' said P'ao, 'there's only old bones.'

Gui turned back to his daughter. For the first time wariness softened the anger in his voice. 'Is this where you chose to spend the night? In a charnel house? With a wild dog? It's b-big enough to be a fox fairy!'

She was too afraid to reply.

'How did the creature die?' he asked, fingering a protective amulet attached to his silken girdle. 'P'ao, how do you think it died? Was it through magic?'

The soldier bent over the corpse.

'Skull crushed inwards, Your Honour,' he said. Then Sergeant P'ao turned to Hsiung. 'Boy, is that how your leg got injured? Fighting this wild dog?'

Hsiung would not answer. He met the sergeant's eye then looked away in contempt. P'ao bent forward and whispered: 'Better to answer Master's questions, son.'

'Honoured Excellency!' cried Teng. 'Our servant saved your daughter! He fought the wild dog when it was attacking her and killed it. Hsiung saved her life! I was too afraid. But not him!'

The bodyguards murmured their approval at the boy's courage. Sergeant P'ao went so far as to slap his back.

'Is this true?' demanded Gui, turning to his daughter.

She nodded. 'It was scared for its pups, Father! Hsiung arrived and . . .'

'Enough!'

The Minister of Salt turned to the silent boy. He raised his abacus and rattled the beads. 'Lucky for you the accounts b-balance. Therefore, you shall not be punished.'

The soldiers grunted approvingly until their master silenced them with his fishy stare.

Deng Nan-shi cleared his throat and smiled affably. 'It appears the matter is settled, Your Excellency! We shall leave you to your delightful daughter . . .'

'Shut up, *you*!' said Gui.

The soldiers reacted to such grave discourtesy with narrowed, expectant eyes. The boys stared miserably at the ground. A dark look transformed Deng Nan-shi's urbane face and his smile froze. Had he possessed the power of his ancestors, things would have gone very cruelly for the Salt Minister.

'Are you aware,' said Gui, crimson with rage, 'what g-grade of human the Great Khan classes *scholars*?'

'I believe we are classified ninth in the ranks of human beings,' said Deng Nan-shi, 'one below prostitutes and one above beggars. At least, according to the Northern Edicts.'

Salt Minister Gui nodded. 'Precisely. And now your . . .' He groped for a suitable word. 'Your *b-brat* has kidnapped my daughter.'

'Teng didn't, Father!' cried Yun Shu. 'Teng urged me to return home!'

'B-be quiet! Cover your feet!'

Deng Nan-shi stepped forward, laying a hand on his son's quaking shoulder.

'He's just a child, Your Excellency. They're just children. Perhaps it is we who should reproach ourselves for not keeping a closer watch on how they grow.'

For a long moment the bamboo grove was silent. Lights glittered on the blue waters of the lake as the overcast sky cleared.

'Do not cross me again,' said the Salt Minister, 'not one of you. Sergeant P'ao! Carry my daughter. I will lead the way.'

'Master,' said P'ao, 'what shall I do with these puppies?'

There were three squeaking plaintively. Salt Minister Gui considered. 'Throw them over the cliff.'

'No!' protested Yun Shu, stepping forward too hurriedly. Her feet screamed with pain and she stumbled.

Again Gui examined her suspiciously. 'Are not these the whelps of a fox fairy?' he muttered to himself. 'Why does she wish to preserve them? Are they her familiars?'

Yun Shu covered her eyes as P'ao hurried to the cliff edge. One by one the puppies were hurled into space. No one stirred.

'Carry her,' ordered the Salt Minister, 'and her clothes.'

She shot Teng a look of pure hatred. The scholar's son met her gaze defiantly. But Yun Shu knew she'd been wronged. He had pretended to be her friend. Now she was forever worthless in Father's eyes.

Before long, only the Dengs were left beside the tower of bones. Hsiung stood straighter and prouder than before. He stared avidly after Sergeant P'ao and the other soldiers until they vanished in the trees.

four

天命

What of Yun Shu's journey through the dark wood, her palanquin a spear shaft held horizontally between two men, her pillow rough, unfriendly hands? So intense was her defeat she entered a thoughtless daze. Father brooded in his sedan chair. He did not acknowledge her in any way. When they reached home he stalked to his bureau without a backward glance.

She was carried through darkened corridors to the same disused section of the mansion where Golden Lotus had attempted to bind her feet. A maid waited with a flickering candle by the open door of one chamber. Even in the soft light Yun Shu detected concern in the girl's face.

'Master told me to tell you, if you leave this room without permission, you must leave his house and never come back.'

Yun Shu entered and the door closed. A bolt clicked behind her.

At first the darkness in the chamber seemed absolute. As her eyes adjusted, Yun Shu noticed the outlines of a window and drape. Hobbling over, she lifted the thick hemp curtain and peered through a lattice of diamond-shaped wooden bars.

Outside was a strip of abandoned garden that terminated in the cliff edge. The lake sparkled with moonlight. The moon revealed her only comforts: a low, sagging divan and pile of blankets. An open chamber pot in one corner. Yun Shu used it, wondering when she would be given water. It took a long while to achieve even a troubled sleep.

The next day brought a dawn summons. Yun Shu was shaken awake by the maid from last night, Pink Rose. Today the girl seemed afraid.

'Quickly,' she hissed, 'your father wants you.'

So urgent a summons allowed no time to straighten her dress or hair. When the maid opened the door to her father's study, Yun Shu's robes were still stained with mud and the mother dog's blood.

Salt Minister Gui sat on a high-backed chair like an emperor, his expression forbidding. Golden Lotus hovered behind. Yun Shu sank stiffly to her knees and kowtowed, resting her forehead on the cool earth. No one spoke.

'You're obedient now,' said Father, finally. 'Let's hope your change of heart is sincere. Otherwise you're no use to anyone.'

Although Yun Shu dared not look up, she sensed Golden Lotus stirring. The concubine whispered in Father's ear.

'Quite right, my love,' said the Salt Minister, 'the only real proof will be lotus feet. That's what my contract with your new family in Chenglingji specifies!'

Again, silence.

'She looks like a peasant girl,' muttered Golden Lotus, unable to hide his contempt. 'Just like her mother.'

Yun Shu sensed her father had grown agitated at the mention of Mother. The Salt Minister clicked bead after bead on his abacus, as though that sum could never tally. Never balance. She was led away like a criminal back to her cell.

Days passed in the room. Hot, dull transitions from morning to night, her only company a bloated spider and its flies. At first Yun Shu slumped miserably on the bed in a pose she hoped would arouse pity if Father saw. No one came. No one saw.

Gradually the tenderness of her feet lessened so that, in her boredom, she walked complex patterns round the room. Soon she could hop, stretch and wriggle her toes; bend the arch of her instep up and down. Freedom to exercise had a contrary effect to the one her gaolers intended. Yun Shu began to love her feet, however large, as something precious, strong, not to be casually discarded – especially to please a future husband she had never seen, whose family were equally unknown.

When Golden Lotus came, he found her barefoot in the hot room, oblivious to shame. His lotus gait held more of a suggestive sway than usual and she detected wine on his breath,

'Hide them!' he whispered. 'Are you a peasant girl in her paddy?'

Yun Shu reluctantly obeyed, head lowered. Golden Lotus beamed through his white mask of make-up and brilliant red mouth. 'Follow me!' he cried in a brittle singsong voice that left Yun Shu warier than ever.

It was a short journey: merely across the corridor.

'Here we are!' cooed Golden Lotus.

Yun Shu's heart beat uncomfortably as they entered the clean room with its stools and chairs and tables and shiny wooden box of bandages. Its bowls of fresh water and reeking pig's blood, putrid in the heat. There was, however, something new. On the table were four lacquered cases with closed lids.

'Sit!'

Golden Lotus's doll-like, painted face remained impassive as he examined her. 'Do you know,' he said, 'I used to pity you when you were small – such an ugly child. Yet I could see a single hope for you. Do you know what it was?'

Yun Shu could guess. She shook her head dutifully.

'That, however plain your face, your feet would give you a little power over men. For they dote on lotus feet, Yun Shu, you cannot imagine it!'

Yun Shu's eyes opened wide as she swallowed a reply.

'Instead,' said Golden Lotus, 'you *want* to be ugly.'

For a while, more silence. Yun Shu conceived a faint hope she might be ordered back to her room.

'Youngest Daughter,' sighed Golden Lotus, with a flutter of his eyes. 'I have something to show you. Something I never show anyone except your Father. You may rise. Come! Come!' Golden Lotus beckoned her to the lacquered cases on the new table. 'Do you know what these contain?' he asked, excitedly.

Yun Shu shook her head.

'I'm surprised. You're not a stupid girl. Come nearer. See!'

There was a peculiar, giddy gloat in his voice as he produced a hidden key and unlocked the first polished box. It opened to reveal nine compartments, each containing a pair of tiny shoes four inches long, like coverings for a deer's hoof. Shoes stitched with silk and gold and silver and pearls worth a peasant's wages for a whole year.

Golden Lotus giggled as he threw back lid after lid: 'See! See! These are a beautiful lady's war chests, her armoury. You may touch them, Yun Shu. There, I must care for you! I never allow anyone to touch them. Oh, look at that turquoise pair! So dainty, such loveliness!'

Nervous tittering agitated the young man. He rocked forward, hiding his mouth. Frightened by his strange behaviour, Yun Shu picked out a splendid golden shoe. For all its costliness, the feel and smell of it sickened her. Luckily, Golden Lotus was incapable of noticing.

'The merest twitch of your dress makes every man who sees such sweet slippers stare! That is power! But you must pay the price for that power.'

With shaking hands, Yun Shu returned the golden shoe to its compartment. One by one, Golden Lotus closed the lids. Tears glistened on his cheeks.

'Now,' he said, composing himself, 'let us begin. And no more nonsense!'

Yun Shu found the courage to speak. She gulped, for her mouth and tongue were parched. 'I . . . I won't. I *can't*!'

Golden Lotus's face lost all emotion in an instant. His white, rice powder face-paint had run from his tears so that the pale cheeks resembled cracked jade.

'Is it the pain?' he demanded. 'I endured it. Why can't you?'

This taunt goaded Yun Shu one more dangerous step towards honesty.

'Do not make me say why!'

'You refuse beauty and power,' pressed Golden Lotus, steadily more furious. 'I promised your father I'd persuade you so the marriage contract would be honoured! Do you not know how much money is at stake? Why?' He seized her shoulders and shook hard. 'Tell me why!'

'Do not force me to speak!' moaned Yun Shu.

'Look at my feet! My lovely shoes!' By now his voice was edged with hysteria. 'You think you're better than me, don't you?' shrieked Golden Lotus so loudly it echoed round the house. 'Just like your mother! You think feet like barges are better than mine, don't you? I've met your envious, spiteful kind before!'

The madness in him frightened Yun Shu. Yet she felt compelled towards defiance. For a long moment she balanced between possible futures then truth erupted. 'I want to run and skip!' she cried. 'I want to dance like the Dao! Oh, I heard its music in the woods! I want to ripple like the stars!' Where these words came from Yun Shu would never know. Later she often meditated on them, particularly her precocious reference to the Dao.

'You think my treasures are ugly!' whispered Golden Lotus. 'Don't you?'

To Yun Shu's eternal horror, she heard her firm reply: 'Yes, I do. They're *hideous*! And so are you!'

For a long moment stillness in the room.

'You're not Gui's daughter!' wailed Golden Lotus. 'You're a fox fairy in disguise! I shall never forgive this!'

He swept from the room, calling out for his maids in a high, agitated voice. Answering cries and rushing feet filled the corridors. Yun Shu fled to her room.

天命

The fierce beating she anticipated did not occur that day – or even the next, or any that followed over long weeks. She had been abandoned to the small, empty room with barred windows. Father's curse would never be reconsidered. Even the kindly servant girl, Pink Rose, regarded her fearfully when she delivered water or food, as though the rumours were true, that Yun Shu was a fox fairy who might cast a wicked spell.

The long summer passed until Yun Shu detected signs of autumn through the latticed, diagonal wooden bars: a certain softness to the sky, stray leaves blown across the garden and long crescents of white birds arriving from the cold north to fish the plentiful lake. Still the punishment she expected did not fall. Neither Teng nor Hsiung came to set her free. She had been forgotten, just as when Mother died, just as always.

five

天命

Teng looked up and down the dusty lane: no one. On either side high walls where yellow, star-shaped flowers colonised gaps between bricks. A drillmaster's bellowed commands drifted over one of the walls.

Teng examined the brickwork for handholds. Pulling himself up, he reached the top with a gasp and peered over.

An ill-assorted band of soldiers, the Salt Minister's body-guards, drilled in the front courtyard of Yun Shu's house. Their numbers had doubled in response to attacks against the Great Khan's officials by Red Turban rebels.

Teng examined the burly men stabbing imaginary foes. At the end of the line stood a diminutive warrior: Hsiung.

Twisting a spear to murder air, his former playmate screamed *Hai! Hai-eee! Ha!* Somehow Hsiung glimpsed Teng's head bobbing over the boundary wall. The young warrior hesitated, perhaps because Deng Nan-shi had impressed upon the two boys that no decent man willingly becomes a soldier, before shouting more loudly than ever, *Hai! Hai-eee! Ha!*

Teng withdrew and climbed down into the lane.

There, aimlessly plucking handfuls of grass from the verge, he listened to Sergeant P'ao shouting. It was weeks since he and Hsiung had explored their favourite haunts together. His old companion had grown indifferent to all they once shared.

Whenever his duties at Deng Mansions allowed – and often when they didn't – Hsiung skipped away to join Salt Minister Gui's bodyguards, who had adopted him as a blend of mascot, slave and butt of their jokes.

Teng trailed home to his study with its worn table and stool, cheap ink cake and writing materials. There he read a woodcut printed volume of poems from Father's library. One in particular, *The Lotus*, seemed so fine that he copied it in a flowing cursive style for display on his study wall.

Engrossed by this work, Teng didn't notice Deng Nan-shi's presence until he was peering over his shoulder. The boy lowered his brush and bowed.

'Ah,' said Deng Nan-shi, '*The Lotus!* I'm glad you found it out for yourself.'

Teng blushed at such rare praise.

'Do you know the poet's name?' asked Deng Nan-shi.

'Yun Cai,' replied Teng, indicating the front page of the book.

'Yes, *Yun*. Does it not strike you as strange he shares his surname with our courteous neighbour's daughter?'

Teng shrugged. He grew uneasy whenever he thought about Yun Shu. Lady Lu Si had heard from one of her friends in Cloud Abode Monastery that Yun Shu was kept prisoner in a room with barred windows.

'The world is full of Yuns,' he muttered, 'as the sky is full of clouds.'

The hunchbacked scholar nodded.

'Perhaps finding *The Lotus* is a sign,' he said. 'Come with me, Teng, there is somewhere I must show you.'

天命

He led his son through courtyards and corridors, emerging at the rear of the compound, where a faithful model of Holy Mount Chang, tall as two men, had been sculpted from rocks and earth. On its summit stood a small moon-gazing pavilion with a high domed roof resting on six carved pillars.

Deng Nan-shi climbed the model mountain, seating himself on a marble bench in the centre of the pavilion. Vines, creepers and moss covered the structure. Teng crouched at his feet, looking out at the lake.

'It is twenty-eight years since I last set foot here,' said Deng Nan-shi.

Teng waited. Father bent forward, his eyes closed as though in meditation. Finally he sat upright.

'Our family,' said Deng Nan-shi, 'has been the foremost in this province since the advent of the Song Dynasty, three centuries ago.'

All this Teng knew. It seemed all he had ever been allowed to know.

'You have heard of our ancestor General Yueh Fei,' continued Deng Nan-shi, 'a great hero and saviour of the Empire against the Kin barbarians, betrayed by cowards, pragmatists, traitors. Yet before his execution, Yueh Fei granted a mountain estate to an unknown infantry officer with the surname *Yun*. I know this because I found a document in our library. It states Officer Yun saved General Yueh Fei at the Battle of T'su Hu Pass, and so earned his reward.'

A ragged vee of honking geese flew overhead toward the lake; both watched silently.

'Officer Yun had a famous son, a brilliant son, a great poet. The author of that poem you found without my prompting: noble Yun Cai. When I was young we loved his poems. They described our deepest feelings – and fears.'

The boy's thoughts raced ahead. 'But Father, Yun Shu . . . Can she really be related to Yun Cai?'

'Yes,' said the scholar, 'impossible as it seems. Though the poet died a hundred years ago, his descendents still exist. Debased, certainly. Diminished, of course. I have established your little friend, Yun Shu, is a direct descendent of the poet, through her dead mother.'

49

Deng Nan-shi settled back on the bench.

'That is the first thing I wanted you to know,' he said.

'What does it mean?' asked Teng.

'Mean? Probably nothing. What does anything mean?'

Teng stirred. 'Why did you bring me to this pavilion, Father?'

'Ah, now that is not coincidental.'

It was for a story Teng knew well, pieced together from hints and indiscretions.

After Hou-ming's defences crumbled twenty-eight years earlier, the Mongol army stormed through its ancient wards. All resistance melted into abject pleading, yet the victorious soldiers' orders excluded the option of mercy. Prefect Deng's futile defiance had cost the Mongol general, Prince Arslan, his brother's life.

'Did Prince Arslan really vow to add the last human, dog and cat in the city to his brother's grave mound?' asked Teng.

'You have seen the size of the mound,' said his father, 'judge for yourself.'

Deng Nan-shi had been a sallow youth of eighteen, the youngest of five sons, disregarded because of his deformed back. Yet he had been married since the age of sixteen to a younger daughter of an impoverished scholar family.

'Did you kill any Mongols, Father?' Teng asked eagerly. 'And my uncles, did they fight, too?'

The scholar shifted, glancing up at the ceiling of the pavilion. It was made of wooden boards sealing off the domed roof.

'No, fighting was for the soldiers. We Dengs were for *policy*.'

His solemn emphasis on the word confused Teng.

'Yet they were entering the city, Father! What other policy could there be than fighting?'

Deng Nan-shi struggled for breath, so that Teng stirred uneasily.

'Where was I?' asked the scholar.

天命

The majority of the Deng clan had gathered in Deng Mansions, pretending not to hear the distant screams from the city below. Prefect Deng and his favourite sons had remained in the Prefect's Residence, where they nobly hung themselves from the rafters using silken cords, to avoid the disgrace of capture.

None of the Dengs in their ancestral home could imagine their clan head's fate. Up on Monkey Hat Hill a mood of un-reality had taken hold. Relative greeted relative, paying graded respects and enquiring politely after each other's health. Servants appeared with trays of exquisite wine from the store-houses, still earnest about their duties – for Prefect Deng was no friend to slackness. Soon a gay, almost festive atmosphere had flowed round the salons and courtyards. Aunts, uncles, cousins, nephews, their servants and concubines, gulped the wine and chattered, or withdrew to corners, staring round fearfully.

The only one of Prefect Deng's sons to remain at home was Deng Nan-shi. At first he pleaded with Mother to seek a hiding place, but she refused scornfully.

'We can be sure that the Prefect will find a way of keeping us safe,' she had said, as though her son was still a small, foolish boy.

Deng Nan-shi had stared at her incredulously. At that moment sounds of slaughter lower down Monkey Hat Hill became unmistakeable. A buzz of panic spread among the hundreds of Dengs and their followers. Individual voices merged into a collective moan.

'Hide!' screeched Deng Nan-shi. 'I command you! I am clan head now, for surely Father and my brothers are dead. Hide!'

No one listened. He hurried to the gatehouse to look for signs of the enemy. There he encountered a single infantry officer with a handful of men. Deng Nan-shi stopped them at the gate. 'Do not come in here,' he warned the soldiers. 'Hide in the woods and hope they do not find you.'

The officer was a little older than himself and had a bleeding gash on one cheek.

'Sir! Prefect Deng sent me to protect you all!'

Again Deng Nan-shi held up his hand.

'Save yourselves! It is too late.'

The officer pushed past him. The sight within the compound forced the soldier to halt. Some Dengs huddled and embraced each other, sobbing or wailing. A great crowd of concubines and other women, over two hundred strong, were being led towards the cliff by Prefect Deng's First Wife.

'No!' shouted Deng Nan-shi, running forward. 'Hide in the woods. Anywhere!'

The women were screaming, crying, chanting prayers for a favourable rebirth, holding hands or embracing a friend. He only had time to extract his wife before they reached the cliff edge and began to leap off the precipice like crazed birds without wings.

He stood in the now deserted courtyard and found the officer beside him. His men had fled.

'Is there nowhere for you to hide, sir?' demanded the soldier.

Then young Deng Nan-shi remembered a place. 'This way!' he cried.

As they hurried from the courtyard the first Mongols entered with bloody swords and axe blades. Deng Nan-shi, his wife and the officer rushed out to the artificial Holy Mount Chang at the rear of the compound then climbed up the mound – Prefect Deng's pride and joy – into the moon-gazing pavilion.

'There is a gap between the domed roof and those wooden boards,' said Deng Nan-shi. 'If we could somehow reach so high . . .'

The officer looked up doubtfully. Fresh screams reached them from the house. The Mongols had discovered those without the decency to jump to their deaths.

'How?' he began. His eye fell on a wooden bench. Seizing it, he held it up like a ramp, his arms high above his head.

'Climb!' cried the officer. 'Quickly, before they see.'

Deng Nan-shi went first, scrambling up, shoved from behind by his wife. The officer roared at the strain of bearing their weight. Pushing aside the loose boards the scholar climbed into the moon-gazing pavilion's dome: a small space, barely enough room for two. His wife nimbly followed, climbing in beside him. Yet when the hunchbacked scholar reached down for the officer, he found the bench back in its place and the soldier gone. At that very moment the first Mongols emerged from the house, dragging out women to violate on top of Prefect Deng's prize orchid beds before casting them semi-naked over the cliff. As the air filled with despair, Deng Nan-shi had pulled the roof boards tight . . .

'So that is how you survived,' said the boy, dully. 'By hiding.'

'Yes.'

'And after the massacre you and Mother climbed down from the pavilion.'

'Yes.'

Teng realised he was tearful.

'Did you . . . have to bury them all?'

'One or two. Remember, Prince Arslan had decreed the people of Hou-ming were to form his brother's grave mound. Most bodies were carted away in wagons dragged by prisoners who were themselves later added to the mound.'

'How many died, Father? How many died that day?'

Deng Nan-shi laid a hand on his son's arm.

'When the next census was taken a few years later, only one in twenty of those who had lived in Hou-ming survived. And yet, as you know, the buildings were undamaged. Such were Prince Arslan's commands. Looted and emptied of valuables, yes, but undamaged. A city of ghosts.'

Teng pictured twenty eggs laid out on the ground. Someone

stamping until the ground was sticky with yoke and egg white and shell. Until a single egg remained.

'There is more you want to tell me, Father,' he said, 'isn't there?'

Deng Nan-shi nodded, rubbing his eyes. 'Another day. Not today.'

The hunchbacked scholar left the pavilion, leaving his son to stare up at the roof boards of the wooden dome.

'It's about Hsiung, isn't it?' Teng cried after his retreating Father.

Deng Nan-shi did not answer.

天命

A week later, Teng perched on the shell of a giant tortoise. The stone statue was ancient, Guardian of the Crossroads halfway up Monkey Hat Hill and a very stern tortoise indeed.

Over the last few days there had been a fury of packing in Yun Shu's house: wagons pulled by donkeys or some of His Excellency Jebe Khoja's immense herd of horses, accompanied by resentful soldiers tired of tramping up and down Monkey Hat Hill. Nearly all the Salt Minister's possessions – and he had gathered an astonishing collection of valuables – had rolled through derelict districts of the city to Prince Arslan's walled palace.

As Teng waited he noticed Hsiung coming towards him, kicking moodily at stones. He was tempted to ignore his faithless friend, but only for a moment.

'Hsiung!' he called, leaping onto the road. 'I'm over here! Sit with me on the tortoise!' The servant boy examined him so coldly Teng regretted his warmth. 'That is,' he added, haughtily, 'if you like.'

It seemed Hsiung did like, though he chose not to acknowledge his master's son. The two boys perched side by side on the stone shell, looking every possible way except at each other.

'Do you think they'll leave soon?' asked Teng, when he could bear the silence no more.

'Maybe.'

'But you must know!'

'Maybe.'

'You're hopeless.'

Mild and ineffectual as such a rebuke seemed it had a gratifying effect.

'All right,' said Hsiung, 'I do know.'

Teng settled back on the tortoise's neck, satisfied to have gained his point. It was one of autumn's last kind days. Clouds of migrating birds blurred the horizons of the lake.

'Why are they leaving the Hill?' asked Teng. 'Why leave a big mansion for a small house in Prince Arslan's palace?'

Hsiung shrugged. Recently his voice had acquired a casual, soldierly drawl.

'No choice. Too many officials killed by Red Turbans this summer. Bastard bandits!' He paused to examine the effect of such hot language on the scholar's son. 'So the big bugs must live in a safe place.'

'How do you know?' asked Teng, scornfully. 'Did Salt Minister Gui tell you?'

Hsiung spat proudly. 'Sergeant P'ao tells me.'

The noise of wheels, hooves, feet, voices interrupted them.

'Here they come!' cried Teng, standing upright on the tortoise shell. Hsiung rose with him.

First a dozen soldiers led by Sergeant P'ao. At the sight of Hsiung some winked and waggled their eyebrows so that the boy flushed with importance. Then he wept silently to see his heroes march away. Next came the Salt Minister's personal palanquin, its curtains drawn. Another followed, similarly shrouded – presumably belonging to Golden Lotus. A larger, open carriage gaudy with tassels carried Yun Shu's two brothers and an aging tutor. More wagons of boxes and furniture followed, surrounded by a dozen porters with burdens so huge they resembled camels. Last of all, carts of servants.

Teng stared at the very final wagon. 'Hsiung,' he whispered, 'do you see?'

Amidst a gaggle of maids perched their friend, Yun Shu, her clothes shabby, hair ill-tended. Teng realised it was over three months since he last saw her – and had so bitterly reproached the girl. All that anger was gone. Now he felt a need to acknowledge her. Perhaps that was why he stepped into the road, staring up into the crowded wagon.

'Yun Shu!' he called. As he could think of nothing else, he shouted: 'Farewell! Do not forget us! Farewell!'

Teng caught a hot, resentful flicker from the corner of her eyes. Then she was past, trundling down the Hill, out of Monkey Hat Ward. He stood in the lane until the last carriage vanished through the ward gate.

'Good riddance!' he cried. 'Good riddance!'

He whispered in case anyone heard: 'Traitors!'

Stray yellow leaves fluttered down from a nearby tree. When Teng turned to speak with Hsiung he found himself alone. The image of proud, brave Yun Shu huddled among low females lingered. It was hard to forget who had betrayed her hiding place and so brought about her disgrace. All too easy to forget why.

six

天命

A cold, hungry autumn followed Salt Minister Gui's departure from Monkey Hat Hill. Deng Nan-shi succumbed to stubborn inflammations of the spleen, manifested in exhaustion and a listless pulse. His earnings from tutoring dwindled as he kept to his bed. Worse still, he was forced to sell what few ornaments and paintings the Deng clan still possessed. The household was constantly on edge. Of them all, only Hsiung remained sleek. He was broader, long-limbed, a buck with budding horns.

Hsiung came to view his bedridden master with the secret disdain of the healthy for the feeble. Had he but known, Deng Nan-shi's withdrawal from the streets of Hou-ming was timely.

It suited him not to travel round the city from pupil to pupil like a spy. A faction of the Red Turban rebels named after the Dengs' great ancestor, Yueh Fei, had raised a serious rebellion in the hill districts surrounding Six-hundred-*li* Lake. When their attempts to drive the Great Khan's servants from Hou-ming Province threatened the valuable Salt Pans, Jebe Khoja led a large force to disperse them, chasing famished bands of rebels across several counties and executing thousands of blameless peasants as a warning to others.

天命

One morning, Hsiung slipped through a side gate of Deng Mansions and hurried down the lanes, out through the ancient Ward Gate into the streets of the city. He did not turn south to the Port District with its busy wharfs and warehouses. Hsiung's route lay among places almost as deserted as Monkey Hat Hill, for the population hereabouts had scarcely recovered since the city's fall. Wards built to house tens of thousands in cramped tenements and slums resembled larders stripped bare. Yet apparent emptiness concealed danger, as Hsiung was well aware.

Most of the houses he passed were overgrown: trees poking through roofs and gardens like thickets. Roads were vanishing beneath grass except where fresh wheel ruts scored the soil. A few birds perched on eaves, gazing beyond the crumbling city ramparts to the fish-filled waters of the lake. Occasionally he passed courtyards where clans or individual families had set up islands of humanity amidst the deserted, rotting houses.

After half an hour's walk he reached his destination: a large, high-walled palace compound occupying the north east corner of the city's rectangle. Here was the site of the old Prefect's Residence. During the previous dynasty it had been busy with bureaux and quarters for officials posted here from all parts of the Empire. Now it was Prince Arslan's palace, as well as home to his highest officials and tax gatherers, including Salt Minister Gui.

The gatehouse was heavily guarded and Hsiung did not care to chance it. Besides, he had an arrangement with someone who dwelt within, someone who came and went at will. Yet it turned out to be a long wait beside the bridge over Jinshui Canal, watching customers visit the astrologers' booths to determine auspicious days. A dry, icy wind set dust devils dancing. Even an excited peal of bells from the nearby Buddhist Temple sounded forlorn beneath a sky so laden with low clouds.

When Sergeant P'ao finally arrived he smelt of spirits. Hsiung looked up at the older man resentfully.

'I see Little Fox Tamer is angry!' said Sergeant P'ao, lowering a heavy sack to the floor with a grunt. Hsiung's frown deepened.

'It will be the curfew soon,' he muttered.

'Brighten up, boy!' Sergeant P'ao clapped him on the shoulder so hard he reeled. 'I've more for you to deliver! Just to the usual places.'

A calculating look crossed Hsiung's face.

'For the usual amount?' he asked.

Instantly, Sergeant P'ao's affable expression vanished and his arm rose to strike. The boy cringed.

'Don't you dare haggle with me! Just make sure they're delivered. When you're done I'll be in that wine shop across the way. Bring . . .' He glanced round slyly, raising bushy black eyebrows. 'Bring *everything*.'

Sergeant P'ao was as good as his word, vanishing into the wine shop where a hearty bellow greeted him.

Hsiung's first destination lay in the ancient Pleasure District round Bright River. Thirty years ago hundreds of restaurants, floating oriole houses, teashops and theatres had competed to empty purses of *cash*, minds of perplexity, hearts of pain. That number had reduced to a few dozen establishments.

Hsiung approached a small restaurant specialising in river serpents and examined the street. Few people were about, though enterprising members of the City Watch sometimes wore disguises. Satisfied, Hsiung went to the back door of the restaurant, poking his head into a steam-filled kitchen. When he left his sack was considerably lighter and girdle purse heavier.

A similar transaction took place at the rear of a theatre where music and clashing cymbals escaped into the street. Then he was walking alongside Bright River, bound for the Port District. Yet Hsiung sensed he was the victim of a poor exchange. Why was he rewarded with a few *cash* coins when he collected hundreds on P'ao's behalf? At least with the Dengs everyone was poor together.

True, Sergeant P'ao allowed him to polish weapons and join drill practice. He also had a noble nickname for him, inspired by his feat of bravery in killing the wild dog. Once the soldiers had got him drunk on cheap rice wine. The drink unleashed a volubility Hsiung did not know he possessed. Also an unguarded tongue. For no sooner had the boy revealed that his master, Deng Nan-shi, called Salt Minister Gui a traitor than the room whirled and he had found himself outside with Sergeant P'ao shaking him up and down. Finally Hsiung sobered.

'What are you doing?' P'ao had hissed. 'That hunchbacked beetle brought you up as an orphan! He feeds you when half the world starves. He's your Father, damn you! Now you've put him in their power.' He indicated the soldiers inside. 'Show some loyalty!'

Hsiung ducked. 'He's not my father!' he had squealed.

'Neither am I, boy,' said Sergeant P'ao. 'Besides, sooner or later we'll be leaving Hou-ming. I've heard Jebe Khoja plans to send my dear Master to supervise the Salt Pans. Not enough salt is coming up from the earth. A firmer hand is needed.'

The soldier had laughed coarsely. 'And maybe Golden Lotus will have to stay behind in Jebe Khoja's compound. I've heard . . . Ha! Best not talk of that! Eh, boy?'

Hsiung's head and stomach had churned. Yet even in the midst of drunkenness he wanted to ask about Yun Shu.

These thoughts distracted him until he entered the Port District. There he grew alert. The shortest way to his final customer involved crossing the Slave Market.

Hsiung glanced up at the sky. Night was approaching and, with it, the Great Khan's curfew. He would be lucky to deliver his wares, collect payment and return to Sergeant P'ao before the curfew bell tolled a thousand times. After that a dangerous journey home through the darkness awaited.

But Hsiung was not prone to fear. He hastened his step, turning from Bright River up a side lane leading to the Slave Market where blacksmiths had set up forges for the manufacture and repair of manacles. At the edge of the market his progress halted. For the wide square resembled a battlefield.

Mongol cavalry were herding scores of prisoners into the square with lance butts and whips. Near the entrance, mounted on a huge black stallion, sat a handsome young man in gentlemanly silks. A sword and bow hung from his saddle; black hair spread over his shoulders. To Hsiung, the Mongol prince resembled a hero from the thrilling tales Teng sometimes read out loud, his eyes bright and voice animated.

Salt Minister Gui and a number of other officials were fawning before the splendid horseman – none other than Jebe Khoja himself.

Dozens of bystanders watched. A blacksmith's apprentice in a leather apron turned to Hsiung. 'Red Turbans,' muttered the lad, pointing at the prisoners. 'They must have been spared for a reason. Maybe they're short of hands in the Salt Pans. I heard hundreds escaped . . .' The blacksmith's boy went dumb for a grizzled man had drawn close to overhear their conversation.

'Interesting, my lads! Who told you that, I wonder?'

Hsiung realised the man was one of the Great Khan's hired accusers. He sidled away.

'You!' called the man. 'What is in that sack?'

Hsiung dodged into the square. It was filling with manacled, shuffling rebel prisoners. Orders were shouted on every side, drowned out by whinnying horses and clip-clopping hooves. No one in the thick press of cavalry and captives noticed his presence. Beaten, downcast faces surrounded him, advancing in columns towards the slave pens, herded by trotting riders like cattle to a shambles. Many were wounded or spirit-broken, a few defiant; all wore heavy wooden neck yokes and chains linking their ankles.

Hsiung looked around for a way out. But he was trapped in

a maze, unable to do anything except flow with the prisoners deeper into the square. Abruptly he came to a circle of braziers and glowing branding irons. Here slaves were being marked on their cheeks with the character *salt*. Beyond them, like an unreachable shore, he spied a clear route to the alleyways of the Port District. A large soldier appeared before him, barring the way.

'You boy! What're you doing here?'

Shrieks and groans, the acrid smell of scorched hair, skin and flesh as branding began in earnest. The soldier stepped closer.

'What's in that bag?' he demanded. He turned to another man. 'Sir, there's a . . .' When he looked round the boy had vanished, leaving his sack on the ground. Out of it spilled solid, grey bricks of pure salt.

Hsiung only stopped running when he was through the broken gates of Monkey Hat Ward. Deep twilight; indigo beneath a layer of low, basalt clouds. Across the city people hurried indoors lest the Watch find them and demand bribes not to report them to a magistrate.

His heart still beat painfully. Sheer luck had saved him. A group of rebels had kicked over some braziers, chanting *Yueh Fei! Yueh Fei!* Sparks and glowing coals poured across the cobbles until the rebels were swiftly cut down. In the confusion he had raced between lines of prisoners, so escaping into a shadowy alley.

Yet Sergeant P'ao's blocks of salt remained behind, each worth a night's carousing. Hsiung did not anticipate understanding or sympathy for the loss. He had no means of recompensing the sergeant and expected, at the very least, a beating.

Night had fallen as he entered Deng Mansions. In the gatehouse he was surprised to find Deng Nan-shi holding a feeble oil lamp.

'There you are!' said the scholar. 'I've been looking for you.

We have a visitor, a most intriguing gentleman. Come, Hsiung!'

The boy almost fled back into the night. When he realised Sergeant P'ao could not have reached here so fast, he followed his master inside.

天命

Their visitor possessed characteristics rarely observed in Hou-ming: a belly bulging like a happy Buddha's and jowls heavy with meat. Good-feeding had swollen his legs and arms. As for his clothes, they rustled slightly when he moved, as only the best, stiffest silks do. Gold and silver thread decorated the hems of his coat.

Such a gentleman seemed too fine for Deng Nan-shi's shabby library, yet his hunched shoulders suggested profound deference towards the scholar.

'Come in, Hsiung,' commanded Deng Nan-shi. 'Don't be shy. Here is . . .' He glanced quickly at his guest. 'Perhaps I should not mention names?'

The visitor's moon-like jaw rose and fell.

'Now, boy, stand before me!' ordered the fat man, chuckling for no apparent reason. His accent was unplaceable. 'My, a fine boy! *My!*'

Hsiung glanced anxiously at the door. Had Deng Nan-shi decided to sell him at last?

'Truly he has grown well,' continued their visitor, rubbing a scar on his meaty jowls, 'a tribute to your care.'

Deng Nan-shi acknowledged the compliment. For a long moment the men regarded him. The long dark room hoarded shadows between smoking oil lamps and racks of scrolls, chests of woodcut printed volumes. The hunchbacked scholar cleared his throat.

'Before our visitor shares his news,' he said, 'I must tell you a story. It is the story of yourself – from a certain perspective.'

Yet he seemed in no hurry to start.

'He *is* tall,' murmured the fat man.

'Listen closely,' began Deng Nan-shi . . .

天命

Ten or so years earlier the scholar's wife had still been alive, though no longer young and almost past son-bearing age.

'We had no child of our own,' said Deng Nan-shi. 'Teng was yet to be born. We wanted a son badly, for I was the last of my line. Without a son, who would tend the ancestral altars when I sought my next incarnation?'

Then, miraculously, a child had appeared. One day Deng Nan-shi's wife had come running, saying a baby was crying in the gatehouse, wrapped in a bundle of coarse, hemp blankets. When the cloth was unwound they discovered two things: a naked baby boy, kicking his limbs as though in rebellion against all confinement, a boy with a bawl loud enough to shake Heaven.

Secondly, a letter wrapped around the child for safekeeping. This was less satisfactory than the splendid child; its ink had run so that only the words *Remember the officer who saved you. I beg you to repay what* . . . and a single character, *Hsiung*, were legible. Whether the character referred to the boy's name, no one could determine.

Hsiung looked up, his face burning with emotion. 'That boy was me?'

'Of course,' said Deng Nan-shi. 'There is more . . .'

The childless couple had not hesitated; for, indeed, an unknown officer had saved them seventeen years earlier. At last his sacrifice could be repaid, life for life.

The fat man stirred as if about to speak, then subsided into his Buddha-like smile.

'A year after you joined us,' continued Deng Nan-shi, 'Teng was born. A miracle, for my wife was past a woman's best. Perhaps that was why she weakened and died a few years later. I have never ceased to mourn her loss, as you know well.'

Hsiung realised he was trembling. 'Why did you not tell me before?' he asked. 'I could have looked for my father!'

The room remained dark. Lantern light softened the older men's faces. It seemed neither wished to be the first to reply. Deng Nan-shi asked kindly, 'Where would you have looked?'

'Anywhere!' cried Hsiung. 'Wherever he is!'

'And where is that?'

Hsiung hung his head.

'I don't know.'

Now the fat man chuckled again, a chesty noise, mirthless as his smile.

'Ha! Ha! The lad has plenty of spirit.'

'Where is he, sir?' pleaded Hsiung. Then more aggressively: '*Who* is he?'

'Ah,' sighed the stranger, raising a plump finger. 'That is what your honoured master asked me to find out.'

The two men regarded the boy in silence.

'When may I go to him?' pressed Hsiung.

Their visitor ran a finger round his collar; he was perspiring though the night was cold. 'All I had to help me find him were two clues: the name of Hsiung and that your father had fought bravely at the fall of Hou-ming. Careful enquiries among – let us call them, associates of mine – revealed there had been an officer among the Yueh Fei rebels who fitted that description. But he was captured not long after you appeared in Honourable Deng Nan-shi's gatehouse and was taken to the Salt Pans. What happened to your father there I cannot say.'

'I am *really* called Hsiung!' marvelled the boy. 'And my father is called Hsiung! I have a clan and my father is alive!'

Now their visitor grew solemn.

'Young man,' he said, 'the Salt Pans is a terrible, terrible place! No one leaves easily or survives for long. My dear boy, I fear you should not expect to see your father. Enough that he ensured you would be protected by the most honourable family in the province.'

'I will find my father,' said Hsiung, fiercely, 'I will set him free!'

The two men exchanged sad glances.

'I hope it has done no harm to tell you the truth. At least, what we can of it,' said Deng Nan-shi, laying a hand on the lad's shoulder. Hsiung flinched and pulled away.

'I know he is not dead!' he said.

'Be comforted your father disappeared for a just cause,' advised the fat man. 'If he was alive today that cause would be his life's work. And if it turns out he is not dead, perhaps your father will reveal himself when it is safe. Perhaps he is a wanted man and does not wish to endanger his son.'

'I will find my father!' cried Hsiung, his voice retreating down the dark corridor. 'You'll see!'

For a long while Hsiung wept on his bed, unable to sleep. Then he rose, wearing his blanket as a cloak, and left the house by a side door. Soon he reached the mound shaped in imitation of Holy Mount Chang and ascended to the moon-gazing pavilion. The night sky had cleared to reveal dazzling webs of stars. Hsiung stared south, looking for signs of flickering flames – the fires of the Salt Pans that were rumoured to never go out. But that dismal place was too far away to be seen except by Immortal eyes.

Inside, Deng Nan-shi and the fat man talked deep into the night. Often the names of Yueh Fei and Hornets' Nest entered their conversation.

seven

天命

The next morning Teng woke to an air of intrigue in Deng Mansions. New things were happening in the abandoned chambers and corridors. Who, for example, was the fat man in silks lurking in a secluded room at the centre of the house? And why did two tall strangers lounge near his chamber, swords discreetly concealed in cloth wrappings?

Above all – and here Teng could not suppress jealousy – what had inspired Father to spend a whole hour with Hsiung last night? Teng held little hope of finding out from Hsiung himself. His old friend had ignored his greeting and hurried out of the courtyard and down the lanes to the city below. He seemed in a great bustle, like a high official on secret business.

Teng waited at the crossroads below Deng Mansions for his return, perched on the back of the giant stone tortoise. The beast was company of sorts and Teng pretended to ride it all the way to the Western Mountains as Lao Tzu had ridden his ox. Next he played at being a *xia* on a magic turtle, sweeping away hordes of Mongols to preserve the honour of . . . what? The Empire? A lady? Yun Shu came to mind, her name trailing guilt. Let it not be Yun Shu but Hsiung. Saving him would renew their friendship forever.

The afternoon passed slowly on Monkey Hat Hill. A few

bird-trappers went by, bound for the bamboo groves with nets and sacks. Families filled the road briefly, seeking Cloud Abode Monastery where they would sacrifice to their ancestors. Otherwise, silence and opaqueness in the chilly air.

Teng's loneliness, his frustration and hidden grief, welled up. He remembered Mother's ghost when he was five years old. How he had cried out, half in fear, half relief, and hid behind a doorframe so only his shaven head with its tufty topknot was exposed. She had not noticed him as he watched her shuffle down cracked marble steps to the garden; down to an ornamental pond guarded by stone dragons. Even then, so close to her lost life, she had been a shadow.

'Mother!' he had called, high-pitched and eager. 'I'm here! I'm here!'

The dark shadow peered in his direction. Teng had stifled a sob and run forward, so intent on embracing her that he misjudged the marble stairs and tumbled, cutting his knee. When he looked up she had gone, never to be seen again, yet always there, forever in midnight corners, sighing in the wind.

Tears pricked his eyes. Hsiung appeared at the bottom of the hill and Teng ran forward to meet him. 'Hsiung! Here I am! I've waited all day for you!'

The older boy cast him a troubled glance and strode past up the hill, vanishing through the gatehouse of Deng Mansions. The pain in Teng's chest tightened.

天命

After a meal with Lady Lu Si, during which she twittered about sutras and divine blessings in Cloud Abode Monastery, Teng withdrew to his study for calligraphy practice. Only then did heaviness lift from his soul. Taking a sheet of cheap paper, he painted the character *shadow*, bordered by swirling infinities of cloud. To give balance, three tiny birds formed an arrowhead, skimming towards distant, snow-capped mountains. He also painted pine, bamboo and plum trees laden with blossom. By the time he finished, the light was fading quickly. Teng became aware of someone watching.

'Hsiung!'

The tall boy leaned forward, apparently fascinated by the painting.

'How can you *do* that?' he murmured. Then he stiffened. 'It doesn't matter. My ancestors were all famous soldiers! I shall paint my way to glory with a sword! A sword always crushes a mere brush.'

Though Teng knew the history of the Empire disproved such a notion, he did not want to argue, secretly relieved to have been sought out by his old companion. Hsiung hovered by the doorpost.

'I will only enter if you swear an oath of secrecy,' he said, fiercely. 'A soldier's oath!'

'I'm not a soldier,' said Teng, 'neither are you.'

'So you refuse to swear!'

'I did not say that . . . Why are you angry? What is wrong, Hsiung?'

'Swear!'

'Very well, I will . . . but not by mere *soldiers*. I swear by my noble ancestor, Yueh Fei. So there!'

'Oh, and *General* Yueh Fei wasn't a soldier, was he?' demanded Hsiung, triumphantly.

Hsiung's agitation lessened. He glanced up the corridor then slipped inside, sliding the door shut behind him with great difficulty for the wooden frame was swollen by rot.

'Teng,' he whispered, 'I went to see Sergeant P'ao today. I owed him hundreds of *cash* – oh, do not ask how!'

Teng nodded reassuringly.

'When I got to Salt Minister Gui's residence, I found Sergeant P'ao and his men packing their belongings. They sail for the Salt Pans tomorrow! Gui has been posted there!'

'Good riddance,' muttered Teng.

'It is not so simple!' said Hsiung.

At times faltering, sometimes rushing forward, he told the same tale their fat visitor had related the previous evening. Teng listened intently. Gone was the cynical, angry boy who had tormented him so often. Tears were in Hsiung's eyes, smeared by a rubbing fist as he vowed: 'I will save my father, Teng! Just you see! I will break his chains or die!'

A long silence followed this terrible oath. Teng felt an urge to giggle nervously. Yet he recognised the vow as sacred, its implications frightening – if taken seriously.

'You really mean to accompany Sergeant P'ao to the Salt Pans?' he asked.

'Yes.'

Teng shook his head. 'Then I will never see you again. He will sell you as a slave.'

The two boys sat with bowed heads. In a far away voice, Hsiung said, 'When I visited Sergeant P'ao, guess who else I met? Yun Shu. She was sweeping the courtyard with the maids. She wouldn't look at me. But her feet were as big as ever.'

'Sweeping?' said Teng. 'That is a common servant's work.'

Realising the implication of his words took a moment. Hsiung's reaction, however, was instantaneous. 'Like me?' he asked, coldly.

'No, not you, I meant . . .'

Their thread of intimacy snapped.

'Remember your promise,' said Hsiung, dragging open the swollen door with an agonising creak and groan. 'Only, please tell Master . . . Honourable Deng Nan-shi . . . where I have gone. And thank him. Thank him for everything. Tell him that when I have found my father I will repay my debt to your family a thousand times over! I will never forget!'

'You won't dare go to the Salt Pans!' cried Teng. 'All you ever do is get angry with me! And boast!'

But Hsiung had gone. Teng's words echoed in an empty chamber.

天命

At dawn Teng sat upright in bed. In a moment he was padding through cold, dark corridors to the kitchen. A familiar smell greeted him and he laughed. The stove was warm, a neat fire smoking. For all his bragging and fierce soldiers' oaths, Hsiung had decided not to leave after all. Teng rubbed his hands before the flames. Though it would be tempting to jeer, he was determined to say nothing. He would even help prepare the morning millet to show he did not view Hsiung as a common servant.

After a while he grew restless and was about to step outside when he noticed something wrong: Hsiung's pile of neatly folded bedding and clothes had vanished. Only a single blanket remained.

'Fool!' cried Teng, dashing out into the courtyard.

A thick lake mist was rolling inland. Droplets beaded plants and wooden surfaces. *Think*, he urged himself, *a scholar of high purpose thinks before he acts.*

Then Hsiung's intention became obvious. If he was to leave for the Salt Pans with Sergeant P'ao they would hardly crawl upon muddy roads for hundreds of weary *li*. Not when a swift passage across the lake was possible. In addition, Teng had noticed a small fleet of river junks gathering in the harbour over the last few days.

He considered rousing Deng Nan-shi. But a perverse desire held him back. Yesterday, on the stone tortoise's back, he had imagined saving Hsiung from hordes of Mongols. Now was his chance to be a real *xia*!

Picking up his bamboo sword, he hurried into the misty lanes of Monkey Hat Hill then out into the stirring city. Although he had only visited the Port District once, Teng did not lose his way.

But when he reached the stone bridge over Bright River, he found a queue of people and carts. Soldiers were searching all

Chinese for contraband or hidden weapons; Mongols or their servants were waved through without question.

'What's happening?' he asked an old peasant woman carrying a basket of winter greens. Luckily, she gave no sign of recognising him as a cursed Deng.

'Rebels,' she whispered, 'spies in the city.'

He joined a small crowd gathered round a poster beside the bridge, discussing a crude picture of a grossly fat man reminiscent of Lord Buddha and the words: *Beware traitors! Beware bandits! Beware Liu Shui, notorious Red Turban and Yueh Fei bandit! Beware the despicable brigand known as Hornets' Nest!* A reward was offered, large enough to buy a dozen farms.

Teng looked round guiltily. He had no illusions where the fat Liu Shui was hiding at this very moment. How could Father be so reckless? To take such a risk after all their years of caution?

A low bell tolled across the city. The Third Hour of daylight: surely the fleet would not delay. He must hurry.

None of the soldiers questioned him as he crossed the bridge. Fog was dispersing beneath a feeble sun when he reached the harbour. A gloomy day was commencing, heavy with drudgery and tedium for thousands in the Port District. For others, a day that would end their future.

The Red Turban prisoners had been chained together in groups of ten, their defiance choked by bulging wooden neck yokes. Most were barefoot and in rags. Nearly four hundred prisoners waited on the wharf for transportation to the Salt Pans. Of those, half would be lucky to last a year.

Many soldiers had gathered to ensure the embarkation went smoothly. This was less straightforward than it seemed. In the winter dry season water levels on the lake fell and one could only berth large junks at the end of long wooden jetties projecting into the water. In between lay fetid, clinging mud, pecked by white birds.

As Teng drew near, a unit of ten prisoners staggered up the wooden jetty, scrutinised by a huddle of officials. After a suitable pause, another ten followed. A crowd of on-lookers had also gathered, held back by spearmen from Prince Arslan's garrison. Teng slipped between longshoremen and merchants until he reached the front, where immediately he spotted Hsiung.

The servant boy lurked near the jetty among the Salt Minister's motley bodyguard, crouching between two large trunks. He had hidden himself behind Sergeant P'ao's broad back.

Salt Minister Gui had been honoured with supervising the embarkation of the prisoners. His silken robes declared fitness for high responsibility, his demeanour a proper contempt for lesser creatures. Yet he seemed oddly distracted, overly absorbed by his abacus. The loading was going well: already three-quarters of the prisoners had shuffled aboard the merchant junks.

Teng wondered how to attract his friend's attention. Hsiung stared constantly at the ground to avoid the Salt Minister's notice. He wore a peasant's wide, conical straw hat to hide his face. Calling out to him would be dangerous. The wharf was silent except for the clank of chains and scrape of feet, punctuated by harsh commands.

At that moment came the trotting of many iron-shod hooves and the rumble of wheels. The crowd parted in alarm as a black stallion pranced across the cobbles, its rump flicked playfully by a riding whip. An exceptionally sleek and handsome nobleman drove the beast forward. A name flitted round the wharf: *Jebe Khoja! Jebe Khoja!*

The rider caught sight of Gui and changed direction. Despite the muddy ground, officials fell to their knees. Yet the Salt Minister was slower than his fellows. He stared past his master at a cavalcade of litters and carriages bumping into the square.

In the lead came Jebe Khoja's personal carriage, gilded and

lacquered, laden with revellers. Its occupants made no effort to conceal themselves. Within lolled half a dozen beauties, peeping out excitedly, their faces white with make-up, fans fluttering like agitated butterfly wings. Among them, to Teng's great surprise, sat his former neighbour, Golden Lotus. Though innocent for his age, Teng sensed the significance of his presence among the courtesans.

Salt Minister Gui surely did, too, for he remained upright to greet his master. Now the silence on the wharf was complete. Everyone watched the two men. Jebe Khoja leaned forward in his saddle, pointed the whip and spoke sharply. Casting a baffled glance at the carriage, Gui finally lowered himself to his knees.

Jebe Khoja trotted over to the remaining prisoners and examined them from his horse. Satisfied, he cantered back to the still kneeling Gui and spoke words of praise. Then he trotted back to his carriage and leaned down from the saddle, murmuring to the ladies inside. Whatever he said provoked a flurry of fans.

Once more the cavalcade proceeded on its way – carriages of acrobats, singing girls, yes-sayers and hangers-on – as well as scores of noble Mongol lords and wealthy Chinese merchants, all bound for a picnic and entertainment to celebrate Jebe Khoja's triumph over the Red Turban rebels. Even now the Pleasure Gardens attached to Golden Bright Monastery were in readiness, pavilions heated by braziers, fire-pits roasting every kind of meat, four-legged and fowl, fish and lake dolphin. Tracks had been marked out for the racing of horses and other feats of skill.

Teng glanced at Gui. The Salt Minister's abacus had reappeared in his hands. He seemed lost, as though calculating an impossible sum.

No one spoke or moved until Jebe Khoja had left and the rumble of wheels died away. Abruptly the silence was broken by a mocking laugh, almost a croak. It came from one of the prisoners: 'Look who's riding the Salt Minister's yellow eel boy!'

A jeer followed from someone hidden in the crowd. Soon dozens were hooting, whistling and calling out Gui's name. The Salt Minister rose to his feet, blinking at his persecutors.

He ordered Sergeant P'ao to drag out the prisoner who had spoken. A savage beating commenced. All laughter ceased. The officers leading Prince Arslan's soldiers grew uneasy. Sensing the possibility of a riot, they gathered their men round the remaining Red Turbans awaiting embarkation. Others levelled crossbows at the crowd.

By now the beaten man's face was mangled, his nose a bloody hole. Gui's fishy eyes stared round and spotted Hsiung amidst the baggage. For a moment there was partial recognition. His expression darkened slowly. The boy's face connected him to another wayward possession: his disobedient daughter, Yun Shu.

'What is *that* b-boy doing here?' he demanded.

Teng did not hear Sergeant P'ao's muttered reply.

'How do you know he is not a spy?' asked Gui, excitedly. 'His family are tainted with treachery! Take away the one you've punished and put this b-boy in his place.'

For a moment it seemed Sergeant P'ao might refuse. Then, with a lowered head, he ordered his men to seize Hsiung.

Teng could barely stir for trembling. Oh, he must not just stand there! He should find a sword and cut his friend free! Capture a horse and gallop into the hills! He watched in horror as Hsiung was chained to another prisoner. Meanwhile the broken body of the man he replaced had been thrown off the jetty to drown in the lake mud.

Hsiung struggled against his new bindings until a sharp command from Sergeant P'ao stopped him. The boy gazed beseechingly into his protector's face. Sergeant P'ao whispered urgently in the boy's ear then moved away to chivvy the last groups of prisoners onto the jetty, his expression unreadable.

Perhaps madness made Teng reckless. Despite his fear, he stepped out of the crowd, first one, then two and a third pace forward. It was not too late. Confucius taught that a good man always admonishes the wicked, whatever the cost to himself. He could yet protest to the Salt Minister that Hsiung was no spy. He would speak out! It was his family's destiny to risk everything for duty. That was the path Grandfather had chosen, the noble path of Yueh Fei. Yet Teng, longing to speak, could only shiver, miserably exposed before the crowd, his head bowed, hands clenched.

Finally his agitation attracted the Minister of Salt's attention. Gui stared, recognising him as his unworthy daughter's other confederate. This realisation broke what little courage Teng possessed. He slunk back and disappeared into the crowd, dodging between tall legs. The cruel hands he anticipated, determined to clutch, hold, hurt never came. Soon he had escaped into the busy streets of the Port District where few noticed a hurrying boy.

天命

Teng did not flee to Deng Mansions. Home was no longer safe since Liu Shui's arrival – and he feared leading an angry Salt Minister Gui to Father's door.

Up the Hundred Stairs he scrambled, chest heaving, dragging himself with his hands. Past the brassbound gates of Cloud Abode Monastery and into the bamboo groves. At once the city seemed far away. He was protected by a maze of delicate stems, shadows, pale winter sunbeams slanting across stone and moss. His pace slowed. Then grief began: images of Hsiung in chains, bound to misery and ceaseless toil forever.

Deeper, deeper into the woods, his steps directed by fate or chance, until he found himself outside the ruined watchtower, its ancient walls besieged by bushes and brambles. For a long moment he dared not enter. This cursed place was the source of all their troubles. But that was why he must enter, at least one more time, to face the hungry ghosts trapped inside.

Wriggling through the crawl-way, now almost completely overgrown, he entered the rectangle of smoke-blackened stone. It had not changed since the spring, except the bones they had patiently buried were more visible than ever. Not a trace remained of the dead dog. Teng realised he was shivering. How did bones always rise to the surface? However carefully one laid them to rest, they broke through the earth like shoots in springtime, seeking a little more life, greedy for the sun.

As he wept silently for Hsiung, gazing out across the grey, still waters of the lake, a large merchant junk rounded the headland from the harbour, followed by another and another. The fleet had set sail for the Salt Pans. Nothing could restore his friend to Deng Mansions.

Teng crept to the very edge of the cliff, examining each ship in turn for the smallest sign of Hsiung. But the slaves were a huddled mass in the open hold.

Soon the last ship had passed; the fleet manoeuvred into a loose diamond formation, their stiff bamboo sails hoisted. For a long while, Teng watched them dwindle into the distant haze of the horizon. He thought of Yun Shu, how he had seen her borne away in a wagon of servants, as much a prisoner as Hsiung. Of the three friends – pine, bamboo and plum – only he remained free.

Part Two

Hornets' Nest

Six-hundred-li Lake, Central China.
Winter, 1314

eight

天命

Yun Shu pondered her next incarnation as she climbed a steep dirt track beside the sluggish Min River. When summer brought the monsoon these placid waters would froth: for now, the winter dry season lingered.

It was a way little-travelled, especially since rebel bands had settled in the district. Fishermen in the port of Yulan, where she had disembarked from a merchant junk carrying salt fish and hemp, had warned her to beware brigands.

'Surely they will not trouble a Nun of Serene Perfection?' she had asked, her eyes wide. Though life had taught her to trust nothing and no one she was a forgetful student.

The fishermen had grinned as they examined the young nun. Yun Shu's hand rose unconsciously to straighten her topknot, flowing in the style of 'whirlwind clouds' and held in place by a modest bone comb. Her blue quilted robe hugged her figure against the chilly weather. She wore a nun's large yellow kerchief round her slender neck. A conical straw hat hung beside a blue satchel containing scriptures and the Seven Treasures she had been given to sustain her journey. Gifts for the spirit as well as body: the two flowed through each other like cloud through air.

One by one the fishermen looked away to hide their amusement.

'Let's just say they *might* trouble you, Little Aunty,' said the eldest. 'And up there . . .' He had gestured at the Bamboo Hills rising toward the distant slopes of Changshan, the Holy Mountain. 'Up there,' he had repeated more forcefully, 'only the gibbons and tigers will hear you cry for help.'

Yun Shu pursed plump lips, then bowed gratefully, 'You are kind,' she said, 'but I have an amulet that will certainly protect me.'

This seemed to reassure them, as well it might, coming from a Serene One.

'Nevertheless,' said the old fisherman, 'I'll send my sons up with fresh fish after the New Year. Just to see how Little Aunty is faring.'

A comforting thought as she climbed the lonely path into the hills.

The road followed the course of the river for many *li*, climbing through limestone ravines clad with moss and trailing vines. The hill country brooded in winter silence. There was no breeze, though the lake was famous for its winds. Bamboo hung motionless, leaves dry and yellow as withered fingers.

Yun Shu paused to drink from the icy waters of a pool – one of many formed by the river. She smelled wood smoke and recalled the warning about brigands.

Yet the smoke heralded the end of her journey: as Yun Shu emerged from a narrow, winding ravine onto a path above the river, she caught her first glimpse of Mirror Lake.

It filled a long, tear-shaped depression in the hills. The reason for its name was obvious. As the sun sank, ribbons of fire shimmered across the silvery surface. Pine trees and bamboo were reflected on the water. Any clouds passing high above could gaze down on their own image.

Tears welled, though Yun Shu had taught herself to never cry in public. A deep quiver ran through her: it was so long since she had felt even an approximation of joy. She savoured and gulped it like water after a parched journey. Then Yun Shu understood that Mirror Lake might reveal everything she needed to cleanse old wounds, however shameful.

She hastened along the shore path until her final destination came into view – and with it the wood smoke's source.

No one knew how long Sitting-and-Whistling Pavilion had perched on the small, rocky island jutting out of Mirror Lake. Since before the Tang Dynasty, certainly. For centuries, any novice seeking to become a Serene One at Cloud Abode Monastery had been sent up here for an extended period of meditation. Here she might renounce foulness and confusion, purify herself through the prescribed rituals and generally maintain the shrine.

Sitting-and-Whistling Pavilion certainly needed maintenance. As Yun Shu drew near, she noticed how the wooden building leaned slightly. It was the size of a large barn. At the front ornate pillars propped up a curving roof of red clay tiles; at the rear were tiny rooms for visitors. A causeway of stepping stones led to the island, otherwise one could easily wade, for the lake was deep only in purity.

A flutter of smoke rose from the rooms at the back. Yun Shu stepped across the stones and followed a path round the outside of the shrine. Within she glimpsed glinting eyes and squat shapes: holy images, best greeted for the first time in daylight.

Round the back were two wooden cells and a covered porch where a fire smouldered in a cooking hearth of soot-stained bricks. A quick search revealed that whoever built the fire was no longer on the small island.

Exhausted from her long walk, Yun Shu slumped by the hearth. The night was cold and she wrapped herself in a blanket, feeding the flames with twigs. The bamboo groves whispered as the night breeze quickened. She could hear the calls of owls and apes, and – far away, she prayed – the triumphant roar of a tiger. Infinities of darkness stretched beyond comprehension, lent shape and meaning by glittering constellations.

Yun Shu knew that one day she might visit those same stars, the Immortals' realm, if she could only transform herself and join the eternal Dao. Then those who had mocked and hurt and rejected and injured her would gaze up in wonder. Yet she would be too rapt on her journey upon a floating cloud, up, up, into Perfection, to even recall their names.

Another, more urgent part of her desired only a friendly voice and face. Yun Shu tried to imagine that such a person sat beside her. Unexpectedly, for she seldom cared to recall childhood, a tousle-haired earnest boy chanting a gloomy poem materialised in her mind. With him, a brooding lad too tall and broad for his age, leaning on a bamboo sword.

Hungry and cold as she was, memories eased her to a deep, dreamless sleep. The glowing embers of the fire dwindled into lifeless grey ash in the hearth.

天命

A few days brought the New Year festival, the first she had ever spent alone. Yet Yun Shu was not truly alone. Clay statues of Immortals and gods surrounded her as she swept the shrine room of the Pavilion: kindly demon officials from the other world; fierce guardians with curved scimitars and angry red eyes. She scrubbed the floor with freezing water from the lake and polished the woodwork with lamp oil. At the prescribed hour she lit lamps and chanted from the sacred books.

On New Year's morning the temple was cleaner than it had been for many months. Yun Shu knelt before the image of Lord Lao, rubbing a shine into his lacquered feet. Then she sensed someone in the doorway.

Turning quickly, she found a young girl peeping round the doorframe. She wore peasant clothing and had a gay, mischievous air.

'Are you the new Aunty?' demanded the girl. 'They said you were young and pretty.'

Yun Shu rose, brushing her knees. She refrained from asking who *they* might be.

'Now you are here, people will come to pray again,' said the girl.

'That would please Lord Lao very much,' said Yun Shu.

'Unless it's Hornets' Nest and his men,' whispered the girl.

'Hornets' Nest? What a funny name! Who is he?'

'You know,' said the girl. She hid a nervous giggle behind her hands, then made a buzzing noise. 'Grandma told me to bring you this. She has too many aches to come herself. Poor Grandma!'

The girl slid a large reed basket into the shrine with her foot.

'You can step inside, you know,' said Yun Shu. 'Lord Lao wouldn't be cross – and neither would I.'

She was answered by another giggle, hidden behind small hands.

'Grandma says it's unlucky here after what happened to the last Aunty. Watch out for Hornets' Nest!'

With that, the little girl vanished and, though Yun Shu called after her, she hopped away over the stepping-stones, disappearing into the bamboo groves.

Inside the basket, Yun Shu found a week's provisions. Simple fare: rice, millet, vegetables, and – no doubt to pour out as a sacrifice – a flask of wine. Yun Shu was not surprised by the food. She had been informed a local wise woman called Muxing, evidently the girl's Grandma, was paid to supply visiting nuns.

As she boiled rice, Yun Shu watched flakes of snow flutter down. The sky was grey as the hardest stone.

天命

All morning the snow fell until, by mid-afternoon, Yun Shu retreated to the shrine for warmth. An ancient fire pit lay in the centre of the earth floor and she built a small blaze. Soon red shadows danced over the walls and watchful statues.

Sipping from the wine flask, blankets round her shoulders, Yun Shu watched the thick, wet flakes swirling until the sky was a restless blur of motion. Though she seemed to look outwards, her whole being turned inwards – if the past may be said to live within a soul, or anywhere, once it has faded . . .

Yun Shu's last New Year celebration with her family had occurred when she was fourteen. By then Father had already spent years posted far across Six-hundred-*li* Lake in the Salt Pans. Even then her memories of him were hazy. All her life he had been too busy to notice her, always hurrying and bustling or, if met by chance in the corridor, a pair of silk slippers and legs glimpsed from a kneeling position.

After her disobedient conduct on Monkey Hat Hill, Yun Shu had been permanently exiled to a tiny room attached to the servant quarters. To all practical intents, she had died as far as Father or Golden Lotus were concerned. Only on New Year's Day or other important festivals was she ushered into their presence, and then merely to perform a silent kowtow. Her two brothers were forbidden to acknowledge her. If she encountered them by chance, she was instructed to face the wall until they had passed. The servants, however, were allowed to address her, as long as they used the title 'Little Fox Fairy'.

So, from the age of eleven to fourteen she was a prisoner. But then, the entire family was confined. His Excellency Jebe Khoja had assigned them a house within Prince Arslan's compound – a great honour. Yet the house was small compared to the mansion on Monkey Hat Hill and lay behind high walls patrolled by soldiers. They had become captives of fear, afraid to venture out in case rebels molested them.

Yun Shu would certainly have gone mad in her tiny chamber except for two diversions. First, she won over a few of the female servants, especially Pink Rose. Hours were spent in the lowly maid's company, helping with dull chores or gossiping.

The second diversion was precious. With the connivance of her brothers' aged tutor, who taught her how to read difficult characters when nobody was watching, Yun Shu periodically crept into Father's library and borrowed books. The library had been abandoned since his departure for the Salt Pans so no one noticed or cared.

But on New Year's morning when Yun Shu was fourteen, she attracted Golden Lotus's full attention.

Outside Sitting-and-Whistling Pavilion snow continued to scatter from a burdened sky. Yun Shu held out her hands to the fire-pit. The heat on her palms warmed a memory . . .

Before her New Year prostration to Golden Lotus, Yun Shu had stopped by the kitchen and held her hands to the stove. It was late morning and the kitchen servants were preparing an extravagant feast in honour of Father's patron, Jebe Khoja, an intimate feast with Golden Lotus as hostess. The Mongol prince was to be accompanied only by his closest retainers.

The servants fell silent as Yun Shu entered, but she knew what they were saying. What everyone would say. Her gut twisted into a hot, helpless serpent of shame.

By the time she knelt before a bored, pre-occupied Golden Lotus, the serpent had grown limbs and claws to become a dragon. It had developed a tongue.

As was customary, she pressed her forehead to the floor while the young man sat stiffly in Father's chair. Only this time, the girl looked up and stood upright, her absurdly large feet in full view.

'Golden Lotus,' she whispered, in case the servants heard, 'someone once told me Confucius says we must speak out when even emperors do wrong.' That someone had been Teng; in a better life it seemed. Golden Lotus watched sulkily, twisting a lock of his silky hair. Yun Shu had realised how young he was, his doll-like face perfect as a lily. She took a deep breath. 'Can it really be that you will entertain gentlemen here, when Father is away?'

Although Yun Shu had no reason to love her father, she could not help defending him. Then she said the worst thing possible, for it rang the concubine's fears like a gong. 'What will people *say*? Will Father ever forgive you?'

For a moment Golden Lotus's white face was blank as porcelain.

'Stupid girl!' he said. 'Did you not realise your Father arranged the invitation to show his gratitude for the favours bestowed upon him by Jebe Khoja this last year.'

'But . . .' began Yun Shu.

His face contorted. 'Your Father calls me his most precious object! Then why am I to be shared? Do you think I relish being served like a dish of meat?'

A cruel impulse forced Yun Shu to speak, 'I thought that was why you want feet like deer hooves! To be served! To be admired!'

'I have every right to be admired!' he screeched. 'Disobedient girl! Get out, Little Fox Fairy! We have ways of dealing with witches!'

In a flash she understood. He was afraid what would happen if he failed to please Jebe Khoja. And equally afraid of pleasing him too much.

All night she heard carousing and shouting in the family quarters, followed by a long, frightening silence. Jebe Khoja left at dawn, having been so overcome he could not manage the short journey to his residence on the other side of the palace.

A few weeks later, as long as it took for letters to circulate round the lake, Golden Lotus sent a servant to inform Yun Shu that her marriage had been brought forward. It seemed Father, though far away, had agreed to hasten his worthless daughter's nuptials to retrieve a scrape of profit from her existence. No loss to him, she thought, tears running silently down her cheeks, a loss soon forgotten amidst his noble affairs.

Tears were back on Yun Shu's cheeks as she sat before Lord
Lao's image. Though certain the wine in the basket was
intended for a sacrifice, she drank deeply. Cheap, coarse wine
that burned . . .

There had been wine on her wedding day, too. One could
hardly avoid the Ceremony of Exchanging Cups, even if every
other rite was neglected.

Yun Shu had been loaded onto a Salt Bureau barge, her tiny
dowry filling a single plain box. Only Pink Rose wept by the gate.
Neither Golden Lotus nor her brothers waved farewell. Indeed,
she had been allowed to see them just once a year – to kowtow to
the little boys in silks before Golden Lotus hurried her out.

Four days of shadowing the lake shore brought her to
Chenglingji, a small port with a garrison, government warehouse and little else. It did, however, possess a singular
characteristic. All commerce in salt and grain for a hundred *li*
was dominated by one clan, the Zhongs. Mutual profit was
assured for anyone supplying the Zhongs with tax free salt –
anyone like Salt Minister Gui. It followed such a deal must be
sealed in a proper manner; and Yun Shu's body was the sealing
wax.

As she entered the Zhong compound a sly-faced man in
gaudy silks looked her up and down. He chewed roast melon
seeds continuously, resulting in a permanent sneer and
narrowed eyes. His name, she soon learned, was First Son
Zhong. 'But you must call me *Dear Uncle*,' he said, leading her
to the woman who would determine her entire happiness:
Honoured Mother-in-law.

Madame Zhong possessed three grown-up sons but no living
husband. Although her eldest – *Dear Uncle* to Yun Shu --
nominally led the Zhongs, it soon became apparent he deferred
constantly to his mother.

The old lady dabbed her nose with a handkerchief as she examined the kneeling bride. An exceptionally bony woman, she wore layer upon layer of padded, scented clothes to fend off unwholesome breaths. The quantity of amulets hanging from her belt, sleeves, head-dress and flat bodice exceeded normal precautions.

'No closer!' she squeaked at her son. 'I've heard bad things about this one!'

Dear Uncle examined Yun Shu with new interest.

'Now,' said Madame Zhong, briskly, 'let us understand one another. I have only allowed you to marry my youngest son because he is worthless. As, I am assured, you are. Also, of course, to oblige our dear friend, the Excellent Gui. Do not ever approach me unless summoned. Even then, never if you are menstruating.'

The wedding ceremony, such as it was, commenced that same afternoon. Dozens of Zhongs gathered to honour the custom of Disrupting the Wedding Chamber. Yun Shu was ordered to lie down and Dear Uncle commenced the jovial games. 'The more fun, the more prosperity!' he cried, citing the ancient proverb. Her feet were poked, pinched and measured by dozens of hands – and declared peasant feet, so that Yun Shu must be treated like a peasant. She was ordered to walk across a 'paddy field' of upside down wine cups and Dear Uncle took it upon himself to spank her behind each time one broke or moved, all the while grinning and chewing. A horde of female relatives yanked at her limbs and whispered in Yun Shu's ear about places of the body she had never dreamt one might mention. In short, everyone was hugely disappointed when Madame Zhong, who had taken no part in the ceremony for fear of noxious breaths, decreed it time to consummate the match.

For the first time Yun Shu met her future lord. He was eased into the room by two brothers, one on either side. Initially she thought he must be very sick – or deranged. His bloodshot eyes rolled slowly as he mumbled incoherent words, suddenly bursting into hysterical laughter.

Yun Shu, still quivering from her recent ordeal, managed to gain Dear Uncle's attention. 'Does Honoured Bridegroom need a doctor?' she whispered.

Dear Uncle's revolving jaw paused.

'Can't you *smell* the problem?' he asked.

Then she did. Quite unmistakeably. The groom was dead drunk. But that which laid him low also lent him the necessary strength for the Ceremony of Cups. Custom decreed the groom should drink four cups of lucky wine and she only two, to denote her frailty. Evidently he considered her very frail, for he gulped down her portion of good fortune as well as his own.

For a long moment the assembled Zhongs went quiet. Perhaps a few pitied the poor girl; perhaps they felt ashamed to see a member of their clan behave without a trace of decorum. Dear Uncle smiled blandly.

'If he manages the next bit I'll drink twenty cups myself.'

His brothers and the other male relatives applauded this vow, offering rival bets. Yun Shu was hustled into a chamber containing a large bed with its covers pulled back. Her husband followed, pursued by a lascivious roar.

Now she had a chance to examine him. He shared his mother's gauntness and sallow complexion. Twice her age, he looked far older. Although they had dressed him in scraps of silk, he wore his usual clothes underneath and stank of soiling. Pity pierced Yun Shu's disgust: with it came power.

'Sit on the bed,' she murmured, aware of ears pressed to door and walls.

They sat side by side. He was looking at her through glassy eyes: yet she sensed he understood far more than his family assumed.

'We must satisfy them,' she whispered. 'We must appear to consummate the marriage or they will give us no peace. Do you understand?'

He nodded slowly.

At her insistence, he jumped up and down on the bed, its creak and groan provoking amusement and applause outside. The effort so exhausted him that he fell into a deep sleep. Yun Shu hesitated only a moment. Remembering Pink Rose's lewd stories about wedding nights, she took a pin from her head-dress and opened a wound in her palm, staining the sheet with blood. Finally she loosened both their clothes and pretended to sleep.

When Dear Uncle and the others peeked in, they exclaimed at the bloody sheet, regarding her with new respect.

'That's the way,' he said. 'Give Mother a male heir and she might decide you're family.'

Once they had gone, Yun Shu realised no one had mentioned her husband's name, other than calling him *Third Son*. Later she learned it was Xuanlu, or 'melody', and laughed bitterly, for she had never met anyone so out of tune with himself.

A draught of cold wind entered Sitting-and-Whistling Pavilion. Yun Shu snuggled deeper into her blanket and stared at the fire-pit. Beyond this room the entire world was dark. She took up the wine flask, drank again . . .

Years merged. She and her husband lived in a hut at the rear of the compound, far from the family quarters, allowed a basic allowance of food and enough wine to keep Xuanlu pacified.

At first Yun Shu tried to be a dutiful daughter-in-law; per-haps to disprove her parents' low opinion of her, perhaps even to dredge a little good from her husband's nature. But he was beyond cure. In the years of their marriage he hardly spoke to her, and never intimately. The one relief was that he made no demands on her body, his *yang* having shrivelled to a worm.

Winter, summer, spring, from a distance seasons merged. Soon she was a tall girl of fifteen, her puppy fat gone. Though she longed to make friends none of the female Zhongs could be trusted, nor their sharp-tongued servants. Yun Shu kept to her miserable hut whenever possible, discovering a secluded corner beside the compound wall that she turned into a garden. Xuanlu was mostly with his brothers, always the butt of their bored, cruel jokes.

Sixteen, seventeen, eighteen, the years of her youth passed meaninglessly. Her dearest companions were a few cheap woodcut printed books stolen from Father's library before her banishment: *The Book of Songs*; a history of the Empire; most precious of all, a copy of Yun Cai's poems given to her by Dear Mother before she died; an almanac; and a Daoist text, *The Way and Its Power*. This she came to learn by heart:

> *Painful to know*
> *we will always be outsiders –*
> *endlessly rolling ocean,*
> *aimlessly blowing wind . . .*

Though the wise book urged passivity, she grew angrier and angrier, until one afternoon when she was barely nineteen years old, Dear Uncle appeared in the doorway of their hut and caught her reading. Xuanlu was elsewhere, getting drunk. She hid the book guiltily but it was too late.

'What is that?' he asked, incredulously. 'A book!'

The Zhong clan were indifferent readers, preferring, like Mongol grandees, to hire scribes. She bowed her head and he sensed advantage.

'Ah! So we have a little secret! Unless you make Dear Uncle happy he might have to take away your little book. He's been watching you.'

This last revelation turned Yun Shu cold. Still she did not raise her head. Dear Uncle's favourite concubine had died recently. She had noticed his eyes following her.

'You want me to be happy? I thought so.'

She looked up sharply.

'I will tell my husband about this.'

Dear Uncle popped melon seeds into his mouth.

'He'd sell you for a jar of wine.'

'Then I will tell Honoured Mother-in-law!' she cried. 'Leave me alone.'

Now he looked less secure.

'She would not believe you,' he said. 'Enough!'

He advanced into the hut, shutting the door behind him.

Afterwards Yun Shu wept on the bed, her clothes torn. In this position Xuanlu found her. For all his drunken idiocy, he guessed at once what had happened – and who was to blame, so that Yun Shu wondered if this was the first time Dear Uncle had taken advantage of the household women.

'Ah,' said her husband, settling heavily on the feeble bed. It creaked beneath his weight.

Unexpectedly, he reached out and stroked her hair until her tears ceased and she stared blindly at the wall.

'You mus' go!' he muttered.

She continued to stare at the wall.

'He won' ever stop now! Go back to y'parents!'

He fumbled at his belt. 'Look! I too' this!'

Reluctantly, Yun Shu turned. He was offering a small purse of coins.

'Go!' he said. 'When it's dark.'

Yun Shu had taken his mottled, bony hand and clutched it. He continued to stroke her hair clumsily with the other, watching the doorway fearfully.

Yun Shu paced up and down before Lord Lao's statue. Did not Lao Tzu teach inaction always overcomes action? That water, apparently meek and compliant, wears away the hardest stone? In Chenglingji she had not been passive. She had tried to shape her destiny. She had fled, deep into the night . . .

* * *

The lands north of Chenglingji were utterly unknown to her. In the five years she had dwelt there, Yun Shu had never been allowed out of the Zhong family compound. If Xuanlu had not led her to the Northern Road and accompanied her several *li* until the lights of Chenglingji lay in the distance, she could not have escaped.

Eventually he halted, shivering though the night was heavy with midsummer heat. Far to the south, she saw a faint glow like a Buddhist hell: the Salt Pans.

'I'll go back,' he said.

They stood awkwardly.

'Come with me,' she said. 'And be free.'

For a moment he hesitated. Then the lure of safety and a known place in this harsh world, however low and painful, overcame his doubt. Flapping a hand in farewell, he shuffled back down the dark road. Yun Shu knew they would not meet again in this world, that her divorce had just been solemnised, that she was young, strong, and blessed with the freedom he had turned down.

Yet by the time Yun Shu reached the ramparts of Hou-ming, twenty days later, she was almost crawling. Her shoes were worn to rags and she had not eaten for days. She passed slowly through the old Pleasure District, crossing canals until the high walls and gatehouse of Prince Arslan's palace reared. Guardsmen leant against their halberds, showing no interest as she approached.

'Is Salt Minister Gui here?' she gasped.

It was her chief anxiety. That he was still in the Salt Pans. The soldier did not disguise his contempt. 'Away from here! No beggars!'

'But sir,' said Yun Shu, through a haze of hunger and fatigue, 'please tell him, tell him his daughter . . . Tell him Yun Shu has returned!'

'Get away!'

'I am his daughter! I *am*!'

Something about her tone made the guards examine her closely.

'She does look familiar,' said one.

'No harm to ask,' offered another. 'We might get punished otherwise.'

So saying, he vanished into the palace, returning with the news her message had been delivered. Yun Shu squatted across the road. The hour bell of the nearby Buddhist monastery chimed. Finally, a maid entered the gatehouse. Yun Shu felt a rush of joy. Pink Rose, older now, her face more careworn, but still her friend! Yun Shu had stepped forward eagerly until Pink Rose's expression suggested a need for caution.

'Where is my father?' she asked.

The maid took her arm, weeping silently.

'Why did you come?' she sobbed. 'A message reached Golden Lotus from your husband's family. How could you, Yun Shu? Everyone knows your disgrace.'

Yun Shu blinked, exhausted and bewildered. 'What disgrace?' she mumbled.

'Is not casting spells on your Mother-in-law a disgrace?' asked Pink Rose. 'You must go somewhere else. Your father won't see you now. He is away down south in any case.'

This seemed so terrible Yun Shu could not accept it. 'I've done nothing wrong!'

'Golden Lotus sent me to say you are no longer the Salt Minister's daughter,' said Pink Rose. 'Oh, Yun Shu, why could you never act like other girls?'

Dabbing her eyes, she hurried back into the palace, leaving Yun Shu swaying on the street. She had stumbled blindly away, not caring where she went.

Did fate bring her back to Monkey Hat Hill? Her only intention had been to reach the cliffs and throw herself off. Yet passing Deng Mansions, Yun Shu paused, wondering if Teng still lived there, whether he might help. She remembered his betrayal at the ruined watchtower and pressed onwards, reaching the Hundred Stairs. Step by step she climbed, each taller than the last. If she had not known oblivion lay at the top, perhaps she would have lain down and given up.

Only at the brassbound gates of Cloud Abode Monastery did Yun Shu allow herself rest. The gates were firmly closed: locking out the world and its cruel, illusory sufferings.

She sat for a long while, head bent over her knees, occasionally staring at the rooftops of the half-deserted city. As her strength returned she knew it was time to find the cliff – and have done with it.

There came a sound of bolts; the high doors of the monastery creaked open.

A lady stood framed by daylight, dressed in yellow and blue robes. Yun Shu shrank back. The lady seemed familiar, known in a lost life.

'Lady Lu Si!' she croaked in wonder.

The Nun of Serene Perfection looked down at her.

'Why, it's Teng's little friend!'

Those simple, kindly words broke Yun Shu's strength. Her head span and she fell back towards the oblivion she craved. Except a hand steadied her before she could topple down the Hundred Stairs.

天命

The snow had stopped when Yun Shu woke. She lay beside the cold fire-pit in the shrine room of Sitting-and-Whistling Pavilion. A dawn of clear skies, night's sorrows and laden clouds having blown far away.

Throwing aside her heavy blanket, she went to the door and looked out across Mirror Lake. A pale blue sky framed the Holy Mountain, Chang Shan. Though snow clung to the pines and bamboo round the lake, it was already melting.

In a fervour to begin her transformation to Perfection, Yun Shu hurried to the statue of Lord Lao and bowed deeply. Then she sat cross-legged, her heels pressed to guard her warmest place. She clapped her teeth thirty-six times and breathed through her nose gently. Though a novice in the Great Work, Yun Shu tried to visualise the Dao's eternal energy rising through her spinal column. She raised her hands in the pre-scribed manner, all the time seeking to form a Pearl of Immortality from her inner force. But try as she might, the golden elixir remained elusive. She sat quite still, slumped in defeat. Someone worthless could never attain the Pearl. Let alone decapitate the Red Dragon.

And so the *ch'i* energy she had garnered through meditation, the life force that breathes and flows through all things, seeped away in grief.

Yun Shu feared she would never have cared about becoming an Immortal if her marriage had been different. If the Zhongs had welcomed her into their family with respect and kindness. If she had children, warm and demanding, to fill her days and heart. In short, if she possessed that precious elixir and magical transformation lost utterly, bitterly, since her mother died: love.

After the failure of her practice, Yun Shu could not settle. She noticed the flask of wine intended as a sacrifice for Lord Lao and shame-facedly poured what remained over his feet. Then she considered all the unhelpful food she had eaten recently. One rarely turned to a creature of pure spirit with a full belly!

But one of the Twelve Rules was *Avoid all melancholy, fear and anguish*. Yun Shu knew she must do something to elevate her mood, and resolved to thank the old woman who had pro-vided her basket of supplies.

The path to Ou-Fang Village was easy to find as it shadowed the river, up past a sluggish waterfall and meadow where a herd of short-horned deer fled into the bushes, their speckled rumps rising and falling.

She came upon Ou-Fang Village quite suddenly and straight away distrusted the place. Perhaps it was the impression of squalor created by huts of damp mud, straw and thatch. In such a woody country it seemed strange no better building materials could be found. Maybe it was the sight of barefoot, hungry children, their faces streaked, their matted heads harbouring generations of lice. Considering a river ran through the village, there seemed no excuse not to wash.

The contrast between her clean, neat appearance and the surrounding dirt attracted immediate notice. Heads poked from windows as she picked a careful path up a street paved with liquid dung, lifting the hem of her skirts. A little way into the village she passed an old man loitering in his doorway. At the sight of her he fingered a lucky charm, as though she might be a hungry ghost in disguise.

'Venerable sir! Where may I find the old woman Muxing?'

This question deepened his suspicion. He spat and gestured at a house opposite. Yun Shu felt his eyes upon her back as she crossed the lane.

Though small, Mother Muxing's house displayed more pride than most in Ou-Fang Village. It possessed clean roof tiles and its own compound, complete with a crude gatehouse. A tiger's fanged skull hung above the entrance. As Yun Shu reached up to touch it, the little girl from yesterday ran round the corner.

'Hey!' cried the girl. 'It's the new Aunty! Grandma, come and look at the new Aunty!'

For a moment no one stirred in the house. Then a large-breasted woman with blue tattoos on her cheeks and extravagantly piled hair emerged. Yun Shu recognised her as one of the Yulai tribe who originally occupied this land, long before the Han Chinese came.

Mother Muxing glanced up and down the street, displeased to find a Nun of Serene Perfection outside her gate. 'Hssss! What are you doing here?'

Yun Shu frowned. 'I came to thank you for sending food. And to make myself known.'

The Yulai woman sniffed.

99

'You've done that all right – and not just to me.'

Yun Shu felt her superiority slipping. After all, was not Mother Muxing a servant of Cloud Abode Monastery? Should she not speak with more respect to an Initiate of the Dao? She remembered the little girl's warning.

'Perhaps you refer to Hornets' Nest?'

A troubled smile crossed Muxing's tattooed face.

'Him and a few others. Best for pretty young girls not to parade around. I'll accompany you home.'

She bustled back into her house, reappearing in a cloak and heavy wooden-soled shoes. Yun Shu noticed two young men in the house, eating their midday meal and watching with open interest through the doorway.

'I must tell you,' said Yun Shu, 'my duties here include finding out what happened to my predecessor. Perhaps you can help me?'

Mother Muxing seemed not to hear the question.

Yun Shu followed the waddling woman through the village. Heads hastily withdrew from windows at the sight of Mother Muxing, who chuckled to herself, making a deep-throated, hoarse sound.

The ill-matched pair halted suddenly where the path re-entered the woods. A large heron blocked the way, regarding them with cold, hungry eyes. In its long beak, a beautiful, glinting trout wriggled. An upward tilt of the beak gulped the fish in one.

Mother Muxing muttered a charm against misfortune, using the dialect of the Yulai, while Yun Shu rubbed her own lucky amulet and prayed to Xi-wang-nu, Queen Mother of the West.

The heron stretched its wings lazily and flapped away.

nine

天命

Spring came and went. If a phoenix or dragon gliding through the pale blue skies of early summer had circled Mirror Lake, it would have noted several things. That the water below was a shiny eye fixed upon heaven; that it was surrounded by curious formations of limestone peaks, slopes, towers and gullies; lastly, that a young man of twenty-one perched on the highest of the promontories, an easel upon his knee and ink-slate, water and brush at his side.

That same curious dragon might have swooped lower and surveyed the young man's work. For he was staring out at Changshan, the Holy Mountain, before executing swift, spontaneous brushstrokes. The composition was gathering force when a loud, taunting voice called up from a gully below.

'Teng! We know you're up there!'

The artist paused momentarily, struggling to retain the flow of his lines.

'Teng!' called a second voice, more insinuating than the first. 'If you don't come down we'll drink your share of the wine tonight!'

The young man on the peak fought for clarity against fresh waves of jeering and a gleeful chant of *We can see you! We can see you!* Sighing, he cleaned his brush and carefully packed away the painting gear. When he rose, his dark silhouette could be seen for many *li* around.

Teng had certainly grown since the day he watched the fleet sail from Hou-ming ten years earlier. He was neither tall nor short, feeble nor broad. His features, too, were midway between handsome and plain. Yet his sensitive brown eyes possessed an unusual intensity. Sometimes it was a cold, proud face, for he had inherited the Deng clan's ancient pretensions.

His expression was particularly scornful as he clambered down to the two young men below, who whistled and pretended to bow. One was burly and the other lithe; both wore the scars of brawls.

'Your Excellency! How gracious of you to . . .' The burly fellow struggled to complete his witticism. His name was Chao.

'To *grace* us?' suggested Teng. 'That might be amusing. Or how about *honour* us?'

Chao's friend, the wilier of the pair, smiled toothily. His name was Hua.

'I'm still going to drink your share of the wine,' he said. 'For dodging work.'

Teng's eyebrows raised. 'You usually do.'

Hua nodded. 'That's how I like it.'

'I've noticed.'

For a moment they examined him.

'How come you always want the last word?' demanded Chao.

Hua roared approvingly and Teng withdrew, more in disgust than defeat. He joined their other companion, a short, sun-burned man, ten years older.

'Any luck, Shensi?'

The wrinkled man shook his head, but continued to glance round. They were in a narrow ravine showing signs of ancient road-building. Except that the road terminated in a sheer wall of collapsed limestone boulders. Teng, who had grown used to interpreting Shensi's silences, nodded at the rock fall.

'Could that hide an entrance?' he asked.

Shensi spat to deter evil spirits who might be listening. Both raised their eyes to the limestone crag above – the same spot Teng had set up his easel. A few shrubs and saplings clung to the slope, otherwise it was unremarkable.

'There is something odd about this place,' Teng muttered. 'Do you feel it, too?'

If Shensi did, he gave no sign.

'Hey, Teng!'

Chao and Hua had been whispering for a while. Teng could predict their next joke with uncanny accuracy. On this occasion, he chose not to anticipate them.

'Hear something growl just then?' asked Chao.

Hua nodded gravely. 'I heard something. Something creeping. Sounded near.'

Early in their relationship, Teng had made the mistake of admitting to a fear of the man-eating tigers said to roam these hills. He had paid a price ever since.

'It was near!' insisted Chao. 'A sort of growling. Eh, Teng?'

Teng gazed down at Mirror Lake in the valley below. A small, rocky island with a shrine rose a little way from the shore. A plume of smoke snaked up from behind the temple. Then a tiny figure in long robes left the shrine and disappeared round the back. Chao and Hua watched the distant movement closely.

'Time to go!' said Hua.

Teng continued to stare. Something about the tear-shaped lake, fed and drained by busy waterfalls, moved him in an obscure way. The lake was a ship of pure, bright water floating on a sea of limestone waves. A ship the imagination might sail upon to wisdom.

They descended the steep, stony road through the hills to Ou-Fang Village. Even there, Chao kept up his favourite joke while Teng washed in the river. Hiding behind a maple tree, he roared and snarled like a tiger. And this, Teng reflected, was *before* the evening's drinking games.

天命

At twilight a wave of monsoon passed over Ou-Fang Village. The rain did nothing to cool the heat. Robes were loosened in the tavern where Chao and Hua held court and the two young bravos bellowed for refreshments. At their call the innkeeper nearly fell over himself.

Teng took his usual seat beneath a thatched porch outside and watched the rain. He could hear Hua berating the innkeeper, threatening to take his custom elsewhere. Significant custom it was. Teng marvelled that so shallow a fellow as Hua controlled so deep a purse. Further proof of the world's corruption. Of course his companion's wealth flowed from their secret employer – whose identity, Teng suspected, was no mystery to Chao and Hua.

Rain continued to fall. The two bravos settled down when food and wine appeared. No one offered Teng any and he was too proud to ask. Besides, Shensi would make sure he received a share.

His mind drifted across Six-hundred-*li* Lake to Hou-ming and back in time. A month ago this dubious expedition had seemed a blessing from Heaven.

Teng had been in Deng Mansions when the merchant had come. He was finishing off a writing class of fifty sweating, itchy, fidgeting boys. The day's lesson: the character for *duty*. He had yawned as he addressed the rows of faces; trays of sand and practice styluses on their grubby knees. It was too deliciously ironic. After all, duty was his only motive for playing teacher, certainly not cash; less than half the boys paid their school fees regularly. Yet when Father was too arthritic to conduct the lessons, an increasingly common occurrence, Teng had no choice but to deputise.

'Up like this. Down like this,' he instructed, tracing out this most essential of characters on a large square of the cheapest paper.

Then he noticed the merchant. After the class, Teng bowed, assuming the man wished to have his son tutored by Hou-ming's most illustrious scholar family. The quality of the man's silks suggested he, at least, might be a paying prospect.

'You are Honourable Deng Nan-shi?' asked the man in a soft voice.

'No, his son.'

The merchant glanced round the schoolroom – once a well-appointed audience chamber, its frescos faded by damp and regret.

'May one see the Honourable Deng Nan-shi?' pressed the man.

'My father is unwell,' said Teng. 'If you wish him to teach your son, I would be honoured . . .'

An upraised hand silenced him. 'No teaching and no son. Just an offer.'

'Then I shall see if he will break his rest,' replied Teng, intrigued.

Deng Nan-shi insisted on his son's presence during the interview. These days the hunchbacked scholar seemed to gain confidence when Teng was around.

'Very well,' said the merchant, 'but I insist on silence regarding all I reveal.'

And he had an intriguing tale.

He claimed to represent an important gentleman who wished to remain nameless. Yet this gentleman had chanced upon another gentleman, unfortunately now deceased – no need to mention his name either – who had possessed a trifling document the unnamed gentleman would pay generously to have translated.

'Very well,' said Deng Nan-shi.

'How do you define *generously*?' asked Teng.

The man laid hundreds of *cash* coins on the table.

After withdrawing to the library and conferring over the document, which was written in an archaic mode, father and son returned to their guest.

'The characters are obscure in places,' said Deng Nan-shi. 'We believe it is a copy of a much more ancient document, itself derived from one older still. It refers to the Kingdom of Chu in the age of Shang. It laments that all the royal family's tombs have been robbed, save those in the *Holy Region*. This being near, let's see, *Eye-look-heaven*, almost certainly a place name. Do you agree, Teng?'

His son nodded. 'It also complains the remaining tombs merely belong to lesser sons, possibly princes. We aren't sure. The author concludes by mourning the fragility of dignity and fame.'

The merchant listened avidly. 'Does it say where this *Eye-look-heaven* place might be?'

Deng Nan-shi had smiled.

'I discern you do not have a historian's interest in tombs,' he said.

The man had huffed and puffed but finally conceded the old scholar was right. He then came to the other part of his proposition. That Deng Nan-shi, or his learned son, sail down the lake to seek these undiscovered tombs. All expenses for the journey would be paid, as well as a tenth share of any profits, and he would hold an honoured position with the other explorers.

'For they lack someone who can read the ancient characters,' explained the merchant.

Deng Nan-shi's negative had been courteous but cold.

'Still, I will give you a few days to consider,' said the man, glancing round at the shabby state of Deng Mansions.

After he had gone, Teng asked excitedly why he, at least, could not go. Here was a chance for easy wealth. Every year one heard tales of tombs being opened and huge fortunes being made. The Mongols paid extravagantly for ancient treasures.

With the profits the Dengs could restore the ancestral home, buy a gentleman's wardrobe of silks. If nothing else, eat meat for a change.

Teng dared not mention his real motive: to escape the schoolroom forever. Then he would paint and dally with singing girls and banter with his friends and applaud in the theatre and contemplate the Ten Thousand Creatures to his heart's content. The vehemence of Deng Nan-shi's response surprised him.

'Are we to become grave robbers? Just because we are poor? Do not take me for a fool. You hope to evade your duty!'

The argument went back and forth until Teng finally gained his way. Deng Nan-shi, for all his ideals had to concede their desperation. Especially since a brace of orphans had taken residence in Deng Mansions after the recent famine, an act of charity they could ill afford.

'Do nothing dishonourable,' cautioned Deng Nan-shi. 'Remember, our family's reputation extends all round the lake and far beyond.'

Teng had sailed down to Yulan Port where he found Chao, Hua and Shensi waiting. Evidently the merchant, or his secret sponsor, had ways of passing messages swiftly. For weeks they had been scouring the lands round Changshan, the Holy Mountain and the district capital Lingling, until Teng heard a rumour of ancient tombs near Ou-Fang Village.

His thoughts were interrupted by a crashing sound from the inn. This was followed by shouting and the thud of a blow. Inside, Teng found Shensi struggling to separate Chao from a villager with blue tattoos on his cheeks – one of the Yulai people.

'You damn savage!' bellowed Chao. 'How dare you bring your blue face in here?'

Teng squeezed in front of Chao, who was hopelessly drunk. Meanwhile Hua roared encouragement to all sides at once. Teng and Shensi urged the villager to leave. This the man did with baleful dignity, and only just in time, for Chao threw Teng aside like a paper warrior and reached for the knife he kept in his boot.

After the villager had gone, large cups of wine were required to subdue Chao. Amidst curses and threats, Teng learned the reason for the quarrel. People were complaining that Chao and Hua bought up all the spare wine, grain, eggs and chickens in the village, pricing out its poorer inhabitants.

'Don't you think,' said Teng, 'it would be better not to offend our hosts? We are unarmed and there are only four of us. Besides, their case is not unreasonable. They have children and elderly relatives to feed.'

Hua snorted. 'They won't trouble us.'

'How can you be certain?'

Now Chao joined in. 'Because they know what's good for 'em.'

'And bad,' added Hua. 'Or, let's just say, who is bad for them. Eh, Chao!'

Though Teng pressed, neither would reveal the name of this bad *who*. As for Shensi, the tomb-finder concentrated on tilting his bowl.

天命

At noon the next day, Chao and Hua were breakfasting when tramping feet could be heard entering the village. They stuck their heads through the ground floor window in time to see a procession coming up the muddy road. Teng, who was reading a woodcut volume of poetry beneath the thatched porch, rose for a better view.

Forty guardsmen bearing halberds and fire-lances headed the column. Their faces shone with sweat from the hot climb. Then came four palanquins, each carrying an official. In the midst was an ironbound box on painted wheels, hauled back and front by lightly armed soldiers. Another few dozen guardsmen brought up the rear.

Hua whistled between his teeth. 'Tax farmers,' he said, softly. 'Going to Lingling.'

'They'll be back through here in a few days,' muttered Chao.

'Unless the rain holds them up,' said Hua.

Before the column drew parallel to the inn, they ducked inside. When the road was clear again, Teng found they had left in a hurry by the back door, though no one knew why. Tomb hunting was off for the day.

Mirror Lake drew him. Perhaps as an antidote to the vulgarity of his companions. Perhaps he sought clarity because he was considering whether to return to Hou-ming. It was not an easy decision. He had almost no money and must either beg a passage home or earn one in too undignified a way for a Deng to contemplate. Then again, he was loath to return empty handed, thereby confirming Father's judgement about the whole crazy venture.

Other reasons for staying lay all around. Until now he had never travelled much further than the burned-out suburbs of Hou-ming. It was wonderful to be in a limestone country as varied and contorted as his thoughts. To stand in holy Changshan's shadow and see peaks rising, cloud-capped, snow-capped, dream-haunted. *That* seemed worth a little low company.

Here he could paint and sketch whenever he pleased – at least until the paper and ink ran out. No more herding classes of grubby children for the sake of duty or Father's conception of it. What about a man's duty to himself? To his own destiny? The answer came back immediately in Deng Nan-shi's quizzical voice: 'Duty is a decent man's destiny. And he is measured by helping others. The Mandate of Heaven must be earned, Teng!'

How many times had he longed to retort that Grandfather's dutiful decision to resist the Mongols cost two hundred thousand lives? Had *that* earned the Mandate of Heaven? But, of course, there were some arguments one dared not deploy. For example, that he was enjoying the distance between himself and Father. That an invisible yoke had lifted from his neck – a realisation provoking instant guilt.

It was a relief to reach the clear waters of Mirror Lake and set up his painting equipment in a shadowy corner of the woods, half way up the hillside. Everything felt simple in an exquisitely complex way. All the disparate provinces of his troubled soul found a temporary ruler. His inner resources, memories, physical skill united for one, sublime purpose as he bent over his easel.

First he painted the shrine on its island, surrounded by blankness so the viewer's higher soul might be reflected in the unstained waters. Then, casting its shadow, the towering, limestone promontory behind which they had found the old abandoned road. He was just about to complete the composition with the stepping stones – thereby connecting the floating island of the spirit to a shore clad with resolute bamboo – when he noticed someone leaving the shrine.

Teng's brush hovered. He was closer to the building than yesterday and saw clearly that the barefoot figure in robes was female. He realised, too, he must be invisible to anyone below. What was she doing? His eyes opened wide. He leaned forward.

For the young woman – she was young, he could tell that much – was removing her robes until her pale body was quite naked. Teng knew he should look away. Somehow the fast beat of his pulse paralysed his will. She stood with her back to him, swaying as she tied up her long hair. His breath quickened. Now she half turned to reveal the silhouette of pert breast. She waded into the water and began to bathe.

'I can see why you like painting!' muttered a sly voice in his ear.

Teng jumped with surprise. His brush slipped and a smear of black ink ruined the careful composition.

'Phew!' said Chao. 'I'm getting so hot I might jump in with her!'

Teng closed his eyes. The excitement in his body had not eased.

'You wicked dog, Teng!' chuckled Hua. 'There we were, thinking you'd got ink for spunk.'

'Phee-eew!' growled Chao. 'Never mind him. Look at that! I wouldn't mind praying with that little missy down there. And when she sees what meat I'm offering as a sacrifice . . . Eh, Hua?'

'Maybe she's one of those nuns who like a bit of meat when the Abbot isn't around,' suggested his friend.

Teng realised they were serious about accosting the nun below.

'That would not be proper,' he said, hastily, 'in fact, I don't think we should even look at her. I regret my own part in this.'

Chao poked him in the back with a thick finger.

'Don't tell *me* what's a good idea,' he muttered. 'Ink boy.'

Teng's temper flickered. 'Even so, I believe . . .'

They were spared further dispute by a slouching figure: Shensi. He strolled up and coughed, noting the aggressive postures of the three young men. Then he spat.

'Where you been?' he asked, sullenly.

Hua scowled. 'None of your business. Here and there. There and here. Visiting old friends.'

'I've found it,' said Shensi.

'Found what?'

Shensi pointed up at the hillside above the lake.

'A shaft,' he said. 'The thing we're looking for.'

天命

Shensi led them round the lake, over the waterfall at its end, well away from the shrine. A winding path through the bamboo groves reached the old roadway. At the top of the gully they found Shensi had set up a tripod on the mound directly above the rockslide. A log dangled vertically from three ropes attached to the tripod.

'We're not digging a well,' said Hua, peering up. 'You're wasting our time.'

The young men heard a grating sound. It took a moment to realise Shensi was laughing – if scorn can be mirthful.

'Get spades, rope, lanterns,' said the older man, suddenly grave.

Chao sneered. 'You get 'em!'

Again the odd grating sound. Teng noticed how few teeth Shensi possessed. The tomb-hunter sat down on a rock.

'Well then,' said Hua, turning to Teng, 'do something useful for a change. Fetch the spades.'

But Teng settled beside Shensi. 'My job is to read ancient characters. I am a scholar. A gentleman. You fetch.'

Something about Teng's tone must have resembled Father's, for Chao and Hua sloped off down the ravine in a foul humour.

It was a pleasant wait in the cool, shady gully. Teng lay back, listening to insects and the cheep of mating birds. An image of the naked woman entering the water kept him amused. Even the rain held off.

Chao and Hua came puffing up the road, burdened with equipment. Shensi rose to meet them and they gathered round a slight, concave indentation in the hillside. Hua kicked at it angrily.

'We dragged everything up here for *this*?'

Shensi manoeuvred the tripod over the depression.

'Listen,' he said.

Then he lifted the log and let it fall. Instead of a dull thud on the stone hillside, there was a hollow sound. A definite echo.

'Shaft,' he said, pointing down.

It took less than half an hour to dig through. The earth fell with a clatter into yawning darkness and Teng was glad he did not fall with it. As their spades broke the crust of soil there rose a deep, mournful sigh of released air.

'Ghosts are escaping,' said Shensi.

'Or trying to warn us,' muttered Teng.

Certainly the air below reeked of brooding decay. Hua retreated a few steps.

'Warn us?' he said. 'Do the books . . . mention *warnings?*'

'Yes,' said Teng, enjoying the effect of his words, 'and terrible curses.'

'How do we know it's not just an old well?' asked Chao.

Teng shook his head pityingly. Sighed. 'Think for a change! One would hardly dig a well through solid stone up here. What would be the point?'

He realised Chao and Hua were examining him in an unfriendly way.

'Wouldn't *one?*' demanded Chao.

'One definitely would *not*,' replied Teng.

They all leaned forward and looked into the dark mouth of the shaft. Chao poked Teng with his big forefinger for the second time that day.

'Your turn now,' he said. 'Seeing *one* knows so much about it.'

Hua, still shaken by talk of curses, grunted agreement. 'Get down there to earn your share. We'll stay here and guard.'

Though Teng looked to Shensi for support, even the tomb-finder's face was blank – presumably because he didn't fancy going first himself. And it was the scholar's job to find any artefacts or writing that might date the shaft.

While they tied a thick hemp rope round Teng's chest, Shensi explained the situation. 'They had holes like this for air while digging. And to take out buckets of stone. See if it's what we think. If it is a grave, see if someone's robbed it already. That's often the way.'

Teng had never heard him so voluble.

'Do your job and I'll let you share the wine tonight,'

promised Hua for a change, whose perspiration exceeded his exertions. It was the acrid sweat of fear. 'Do they curse people who are just watching?' he added.

'Every time,' said Teng.

'Down!' he called. 'Down a little further!'

The lamp he held sputtered, illuminating walls of solid stone with a pale, dancing light. Every so often he tested the walls with his booted feet.

'Down!' he cried.

Suddenly his probing boots connected with air.

'Stop!' he screamed. 'Stop!'

Perhaps he had descended so far they could not hear him. A moment later he was on solid ground, surrounded by darkness. Instantly the light went out.

A rushing noise like beating wings filled his ears. He began to breathe rapidly. Any moment demons would lunge from the blackness. He had no defence.

Teng tried to slow his heart, counting breaths, screwing his eyes tight to shut out circling ghosts and demons. Finally he calmed himself. He became aware of distant shouts from above, unrecognisable words. With his eyes still closed, he prepared to tug at the rope three times, the signal to haul him up. Only the memory of Hua and Chao's jeering faces gave him pause. How could he depart without confirming whether it was a tomb or just an ancient mine? Whether thieves had already emptied its treasures?

Teng forced open one eye, then another. No red-faced demons watched from the darkness. The black air swirled with infinitesimal motes of light. He needed a flame.

Gingerly, as though the dark was quicksand that might drown him, he knelt, taking a flint and tinderbox from his belt. Then he set the lamp against his foot so he could find it easily. He felt for the oily wick and struck the flint. Sparks. Struck again and again. The kindling caught, followed by the wick.

Silently, like a giant hand opening out, light seeped across a huge oval chamber carved from solid rock.

A moment later Teng closed his eyes. He had seen enough. Too much, if the old stories of curses were true. He tugged sharply at the rope three times. Nothing stirred. Again, more forcefully. Nothing. A dreadful certainty they would throw the rope down on top of him set Teng trembling. Then, with a jerk, his feet left the ground and he was rising. Up into the dark stone shaft. He helped those hauling with scrabbling hands, desperate to breathe pure air, until a ring of light appeared.

They dragged him into the sunshine and he lay face down, ignoring their excited questions. He sought out Shensi's face and nodded.

The tomb-finder responded with a low, grating laugh that revealed all five of his teeth.

ten

天命

The limestone country was a maze: valleys, lakes, spiralling misshapen hills, ravines terminating in caves that sucked down muttering streams only to release them as singing waterfalls. A place of transformation. Here monsoons dripped through rock to grow fingers of stone, millennium after heedless millennium. Precipices collected windblown earth to host tiny forests high in the air. The people of this barren land were used to clinging: sometimes their fingers slipped.

Hsiung did not imagine losing his grip as he swaggered up a narrow path bordered on one side by a solid cliff wall and on the other by an inglorious fall to jagged rocks. The young man's walk was all loin and shoulder swing. A long sword with a tasselled hilt hung from a scabbard on his back and throwing knives protruded from his girdle. He wore a leather coat sewn with plates of iron. A bright red headscarf held flowing black hair in check and proclaimed him a criminal: a Red Turban rebel, eternal foe to the Great Khan.

Half way up the cliff Hsiung paused. Silver-backed monkeys scuttled along a ledge and he envied their freedom.

The path climbed to a wide opening in the mountainside, carved by ancient rivers that had long ago changed course. The result was a huge, echoing limestone cave. A shadowy, bat-haunted world. Here, other two-legged creatures had built nests; it was to them Hsiung was bound.

A one-storey wooden house had been constructed on the floor of the cave, its presence rendered doubly incongruous by a gaudy, festive style of architecture. One might have mistaken it for the dwelling of a vulgar merchant, except for the constant squeak of bats and sticky rain of their droppings.

Hsiung paused to greet half a dozen crossbowmen and archers guarding the cave entrance. All wore red headscarves like his own.

'Is Hornets' Nest within?' he asked.

'Yes, Captain!' shouted a sergeant with a proper display of military enthusiasm. It was a watchword among the rebels that Hsiung inspired common peasants to act like soldiers, while other officers inspired them to act like brigands.

He nodded and crossed the cave floor to the house, where more guards bowed. Hsiung strode past them into a chamber the size of a long, low-roofed barn; and like a barn it garnered a harvest. Bolts of silk filled one corner. In another, piles of bronze and silver objects looted over Hornets' Nest's long career. There were antiques of great value: tripods and vessels from tombs sealed a thousand years ago. Padlocked chests contained copper, silver and gold coins.

In the centre of the room stood a lacquered throne, also looted. Here, accompanied by secretaries, guards, a pet eunuch, officers and a painted girl who stared fixedly at the ground, lolled a man in dazzling silks: Hornets' Nest.

For a rebel feared throughout the province, he had un-prepossessing features. His face belonged anywhere – a great advantage considering the Great Khan had placed a huge bounty on his head. A decade earlier, his band of Red Turbans had swarmed in their thousands until Jebe Khoja broke and scattered them. Since then Hornets' Nest had lived a fugitive existence and his once-formidable army shrunk to barely five hundred. None of which diminished the absolute obedience he expected from his followers.

'Ah, Hsiung! You are last to arrive.'

Was there reproach in the chief's voice? Hsiung's face stiffened. He saluted with fists meeting across his chest. His glance flickered as he examined those round him: the usual assembly. Many had been loyal to Hornets' Nest since he first earned that nickname through his prowess dismembering Mongols, an axe in each hand.

'Well?' demanded Hornets' Nest.

Again Hsiung saluted. 'Those who it was right to punish have been punished!'

The chief's expression hardened.

'Where are their heads?'

Hsiung could hardly admit they were still attached to their owners' necks. He had been instructed to execute some village elders who were refusing to pay Hornets' Nest's grain tax. They had pleaded their people would starve – and when Hsiung ransacked their houses he had to admit they were right, at least until the autumn harvest. It hardly seemed justice to starve a whole village (and Hsiung knew the horrors of famine only too well). Besides, their fawning gratitude had pleased him. Now it seemed that sparing their heads might cost his own.

'I left them in the village, Sir!' he bellowed.

Hornets' Nest nodded as he examined his youngest captain, smiling without a trace of warmth. 'I have a feeling we might talk about that later,' he said.

Everyone in the room tried to appear inconspicuous. Hornets' Nest's calm was often a prelude to savage violence. This time he merely clapped. Several of his followers flinched.

'No time for that now! I have special information,' he declared. 'Yesterday, a group of the enemy marched through Ou-Fang Village to Lingling. They will return soon with a fortune in taxes and join ships awaiting them at Yulan Port. At least, that is what they think.'

Hornets' Nest produced a large whisk and lazily swept away an offending mosquito.

'Where may I attack them, sir?' asked his most senior captain, a stout man with the bulbous nose of a fierce drinker, who had a reputation for leading from the rear.

'At Ou-Fang Village,' said Hornets' Nest. 'We shall hide in the houses and rush out.' He laughed, signalling that everyone should join in. 'And I'll give them a sting!'

The chuckling took some time to subside. Time enough for Hsiung to consider the implications of Hornets' Nest's plan. In military terms it was sound: surprise the enemy where their missile weapons would be least effective; trap them in a narrow space. The consequences for Ou-Fang, however, a village of seven hundred souls, would be dreadful. If the Red Turbans were victorious, a terrible retribution would follow on the assumption that the villagers had conspired with rebels. And if the Red Turbans lost, exactly the same massacre would follow. In either case, what little goodwill the rebels still retained in the surrounding countryside must surely perish with Ou-Fang Village.

'Sire!' he cried, bowing and saluting with his fists. 'Might not the enemy fight to the end if trapped in a narrow space? Not only would our losses be high, but we might not seize the prize.'

By this he meant the coffers of *cash*, gold and sundry valuables collected in taxes. Hornets' Nest regarded him suspiciously, but did not speak.

'Sire! Let us attack them in the ravines east of Yulan Port. First, they will be tired from their long march. Second, they will be tempted to abandon their duty and flee to the safety of the Port. Third, we may surprise them from the forest.'

A few officers nodded their approval. Hsiung added hastily: 'Sire! It was you who taught me it is a fine place for an ambush. I beg to be allowed to take the most dangerous position in the attack!'

Hornets' Nest relaxed a little. This was the kind of spirit he liked. Still his apparent calm was unnerving.

'I will decide in due course,' he announced. 'Go now and prepare the men!'

So saying, he stalked off to his personal chambers, followed by the concubine who cast a sharp, backward glance at Hsiung.

The other officers retreated to a hut behind Hornets' Nest's house. Here they would drink and boast until midnight about their deeds in the coming action.

Hsiung strode to the cave entrance and inspected the valley below. It nestled between mountain slopes, walled on three sides by cliffs draped with vines and shrubs. On the fourth side, the valley widened as it descended and twisted its way north, still overhung by precipices and greenery.

After his defeat at the hands of Jebe Khoja a decade earlier, Hornets' Nest had chosen to build his hideout here, attracted by its remoteness and the defensive possibilities of the cave. Certainly it was impregnable as long as one had food and brave men to defend the entrance.

But as Hsiung's eye descended to the valley floor he noted, for the hundredth time, the disadvantages of their position.

The rebels had constructed a village of wood and thatch houses in the valley, packed close together and easily set alight. In addition, a large natural fissure broke the stony floor of the valley right in the centre of the village. Long ago, when a river had flowed from the cave, it had discharged itself through this fissure into an underground lake, hundreds of feet below the earth. Now the fissure was dry, save for a few trickling streams. Those brave souls who had been lowered on long ropes into the earth's belly had reported a fairyland of crystals and frightening echoes. Some described it as the gateway to one of the Buddhist hells, hence its inauspicious name throughout Lingling County: Fourth Hell Mouth.

Hsiung's gaze shifted to the head of the valley where a ditch and low palisade sealed off the camp from attackers. It seemed as much trap as defence: once besieged, the rebels had no escape other than leaping into the fissure and hoping for a soft landing on the stalactites below.

Yet no government troops had ever approached the remote hideaway. Perhaps Hornets' Nest was right to fear nothing: he, at least, was protected by his cave and cliff. The safety of the camp below was less certain. If it perished the last ember of rebellion around Six-hundred-*li* Lake would fail – and, with it, Hsiung's purpose in the world.

As he stared gloomily, Hsiung noticed a procession of silver-backed apes following a network of ledges across the cliff face. Similar ledges ran all round the apparently impassable walls hemming the rebel village. Though he could not say why, the monkey paths seemed significant.

At the bottom he found a single soldier waiting for him, an older man, grizzled and scarred. Perhaps his seniority in age explained why he did not bow to Captain Hsiung. Neither did the captain expect it.

'Ah, P'ao,' he said. 'Everything as it should be?'

Sergeant P'ao had changed little since he first adopted Hsiung ten years before. All the change was on the other side.

'No,' he grunted, 'same as always.'

Hsiung glanced round. Luckily no passing soldier had heard the lack of a *sir*.

'What's wrong?' he asked.

Spreading his hands Sergeant P'ao sighed. 'While you were away a fever set in. See for yourself. Only don't catch it.'

Hsiung placed a restraining hand on P'ao's arm and held his eye. For a moment the older man stood firm, then shrank a little.

'Call me *sir*,' said Hsiung. 'Always *sir*.'

A peculiar, lifeless glitter in his eyes argued against defiance. 'Yes, sir,' mumbled P'ao.

'Come then,' said Hsiung more softly, 'show me this fever.'

A dispiriting tour followed: filthy huts of bored, hungry men, some shivering on blankets though the day was hot. Yet Hsiung judged torpor and boredom were worse dangers. It was over a year since many had seen action.

He strode over to the huge fissure of Fourth Hell Mouth and gazed down into the void below. Was darkness his only route of escape from this narrow, dismal valley? Unless, of course, he simply abandoned the Red Turban cause and the ever-dwindling band of rebels. Yet where could he go? Back to Hou-ming and the kindness of Deng Nan-shi? No, that way was lost forever. For a moment images of the Salt Pans filled his mind and he began to pace angrily, one hand touching the scabbard of his sword. Back and forth before the dark fissure he paced, dreaming of revenge, until movement on the cliffs caught his attention.

The monkeys again. How easily they swarmed from ledge to ledge! Then he had a disconcerting vision, that the monkeys were men – and men mere apes.

'P'ao,' he called. 'Gather all those fit enough for a parade. I have work for them.'

An hour later scores of soldiers were clambering on ledges round the three sheer cliff-faces surrounding their camp, con-structing walkways between gaps with bamboo poles lashed together. All day work parties cut and carried the long saplings from groves far down the valley. Many of the men sang as they laboured. This unexpected noise brought the other officers from their hut behind Hornets' Nest's residence. They roared with drunken enthusiasm to see Red Turban soldiers scuttle across the cliffs like apes.

Hsiung, hand on hips in the valley below, grinned up at them. A hot, masterful pleasure filled his soul as he watched hundreds of men obey his commands. Sergeant P'ao stayed close, looking important.

Hornets' Nest did not emerge that day or the next. But two young men in the gaudy clothes of city bravos visited him, travelling on foot with an escort of the rebel chief's picked bodyguard. An hour later Hsiung watched them leave in the direction of Mirror Lake.

天命

He crouched in a stand of bamboo, peering down at the road to Yulan Port. Rain fell continually, dripping through the branches and turning the track below into a slick of mud. Heaven itself favoured them, for with each *li* of struggling through the mire, the enemy's strength must lessen. Soon they would face a pitiless assault led by the bold Captain Hsiung.

He glanced round to inspect the men. All lay hidden, keeping bow and crossbow strings dry. The enemy might be far away for all he knew. Patience must seep from him to his troops. Above all, he must not betray the uncomfortable, fluttering tightness in his gut in case someone called it cowardice.

Still the rain fell. A puddle had formed on a flat limestone boulder near his hiding place and Hsiung watched drops break the surface and bounce. Exhilaration crept from suppressed corners of his soul, wild feelings he revelled in and feared. With them came unbidden images – unwelcome pictures of the past, sometimes distorted, sometimes true, if memory can be more than a flickering shadow. When the dark lights sparkled in his spirit he could hardly tell truth from dream . . .

Yet he remembered a soft squelch of mud between his bare toes. Long ago. Another incarnation, surely. He had managed to evade Overseer Pi-tou and hurried through a landscape of flame and steam stretching along the lake shore. Blue fires flickered beneath giant, crystal-crusted iron pans. Everywhere the stench of raw, seeping gas. Wretches in rags huddled or toiled according to the whim of those set above them. One thought in his head: *Father! He must find Father amidst this crowd of the damned. That was why he had come. To find Father and set him free.* Back and forth he wandered, asking for anyone named Hsiung, searching all night until dawn

123

returned him to his own bubbling salt pan. So exhausted, he could not dodge the sudden harsh grip on his arm, twisting him to stare into Overseer Pi-tou's pocked face. Then came his first proper beating. Fists rising and falling while the other members of his work gang pretended to sleep. Afterwards, Pi-tou dragging his limp, cringing body into a nearby ditch . . .

A noise had startled Hsiung to watchfulness. Long-legged cranes had flapped into the trees on the other side of the ravine and perched, preening themselves in the steady rain. Another memory danced behind his eyes: dusk on the great lake. Standing on the shore, gazing at the vast, burning orb of the sun as it sank behind distant mountains, setting them ablaze. Birds on the lake, chirruping and dipping and piping. Pairs of white cranes cawing and twining long necks in courtship. Lanterns twinkling far out on the waters. No fishermen dared approach the Pans, lest they be seized to replace someone worked to death. The endless peace of sunset spreading across the troubled land. Its beauty made him weep for the first time in years. And one did not weep casually in the Pans, where any sign of weakness invited aggression . . .

Still the rain fell, its smell earthy yet pure . . . In the Salt Pans he had learned the many aromas and textures of mud: sticky, grainy, liquid. As the dark lights danced across his mind he became a youth again, pressing his forehead into soft mud at Overseer Pi-tou's orders. A splendid palanquin surrounded by guards was bobbing past: Salt Minister Gui conducting an inspection. Involuntarily, Hsiung had looked up, searching for his old friend Sergeant P'ao in the entourage. He had not been there. Once His Excellency was past, Overseer Pi-tou set about him with a thick club for staring brazenly at superiors. As he was beaten the dark lights had appeared for the first time . . .

*   *   *

Hsiung felt a compulsion to rise, to display himself to any enemies. His muscles tensed, taut as bows. He mastered the impulse, aware he would betray his men's presence when the enemy arrived. His hands shook slightly. For they were no longer gripping the hilt of his sword. They had hold of Overseer Pi-tou's neck. A gag had been stuffed into the man's mouth to prevent him screaming. Hsiung had him by the hair, lowering his pock-marked face towards the boiling water of a brine pan, slowly, slowly. Closer, closer. The Overseer's terror left Hsiung shivering. Closer, closer, then up again, until, quite suddenly, he dipped his nose into the boiling brine. Just his nose! Enough for him to feel the pain and buck comically. Tiring of the game, Hsiung pushed his tormentor's face deep into the boiling water and the dark lights danced for joy . . .

'Hsiung! Captain! Can you not see them? They are here!'

Sergeant P'ao was whispering in his ear. He cleared the image of the Overseer from his mind but felt sick with confusion. Was that a memory or dream? Had he really boiled Pi-tou's face as one blanches strips of fish?

'Hsiung, what is wrong?'

Sergeant P'ao had hold of his arm, a look of fear and concern on his face. Hsiung shook him off. He was breathing heavily. The dark lights were still dancing. He focussed on the road below. The enemy column was nearly upon them, toiling through mud and rain. He did not notice or care their numbers were three times those initially reported to Hornets' Nest. That they were trained, well-equipped soldiers set against hungry, desperate rebels. All he remembered were his orders to halt the enemy and drive them back down the ravine.

Hsiung rose to his full height, held his sword aloft and bellowed: 'Red Turbans! Yueh Fei!'

At first a trickle of arrows flashed down from the ravine's slopes. Then a steady stream. Yet Hsiung could contain himself no longer. Leaping down the slope, he rushed at the cowering guardsmen before they could form ranks, desperate to release his burden of rage. He did not hear Sergeant P'ao hollering: *Captain Hsiung! Follow Captain Hsiung!* His sword swung back. Descended. A man went down. Now he was ankle deep in mud. One by one, Hsiung swept clambering, slipping, screeching men aside, forcing a way into the enemy ranks.

天命

The executions started soon after the prisoners had been marched back to camp. There were only fifty captives, the rest of the government troops having fled or perished near Port Yulan, their stripped, beheaded corpses left in the mud.

It was still raining when Hsiung emerged from Hornets' Nest's subterranean house. Slanting lines of monsoon cast a shimmering veil across the cave entrance. In the valley below Yueh Fei rebels were celebrating their first noteworthy victory in years. Rumours of the battle would spread all round Six-hundred-*li* Lake and far beyond: right to the Great Khan's court in the distant capital. With it, he hoped, the name of brave Captain Hsiung. Perhaps his lost father would hear; and learn how to find his son.

For now he was a hero. The men had chanted his name as they marched away from the battlefield. Even Hornets' Nest had embraced him. No one doubted the rebel leader's foremost captain now!

Despite so much triumph, his soul and stomach sickened. Had it been necessary to torture the prisoners before throwing them into the dark fissure in the centre of the village? Or even to execute them? He did not care to think what his old master, Deng Nan-shi, would have called such executions. Murder, most likely.

The majority were conscripts from Lingling with families in the limestone country. Surely it made sense to spare the officials, or at least offer them an amnesty to serve the rebel cause. How could the Red Turbans govern without officials to administer justice and tax the peasants fairly? Without scholars they would be little better than bandits.

Hsiung rubbed weary eyes, staring out across the rain-filled valley. When he had asked Hornets' Nest how they would spend their new wealth, whether to raise a new army or help the hungry peasants, his chief had winked. 'It'll do very well in my chests,' he said. 'Soon I'll have enough to buy a pardon from the Great Khan!'

Of course it was a joke. Certainly his chief had laughed. But there was no mirth in his eyes and, quite suddenly, Hsiung understood. Hornets' Nest was a mere brigand, whatever he had been when younger. He had no intention of challenging the government forces in Hou-ming, of driving the Mongols from their province.

His mind had reeled – and not just from the wine he had drunk. Complaining of a heavy head, he left his chief gloating while the officers toasted him until they were insensible.

Now, in the twilit cave, images of that day's killing and other fights as desperate and ruthless throbbed in Hsiung's temples. He retched up a stomach load of rice wine. A familiar hopelessness, one he could only appease with action, made him yearn to be anywhere but this narrow valley. It would not be long before Jebe Khoja sought a suitable revenge for today's work.

When he looked up, a large round figure was emerging from the steep path leading up to the cave, half-hidden by a huge, pink umbrella. Hsiung wiped his mouth and frowned. This stranger was not so strange. He recollected the fat man who called on Deng Nan-shi ten years earlier. And the visitor recognised him, too, for he nodded solemnly: 'Brave Captain Hsiung!' he said, bowing with a Buddha-like smile. 'I hoped to find you here.'

eleven

天命

Yun Shu adjusted her coiled hair, deftly inserting an extra pin. As she did so, she called to the children assembled on the wide porch of Sitting-and-Whistling Pavilion: 'Shicheng! Tan! Pingxin! Do not dance so close to the edge, you'll . . .'

Too late. Three little boys flapping their arms like cranes in time to a drum splashed into Mirror Lake with a delighted scream. All was confusion. Fortunately, several mothers from Ou-Fang Village accompanied their offspring so the young Nun of Serene Perfection was not without help. Rough hands dragged out the wriggling, protesting boys and rougher tongues admonished them.

Yun Shu had decided to establish a school in the porch of Sitting-and-Whistling Pavilion. Partly to attract people back to the shrine and encourage offerings. Most of all to bring a little laughter to the lonely valley, thereby pleasing Lord Lao as he gazed through his clay image at the passing seasons. Besides, she liked the children and their innocent noise. They unfurled small buds of happiness she kept closed to the world.

Persuading the villagers to spare their children from work for a few hours each day had been surprisingly easy, especially with Mother Muxing's grudging assistance. Half the district feared Mother Muxing. At first four, then, as word circulated, six, ten, twenty-four pupils emerged each morning from the bamboo groves, filling the valley with games and chatter.

For all their poverty, or because of it, the people of the lime-stone hills viewed any scholarship with awe; and their expectations were Yun Shu's chief anxiety. She had no money for paper and ink, let alone books. Her lessons consisted of chanting Daoist prayers and ancient songs. Ritual dancing was also a favourite. She taught them to memorise and recite lists of Emperors and dynasties, Immortals and heroes. But, of course, the most popular lesson was writing. This she contrived by spreading fine sand across a board and teaching each child the characters of their clan name. So precious did this skill seem to families who could barely afford clothes they sent grateful baskets of flowers, vegetables, wine and fruit.

When the children had gone, Yun Shu succumbed to melancholy. Hugging her knees, she gazed at the shimmering reflection of hills and trees in Mirror Lake. Loneliness seemed failure when one was supposed to be cultivating supreme detachment. The children's voices and games reminded her she would never become a mother herself: not if she was to complete the Great Work necessary for transformation into Pure Spirit.

That afternoon Yun Shu busied herself in the shrine until the sound of whistling made her pause. Perhaps one of the children had returned. She went out to find a young man in shabby silks perched on a rock, trilling a popular song. He had wet lips and sharp, appraising eyes that looked her up and down.

'I'm sure you don't mind my tune,' he said. 'This is Sitting-and-Whistling Pavilion after all! And look, I'm doing both. Ha! Ha!'

Yun Shu waited. The Pavilion was a public shrine and he had every right to pay his respects to Lord Lao. Yet something about his manner displeased her; she grew nervous.

'Perhaps you wish to offer a sacrifice?' Her question sounded shrill.

'Who to, Aunty?' he asked.

Although Nuns of the Dao were often addressed as 'Aunty', along with matchmakers and widows, he savoured the title as he examined her. Yun Shu's cheeks coloured.

'A sacrifice to Lord Lao,' she said, 'and the other Immortals who dwell here.'

'Ah! Does that include Chuang-Mu?' he asked, referring to the Goddess of the bedroom and sexual delight.

'No.'

'Then come to think of it, I don't,' he said. 'I do have a few words of advice though.'

She edged back towards the shrine. 'Indeed?'

'Just a few, Aunty. If I were you I'd stop all those brats coming here every day. All they need to learn is how to dig and chop wood for their betters. It's not nice to have little eyes looking round where they're not wanted.'

'Nice for whom?' she asked.

The young man laughed and stretched. He seemed to be enjoying himself.

'People who aren't nice either.'

Yun Shu had noticed groups of men moving quietly through the woods and assumed they were gathering bamboo. Now she wondered.

'What's your name, sir?' she asked.

'Hua. What's yours?'

'Aunty will do fine,' she said, firmly. 'And if I choose not to close my school?'

His gallant smile stiffened.

'You might find there are others less polite than me. Others who prefer Nuns on their backs.'

Shocked by his coarseness, Yun Shu took another step towards the shrine. She thought of her predecessor. Had the poor girl ended up on her back before vanishing? Yun Shu dared not ask.

The young man rose languidly. She followed his upward

glance to two watchers high above them on the craggy, limestone peak looming over Mirror Lake. Two dark silhouettes against the azure sky. Hua wagged a finger at her.

'If you're a lucky lady,' called the man over his shoulder, as he hopped across the bridge of stepping stones, 'I might even decide to know you better.'

Yun Shu shielded her eyes and gazed up at the silhouettes. Only one remained. Though she could not begin to say why, it seemed familiar.

天命

Shadows gathered into twilight over the limestone hill country. Birds flapped to roosts or swirled in noisy clouds over Mirror Lake, before departing for favoured cliffs and caves. Yun Shu felt lonelier than ever as the stars appeared. Her visitor's warnings lingered, despite hours of intense meditation and prayer.

She sat on the steps of the shrine, seeking cool breezes after the hot, uncomfortable day. Her eye was drawn up to the promontory on which the two silhouettes had stared down. A glow was coming from behind the peak. Was it a flicker of fire? Perhaps it came from the eyes of a dragon. She had also read of magic fungi glowing in the night. Eating their white flesh conferred Immortality, but one might only find them with divine help.

For a long while she glanced up, until curiosity and the impossibility of sleep tempted her across the stepping-stones into the bamboo groves. A bright quarter moon hovering over Holy Mount Chang showed the path. She followed the lake shore, wading over the lip of a waterfall frothing silver in the moonlight. Then she was back in the groves, climbing toward the rear of the promontory, seeking the red glow's source.

The footpath joined a wider track into the limestone hills. Here Yun Shu hesitated and pulled her nun's cape close.

131

Although overgrown, a path had been trampled through the foliage – and recently, for severed plants lay on either side, barely wilted. Who would take the trouble to clear a road in so barren a place, one leading nowhere? Certainly not a dragon. And magical fungi had their own mystic means of transport, appearing and disappearing at will.

It was lucky for her she did not step out onto that trampled path. Lucky, too, she was standing still as a graceful sapling when she became aware of feet moving towards her. Yun Shu barely had time to crouch in the shadow of a nearby rhododendron bush before a tall man carrying a halberd came into view. One by one other soldiers followed.

Behind the soldiers came a procession of more lightly armed men. All wore headscarves, though she could not tell the colour in this shadowy place. Some carried bundles of tools and large wicker baskets. She counted dozens passing within a few yards of her hiding place, and trembled, awaiting a harsh cry of discovery. Hardly daring to breathe, she narrowed her eyes lest they reflect a glint of moonlight. Feet continued to shuffle. Breaths panted from heavy burdens. Surely the loud beat of her heart would betray her. None of the passing men spoke or complained, and soon they had gone like a wind through the darkness. Still Yun Shu dared not move for a long while. When she rose, her muscles quivered from crouching so long.

Were these soldiers also drawn by the red glow? Whatever their motive they came in great secrecy. Yun Shu returned to Sitting-and-Whistling Pavilion. No one waited for her there. Yet the door was slightly ajar and she was sure it had been closed when she left.

The red glow continued all night. Only now it was accompanied by faint, rhythmic echoes beyond the edge of hearing, more a disturbance of the soul than an identifiable sound.

天命

The echoes guided her dream across the still, moonlit waters of Six-Hundred-*li* Lake. Back to the Hundred Stairs. Back through distance and time to the day she had intended to leap off the cliffs of Monkey Hat Hill. An insistent gong beat a low, sonorous summons to prayer. Lady Lu Si's mouth, puckered by concern, was ordering a bald man with a wrestler's burly physique to carry her to the nun's quarters.

When Yun Shu had awoken the man sat beside her, apparently dozing. Memories of Dear Uncle made her afraid to be near any man. He opened a single quizzical eye and examined her, before closing it again.

'Don't worry about me, Little One,' he said. 'I lack that which gives a woman both pleasure and pain.'

In no time at all, he began to snore.

Yun Shu had glanced stealthily round the clean room, its varnished wooden walls dark with age. The bald man was an odd-looking creature, strong yet effeminate. His moon face reminded her of the Egg of Chaos where *yin* and *yang* contain each other's seed. An odd thought; one of many triggered by the unworldly atmosphere in Cloud Abode Monastery.

She learned his name was Bo-Bai and that in his youth he had served as a minor eunuch in the Imperial women's quarters of the old, failed dynasty. He had fled west when the Song capitulated and been allowed to serve the nuns precisely because he lacked *yang*'s weapon and could not threaten their composure.

As for Lady Lu Si, it seemed more than just her appearance had changed. Now she wore the yellow and blue robes of a *sanren*, Abbess of Cloud Abode Monastery. There was a new confidence about her, a new authority. The forlorn, nervous, broken woman from ten years earlier had acquired inner power through her devotion to the Dao.

Yun Shu had agreed to whatever the older lady said. Everything was so novel she dared not ask questions. Instead she lay in the bed for two days, eating simple food from wooden bowls, listening to chants and gongs from the nearby temple. Scents of bitter incense drifted through her open window, along with whispered conversations. The contrast between the coarse, vulgar bedlam of the Zhong household and this mansion of peace could not be more marked – nor more welcome . . .

Yun Shu's dreaming body curled tightly. She murmured in her sleep, rehearsing an argument conducted within herself every day during those first weeks: whether she truly belonged among the Nuns of Serene Perfection. Whether chance or fate had deposited her there just when they needed a new acolyte.

Abbess Lu Si seemed to have no doubt: 'How else can you recite *The Way and its Power* by heart? An Immortal must have taught you while you were dreaming. One may not deny one's destiny! It will always pursue you.'

Yun Shu had meant to explain why she knew the book so well. That Lao Tzu's holy volume had been almost her only agreeable companion for years and she possessed an unusually good memory. Instead she kept silent.

'It is a miracle and a sign,' agreed the other nuns: Gold Immortal, Earth Peace, kindly Jade Perfected, even sly Three Simplicities, the youngest of the Serene Ones, who Yun Shu distrusted instinctively.

'You shall join us,' Abbess Lu Si said, 'it is inevitable.'

Lady Lu Si's whispered revelations concerning the Great Work set her imagination ablaze. Could she, too, perfect herself and become Pure Spirit? An Immortal granted the power to change shape and fly, to walk among the stars, weave magic at will? It seemed the supreme triumph over Dear Uncle and the hateful Zhongs, over the father she could not forgive. How he would long to acknowledge his big-footed daughter then!

Her heart hid a final reason, one that had nothing to do with the Dao. In truth, Yun Shu had nowhere else to go. Cloud

Abode Monastery offered spaces to feel safe. The world bore little regard for women in general, even less for poor girls without family. The nuns might become her new family.

So Yun Shu had donned an acolyte's robes and learned the ways of the ancient monastery. When the gong sounded she hurried to the temple bright with candles and gaudy images of a hundred Gods, a place alive with power. There they chanted and danced magical steps. All applauded her swiftness in learning the rites except for Three Simplicities who invariably noticed some error.

Between rituals she explored the many buildings within the high brick monastery walls: here were courtyards and meditation pavilions dating back five hundred years; a vegetable garden tended by faithful Bo-Bai; rat-infested wooden pagodas ten men high whose stairs creaked alarmingly. From their topmost balconies one could gaze beyond the city to the mountains ringing the great lake.

She also discovered a flight of stone steps cut into the limestone cliff, leading down to a jetty that gave access to the monastery by boat. No one tethered there now, not even fishermen. Yun Shu often sat on the jetty when she desired solitude, hugging her knees and staring out across the waters, re-enacting in her soul a hundred old sorrows that threatened to drown her new-found peace.

After two years of this life, Abbess Lu Si had summoned Yun Shu to the temple. She found the four senior nuns sitting on mats. All were unusually animated: even old Earth Peace was muttering in Jade Perfected's ear.

'Please sit,' twittered Gold Immortal.

'We are pleased with your progress,' said Jade Perfected. 'Do not think we mean to criticise.'

Yun Shu had knelt on a mat and waited. Abbess Lu Si glanced uneasily at her colleagues.

'I really think we owe Yun Shu absolute frankness,' she said. 'There may be danger.'

The other two nodded.

'Dangerous times outside our walls,' croaked Earth Peace, who had not stepped beyond them for decades.

'You see,' said Gold Immortal, in her fluty voice, 'we know you are resourceful and have seen, well, rather more of the world than some of us.'

After that, their tale – and request – came out gradually. How an acolyte had been sent to an out of the way shrine at Mirror Lake near Holy Changshan to purify herself following certain laxities uncovered by Three Simplicities. No one chose to elaborate the nature of the poor girl's lapses. For the first year, regular if infrequent reports had come via travelling merchants and monks heading for the shrines at Changshan. Yet no word of her had arrived back in a long time.

'We would like you to see how she fares,' concluded Jade Perfected. 'After that, dwell in the shrine at Mirror Lake and see what good you can do. When you are ready, take the poor girl and visit the shrines on Holy Changshan. We will send a message to a wise woman in the nearby village who will ensure you have sufficient food. When you return fully purified, we shall apply to the provincial authorities for your certificate as a Serene One.'

Yun Shu had bowed with gratitude. To be appointed a *sanren* so young! She had insisted on leaving for Mirror Lake without delay, even though winter had not fully turned to spring. There must be no slacking in the Great Work! For when concentration lapsed, melancholy and rasping, grating memories crept in. And her spirit felt sick, raw . . .

At dawn Yun Shu woke in the shrine room of Sitting-and Whistling Pavilion. The dream had been a warning, perhaps even an admonishment. Today she must fulfil the first of her allotted tasks, one she should have pursued with greater vigour. Namely, to discover exactly what had happened to her predecessor.

So far, all Yun Shu's enquiries among the villagers had met with frightened silence. It seemed the only person likely to know was Mother Muxing. Yet even she had avoided an answer by rambling in the obscure Yulai dialect or pretending to be deaf. This time, however, Yun Shu was determined to get her way.

Besides, if anyone would know about the red glow in the hills and the secret procession of men, it would be Muxing. Her sons were hunters and familiar with the whole limestone country. Accordingly, she hurried off to Ou-Fang Village as soon as her morning devotions were complete.

天命

The village had been a gloomy, suspicious place when she last visited; now its peasants peered from their houses as though destruction would fall any moment.

Four weeks had passed since Hornets' Nest ambushed the tax farmers near Yulan Port. Everyone with access to news in Hou-ming Province had heard the story – and it had grown in the telling. Instead of three hundred soldiers, five times that number were rumoured to have lost their heads before being cast into a deep pit leading directly to the Fourth Hell. If Hornets' Nest had been prone to worry, he might have wondered how so accurate a description of his secret hideaway was in circulation. Fortunately for his equanimity, he wasn't. As for the haul of taxes, it had grown huge. Enough, whispered wits, to feed the Great Khan's dogs for a week – or provide his princes and nobles and countless yes-sayers with a single breakfast.

Little surprise the hapless people of Ou-Fang Village considered themselves fortunate to greet another dawn. Four weeks was plenty of time to gather a large force and transport it to Yulan Port. And no one expected anything less than savage retribution.

* * *

Yun Shu picked her way through the narrow, muddy lanes, expecting a discourteous reception. This time, however, she was known. Mothers of children attending her school left the riverbank where they were singing as they washed clothes. All lined up and bowed in unison. One old man nodded from a doorway, aware the Nun had taught his grandson how to write their clan name.

A small crowd of children followed her to Mother Muxing's house. The girls viewed the handsome young Aunty with blatant awe and longed for a large yellow kerchief of their own.

She found Muxing winnowing rice in the front courtyard. The same granddaughter who had visited her at the shrine on New Year's Day was helping crank the handle. Much sun and rain had occurred since then and a fine first crop in the paddy fields was the result. Now husk must be separated from grain.

The blue-tattooed Yulai woman waved her to a nearby bench but continued to feed the winnowing fan. For a long while neither woman spoke. Stillness was a game Yun Shu had mastered in Cloud Abode Monastery. As a family woman, Muxing was less adept. When the prolonged silence got uncomfortable, she remarked: 'I thought you would have moved on. The Nuns they send here never stay long.'

Yun Shu stirred. 'I wish to ask some questions, Mother Muxing.'

'Oh?' said the Yulai woman, suspiciously. 'Crank harder, girl!'

'You see,' said Yun Shu, 'strange things happen at Mirror Lake. A red glow in the hills. Armed men moving at night. I wondered if you know anything.'

Muxing's laugh was coarse and loud. 'I know lots of things,' she said. More grain entered the hopper; more husks blown out by the cranking fan.

'Perhaps you might share those things?' said Yun Shu.

'Perhaps not,' retorted Muxing. 'I keep myself to myself. It's the safest way in Ou-Fang.'

'I see,' said Yun Shu, glancing round at the Yulai woman's house, which was notably larger and better appointed than its neighbours. 'Then I shall advise Cloud Abode Monastery to cancel your annual stipend for acting as their agent here.'

Yun Shu rose slowly and gracefully. For the first time Muxing paused in her work. Anxious thoughts betrayed themselves on her face.

'Sit! Sit!' she urged. 'Of course I'll tell you! Hornets' Nest's men have found something in the hills, that's all. Something they wish to keep secret.'

So her suspicions had been right! 'Something valuable?' she asked, eagerly.

Now Muxing frowned.

'Don't go near them! Hornets' Nest has four of his spies in this village. Bad, wicked men! Now they're up in the hills and no doubt up to mischief.'

With a sudden insight Yun Shu asked: 'Was one of them called Hua?'

'Yes, he's their leader. His friend, Chao, struck my son in the tavern! Curse them! If it was not for Hornets' Nest . . .' The consequences for the unfortunate Chao dangled like a noose.

Muxing ordered her granddaughter to crank. Once again she fed grain into the chute. Clouds of chaff drifted across the courtyard.

'That is not all I wish to know,' said Yun Shu. 'Once I asked you about my predecessor here. I have been instructed to find out what happened to her.'

Muxing shot her a sharp glance.

'That is no secret,' she said. 'She disappeared a year after coming here. No one knows where for sure.'

Yun Shu sensed evasion.

'You have suspicions?'

'Of course.'

Crank. Crank

'Then tell me, please.'

The cranking stopped.

'Go and play in the gatehouse until I call,' Muxing instructed her granddaughter. Once the child had gone, she turned to Yun Shu. 'Your predecessor was far prettier than you. And younger. She told me men had brought gifts of wine and fine food. As well as silks. She was flattered rather than afraid, foolish girl. It seemed someone had watched her bathing in the lake . . .'

Yun Shu blushed at the thought that she, too, might have exposed herself to unseen eyes.

'That particular someone is said to value virgins highly,' concluded Muxing.

'You mean Hornets' Nest again, don't you?' said Yun Shu. 'He seems everywhere in these hills. And behind everything.'

Muxing nodded significantly.

'He bought a virgin from Ten Pine Hamlet and two from Shang Village. None were heard of again. Perhaps he also bought the nun.'

Yun Shu needed no more: Dear Uncle had taught her how virgins are put to use. 'Then I will inform the senior nuns she is lost,' she sighed.

Mother Muxing leaned forward earnestly. 'You must leave!' she urged. 'Do not stay here! Soon government troops will come seeking revenge. And if not them, Hornets' Nest won't like witnesses round Mirror Lake. Even my sons are afraid to hunt there. Whatever he's up to, it's of great importance to him. Go while you can.'

Yun Shu hesitated. 'What of you?' she asked. 'Why do you stay?'

This time Muxing's laugh was proud.

'I am Yulai. My people are Yulai. Where do we belong, if not here?'

As Yun Shu bowed gratefully, the little granddaughter came running.

'Grandma,' she whispered, 'there's a man at the gate. He says he knows the nun is here and that he wants to speak to her.'

Muxing gestured for Yun Shu to hide. Inside the house, she crouched near a curtained window, listening to a familiar, insinuating voice enquire where the nun had vanished and why she went missing from Sitting-and-Whistling Pavilion last night. The voice belonged to Hua.

Yun Shu realised he must have visited the shrine yesterday evening, while she was seeking the source of the red glow. No wonder she found the door ajar. Yun Shu fingered her lucky amulets: she would not like to trust herself to such a fellow's power, especially after hearing what had befallen her predecessor.

'Do you know,' he declared, in an amused tone, 'I think my Holy Aunty can hear every word I'm saying! Are you hiding her in the house? Bring her out!'

Muxing replied hotly, 'Leave! You are not welcome!'

'Careful, you old . . . Oh, my! What do we have here?' Hua's bluster took on a brittle edge. 'If it isn't more of my blue-faced friends.'

For the first time he sounded unsure and Yun Shu risked a peep through a tiny gap in the curtain. Four of Muxing's sons had appeared from behind the house. Each carried a hatchet or bamboo club. Hua touched his sword then backed away.

'Well, well!' he said, whistling. 'We're growing bold! I'll be back soon, Mother. Only next time I'll bring friends.'

So saying, he swaggered away as though he owned all Ou-Fang Village.

When Yun Shu ventured outside Mother Muxing said, 'You see how it is! Go now, while you still can. For all our sakes.'

But the young woman looked at the winnowing machine and wondered if she, too, was to be blown from place to place like rice chaff.

'Perhaps,' she said. 'First I will pray to Lord Lao for guidance.'

Muxing shook her head sorrowfully. 'Let's hope he's in a sensible mood.'

twelve

天命

The fat man's name was Liu Shui, Hsiung remembered that much. Yet the terrible day he had been enslaved and shipped to the Salt Pans was something he chose not to remember. Or the months spent scavenging like a wild dog after he escaped, desperate enough to rob peasants of precious seed corn, widows of their last coins, ever more bold and indifferent to capture. Sixteen years old and already despairing of life. If hopelessness and anger had turned him cruel, better not to remember that either.

He paced up and down his hut, heart beating excitedly. A dog barked outside. He imagined twisting its neck sharply, so that all annoying noises ceased. Then he felt ashamed and confused. As so often, Deng Nan-shi's watchful, patient face flickered across his mind. He almost heard the old scholar's voice: 'Of course one does not kill a guard dog for barking. Its nature is to bark.' Of course. Of course.

Hsiung strapped on his sword and strode into the camp. Instantly his shoulders went back, chest puffed out and buttocks moved in a decisive manner. His hand steadied the hilt of his long sword as he walked. Whenever soldiers or camp-women encountered him they bowed low, for young Captain Hsiung was held in awe since his courage at Port Yulan.

Perhaps such deference should have been enough. He knew he should be happy, proud, pleased, all three at once. But doubt crawls behind every triumph – and always catches up. So what if he was brave? Were not many men? He wanted respect as a leader, a master of tactics. He wanted . . . he couldn't say what, except that for now it eluded him.

As for this fat man, this Liu Shui, his false information ten years earlier had sent Hsiung to the hell of the Salt Pans. Not a trace of Father had been found there, not even a rumour; he wondered if Liu Shui was a liar and deceiver who deserved a harsh punishment.

More vexing still, the fat man was obviously avoiding him. Ever since his arrival he had stayed hidden in Hornets' Nest's house in the cavern, engaged in secret conferences. Whispered words in the camp identified Liu Shui as a leader of the Red Turbans in Chiang-Che Province, far to the east; he was said to be seeking an alliance with Hornets' Nest after his victory outside Port Yulan. Hsiung, however, knew this could not be true. For one thing the journey to Chiang-Che was long. Liu Shui could hardly have heard of the battle and then rushed here in so short a time. For another, the victory itself was far from decisive. In his more honest moments, Hsiung conceded it was akin to an act of brigandage.

What agitated him was that the fat man had known his name and even claimed he hoped to find him here. Why then did Liu Shui avoid a meeting? After all, Hsiung was easy enough to find.

His voice boomed round the camp at regular intervals, instructing scores of recruits who had arrived since the victory at Port Yulan. Over two hundred impoverished peasants so far – and many thousands more were rumoured to support the Red Turban cause, assured that the Buddha Maitreya would sweep away the Mongols if the people enticed the Divine Messiah to appear. Hornets' Nest should be sending out men to all districts and encouraging recruits by returning some of the taxes stolen by the Great Khan's tax-farmers. To waste such an opportunity damaged their cause.

Later that day his desire to glimpse the fat man was satisfied. Hornets' Nest summoned his officers and advisers for an audience. As usual they gathered in the rebel leader's treasure house, kneeling before the raised, lacquered throne. Hsiung noticed that Liu Shui sat to one side, hands hidden in his trailing silk sleeves, apparently deep in thought.

Hornets' Nest regarded the officers, his eyebrows jutting fiercely.

'Which of you is the most loyal to me?' he demanded.

Though all the officers might have been expected to shout out, they glanced nervously at wall and floor. A declaration of superiority in this regard might lead to one of their chief's cruel – and fatal – tests.

'What!' roared Hornets' Nest. 'None of you are loyal!'

Now his oldest and stoutest officer took a chance.

'What is your command? I am the most loyal, sire! Twenty years I have served you, and grown gaunt for your sake!'

This last statement was contradicted by the old veteran's bulging girdle.

'I see,' growled Hornets' Nest. 'What about you, Captain Hsiung? Are you not the most loyal? Or just the most eager for your own glory?'

At this question the fat man dozing to one side glanced up.

'Tell me your command!' bellowed Hsiung. He was saved from further questioning by other officers taking up the shout, their fists placed together in salute.

'Good! Good!' said Hornets' Nest. 'Then how is it you fail in your duty?'

No one wished to address that question. Luckily for them, Hornets' Nest was tiring of the game and rose to his feet. At his full height he towered over most, his limbs thick as logs and chest solid as a bull's. Only Hsiung was as tall – or would have been if he hadn't bowed low like the other officers.

'Not one of you told me the enemy has landed a thousand warriors at Port Yulan! Fools! If I did not have spies everywhere, we would be taken by surprise. I should have the lot of you beheaded for negligence!'

The rebel leader sat down again with a crash that made the throne vibrate on its wooden platform. He seemed uncharacteristically agitated.

'Prepare all the men for battle!' he declared. 'At a moment's notice! These Mongol scum might attack any time. And when they do, I shall crush them!'

'Sire,' ventured Hsiung, once Hornets' Nest had subsided and was mopping his brow. 'Who is their leader?'

The rebel chief glowered.

'Jebe Khoja, of course! This is why Hornets' Nest is glad. I beat that fool once before and will do so again!'

No one chose to challenge this outrageous lie. The officers were quite content to slink away when dismissed.

Outside Hornets' Nest's house in the high, echoing cavern, Hsiung found a servant waiting. He recognised him as one of the fat man's entourage.

'Captain Hsiung,' whispered the man, 'I have a message. Liu Shui requests that you meet him at dusk in the entrance of the cave.'

'Why?'

But the messenger merely bowed and returned to the outlandish mansion. Hsiung noticed an injured bat on the floor, dragging its wings. On impulse, he carried it to a ledge where others of its kind slept, awaiting dusk.

天命

Every sunset the huge cavern was transformed. Hsiung arrived early to watch, taking a seat on a limestone boulder near the soldiers on guard. He enquired whether they had eaten then gazed silently across the narrow valley hemmed in by cliffs.

Below, smoke rose from cooking fires outside hovels crammed with men and their equipment. In the centre of the valley floor was the sinkhole like a gaping mouth in the earth. As Hsiung watched, women emptied buckets of waste into the abyss, where it would fall hundreds of feet, landing on the corpses of those executed after the battle of Port Yulan.

He raised his eyes, alerted by a change in the light, high-pitched sounds at the edge of hearing. Dark, flitting shapes appeared all over the valley, skimming thatched rooftops to form a dense, swirling cloud of swallows. The birds were returning to ancient roosts in the cave. And as they flowed in like a dark stream, another cloud of creatures flapped out – bats, thousands of small wings making the air rustle like a forest in a gale.

Hsiung marvelled at the co-operation that allowed two different kinds to share this place so amicably. Men would not be satisfied with less than complete mastery. Only then would they feel secure.

A chuckle disturbed his thoughts and he glanced round. For all his girth, the fat man could move quietly when he chose. Now he joined Hsiung and for a while they stood in silence, watching the last few bats leave and swallows enter.

'You wished to speak with me,' said Hsiung, haughtily. He was determined the fat man would know his displeasure. The latter, however, seemed quite at ease.

'Well, well,' he said, with the same Buddha-like smile Hsiung remembered from ten years earlier, 'how you have grown!'

'And what of that?' demanded Hsiung. Without realising it, the young man began to pace, one hand on his sword hilt. 'I do not know why I should talk with you,' he said. 'Because of you I was in the Salt Pans for three years. And never once heard a mention of my father.'

'What name did you ask for?' replied Liu Shui.

'The one you told me! My father's name. The same name as my own.'

'I see. Do you think your father was so foolish as to use his real name there?'

Hsiung fell silent.

'It was wonderful of you to seek your father,' said Liu Shui. 'Noble and stupid. A sign of great character. Only, don't blame me, Captain Hsiung. Your own impatience was the culprit. But that is not what I wished to discuss.'

'Yet I do!' replied Hsiung, angrily. 'Where is he? Did he hear of my prowess at Yulan Port and send you?'

The fat man shook his head. 'I have no idea whether your father is even alive.'

Hsiung examined him suspiciously. Could he trust anything this man said? Liu Shui glanced round for spies. Only dark clusters of swallows on their ledges were listening.

'I came to see how the cause of Yueh Fei fares in this district,' he said, quietly. 'I must report great disappointment. Especially with your chief.'

Now Hsiung looked round anxiously. Such talk could cost both their heads. Yet he did not contradict the fat man.

'Hsiung, you should know Hornets' Nest's leadership no longer advances our cause. This is the most dangerous time for us. I want you to remember this: ridding our land of barbarians is more important than any single man, however brave and useful he may have been in the past. That is true of you, me, any one of us – even Hornets' Nest. No, *especially* Hornets' Nest.'

Before Hsiung could reply, Liu Shui placed his hands in his long sleeves and bowed.

'I leave tomorrow,' he said. 'When the time comes, remember what I have told you.'

Hsiung watched him shuffle back to the bizarre house in the cave, trying not to soil his embroidered silk slippers with bat and bird guano. Then his pulse quickened. Was that a furtive movement in one of the lighted windows? Yet the shadow crossing the window was slender. It belonged to Hornets' Nest's concubine.

天命

The fat man left before dawn the next day and those who saw him go remarked on his haste. Perhaps rumours that the government forces in Port Yulan had advanced into the lime-stone hills sent him scurrying; perhaps he feared another night of Hornets' Nest's hospitality.

That same day Hsiung noticed the plump officer who had declared himself most loyal to their chief marshalling a force of a hundred men by the gate. In addition to their usual weapons, many carried spades, pickaxes and large wicker baskets. Though Hsiung tried to learn their mission from his fellow officer it appeared the subject was forbidden.

'I must do my special duty,' declared the older man with self-satisfaction.

With that he marched out of the camp, heading north. Hsiung was surprised so large a force, especially of experienced men, could be diverted from their small army when a battle seemed imminent.

A few days later there was another departure, one that caused consternation. The rebel chief himself left his house in full armour, both of his famous battleaxes strapped to his back, and strode down the narrow pathway from his house in the cavern to the valley floor. A sizable procession followed: his personal bodyguard of 'bravest and best'; three secretaries; a wine butler; two chefs (one for wet dishes, the other for dry), and two servants with large silk fans on poles resembling striped insect wings.

Hsiung, who was drilling the new recruits higher up the valley, watched in amazement as this cavalcade emerged from the camp. More astounding still was that another hundred soldiers carrying spades and baskets followed behind.

Hastily ordering his men to attention by the roadside, Hsiung rushed forward and knelt in the dust. His chief approached on a lacquered throne attached to two thick poles. Twelve burly soldiers were needed to carry it.

At first it seemed Hornets' Nest might not notice his brave young captain, looking up from the roadway with loyal, expectant eyes. Then a thought visibly crossed his face and he ordered the bearers to halt. They swayed slightly while Hornets' Nest squinted down. A fresh wind blew through the valley, making young bamboo stems shiver. The sky overhead was a deep, flawless blue, yet grey clouds with golden sunlit edges rimmed the horizon.

'Well, Hsiung,' said Hornets' Nest, coldly, 'I am entrusting you with the defence of the camp while I am away. Protect it with your life! As for the cave and my own house, no one is to go near. No one! I have left half my bodyguard up there with orders to shoot anyone who disobeys me. Do you understand?'

Hsiung nodded, consumed by a question that prudence could not repress.

'Sire, why are you leaving us?'

Hornets' Nest lolled back in his elevated seat and chuckled.

'When I return all will be clear,' he said. Then his eyes hardened. 'Do not fail me! Keep the camp safe in my absence.'

He did not need to mention the consequence of failure. Broken skeletons belonging to former officers lay in the bottom of the sinkhole. Falling from favour took a literal turn in Hornets' Nest's camp.

Hsiung watched the column march up the valley until it rounded a corner. The new recruits, hundreds strong, muttered amongst themselves like his thoughts.

All that day Hsiung kept glancing up at the huge cave entrance in the cliff. Had Hornets' Nest really meant no one should go there? This stung his pride. If he was trusted with the welfare of the Yueh Fei camp, he should have access to every part of it. When Hsiung complained of this to Sergeant P'ao, the older soldier laughed: 'The camp can burn as far as Hornets' Nest is concerned, as long as his treasury is safe up there. And with fifty men to guard the path, it's safe. Do you think he'd let you or any man come near? What do you expect?'

'I'll show him what I expect!' said Hsiung, his temper flaring.

With that he marched off towards the pathway winding up the limestone precipice to the cavern.

'Hsiung! I mean, sir, I wouldn't do that if I were you!' called P'ao, struggling to keep up.

Hsiung, however, ignored him. He purposefully mounted the narrow track as he had so often before. Only this time his chest itched with the possibility of a crossbow bolt. As he approached the cave entrance a gruff voice called out.

'Halt, sir! We are forbidden to allow you further.'

Reluctantly Hsiung slowed his pace but did not stop.

'Halt! We have orders to shoot any who come near.'

Still Hsiung kept going, shouting up as he walked.

'What nonsense is this, Jin! You did not speak so foolishly at Port Yulan. There we stood shoulder to shoulder.'

This recollection was a potent weapon. For Hsiung had saved Lieutenant Jin from a big Mongol with a mace when he had been beaten to his knees. It also allowed Hsiung time to reach the top. There, he found fifty men gathered, all veterans of Hornets' Nest's numerous campaigns. Yet they seemed unusually worried. And Hsiung noticed their crossbows were still pointed at his chest.

'What is going on, Jin?' he demanded, with a slight smile. 'Are we all to become deadly enemies because Hornets' Nest is elsewhere for a few days?'

Still Jin was uneasy. 'You should not be here, Hsiung. I will be punished for disobeying orders.'

'Set your mind at rest. I only wish to inspect Hornets' Nest's house and ensure it is secure.'

So saying, he marched over to the long wooden building and entered without ceremony. A few servants vanished into side chambers as his long strides echoed through the long central wooden corridor to Hornets' Nest's treasure house. The doors were locked and barred and a guard had been posted – or had posted herself. For Hornets' Nest's concubine sat on a stool before the doors, propping her elbows on her knees to cradle her chin in small white hands. Her dark eyes narrowed a little as Hsiung approached, but she did not move.

'*Someone* would not like to see you here,' she said.

Hsiung glowered. He detected wine in her voice.

'Probably not,' he said, stiffly.

'Then why are you here, Captain Hsiung?'

He was not surprised she knew his name; that was his due.

'For answers. Why has Hornets' Nest left in such a hurry?'

Only then did he notice silent tears rolling down her cheeks. Hsiung felt suddenly unsure of himself. He'd known few females and this one was eye-catching. A furtive memory of another girl arose, long ago when the world was green shadows and light, when he had sworn to be a *xia*, her noble hero

'Why are you crying?' he mumbled. 'I order you to stop.' She did not. His question seemed to make it worse. 'I'm sure he'll return soon,' he said, lamely.

'That is what I fear!'

'But why?'

Then she turned her back to him and lifted her silk robes to reveal patterns of whip marks on pale, luminous skin, like an illiterate's senseless brush strokes on precious paper. She let the clothes fall back into place and looked at him boldly.

'That is why,' she said.

A dark flush coloured his high cheek-boned face.

'Where has he gone?' he said.

She laughed and covered her eyes.

'To Mirror Lake! Oh, how he gloated!'

'I do not understand.'

She replied with growing hysteria. 'I wish I had never left Hou-ming! I hate these hills!'

'Speak more clearly,' he ordered. 'Why has he gone to Mirror Lake?'

'To hunt for more treasure,' she said. 'To steal an old king's precious things! That's what he told me. Do you know what he hopes to buy?'

Hsiung shook his head.

'A pardon from the Great Khan. He told me! He has sent messengers to the capital enquiring about a price.'

He stared at her in disgust. What filth! Lies of the kind spread by the rebel leader's enemies! How could such a gross slander be true?

Yet in his heart he knew, he knew. For years Hornets' Nest had gathered every *cash* coin available and stored it in his treasure house. A pardon would betray all his comrades who had struggled and starved and died to win that wealth for the noble cause, thousands upon thousands of honest men. For whatever pardon Hornets' Nest purchased could never apply to his followers – they would remain hunted outlaws, while he set himself up in style as a prosperous country gentleman.

'You are lying!' he retorted.

And truly, he could not, would not believe his leader, the man who had promoted him for his bravery and resourceful-ness, might turn traitor. Hornets' Nest had sacrificed his whole life to drive the barbarians from their native land. For the Red Turban Brotherhood and the Second Coming of the Buddha Maitreya. For the cause of Yueh Fei. Yet a vague recollection of Deng Nan-shi's lost voice came to him: *Without the Mandate of Heaven not even a village headman is fit to rule. Never forget that, Hsiung.* And he recollected the hungry, ill-housed men in the camp below and the treasure house gorged with enough *cash* to avert a famine.

A clatter of booted feet in the corridor made him turn with one hand on his sword hilt. It was Jin. The lieutenant glanced at the girl and young man in alarm.

'You should not be talking with each other!' he wailed,

though that was clearly not the only source of his distress. 'Listen, Captain Hsiung, a scout has returned. Jebe Khoja and a large column are only forty *li* away! They are approaching Dragon Whirl Gorge!'

Hsiung looked down at the weeping girl. Unfamiliar emotions stirred. 'I shall ensure everyone's safety,' he said. 'Do not be afraid.'

Her look of gratitude encouraged him to deserve it. He strode back up the corridor, Jin in close pursuit. She watched his broad back with slightly parted lips.

天命

On the afternoon of that same day Hsiung ordered a rest. The command passed down the column from officer to officer and four hundred men gladly obeyed, laying down stores of provisions and bundles of arrows. They had stripped the camp to maintain themselves in the limestone hills, a ground unforgiving to anyone ill-prepared.

Hsiung strolled among huddled soldiers, praising some, rebuking others, his face and voice entirely free of doubt. Yet face hid heart.

Leaving the apparent safety of the camp had not been easy, but he knew it was more cage than haven. Even if the palisade and ditch had been stouter, a few volleys of fire arrows would set the thatched hovels ablaze, driving the defenders to take shelter beneath the cliffs at the end of the camp where they would be trapped. Even the monkey paths he had established on the encircling cliffs offered the slimmest chance of escape.

No, he knew their best hope lay in defeating, or at least delaying, the Mongol force before it sealed them in. Yet to do so meant disobeying Hornets' Nest's order to protect the rebel camp at all costs – and so, by implication, his treasury up in the cavern.

Hsiung had sent runners to their chief at Mirror Lake with a simple appeal: return at once or find the Red Turban cause destroyed. Then, conscience appeased, he had made his decision: march out and fight, while they still could.

Hsiung walked down the column, pausing at a group of new recruits. All saluted or bowed in a pleasingly obsequious way. A few wore the blue tattoos of the Yulai tribesmen.

'You,' he said, addressing one. 'Are you familiar with Dragon Whirl Gorge and Market?'

The man nodded, looking at his comrades.

'We all are. It is our home village.'

'Come with me.'

Hsiung listened to their tale then led them to the front of the column for a conference with his officers. Many of the older men clearly viewed his authority with suspicion but dared not protest. Others regarded the tribesmen as semi-barbarous and scarcely concealed their distaste.

'The fact that Jebe Khoja has chosen to approach our camp via Dragon Whirl Gorge shows he has local guides,' he announced. 'Good! So do we. And better ones. These men are from Dragon Whirl Market and will lead us directly there. Order the column to reform.'

They resumed their weary climb and descent through the hills, directed by the Yulai onto barely perceptible trails. With every step Hsiung brooded over what they would find at the Gorge. If Jebe Khoja's force had managed to cross the river in large numbers disaster must follow. The Red Turbans' most capable fighters were with Hornets' Nest near Mirror Lake; a straightforward battle on equal terrain could have one result. Yet he hid his fears and stayed near the front, sometimes passing up and down the column to encourage the men.

Towards dusk they entered a twisting, snake-like valley through hills clad with sombre pines. It was a gloomy path, carpeted with thick layers of decaying pine needles. At the

155

end their Yulai guides paused, waiting for Hsiung to catch up.

'Not far and you will see the gorge,' said one.

'And the village,' added another. 'It is built on the hillside, like so.'

He modelled the layout with callused hands. Hsiung turned to Jin.

'Order the men to prepare their weapons. The hundred I have selected must be ready at the front. All orders are to be whispered, not shouted. Anyone who betrays our position will be thrown off the gorge as a traitor.'

Jin saluted with both fists across his chest. 'As you say, sire.'

Hsiung's heart quickened. It was the first time he had been addressed by a noble title.

'Good,' he grunted. 'Good.'

The Yulai led them deeper into the wood. From its eaves he stared down into Dragon Whirl Gorge and groaned with disappointment.

天命

From this vantage point Hsiung could see everything: the gorge a dozen *li* long and one wide, white water foaming and singing between limestone precipices. On the nearest shore, a village of houses with clay-tiled roofs clinging to the green hillsides – Dragon Whirl Market. On the opposite cliff were other wooden houses, linked by a sagging bridge constructed entirely of bamboo. That was not the only way over the rapids below. Sturdy cables had been strung across in diagonal patterns. Along these one might slide from one side of the gorge to the other in less time than it took to cross a crowded city square.

All this might have been a pleasure to witness at dusk, the low sun framing Holy Mount Chang in the distance, flocks of birds congregating round their roosts, shadows forming unusual shapes, except that both the bamboo bridge and sliding ropes were unusually busy.

'Damn them!' cursed Hsiung, ducking out of sight.

Jebe Khoja's army was in the process of crossing the gorge. As he watched, soldiers slid down the taut, slanting ropes in broad baskets, clutching the sides for dear life. Normally such baskets were used to transport trussed animals to the market on the other side. A dizzy way to travel: falling into the river below had a single consequence, for if the whirlpools and currents did not snatch you, the sharp stones would. A more conventional way of crossing, the bamboo bridge, was also swaying from the exertions of booted feet and armoured bodies.

Hsiung estimated nearly a hundred enemy troops had already crossed. They seemed quite at ease, slowly fanning out into the village market square, where wooden crates of chickens and piglets had been stacked among the other stalls. He noted bows strapped to their backs and weapons undrawn. Hsiung hesitated. There was still time to withdraw and establish a defensive position further back in the hills. It would give his own men a chance to rest. But well over a thousand Mongols and their Chinese auxiliaries were waiting on the opposite bank. Once they crossed, the Red Turbans would be outnumbered two or three times over.

'Lieutenant Jin,' he whispered, for sound carried unpredictably in that country, even above roaring water. 'Signal the hundred 'bravest and best' to move forward. Our guides will lead us into the village by the most unobtrusive way.' The Yulai tribesmen nodded to show they understood. 'We attack at once,' he added.

His instinct was to lead the assault. But if he fell, what would happen? He could not trust Jin to be decisive.

'Advance now! I shall join you with the main force as soon as you engage.'

War is vast boredom and moments of aching, fearful tension: the latter consumed Hsiung. From his hiding place he watched the 'bravest and best' sneaking into the village. Behind him in the wood he could hear the main body of Red Turbans forming up. When the time came he would lead their charge himself.

'Closer!' Closer!' he muttered. It was essential the advance party below surprised the enemy. Luckily, the Mongols did not seem to be crossing with any haste.

How many of the enemy were on the Red Turban bank of the gorge now? He estimated a hundred and fifty, perhaps two hundred. He could even see Jebe Khoja himself on the opposite cliff, conferring with officers in splendid suits of armour, flag-bearers and drummers around them. Then Hsiung remembered the terrible day, ten years, a lifetime ago, when he had watched this same handsome man ride onto the wharf at Hou-ming on a black charger, admired by all. And now that frightened boy stood ready to fight the Mongol prince – and take his head if he could.

Perhaps Jebe Khoja sensed his intense, hostile gaze, for he shielded his eyes against the sun and stared up at Hsiung's hiding place in the trees. At exactly that moment a scream rose from the village. A clash of weapons. The 'bravest and best' had been discovered.

Instantly Hsiung was on his feet. He surveyed the ranks of halberdiers and swordsmen looking up at him, many fearfully. Most had never seen a battle more dangerous than cock-fighting or childish brawls. He raised his sword.

'Maitreya!' he bellowed, appealing to the deity who favoured the Red Turbans. Then to their great inspiration: 'Yueh Fei!'

Other voices took up the cry as he charged down the hill and into the village. Almost immediately he encountered a Mongol cocking an arrow. Too slow! Hsiung cut off his arm with a sword sweep and threw the man aside. He joined the 'bravest and best' Red Turbans, forcing a way down to the gorge and the bamboo bridge.

The rebels' sudden attack caused instant panic amongst an

enemy already wearied by a long day's march and dispersed over a village they had been happily looting. Moreover, help from their comrades lay beyond an impassable stream.

'Split their forces! Do not let them form ranks!' shouted Hsiung, directing a company into the central market square, now a tangle of struggling bodies, dust and panic-stricken fowl. Piglets squealed underfoot as men butchered each other.

Almost immediately, after storming a steep roadway, the Red Turbans reached the bamboo footbridge. Hsiung could hardly believe how easy it had been. Only a few dozen Mongols were gathered to defend it. The walkway swayed and bucked as more enemy troops hurried over to join their beleaguered comrades. For a while the fight was uncertain and the Red Turbans were forced to pull back a short way.

'Over there! Archers!' cried Jin, gesturing at lines of men on the opposite shore.

They heard running feet and turned as a large company of their own troops arrived from the market, led by Sergeant P'ao.

'Form up on the hillside above us!' ordered Hsiung. 'Shoot anyone crossing the bridge!'

Moments later the air was thick with arrows, for the Mongols also began to loose wildly, inadvertently killing some of their own men defending the bridge. A final desperate rush led by Lieutenant Jin overwhelmed the rest.

'Cut the bridge!' bellowed Hsiung. 'And the slide ropes! No more must cross.'

Axes hacked at cables and he laughed exultantly as a Mongol warrior sliding down one of the ropes in a basket fell into the river. The first bridge cable parted, sending a dozen more of the enemy after their brave comrade. Others clung to the see-sawing walkway then it, too, broke, casting them into the cataract.

Hsiung jumped onto a boulder and stared defiantly across the gorge, the tip of his bloodied sword resting on the stone. He could see Jebe Khoja on the opposite bank, shouting orders to a squad of bowmen. Hsiung lingered one more taunting moment before jumping off the rock to safety. A dozen arrows skipped where he had stood.

Cheering had begun in the village – and with good cause. Not only had nearly two hundred enemies been trapped or killed, it would take Jebe Khoja days to find another route over the river. With luck, he might be delayed considerably longer.

Sergeant P'ao ran up. He was panting and a gash had been torn in his armour.

'Hsiung! Sir! We have captured nearly a hundred of them! Lieutenant Jin begs to know what we should do.'

'Kill all the Mongols except one and throw their bodies into the gorge,' said Hsiung. 'Offer the Chinese a chance to join us. Behead any who refuse. And see that last rope? Make sure no one cuts it.'

A single slide rope slanted down to the opposite bank. 'Why not, sir?' asked P'ao.

'Use it to send the surviving Mongol back to his friends with this message: *Captain Hsiung looks forward to our next meeting.*'

Hsiung smiled as those around him chanted his name and gestured at the grim ranks of Mongols watching from the opposite hillside. He knew he had just ordered his own execution – and a conspicuously painful one – if he ever fell into Jebe Khoja's power.

thirteen

天命

All day chains of men in grimy red headscarves carried baskets of earth and rubble from the rockslide at the end of the ravine, dumping it further down the hill. In the humid, midge-clouded air, sweat dripped from nose and chin. The pace of work was frantic, driven by a fat officer who kept glancing expectantly down the ravine.

'Quicker!' he berated a soldier stumbling with his heavy basket. 'You'll pay if you drop it, damn you!'

As bellowing in the midday heat is thirsty work, the officer withdrew to a canopied area away from the dusty rockslide. There he mopped his red face while a servant poured wine. Even in this oasis, his glance flicked back down the ravine.

Teng perched with Shensi in a shady nook on the hillside, observing the incessant motion below.

'When Chao mentioned a few men were on their way to help us,' he said, 'did you expect this many? There's at least a hundred.'

Shensi nodded but did not reply. Both watched Chao join the red-faced officer; both took turns shouting at a sergeant who bowed before them, evidently reporting bad news.

'Oh ho!' said Teng. 'All is not as our dear comrade Chao would wish! Work is going too slowly, I suspect. I wonder why.'

They examined the rockslide below. Already tons of stone had been cleared and carted away. The larger limestone boulders were manoeuvred onto pine logs and rolled to one side, a back-breaking effort that had already resulted in a fatal crush and a severed arm. Shensi stirred uneasily and spat.

'They've reached the door,' he said, 'that's why.'

As the last few boulders of the rockslide were removed, a rectangular stone entrance emerged and Shensi leaned forward intently. Teng could imagine his companion's pride and satisfaction. It seemed everyone was given a chance to achieve something, however unpromising their circumstances. Even his father had maintained a shadowy semblance of the Deng clan's lost glory. What then of himself?

Teng longed to be far away from this ravine of reckless greed. Soon their mysterious patron would arrive: and he suspected the man's identity promised terrible danger.

By dusk the tomb entrance was fully revealed. Still Chao and the officer drove their men to greater efforts, so that the narrow space rang with the chime of chisels on obdurate stone.

'Ah!' said Teng, uneasily. 'Look.'

A column of soldiers was advancing up the ravine, guarding a throne covered by a striped yellow and black silk canopy and lashed to two long poles. A dozen men had borne it through the tortuous limestone country, and they moved quickly.

'I believe,' said Teng, 'we behold our patron. A burly sort of fellow. One might almost mistake him for a villain. What do you say, Shensi?'

Shensi spat, only this time surreptitiously.

'Didn't you realise he was Hornets' Nest?' he asked.

'Of course,' said Teng, 'I'm not a fool.'

'Maybe we both are,' muttered Shensi.

Up the ravine came Hornets' Nest's cavalcade.

'Look!' said Teng, pointing. 'Just in time.'

None other than Hua scrambled from a steep pathway

leading to Ou-Fang Village, rushing forward to greet his master.

Teng's mouth tasted disconcertingly dry. To be so near the rebel chief who had beheaded hundreds only a month earlier. To be the hired servant of such a man! He dreaded what Father would say. For although Hornets' Nest called himself a patriot in the mould of Teng's noble ancestor, Hero-general Yueh Fei, one might as well compare tiger to rat.

After an extended period of fawning by Hua, Chao and the officer, Hornets' Nest's portable throne was carried to a canopy near the tomb entrance.

Though night came swiftly many guttering lamps and smoking torches were lit and the work continued at the same pace as before. Teng and Shensi maintained their station on the hillside, eating rations the tomb-finder carried. It seemed Chao and Hua had forgotten them.

'I bet they haven't mentioned our part in finding the tomb,' said Teng. 'Do you think we'll see our share?'

The tomb-finder had been engaged on the same terms as himself: a tenth share of the profits. Shensi shook his grizzled head. But it seemed he might be wrong, for Hua came rushing over.

'Hey, Ink Boy! You there!'

Teng pursed his lips and stared up at the constellations.

'Ink Boy! I can see you hiding up there.'

Still Teng did not stir and the reason dawned on Hua.

'Alright, Master Honourable Deng Teng, you know I mean you.'

Now the scholar acknowledged him with a curt nod.

'You're needed,' said Hua, sullenly. 'And don't keep me waiting again.'

He was led across the rock-strewn floor of the ravine, straight to the tomb entrance. Shensi followed close behind. Quite a crowd had gathered in a semi-circle. There were officers and secretaries with scrolls and ink; Chao and Hua, of course; most notably, at the front, Hornets' Nest.

Close up, Teng was surprised by the rebel leader's ordinariness. He resembled a shopkeeper in silks, laden to the point of vulgarity with gold and jade ornaments. Yet the intensity on his cold, watchful face as he stared at the entrance was far from ordinary.

Certainly, the continued labours of his followers had uncovered an interesting sight. Once the stone was removed, another door blocked the way. Except this was made of solid grey metal. Characters had been inlaid onto the door, wrought in some shiny material that caught the red flickering torches and oil lamps.

Before the wonder of such a discovery, all living men were equals. Who could claim ownership of something so ancient and strange? Perhaps that was why Teng neglected to bow to the rebel chief or even acknowledge him. Instead, assuming his part as scholar without prompting, he approached the metal door and ran a hand over the surface. It felt dusty, oddly malleable. A murmur of alarm at his boldness rippled through the watchers. Many stepped back, including Hornets' Nest.

'The door is fashioned from lead,' Teng announced.

He traced the characters with his fingers. The first two were known to him, though rendered in an obscure style, for the Deng family library contained many ancient documents describing the fall of emperors and dynasties, how cities with walls a hundred *li* in circumference burned until their ash blew away in the breeze.

'What does it mean?' called a deep, gravelly voice.

Turning, Teng realised it belonged to Hornets' Nest himself.

'It means *death*, Your Honour,' he said.

Again those watching muttered fearfully.

'Strange,' he continued, thinking aloud, 'for the character, *xiaowang*, means the death of a tradition or way of life. One would expect *siwang*, would one not?'

Hornets' Nest nodded and a slow, scornful smile crossed his face.

'A scholar!' he chuckled. 'Well then, what of the other characters?'

Teng could not answer with integrity. 'They are familiar, but somehow contradictory. I need time to think.'

Silence in the ravine except for the crackle of pine torches.

'Break open the doors!' ordered Hornets' Nest.

'That is not wise!' cried Teng.

All froze in amazement. No one outside his inner circle had contradicted the rebel leader so blatantly for years – much to the damage of his character.

'We should wait until dawn,' said Teng. 'If there are angry ghosts within – and they will hardly relish Your Honour's designs upon their valuables – they will be invisible at night. At least one may see them as vague shapes by day and so gain some warning.'

For a long moment Teng's fate hung on an impulse, a whim. But Hornets' Nest was a practical man by nature and knew better than to tangle with unseen spirits on their native ground. He had also not commenced that night's drinking.

'Very well,' he said. 'Break down the doors at dawn. The scholar goes in first.'

With that he withdrew to his canopy, where wine and sizzling, grilled meats of various kinds awaited him.

天命

Towards dawn it began to rain. Teng woke to a wet trickle on his cheeks. He and Shensi crouched beneath a large umbrella – Deng Nan-shi's only gift to aid his son in the wild, tiger-haunted mountains – while Teng mixed ink using raindrops. This he applied to paper scrounged from Hornets' Nest's secretary. After an hour's work he possessed over a dozen spells and admonitions written in the oldest characters he could recollect. The most powerful he placed beneath his shirt as armour. Then Teng approached the tomb entrance and studied the inlaid characters: *death*, certainly, but what was the second set?

Dawn sowed brightness into the rolling clouds above. Now was the time to brave an entry: a meeting point between *yin* and *yang*. Teng took his spells and nailed them into the lead door until they completely obscured the characters for death. It was disquieting how easily the nails went in, as though some force tempted him onward. Shensi, who was breathing over his shoulder, grunted.

'Lead doors are only good for keeping out water, not robbers,' he said.

He called to one of the soldiers: 'Bring an axe.'

The first blow left a shiny scar across the grey metal. Soon a man-size silver gash split the sealed entrance from top to bottom. A stout pole was applied to lever it wider so a man might slip through. Teng became aware of a fetid, vile odour beyond the gap – darkness, profound and undisturbed, a pool of night concealed by layers of stone, dust and brooding time.

'Is it so easy to enter the past?' he murmured, wonderingly.

The tomb-finder shrugged. 'It's getting out that's hard.'

They were interrupted by Hua and Chao. Both were pale and dishevelled from last night's carouse.

'You two! What are you doing?' Chao called angrily, grabbing Teng's arm.

He tried to shake him off but Chao's grip was strong.

'Following orders,' said Teng. 'And you're disobeying them. Remember, *the scholar goes in first*.'

A loud, grating voice made everyone jump. It belonged to Hornets' Nest, and he sounded hungover. 'Let him go, you fools! That's why he's here.'

Chao and Hua leapt away from Teng as though he burned. They bowed low to their red-faced chief. A glint in their eyes indicated who they blamed for Hornets' Nest's displeasure. And who they were unlikely to forgive.

'I need a lamp,' said Teng, addressing Hua. 'Get it now.'

'Two lamps,' called a new voice. Shensi rubbed his stubbly chin and raised two fingers. 'I go in with the scholar.'

'Two lamps,' ordered Teng. 'Quickly!'

Under the impatient eye of his chief, Hua could only obey.

天命

As Teng stepped through the oval rip in the lead sheet he thought, quite oddly, of a woman's cinnabar passage. After all, he was entering a tunnel steeped in shadowy female *yin*-essence. To proceed further meant entering a kind of womb, gestating . . . what? The character on the entrance promised *death*. If he and Shensi were the seeds, what monstrous egg awaited them?

Shensi, however, had less fanciful matters on his mind. 'Chao and Hua are turds,' he muttered, 'I can tell they're angling for our share.'

'Why did you offer to accompany me?' asked Teng.

'Because Hornets' Nest is a bigger turd. I want to see what my tenth looks like.'

Both held up their lamps. A long corridor sloping downwards had been cut into the solid rock, an inconceivable labour, especially as the curved roof was taller than a man could reach. The lamp flames stirred slightly, bending back towards the entrance: an indication of air movement. Most notable was the smell. Teng sniffed repeatedly – earth-scents, incestuous generations of mould and something unfamiliar, perhaps dangerous. He touched the written spell guarding his chest. It was well known one might detect demons by their peculiar fragrance. Teng placed a warning hand on Shensi's arm.

'If we meet a beautiful lady who smells of warm jade, we must not trust her,' he cautioned. 'She will be a fox fairy.'

The tomb-finder shrugged. 'If she's carved from jade, I'll sell her. Come on.'

He led the way down the corridor, tapping the floor in case of ancient pits. Darkness closed around them and soon the slit of daylight from the entrance faded. Their feet slithered on the uneven stone floor. Teng marvelled that once, millenia ago, a funeral cortege had followed this same road.

'We are the first!' he whispered, eagerly. 'Imagine it!'

'We better be,' replied the tomb-finder. 'If we're not, Hornets' Nest will have no use for us.'

Soon the floor levelled and they reached a high, semi-circular arch. Shensi paused, sniffed. Whatever he detected gave satisfaction for Teng caught a glint in his eye.

'Come!' he ordered.

They advanced into a small, hand-chiselled cavern. Side tunnels stretched on either side. Now Shensi was chuckling. 'See!' he said. 'We *are* the first!'

Waving the lamp revealed a passage to one side lined with jars, cooking utensils, storage gourds.

'All so His Mightiness should not starve in the Beyond,' said Shensi. 'Pah! And, look, he wanted to ride in style, too.'

The other passage contained more: the low shapes of carriages and wheels on the sand-strewn floor, all rotted away except for metal fittings and stray pieces of wood. Teng noticed pale sticks beside the chariots and went over to investigate. The grey, decayed bones of horses lay in piles. His breath hissed. 'Shensi! Look!'

The tomb-finder came over. Beside every pile of horse bones lay the remains of a smaller skeleton, its flesh and garments reduced to dust. Sightless eyes stared up at Teng. He remembered the ruined watchtower on Monkey Hat Hill and proud, brave Hsiung. The thought, as always, touched him with guilt.

'His Majesty required drivers for his chariots,' he said, dully. 'Do you think they died willingly?'

Shensi shrugged.

'Bones are everywhere,' he said. 'This way.'

Holding his lamp high, Shensi proceeded through the small cavern to another high entrance. Darkness blocked their way.

'Should we go back and tell them it has not been robbed?' whispered Teng.

Shensi held the lamp close to the scholar's face so he could examine him.

'Scared?'

'Of course! Aren't you?'

The older man considered this, then said: 'Follow me closely.'

Raising his lamp, Shensi walked boldly into the dark, disturbing jars and vessels laid out for some ghostly feast. After kicking over the first pot, he was more careful. The sound echoed. They were in a huge chamber dug from the rock. Its roof rose many men high and Teng noticed a small, black circle in the centre – evidently the shaft he had been lowered down days earlier.

A perfunctory examination revealed the chamber's purpose.

'A banqueting hall,' he whispered. 'Look! There is the stone chair where His Majesty sat, all his scholars and princes round him, to enjoy the feast. I wonder who he was. Perhaps the ancient records mention his deeds.'

Shensi was poking round the floor.

'Some good stuff here, lots of bronzes,' he said. 'More bones, too. Probably servants. We're nearly there.'

Crossing the banqueting hall seemed a long journey to Teng. It ended in a low, rectangular stone doorway.

'The tomb will be beyond that,' said Shensi.

'Let us call Chao and Hua,' said Teng. 'A solid stone door requires many men to thrust it open.'

'Maybe not,' said Shensi. 'The earth sometimes moves. Even mountains breathe in and out. Hold this.'

While Teng trained the lamp, Shensi shoved steadily at the

door with his shoulder. At first there was just his grunting, panting breath, then a grating sound.

'Stand back!' warned Shensi, nimbly following his own advice.

With a crack and creak the stone panels fell inwards. The crash as they hit the ground echoed round the cavern. Both lamps flickered and almost expired. Clouds of clammy dust rolled into the banqueting hall.

'If that doesn't bring them down here, nothing will,' muttered Shensi, glancing back the way they had come. 'We'll have to be quick.'

But no sound of rushing feet or bobbing lights disturbed them. Gradually the dust cleared. Seemingly unaware of his companion, Shensi stepped into a small chamber lined with slabs. At the end stood a carved, open stone coffin.

Faced with the ruler of this lifeless kingdom, even Shensi grew nervous. He turned to Teng.

'Go and have a look at him,' he murmured, 'there might be some writing.'

Teng's heartbeat seemed to fill the chamber. Again he thought of *yin*'s womb. Was this coffin the egg he had imagined?

'Go on!' urged Shensi.

Step by step, Teng obeyed. When he came to the tall coffin on carved dragon legs he paused, trembling. The lamp shook in his hands, making the light dance.

Unexpectedly another memory of the watchtower came and he muttered slowly, like an incantation:

Autumn wind rises,
Plump clouds burn . . .

The words lent him courage. He repeated them more loudly and stepped up to the coffin. What he found surprised him. Nothing! No body, not even decayed bones had survived. Instead, hundreds of carved jade pieces in the shape of a body, the remains of a suit guaranteed to preserve His Majesty forever. Yet not a shred or hair remained.

Teng stepped back and turned to Shensi. When he spoke his voice was calm, even sad. 'I shall endeavour to find characters that at least tell us his name,' he said. 'Perhaps he was a kindly ruler, for all the sacrifices of the charioteers and drivers.'

But Shensi had found a storeroom at the side, and was chuckling: 'A tenth of this would set us up as princes for life!'

When Teng peered over his shoulder he, too, gasped. The little room was stacked with dusty treasure: gold and bronze leopards with red jewels for eyes; lamps moulded in the likeness of yielding slave girls; everywhere bronze vessels inlaid with gold and silver. In one corner, a large pile of bamboo strips bearing columns of characters; and old tortoise shells and ox bones covered with writing. Instinctively, Teng reached down and picked up a tortoise shell, tucking it into his girdle. A familiar voice echoed behind them.

'Hey! Don't touch anything if you know what's good for you!'

It was Hua, accompanied by soldiers and secretaries, peering round fearfully.

天命

At Hua's command they were marched out of the tomb, their guards only too glad of a duty leading to daylight. Outside Teng averted his eyes from the sun. For a long moment he stood squinting, until a brutal shove forced him to stumble forward.

They were prodded past Hornets' Nest on his throne. The rebel chief seemed unaware of them, as though they were invisible. He gazed eagerly at the dark rectangle of the entrance, awaiting news. Only then did Teng realise the extent of their danger.

A short journey led them to a wide crack in the limestone side of the ravine. It went back quite a way, forming a natural prison of sheer walls guarded by soldiers. They were not the only captives. Two Yulai hunters with blue tattooed faces crouched on the floor. Teng recognised the eldest as the man who had remonstrated with Chao in the tavern at Ou-Fang Village – and been beaten for his boldness.

Both pairs of prisoners ignored each other and fell to muttering.

'This is bad,' Teng advised Shensi. 'Very bad.'

The tomb-finder did not seem to be listening. 'No one makes a fool of Shensi!' he said. Given the circumstances, Teng was inclined to disagree.

Later, Hua and Chao appeared at the entrance.

'Shame we caught you and Shensi trying to steal Hornets' Nest's treasure!' said Hua.

'Big shame for you,' agreed Chao.

'Our chief won't let you off easily,' said Hua.

'We won't let you off at all.'

They both laughed and withdrew, leaving their ex-comrades to fume.

All that hot day they sat in the shady, narrow crack in the limestone. Shensi found fresh rainwater in a hollowed rock, otherwise they were given no sustenance. The Yulai huntsmen, accustomed to not stirring for many hours, restricted their movements to noticing everything and communicating by shared looks.

Something hard poked into Teng's ribs and he extracted the tortoise shell from his girdle. Of course he had seen such things before. His father, wise Deng Nan-shi, possessed several. He had even taught his son how to decipher them.

A lattice of delicate lines and cracks spread from a burn-mark in the centre of the shell, seared by a red-hot poker. Columns of characters were carved and stained on the surface. Sighing, he stared at each character in turn.

All day Teng studied the writing, recognising at least half the words. As one would expect, there was a question: *Will the clan of Xue . . . prosper . . . regain the Emperor's favour?* And an answer, interpreted by priests from the patterns of the cracks: *When tears . . . salt . . . heavy . . .* did that say *break back?* He couldn't be sure . . . *Xue clan . . . regain . . .* he couldn't read the rest. What exactly they would regain was a mystery. Teng frowned, for Xue also meant scholar as well as a clan name, and he could not help thinking of the blighted Dengs.

He fell into an exhausted sleep, propped against a boulder. At once he was back in the dark tomb of echoes: an eternal feast filled the central chamber with scents and voices. Wine, starchy rice, roasted animals of every description, fishes steamed in their scaly armour, every platter laden for the guests, while favoured concubines served His Majesty who sat beneath a yellow and black striped canopy. Then acrobats were wheeling across the banqueting hall; gongs and pi-pa playing. For all the wild revelry, Teng could not help being afraid. Something was wrong with the smiling, nodding prince in his suit of jade plates . . .

Teng stirred fearfully in his sleep, clutching the tortoise shell close to his chest; Shensi and the Yulai hunters glanced over curiously.

Could it really be Deng Nan-shi in the jade suit? Did Father wish to live forever? Teng realised in horror that all those feasting had been sacrificed at Grandfather's command, to preserve his dignity as Prefect forever . . .

'No,' he muttered in his sleep. 'Our family will redeem itself!'

Now the empty jade suit strode through the tomb world. Chariot drivers cowered by their dead horses while guards without faces cut them down. The concubines wailed in terror, forced by eunuchs to swallow cups of acrid poison. And Father was back on his throne, watching all that passed with a disdainful expression. Priests applied burning pokers to ox shins and tortoise shells while others wrote on bamboo strips. Teng could read their messages with ease: rumours of forgotten princes, kingdoms destroyed, oh, he must not linger in this dreadful tomb! To stay here was death! Acrobats somersaulted past. He must awake, awake . . .

'Wake up!' Shensi was whispering to him. 'Wake up!'

Teng opened his eyes to semi-darkness. It was dusk in the limestone country. He must have slept for many hours.

天命

'What has happened?' he asked, between one dream world and the next.

'Quiet,' urged Shensi. 'A messenger arrived here a few hours ago. Ever since they've been running round like angry wasps.'

'But why?'

Teng crept nearer to the guarded entrance of their makeshift prison and saw dozens of soldiers with baskets hurrying to and from the tomb. Others were piling treasures on the ground, where secretaries inventoried the objects before assigning them to numbered chests. Whatever the reason for haste, it seemed Hornets' Nest was determined not to lose a single bronze bowl or jade disc. Inexperienced as he was in valuing antiques – the Deng clan's collection had been dispersed decades ago – Teng could not estimate their worth in *cash*.

'Shensi, do you think this tomb will make Hornets' Nest rich?'

The older man nodded. 'Rich enough to re-equip his army many times over.'

Such a notion had not occurred to Teng. 'Do you think that is his intention?'

Shensi shrugged.

Dusk became night and still the soldiers harvested anything valuable. Teng wondered if their greed would include the ox bones and tortoise shells, the books of bamboo strips covered with ancient characters. These aroused his curiosity more than any of the lacquered, splendid objects he had glimpsed. For the bamboo strips were tongues, voices two millenia old. What secrets and wisdom they might utter! The ancient kings had possessed knowledge lost to later, debased generations, formulae for elixirs of Immortality, maps to the Magical Isle of Penglai, spells guaranteeing health and prosperity for a dozen generations.

As Teng watched the treasure being removed, he saw no bundles of bamboo strips. It appeared no one but himself guessed their value.

Shensi maintained his own vigil, occasionally grumbling about his tenth share.

Towards midnight a fresh commotion arose. Even the Yulai huntsmen, who had shown no sign of distress at their captivity, muttered anxiously. Dozens of voices were bellowing orders, urging exhausted men to form ranks.

Guards appeared outside the crack in the ravine wall. The prisoners were led out, their hands lashed in front of them with tight leather thongs. Teng glanced fearfully round the ravine. They were at the rear of a long column, at least two hundred strong. Flaming torches revealed shadowy figures. In the centre of the column were large chests attached to poles carried by soldiers. Ironically, those same chests once contained the Great Khan's tax revenues from Lingling.

Teng kept beside Shensi. 'Where are they taking us?' he whispered.

Shensi seemed not to hear. Indeed, there was no time for talk. A shout from Hornets' Nest set the whole column in motion, jogging down the ravine. Where the ancient pathway passed Mirror Lake they found more prisoners surrounded by guards. Teng recognised Hua, his cheekbones gaunt in the torchlight. Their former comrade appeared to be in charge, for he ordered the captives to take up position near the treasure chests. At once they were on the move again and Teng forgot everyone's misery but his own.

A night of unaccustomed hardship for the young scholar. On

and on they stumbled, constantly afraid of slipping and being trampled by those behind. To maintain balance with hands lashed together was not easy; walking without rest or proper food for hour after hour became harder with each step. Hornets' Nest's fear goaded him to drive his men mercilessly.

Dawn rose through the jumbled peaks and crags. With the growing light birds and apes found voice. Still the column advanced through the hill country. Only when his men began to faint, first singly, then in twos and threes, did Hornets' Nest order a halt, cursing them as weaklings. He even descended from his palanquin to beat an unfortunate straggler to death with the man's own halberd butt.

As soon as they stopped, Teng curled on the dew-sodden ground and span downwards into a painful doze. Through thick clouds he heard Hua's voice from further up the column: 'If you'd been nice to me, who knows, Aunty? Blame yourself.' Even in his half-conscious, swirling state, Teng detected unease in Hua's tone. He didn't care. Only sleep mattered. It might be good to never wake at all.

天命

The respite was brief, the next march long. Yet the column made rapid progress through the limestone hills, taking paths known to few and used by fewer still. Teng concluded that during their halt Hornets' Nest had received further bad news, for he urged his men onward whenever they slowed, often looking round anxiously from the elevated position of his portable throne.

'I believe he fears government troops,' Teng whispered to Shensi. 'Jebe Khoja and Prince Arslan must be thirsty for his blood.'

Teng had also noticed a small group of female prisoners roped together near the treasure chests, too far up the column for him to see their faces. Perhaps Hornets' Nest hoped to increase the profits from his expedition by rounding up a few slave girls.

Towards dusk, they entered a long, winding valley fringed with vines and tree stumps, as though stripped bare for fire-wood and building materials. Sentinels on crags were also visible, signalling to one another with yellow flags. Teng and Shensi exchanged glances.

The valley echoed with shuffling feet as the column turned a final corner, revealing Hornets' Nest's lair. At first Teng was surprised that so notable a rebel, leader of all the Yueh Fei and Red Turbans in the entire province, should be content with flimsy wooden palisades for his ramparts and thatched huts for his barracks. Then his gaze climbed sheer cliffs to the huge open mouth of a cavern. Hornets' Nest's house was clearly visible, tucked into the vast space like a gigantic fungus planted by magic.

'Why bring us here?' he murmured to Shensi.

But Teng knew very well why they were here: as experts who might help to date and value the treasure Hornets' Nest wished to sell; as witnesses who knew far too much; most of all, as men promised a tenth of the spoils. A contract easily cancelled by an executioner's sword. Their one hope lay in remaining useful.

A group of officers waited beside the open gates as the column limped through. Hundreds of Red Turban rebels had also gathered to greet their chief and a loud cheer echoed round the sheer walls of the small valley, making birds rise from perches on the cliffs and apes screech.

The officers bowed as Hornets' Nest's palanquin bobbed past, its bearers close to collapse. The lead officer at the gate, a tall young man in scuffed armour, straightened once his chief had gone and marched into the camp before Teng drew near.

The prisoners were herded into a dense village of wretched hovels and houses, down narrow lanes where bony chickens clucked in alarm. A cave entrance at the foot of the cliff was their final destination.

Once their hands were unbound, they were pushed towards a narrow, dark tunnel. Teng managed a single glance up the cliff before he entered the prison. A line of female captives was being chivvied onto a steep path leading up to the huge cavern he had glimpsed. Then he was in the tunnel, stumbling over coarse, flinty ground. Guards holding lanterns directed him through a door constructed of bamboo poles lashed together. Unwholesome odours engulfed him, as they had in the dead prince's tomb.

Teng's last thought before he lay down in the darkness was that His Majesty's curse had come quickly, karma had come – as did sleep's oblivion.

fourteen

天命

While Teng slept in sheer exhaustion, unaware of danger, Hsiung was allowed no relief. Hornets' Nest's cold stare as he bobbed past had revealed his chief was unlikely to forgive the victory at Dragon Whirl Gorge. An underling showing initiative led to questions; and Hornets' Nest answered such questions in his own way.

He must give the rebel leader no excuses, no pretence for punishment. With this in mind, Hsiung summoned Sergeant P'ao.

As soon as he came over, he glanced up shrewdly at the cavern. Hornets' Nest's residence glowed with lights and sounds of celebration: shouting, a wildly beating drum, a pi-pa and flutes playing at double-quick time. Hsiung and P'ao stood side by side. Night and their intentions thickened.

'Odd the Chief hasn't asked you to report about Dragon Whirl Gorge,' remarked P'ao.

'Hmm,' said Hsiung.

'They'll all be drunk up there soon,' said P'ao. 'Maybe that'll improve his humour. Perhaps you should beg forgiveness for winning before he gets a hangover.'

'Maybe.'

'I hear he has lots to celebrate,' said P'ao. 'A dead prince's treasure! If what you told me about buying a pardon is true, he has enough now. No wonder he's happy.'

'Yes.'

'The men who had to dig like slaves aren't,' continued P'ao, quietly. 'I heard they haven't eaten properly for days. They might not like it if he moved against you. After all, you've won a *real* victory for our cause.'

'Perhaps so.'

Both waited in the darkness, looking up.

'P'ao,' said Hsiung, after a while, 'do you remember how you came to be here?'

The old soldier grunted. 'Of course! I got captured during one of Hornets' Nest's salt raids. Four years ago.'

'And I managed to persuade Lieutenant Jin to let you live, didn't I?'

'You saved my life.'

'Does that make you beholden to me?' asked Hsiung, his voice troubled.

P'ao muttered as though affronted, then said, 'Of course!'

'Hornets' Nest saved *my* life,' said Hsiung. 'Shouldn't I be loyal to him? Whatever he decides?'

P'ao chuckled. 'Not *whatever*. Never *whatever*. Don't let him take your life because once he saved it, boy! That doesn't make sense.'

For a moment Hsiung was an eleven year old lad instructed by big, bold Sergeant P'ao. Only a moment. He clapped P'ao on the shoulder.

'I'm going up there to see the old devil,' he said.

'Then I'm going with you,' said P'ao. 'And I'll bring a few others, just to be friendly.'

As the young captain didn't contradict him, P'ao strolled off into the camp.

Hsiung climbed the steep, winding path, one shoulder close to the cliff. It would not do to slip and tumble into the valley below. He had no intention of being pushed either, at least, not without a fight.

His mouth was dry as he approached the top. Although he had undertaken this journey many times, at every hour of day and night, he sensed something had changed. Retreat into old certainties was impossible. P'ao was right – Hornets' Nest did possess enough treasure to purchase a full pardon. Yet Hsiung believed the change was more in himself. The victory at Dragon Whirl Gorge had been no accident, nor a matter of mere skill or luck with his sword. Success watered seeds subtly planted by Liu Shui. The fat man had urged him to oppose Hornets' Nest 'when the time comes'. Perhaps that time had come.

A dozen yards from his destination, Hsiung halted. The twenty men following, all armed and led by Sergeant P'ao, paused along with their leader. Instead of Hornets' Nest's usual bodyguard blocking the pathway to the cavern, a beaten, bloodied man hung from iron rings in the rock. Weary swollen eyes flickered open. Hsiung lifted the man's chin with his gauntleted hand.

'Jin! What has happened? Why are you tied like this?'

It took a struggle for Lieutenant Jin to speak. 'I abandoned my post . . . I went to Dragon Whirl Gorge . . . He said I could not desert again if I was tied like this.'

Hsiung felt a lurch of guilt. He had assured Jin no harm would befall him, that the only way to defend was to attack, that every experienced officer was needed to save the camp. Yet if he interfered now on Jin's behalf it might enrage their chief further. Then a voice came to him: Liu Shui's perhaps, or Deng Nan-shi's, repeating *something changed, something changed* . . . And the voice stirred a thrill of power, the same joy he felt in battle.

'Release Lieutenant Jin,' he ordered, 'there has been a mistake.'

While two of his escort sawed at the prisoner's bindings, Hsiung marched up the final section of path, emerging so suddenly the dozen soldiers posted on guard had no time to stop him. All had been drinking and were engrossed by a spectacle inside the cavern.

The rebel chief had set up his throne on the cavern floor and laid out scores of ancient bronzes, silver platters, statuettes, heaps of *cash* coins from his treasury. A hundred lanterns made the cavern dance with shadow and light, an effect intensified by circling swallows alarmed from their roosts by the echoing, driving music. Frantic drums, twanging pi-pa and trilling flutes. More than just shadows danced. Hornets' Nest's officers and advisers, wild with drunken triumph, swayed and clapped. Even their chief had left the dignity of his lacquered throne and was capering beside two golden statuettes of leopards, dragging his slender concubine behind him, one hand clamped on her white wrist. Uproar and exultation dripped from every face.

For ten years Hornets' Nest and his closest followers had been prisoners in this cave. Ten years of living like rats the farmer hasn't got round to poisoning. Ten years of noble dreams turning rancid; of mocking ideals and vows once held sacred. Hsiung almost pitied them as they jigged. Except that now they held the means to free not just themselves, but to equip an army capable of freeing the entire province.

One by one the guards stopped clapping and hastily put down their cups. But Hsiung's escort had already taken up position in the cavern.

Finally Hornets' Nest noticed his uninvited guests. His ungainly dance ceased. The drummer went still. Silence would have filled the cavern if the swallows had not twittered and beat their wings in alarm.

Casting disdainful glances round him, Hsiung strode through the banquet, servants and fellow officers moving aside to let him pass. Sergeant P'ao attempted to follow but was ordered back by the younger man.

Before the throne Hsiung bowed perfunctorily and executed a crisp salute with fist and palm across his chest. Hornets' Nest, who carried no weapons, cast a wary glance at Hsiung's armed escort and chuckled. 'The hero of Dragon Whirl Gorge joins us! Why is he so late? Bring him wine!'

A servant scurried forward with a loaded tray and Hsiung shook his head.

'I will not feast until our brave men have eaten and drunk! They are thin as hares when there is enough silver here to feed Lingling County for a decade! How can this be right?'

Hornets' Nest chuckled again.

'I see! You would like to take charge, eh? Then the entire world can dine at my expense.' His confidence was daunting even to Hsiung; it emboldened his officers and closest supporters to jeer and laugh. 'Or perhaps,' added Hornets' Nest, winking at them, 'you'd like it all for yourself?'

The wily old rebel smiled. He could tell from Hsiung's confusion that the boy had no idea how to become master.

'How can this be right?' repeated the young man. 'There are rumours you have sent agents to buy a pardon from the Great Khan! Deny it if you can.'

Amusement instantly left Hornets' Nest's face. 'Who told you that?'

'Your concubine,' replied Hsiung, at once regretting his indiscretion. The girl moaned with fear. Then he knew he could not walk away from this argument with Hornets' Nest still ruler here: or the girl, Sergeant P'ao, Lieutenant Jin, all who had trusted him, would pay for his weakness with their lives. He knew what he must do – and soon. Yet still he was tormented by a desire to prove himself more regal than his chief.

'Because you once saved my life,' he said, 'and once served the cause of Yueh Fei well, I will allow you to leave unharmed.' He added contemptuously. 'You may take as much wealth as a single man can carry.'

A foolish, insane offer, he knew. An offer allowing Hornets' Nest the little time he needed to arm himself and gather men. Already the rebel chief had relaxed, his glance passing from

Hsiung's supporters to his own, assessing strengths, calculating odds. No doubt he would have accepted this merciful offer if not for a cry from one of the guards.

'Sire!' shouted the man. 'Look! Lights in the valley!'

Instantly all quarrels were doused by a greater threat. Attention turned outwards. Hsiung hurried over to see. There were scores and scores of lights – red pinpricks of flaming torches in the darkness.

'Where are our scouts?' cried Hsiung, turning to the plump officer who had accompanied his chief to the prince's tomb. 'I asked you to arrange the usual scouts! We should have received warning of the enemy hours ago!'

'I don't take orders from a boy like *you*!' replied the other, his voice slurring. 'So I didn't.'

Hsiung resisted an urge to cast him face first over the cliff. Instead he gestured at the advancing lights.

'That is why Jebe Khoja is our surprise guest,' he said.

天命

Jebe Khoja's unexpected arrival at the rebel camp so soon after his defeat at Dragon Whirl Gorge came at a price.

The first cost was to his pride, for he had promised his uncle, Crown Prince Arslan, he would avenge the royal honour within a month. Prince Arslan had many virtues and vices, not least impatience. His Highness also abhorred mockery from his fellow princes at court; losing an entire county's revenues had certainly inspired that.

The next cost had been paid by humbler folk. In accordance with established methods, Jebe Khoja rounded up his local guides and accused them of leading him into a trap at Dragon Whirl Gorge. Furthermore, that if they failed to ensure his passage across the perilous Min floodwaters within two days, they and their extended families to the third generation would be executed. To prove his sincerity, he selected one of the guides at random and had him beheaded on the spot.

But rivers are no respecters of threats. They existed before men and will outlast them. Though their guides struggled night and day to find a crossing place, it was only achieved after two days' march in the opposite direction to Hornets' Nest's camp. Luckily for them, Jebe Khoja was a reasonable man. He saw they had done their best and only executed their leader, with the added mercy that the man's family was spared. Flexibility of this kind confirmed Jebe Khoja's reputation as a moderate lord. Others, envious of the Provincial Governor's high standing with Prince Arslan, called it a lack of resolve.

The next cost had been borne by his entire army. Determined to achieve three days' progress in two, he commanded a brisk pace along the Min, arriving at the rebel camp a little after dusk, having observed no scouts or even watchmen. Naturally, Jebe Khoja assumed the apparent unpreparedness of the rebel camp proved its opposite and that Hornets' Nest hoped to lure him into a trap. As a result, he ordered his flying column of fifteen hundred to rest on the dew-soaked, stony ground before an attack at dawn. Had he launched a probing night sortie, as some of his officers advised, he would have discovered that the rebels were in complete disarray and outnumbered almost three-to-one.

Instead the Mongol nobleman climbed a tall rock and looked at the lights of the rebel camp in the distance. Memories of defeating Hornets' Nest a decade earlier mingled with subtle mourning. Then he had been thoughtless with youth, eager for glory, ablaze with lusty enthusiasm. Now, awaiting a victory no one doubted – least of all himself – Jebe Khoja felt the weariness of one who has known only success. Even the setback at Dragon Whirl Gorge could not infiltrate his assurance.

'Make sure that upstart Captain Hsiung is brought to me when the rebels surrender!' he called down to his retinue.

He resumed a brooding watch over Hornets' Nest's camp.

185

天命

Rays slanting from below the horizon merged into beams then fields of light. The upper silhouette of Mount Chang glowed. An hour would bring a clear dawn, a cloudless dawn, exactly the sort Hsiung dreaded. Last night he had even ordered sacrifices of precious sheep to various local deities, begging for rain. Torrents would slow the Mongols, make the thatched huts harder to burn. But the mountain gods and demons weren't listening. Well then, they would do without divine assistance, though it had never been more needed.

A bizarre rift among the Yueh Fei rebels had weakened their ability to resist the coming attack. P'ao, hoping to dispel Hsiung's gloom with a joke, dubbed it a quarrel between 'high' and 'low'. All one need do was look up at the cavern containing Hornets' Nest's house to catch his meaning.

The rebel chief had spent the night seizing supplies of food and arrows from the camp below while Hsiung bullied the troops into three clearly defined units, appointing officers loyal to himself, signallers and message-runners. In short, a simple triangle of command.

Meanwhile, Hornets' Nest expelled scores of servants and prisoners unlikely to add to his personal safety, dispatching the latter to the same gaol where Teng still lay dreaming of bamboo strips bearing secret messages from the Immortals. Among the prisoners were females of every age and type.

In the hour before sunrise, Hornets' Nest gathered a force of fifty picked men to garrison the cavern in the precipitous cliff and his plan became obvious to everyone in the camp. Those in his unscalable eyrie – P'ao's 'high' – could resist a siege indefinitely. Even if food ran low they would devour the birds roosting there each night. Just as importantly, there was rumoured to be a secret escape route at the back of the caves known only to Hornets' Nest. Finally, to guard the privileges enjoyed by these 'highs', a sturdy barricade was placed on the pathway to the cavern. A few servants foolish enough to seek re-admittance were shot down with crossbows, their corpses left on the steep path as a warning to others.

Conditions were less favourable among the 'lows'. When Hsiung finally paraded the rebel forces he counted five hundred men. Dawn was almost established in the shadowy valley. Hsiung stood on an upward-thrusting boulder before this limp force. In his heart he paced nervously; yet no one, except perhaps old intimates like P'ao and Jin, would have noticed.

He examined the ranks until some began to murmur. Above his head the first bats were returning and swallows flew from the cavern. At this sign he raised his clenched fist. 'Today will be a great victory!'

'For who!' shouted a voice from the ranks.

The murmuring became a quarrelsome clamour.

After the doubter had been dragged out and beheaded by P'ao, who had been promoted to Lieutenant overnight, Hsiung resumed his tirade. 'A great victory!' he repeated. 'First Port Yulan! Then Dragon Whirl Gorge! Soon we will control Lingling County! Obey your officers! Kill any who show their backs to the enemy! Remember, we are trapped and there is nowhere to escape but death! That is why *we* shall trap *them*!'

At this many chanted the name of Yueh Fei, especially when Hsiung revealed all except the 'bravest and best' were to retreat as soon as the enemy attacked. Others, who listened more carefully, remembered how Captain Hsiung had instructed them to build walkways among the monkey paths on the cliffs encircling the camp. The more imaginative tacticians squinted up and glimpsed his intention, how one might trap an incautious enemy. Hope flared as they muttered to each other. Most were brothers and cousins, uncles and neighbours who had left their villages to fight the Mongols, and these bonds strengthened resolve.

'Remember Fourth Hell's Mouth!' Hsiung called. 'Today it will be our greatest weapon!'

With this cryptic prediction, the three companies marched off to their designated positions. General Hsiung (he, too, had awarded himself a promotion) tried to raise morale by sharing out whatever food and wine Hornets' Nest had overlooked.

天命

Too late for further preparation. Just time to inspect the three units of the Yueh Fei army. The largest he called the Ram's Body. It numbered three hundred men led by Lieutenant P'ao and stood in formation at the rear of the camp, its back braced against the cliff walls. The other two units, each a hundred strong, he called the Left Horn and Right Horn. These were the 'bravest and best', whether with bow, halberd or discipline. With these two Horns he hoped to gore Jebe Khoja's flanks while the Ram's Body trampled them.

Dawn advanced remorselessly; likewise the Mongol army moved towards the flimsy wooden palisade and ditch of the camp. Signal drums echoed round the precipices, filling the valley with startled birds. Though tired by marching and a rough night on hard ground, Jebe Khoja's force made a bold show. Mongol and Uighar guardsmen in lamellar armour and plumed helmets formed the core, bearing pole axes, swords and bows strengthened with bone. The rest were Chinese mercenaries from the north, contemptuous of southern rebels and bearing a variety of weapons: leaf-shaped swords and crossbows; two-pronged spears; rocket-arrows; fire-lances; all the superior inventions once possessed by the previous dynasty and now serving the Great Khan. Well over a thousand Chinese led by Mongol officers, for Jebe Khoja insisted on separating the races in strict accordance with the law.

A hundred paces from the palisade a swarm of arrows flew up, curling down on the advancing lines. An attack clearly anticipated, for disposable Chinese formed the front ranks; and though dozens fell, the rest of the army broke into a jog that became a dash as they neared the palisade and wooden gate. Here the Mongols paused, loosing arrows and crossbows of their own at the defenders on the walls. Fire-lances sent up spurts of flame. For a short time the exchange of missiles continued, then the rebels seemed to lose heart, vanishing behind their ramparts.

A great cheer rose from the government troops. Jebe Khoja ordered his drummers to beat a special signal and a dozen guards rushed from the ranks to the gates, carrying a large wooden box. This they leaned against the gate. Lighting a fuse, they scurried back – and just in time, for the thunderclap bomb exploded early.

Every living thing in the valley quaked at its roar. Even the plants appeared to shimmer. Waves of sound echoed back and forth across the cliffs and peaks. Splintered wood, dust, and stone rose in the air along with billowing grey smoke. So loud a noise in the limestone hills was greeted with watchful silence. Creatures froze in valley after valley – tigers, mountain goats, foxes.

As for the rebel defences, a gash had been torn in the palisade. Once the smoke and dust cleared it became clear the camp's defenders had abandoned their ramparts.

A roar rose from the Mongol army, almost to rival their thunderclap bomb. Here was the kind of victory everyone liked! They had sacrificed nearly fifty men to seize the walls, but what was that?

Boom. Boom. Boom. The signal drums ordered a final, decisive advance. Through the still smouldering gateway they poured, this time led by the guardsmen in shoulder-to-shoulder formation. More arrows and crossbow bolts met them, for the rebels had gathered in the gaps between the houses. Good! An enemy within cutting reach! The guards rushed forward to engage the village's defenders.

For the next half hour desperate fights flowed back and forth in the alleyways and narrow roads, the Mongol forces hampered by sheer numbers in so confined a space. Skirmish by skirmish those numbers inevitably forced back the rebels. Deeper and deeper into the streets, through pig sties and yards, thatched hovels and storehouses, the two sides fought.

Finally, trumpets blared out from behind the camp, a long, beseeching, mournful sound, and the rebel soldiers broke off and retreated in close order, leaving the densely packed village to its new owners. Again, a cheer rose from the victors, though less confidently than before. Scores lay in the narrow places of the camp, corners well known to the rebels but a hostile maze to their conquerors.

Again and again the trumpet sounded. When it fell silent it seemed the entire valley waited for the next voice to speak.

Jebe Khoja cantered to the front of his troops, a large man in gleaming armour, the blue plume of his helmet nodding like a peacock's tail. Furious at the losses he had suffered, he issued orders to take no prisoners – every last traitor to the Great Khan must suffer separation of head from neck.

Once more the Mongols moved forward. They had begun to regard their opponents with more respect. At the fissure of Fourth Hell Mouth many touched lucky amulets. Rumours had spread throughout the Mongol army concerning Hornets' Nest's personal entrance to the Underworld and his friendship with demons who came up to drink and enjoy virgins in his company.

The village was ominously quiet. Armour jingling, they reached its outskirts.

A limestone cliff covered with vines towered at the rear of the village; a steep hillside of broken boulders climbed to meet its base. Here the Red Turbans had gathered for a last, desperate defence. The Mongols stared up at them in surprise;

they had not expected so many well-disciplined troops, at least five hundred, ready to defend their toe-hold with arrows and bristling halberds. Their backs were literally to the wall. Nothing left to lose, nowhere to go, what the ancient commentators called 'dying ground' where one either perishes or triumphs. Jebe Khoja examined the rebel formation and laughed.

'The fools!' he shouted to his officers. 'We will clear them from Hou-ming Province forever! They have lined themselves up nicely! All we need do is wait.'

This sentiment went down well. His officers hurried off to ready their men for a final assault, one Hsiung had not anticipated.

天命

With each flight of arrows from the village below Hsiung felt the resolve of his men weaken. The Mongols were fine archers, perhaps the finest, and soon the Yueh Fei lines were shedding corpses. He had trusted the enemy would rush up the slope in a fierce, reckless charge, so that his two Horns, Left and Right, might fall on their flanks and rout them. Instead they were bleeding away his strength.

'Loose! Loose!' he ordered, urging his crossbowmen and archers to respond in kind. But the Mongols were using houses and fences as cover: an unequal exchange of fire. Lieutenant P'ao rushed over.

'Sir! I beg you to order a charge!' he cried. 'We cannot just stand here to be skewered.'

From their elevated position, Hsiung could see that the streets below harboured waiting columns of Mongols. Any charge by the rebels would soon be halted by the weight of their guardsman. He glanced up nervously at the cliff walls on either side of the valley. This was the moment he had feared, the moment of decision. Could he trust his fanciful plan? So many things might go wrong. But the alternative was to crouch here while Jebe Khoja whittled his forces as a carpenter planes wood.

'Tell the men to take cover where they can,' he ordered. 'Prepare the fire arrows. We will burn the village.'

At first P'ao seemed inclined to argue, then he shrugged, placing fist against palm in a salute. With a grin he whispered, 'Why not, young Hsiung? I have enjoyed being a Lieutenant, even if it was only for a few hours. Let us go out with a blaze!'

He bowed low to the younger man.

'It *will* work!' whispered Hsiung fiercely, glancing round to see who overheard. 'Just keep the Ram's Body whole, and when you hear the trumpets, charge with all your might.'

Lieutenant P'ao nodded and hurried off to issue orders.

Soon afterwards, scores of fire arrows trailing smoke flew from the rebel lines, a stream of tiny meteors landing on the straw roofs of the village. Now the absence of rain turned to Hsiung's advantage: buildings began to smoulder and catch flame, smoke drifting lazily upwards.

Hsiung had gathered the Left and Right Horns near the base of the cliffs surrounding the village, each positioned on opposite sides of the valley. He raised his sword as a signal and Lieutenant Jin, bruised and injured by Hornets' Nest's maltreatment, but refusing to surrender his command, replied in the same manner.

A hot fury filled Hsiung. If his cause and dreams were to burn he would die sword in hand and drag a hundred hated Mongols with him to Hell! At this prospect he felt the dark lights begin their dance. Yet he knew his head must be clear!

The smoke was thickening, filling the narrow valley, obscuring the visibility of those in the village. Hsiung turned to the Left Horn, crouching with armour and weapons ready.

'To the Monkey Paths!' he cried. 'Follow me!'

In a bound he scrambled onto a narrow ledge and started edging along the side of the cliff, climbing steadily until the burning rooftops were some distance below. He had no eye for anything other than the next hand and toe hold. A miscalculation would cast him onto the rocks below. Like spiders on a wall the rebels slowly traversed the cliff – no great distance, perhaps a single *li*, but an eternity when exposed to the bows of a thousand men milling around in the village below. Acrid smoke obscured Hsiung's vision and he choked back tears. Even in his temporary blindness he could make out the dark hole of Fourth Hell Mouth in the centre of the village, and he had a sudden vision of its potential – so exhilarating it took all his will to hold back the dark lights. Not yet, he promised himself, but soon . . .

In the village below Jebe Khoja faced a decision. Should he attack the rebels gathered at the foot of their last cliff and so escape the smoke and flames swiftly spreading around him? Or order a hasty retreat through the burning village and reform back at the palisade? Then, once the place had turned to ash, he could order a renewed advance.

He sensed his decision must be instantaneous and longed to attack. But he had already lost too many in this campaign and was loathe to waste more.

'Order a withdrawal!' he barked at his drummers. 'No, hold! Hold, damn you!'

To his surprise a crude horn trumpet was sounding in the rear of his forces, then another and another, rebel trumpets if he wasn't mistaken. He turned to confront a further surprise: Yueh Fei rebels surging down the hillside from the rear cliff in a wild charge, flags waving and halberds levelled. Jebe Khoja's proud blood flushed at such a challenge from this rabble.

'Stand and meet them!' he bellowed.

His best men, the guards companies, duly shuffled forward to receive the Red Turbans' reckless attack. Instantly Jebe Khoja sensed his mistake. The village was burning more fiercely and half his army remained trapped in the flames . . .

*   *   *

Moments earlier Hsiung had emerged from the monkey path near the wooden palisade at the front of the camp and rejoiced to feel his boots on firm ground. More soldiers landed beside him, raising tensed crossbows or steadying pole arms. But the only enemies in view were a dozen military officials and their guards gathered round a portable map table. All were staring into the burning village like fishwives fearfully awaiting a fleet's return from a pitiless storm.

'Shh!' urged Hsiung, ducking out of sight behind a boulder as more and more of the rebels appeared from the cover of the smoke-cloud. When enough had assembled he ordered an attack, dispatching the few enemy on this side of the village with ease. While withdrawing his sword from a man's chest, he met Lieutenant Jin, who had successfully travelled the monkey paths on the opposite cliff with his Horn. Combined, they formed a force of nearly two hundred, the 'bravest and best' of the Yueh Fei cause.

'Sound the trumpets!' ordered Hsiung.

How they rang out! Mountain trumpets made of ram horns, blown by blue-tattooed Yulai tribesmen.

On the other side of the village, Jebe Khoja felt panic sweep his troops. The very air was barbed with sparks, floating, smouldering wisps of straw. He turned to find his drummers, all picked, seasoned men, crouching in fear, staring round at the fog of smoke through which rebels occasionally darted to stab at the heavily armoured Guards.

'Sound a withdrawal!' he called.

Slowly at first, then with desperate passion, the signal drums beat out: *boom dum boom* . . . And what should have been an orderly withdrawal became a terrified rout through lanes choked with fume and flame. Where men encountered the hungry lips of Fourth Hell Mouth they toppled over, pushed by the weight of those who came behind, spinning and screaming into the void below. Others, more resourceful, sought the cliff walls and used them as a guide through the smoke. Still more charged down the narrow alleys like maddened beasts gasping for air.

Because the village was not large, it did not take long to emerge from the smoke clouds in ones and twos, then tens and scores. If Hsiung's 'bravest and best' had not been waiting for them, assuredly they would have lain on the ground gasping until fresh air filled their lungs, and their eyes ceased to weep. As it was, they emerged like deer driven through thickets onto hunters' spears. The sudden flash then agony of arrows greeted them. Those who survived the arrows were cut down by swords and halberds.

But not all. Stray groups of coughing soldiers broke through and fled up the valley while Hsiung's Horns were busy else-where with their pitiless work. Amongst them were five wretches in rags, evidently escaped prisoners, or perhaps Hornets' Nest's servants, for one was female, though she ran with the same desperate determination as the men.

Thicker and thicker billowed the smoke. A heat haze gathered, making the air shimmer and distances distort. The need to breathe whipped more waves of men forward, only to emerge on a shoreline of corpses littering the ground. A few stumbled back the way they had come, colliding with dozens more seeking a way out of the cloud.

Hsiung strode up and down the ranks, goading on his men to more efficient acts of slaughter, occasionally cutting down a Mongol or Chinese mercenary.

Finally, like the swallows who streamed each night into Hornets' Nest's cave, the flow of men slowed and ceased. Hsiung turned to locate Lieutenant Jin. He was leaning on a spear, exhausted by his injuries at their former chief's hands. Could all the enemy be dead? Hsiung heard distant sounds of fighting from the rear of the village: proof P'ao was still lead-ing the Ram's Body.

He stepped out of the rebel ranks, over to a boy who lay shivering on the ground. Was he barbarian or Chinese? One could hardly tell from his appearance. Hsiung leaned over the sobbing child. How old was he? Eleven, twelve? A useless boy dragged where he did not belong . . . Hsiung recalled himself as a boy of twelve, staring fearfully up as Overseer Pi-tou raised his whip. He gasped, stepped back from the harmless child.

At that moment a group of coughing, limping Guardsmen emerged from the smoke. Some had abandoned their weapons. Those who still bore arms were barely capable of raising them. In their midst was a wounded man in noble, splendid armour, his silver and gold helmet askew, its blue plume scorched and soot-grey. Hsiung sensed crossbows and bows levelling behind him.

'No!' he cried. 'Do not loose!'

The roar of flames in the burning village almost drowned his words. Otherwise all was quiet apart from the cough and retch of the Mongols. Hsiung knew there was no question of surrender. Such a disgrace for Jebe Khoja's bodyguard would be worse than death, both for themselves and their families. And the Mongol nobleman, though he had to be held upright because an arrow protruded from his chest, still clutched his sword.

Hsiung walked closer to the group and examined the injured man. His gaze found Jebe Khoja's face, puckered by pain. As soon as the Mongol became aware of his enemy, he smoothed his features into the barbarians' notorious 'cold face', though the pain of his wound must have been unbearable. Hsiung bowed stiffly and pointed with his sword at the still smouldering gates. Why did he spare so notable an enemy? He attempted no explanation. Except perhaps, that a forgotten memory lingered in some corner of his soul of gawping as a boy at the Mongol noble on his prancing charger, and of longing to be like him.

Slowly Jebe Khoja and his entourage limped through the

broken gates and up the valley. Many of the Yueh Fei soldiers who had suffered at Mongol hands muttered at this clemency.

'Do not kill all those who escape from now on,' ordered Hsiung in a tired voice. 'If they are Chinese give them a choice: join us or die. If they are Mongol, execute them.'

He found a boulder to sit on, the same rock from which he had addressed the troops hours earlier, and watched the herding and beheading of two hundred or so survivors. At last the flames in the village died back and, as the smoke cleared, Hsiung looked up at the dark entrance to Hornets' Nest's cave high above. Despite the swirling heat haze he spotted dark shapes and knew the rebel chief was returning his scrutiny, looking this way and that to discover what had happened beneath the smoke's cover.

fifteen

天命

The freedom to fight and be killed may seem unenviable. For Teng and Shensi, resting against a rough wall in constant darkness, it lay beyond envy. Droplets bitter with minerals fell constantly from the ceiling: their only drink. Air their only grain.

The long room echoed with moans and shuffles, cries of distress from the other prisoners. Their numbers had swollen during the night and Teng had noticed females among the new inmates. The soldiers had held their lamps high as they shoved the shadowy, cringing forms into the cavern. Then the door, a rectangle of bamboo poles lashed with wire, grated shut. Its huge rusty padlock had been fastened and checked before the soldiers withdrew up the dark tunnel. Yet sounds still reached them from outside and a few hours later Teng stirred uneasily.

'I believe they're fighting out there,' he whispered. There had been an explosion. Shouts. Faint tinkles suggested clashes of steel.

When sight is denied other senses take its place. Teng had already habituated himself to the stench of unwashed bodies, urine and diarrhoea; so much so, he could pick out less obvious odours. Up to now they had consisted of diseased breaths. Not long after the sounds of fighting ceased he detected something new.

'Burning wood and grass,' he mused, 'drifting in from outside. A hut on fire. But who's fighting who?'

Perhaps the rebels were quarrelling over their spoils from the Prince's tomb. A notion that gratified Shensi so profoundly he felt moved to describe Hornets' Nest's parentage in some detail. Teng sensed other prisoners listening to their conversation.

'There are many precedents,' he pondered. 'Take the conflict of Zhao Gao and Li Si. One might call that a squabble over looted treasure, for all their pretensions to possess the Mandate of Heaven.'

He might have elaborated on these learned matters had not the smell of smoke intensified. Soon people were coughing rather than moaning.

'Quiet, Teng!' commanded Shensi. 'Come with me to the entrance.'

They picked a cautious route across the cell, avoiding prone bodies wherever possible. Teng had no such luck with a pile of human dung in a drainage runnel carved into the stone floor.

At the door they halted. Reaching through gaps between the lashed bamboo poles, they rattled the padlock uselessly until it became clear they were not alone. Three others had followed them, no doubt with the same aim of testing their only means of escape. In the feeble light Teng detected a familiar profile.

'Tell me, sir,' he said, cautiously, 'weren't you our fellow prisoner at a certain tomb near Mirror Lake? In short, aren't you one of the Yulai hunters with blue cheeks?'

'Yes, we're Yulai,' came the terse reply. 'I remember you, scholar. Also from the inn at Ou-Fang Village.'

Then it came back to Teng. He and Shensi had prevented Chao from beating this same Yulai.

'We are allies,' he suggested. 'Well then, how are we to escape?'

A crashing echoed down the shadowy corridor that led out-side. A wounded Mongol warrior stumbled into sight, coughing, coughing as though his lungs would burst. He staggered to the bamboo door and clung to it, gasping the foul air.

Instantly, the two Yulai seized his arms through narrow gaps between the poles, crying, 'His knife! Get his knife, scholar!'

Teng did not move. 'Is that wise?'

He was brutally thrust aside by Shensi.

'Quicker!' urged the Yulai.

Shensi needed no encouragement: fumbling wildly, he drew the unfortunate soldier's own dagger, stabbing and twisting the blade until the man went limp.

Stunned silence in the long cell. Then a fearful, incoherent clamour filled the air.

'Can you break the lock?' demanded the Yulai.

His question was addressed to Shensi, who had knelt by the huge, ancient padlock, using the dagger's point as a lock pick. For a long while none of the men round the door spoke or moved. Everything depended on this. Teng grew aware the Yulai had another, as yet silent, companion and felt an odd frisson. Something about the stranger – who hung back in the darkness – disturbed him. He could not explain why.

'Damn you!' grunted Shensi.

Something deep in the mechanism snapped. The padlock opened with a creak. Gently, Shensi pushed the door right back.

They wasted no more time. Dangerous as it might be outside, better to risk anything rather than stay in that noxious trap. Creeping up the tunnel, the group turned a sharp bend. Daylight spilt over the stone floor, the sweet, intoxicating, mid-morning sunshine of a fine summer's day. Except that the light glowed in waves, intermittently darkened by dense smoke. Teng exhaled deeply and clenched his fists, rubbing them against his eyes. The sun, obscured as it was, blinded him with hope.

When he could see clearly, he was confronted by a stranger's face. For a long moment he examined the young woman's nose, eyebrows, chin. Her naturally plump cheeks. Above all her eyes were familiar, though he did not remember such an angry, even disdainful, fire in them. Surely she was a delusion sent by a mocking demon, one he had angered when disturbing the Prince's tomb.

He turned to the two Yulai. They were looking at the young woman with signs of respect. Teng noticed she wore a Nun of Serene Perfection's blue robes and yellow neckerchief. A name escaped as an involuntary, astounded squeak. '*Yun Shu?*'

She met his eye. Looked away, hugging herself. He remembered the gesture only too well. A glance at the size of her feet settled the question.

'Let's not delay,' muttered Shensi.

They followed his lead. Although the world outside the prison entrance was a fog of choking smoke, Shensi scurried along the side of the cliff until they emerged at the perimeter of the rebel village. The sight greeting them was enough to persuade the prisoners to turn back.

A savage melee was taking place in the gap between the palisade gates and the huts. Teng shrank from the slaughter, but could not help staring. So *this* was war! No wonder Grandfather had preferred policy. A hand gripped his arm and they were running like hares through morning mist, up onto the wood and earth ramparts, lowering each other down. No one tried to stop them.

Now they stumbled up the valley, away from Fourth Hell Mouth and the wrecked rebel camp, alongside other refugees in uniforms that Teng recognised as belonging to government forces. The Yulai hunter spotted a deer trail into seemingly impassable hills. 'Up this way!' he called. 'Quicker!'

They had advanced a short way along the path, which steadily widened, when a group of twenty soldiers blocked their route, escorting a man upon a mountain ass.

'Out of their way!' commanded Shensi.

Just in time. The soldiers panted past, ignoring the refugees who crouched in the undergrowth. Teng caught a glimpse of an exceptionally fat man on the donkey, an anxious expression tightening meaty jowls, then they were past, heading for the rebel camp.

'Come!' urged the Yulai. 'We must be far away before dusk.'

天命

'Do not!' urged Lieutenant P'ao.

'No!' echoed Lieutenant Jin. 'No!'

Hsiung's demeanour remained implacable.

'He will shoot you down with arrows,' warned P'ao.

'Do not trust him!' added Jin.

'Did we suffer to allow you to throw away your life – and ours with it?'

P'ao seemed genuinely distressed, and well he might. Hsiung, however, saw no other way. The fires in the village were dying down to reveal blackened, smouldering timbers, ash and scorched humps that had once been upright men. He could not expect his forces to stand at arms for much longer: they deserved rest, the release of celebration. With the destruction of their homes all supplies had perished. Hsiung knew he must lead what remained of the rebels to the Min River in search of food and shelter. Yet to do so would leave Hornets' Nest safe in his cave, sat upon the treasure Hsiung desperately needed to re-equip the army and encourage new recruits.

'Tell me,' he said, 'how are we to persuade the old devil to come down? He has enough food up there to last months.'

Now Jin and P'ao were less generous with their opinions.

'So you see,' said Hsiung, 'since he is unlikely to come to us, it seems I must go to him.'

He did not add another, entirely foolish reason for marching boldly up the steep path on the cliff to Hornets' Nest's door. With the melancholy he invariably suffered at the end of battle had come guilt. He dreaded what had befallen the old brigand's concubine after the disastrous revelation she had betrayed her master.

Hsiung was wearily tightening the stiff leather straps of his armour when unexpected visitors distracted him. Two dozen soldiers wearing red headscarves entered the camp at a jog. Behind came a donkey and bobbing rider he recognised at once, led by a monk in a Buddhist's orange robes. A large, round face looked eagerly from side to side and Hsiung paused.

'Perhaps I shall not climb the cliff just yet,' he said. 'It seems the situation has changed.'

Night brought huge bonfires. The shattered wooden palisade was being used for fuel. Defences were meaningless with nothing left to protect and Hsiung preferred to keep the men warm. He went from campfire to campfire, praising those he recognised and many he did not. Above all, he sought to reassure those Han Chinese who had defected from the Mongol forces. At his command they had been spread out amongst the Yueh Fei rebels, yet he anticipated many would disappear during the night and quietly instructed the guards to let them go.

So much for fires on earth. More numerous were those in the clear night sky; the drought still held and the monsoon's next wave gave no hint of appearing. Hsiung stared up at ribbons and patterns of stars, each an Immortal or God. What did they think of men, hacking at each other until one or another perished? Did it matter who rose or fell?

Tired of loneliness, Hsiung wandered to a large fire near the base of the cliff. Here he found Lieutenants P'ao and Jin eating strips of grilled donkey and toasting their victory with wine P'ao had somehow salvaged. It was of the roughest kind, but Hsiung gulped it as medicine for doubt. He could not understand why victory did not elate him. When he glanced up he found the fat man's bright eyes watching.

'How can you be happy until Hornets' Nest is dead?' asked Liu Shui, softly. 'What use is all of this?' He waved contemptuously at the burned camp littered with enemy dead, eight hundred at least, though no one could count those who fell into

Fourth Hell Mouth. 'What use is this?' he repeated, 'until you have undisputed leadership of the Yueh Fei rebels in this province? Until you have sufficient treasure to pay for your conquests?'

Hsiung laughed harshly and swallowed another burning cup.

'That is all very well,' he said, 'but he will not come down! I tell you I must go to him.'

Liu Shui shook his head. 'Inadvisable!' He added, 'I rushed back here after I heard of the victory at Dragon Whirl Gorge. At last, I thought, a real leader for our cause! But you are young, Hsiung, and need guidance.'

'You have not answered my question,' said Hsiung. 'How are we to persuade Hornets' Nest to come down?'

'But I have,' answered Liu Shui, coldly, 'except you did not hear. I shall say it again. You need an adviser. And the first thing I advise is to drink no more of that poison. There will be plenty of fine wine when you possess Hornets' Nest's head. Besides, I have a plan.'

And Hsiung had to concede the fat man was right on all counts.

An hour after dawn the next day, having been thoroughly drilled by Liu Shui, Lieutenant Jin proceeded to the bottom of the path leading to Hornets' Nest's cave. He did not go alone. Hundreds of Yueh Fei rebels accompanied him, led by Captain P'ao (he had received another promotion overnight, his second in two days).

They stayed below, waiting in disorderly groups, many lolling on the ground while Lieutenant Jin climbed the winding path up the cliff. No one punctured him with crossbow bolts and at the very top he was allowed admittance.

Hsiung and Liu Shui watched from a concealed position on the other side of the valley.

'He's been a long time,' whispered Hsiung, though Hornets' Nest was hardly likely to hear.

'Not that long,' mused Liu Shui.

'What if he doesn't believe Jin? Or has him beaten like last time?'

'That is unlikely. He needs Jin now. But if it happens you will need to appoint a new lieutenant. And I will think of a new strategy.'

Still there was no sign of either Jin or their quarry. Even Liu Shui grew restless. 'It seems we must devise a new strategy,' he said.

Within moments, Lieutenant Jin appeared on the top of the path, bowing to someone out of sight. He retreated to the bottom and had a brief conversation with P'ao, who dismissed the assembled soldiers, instructing them to forage for food.

'Well then,' said Liu Shui, after Hsiung, P'ao and Jin had gathered in a sheltered corner outside Hornets' Nest's view. Jin was still mopping his forehead and seemed unlikely to recover from his experience in the cavern for a while.

'Speak up!' commanded Hsiung.

Jin smacked fist against palm. 'Sir, I told him you were dead, as instructed. I do not know if he believed me. I also said we desperately require his leadership. On that point he was easily convinced. He asked how many men were left, their strength and determination. Then he told me that he – not you – had planned the whole victory and that all its glory belonged to him.'

Hsiung's face darkened. 'How do they fare up there?'

Lieutenant Jin grew more thoughtful. 'He talked with me outside his house. I saw at least twenty corpses hanging from the eaves. As a warning to others, I think.'

'Why?' asked Hsiung. 'How is this?'

Jin shrugged, but Liu Shui smiled his Buddha-like smile. 'Because some of them must have opposed his will,' said the fat man. 'A large share of his followers, and he only had fifty to begin with. Perhaps they regretted betraying their oaths to Yueh Fei. Or recalled the Buddha Maitreya's promise to cleanse the Middle Kingdom. Who can say? Let us take it as a good sign.'

'Yet Hornets' Nest is just as safe up there with thirty men as sixty,' said Hsiung. 'It would take only a handful to hold off an attack up the cliff path!'

Liu Shui stroked his wispy beard, his smile broadening.

'No doubt. But his position is dangerous. Consider, Hornets' Nest has sent messengers to the Great Khan hoping to purchase a pardon. Yet without an army to support him, how can he negotiate from a position of strength? Without an army, how can he even transport his carefully gathered treasure to the Great Khan's officials, even if an agreement has been reached? So you see, he dare not skulk in his cavern for long, however safe it might seem.'

The other men listened in silence.

'There was a naked girl hanging among the corpses,' said Jin, thinking aloud. 'His concubine, I believe. A bad business.'

No one was interested in a mere concubine apart from Hsiung. His teeth clenched involuntarily; he said in an odd, dull voice: 'I must fight him at once. He clearly does not believe I am dead.'

Liu Shui was less sure. 'Jin, did he *definitely* refuse to descend and lead the army?'

'He told me he would consider my message and descend when it suited him.'

'That is a kind of agreement!' cried P'ao. 'No reason then for you to go up there, Hsiung!'

Liu Shui nodded and recited: *'The fish nibbles its own hunger; the patient fisherman stirs.'*

'Ah, to be a scholar,' sighed P'ao, 'that sounds like a poem, sir.'

'It is,' replied Liu Shui with a faint smile, 'one by Yun Cai.'

Though Jin and P'ao exchanged dubious glances, Hsiung did not conceal his pleasure at possessing so learned an adviser.

天命

Hours passed while the rebel army foraged. Hsiung knew he must march them to the Min River tomorrow at the latest, before hunger set in. Yet Liu Shui insisted Hornets' Nest would certainly quit the safety of the cavern.

'We must tempt him until his nibble becomes a bite,' he said. 'We must offer tasty bait.'

What did they have that Hornets' Nest desired? P'ao came up with the solution. 'Tell him we've captured chests of Mongol coins but that he won't get them unless he allows us to swear allegiance. Tell him we're desperate for a leader. Otherwise the army will disband.'

'Don't ask me to pass *that* message,' muttered Jin.

Liu Shui, however, applauded the suggestion. 'Gather the men as before and prepare a case of *cash*. Lieutenant P'ao shall be our matchmaker.'

P'ao's smile showed more teeth than usual. 'It is *Captain* P'ao.'

Once again the troops were paraded for Hornets' Nest's inspection. P'ao abandoned his gift near the cliff top, shouting from the pathway a threat to disband the army. Trembling, he awaited arrows in response. None came. After a suitable delay he bowed his way back to the bottom.

Liu Shui refused to be discouraged by Hornets' Nest's silence. 'Something's going on up there,' he muttered.

An hour later their patience was rewarded. The rebel chief wore full armour, both of his famous battle-axes on his back. His burnished helmet, though small for his head, glittered in the noon sun.

Hsiung, who had been watching with Liu Shui from a hidden corner, leapt up, fumbling for his sword. The older man clutched his arm.

'You will ruin everything!' he hissed. 'Let him gulp the bait!'

Reluctantly, Hsiung subsided.

Step by step Hornets' Nest descended the path, halting halfway to survey the valley with haughty suspicion. Hundreds of faces were looking up at him and perhaps he felt unnerved by their collective gaze; perhaps he glimpsed his cowardly role in the recent battle and that no sensible man would want such a leader – in peace or war – ever again; perhaps, too, he sensed a trap, as deer will halt at the edge of a clearing ringed with hunters they cannot smell. Then P'ao rushed forward.

'Kneel for our Lord!' he cried, thrusting down the rebels around him. 'Kneel, damn you! We're saved! Hornets' Nest will lead us!'

At first only a few obeyed. But they were more used to obedience than defiance, and even those who had every reason to despise Hornets' Nest as a leader undeserving of Heaven's Mandate, gradually joined the hundreds on their knees. Still Hornets' Nest hesitated on the cliff path until, with a masterful glance at his supporters crowding behind him, he swaggered down the final steps onto the valley floor.

Meanwhile Hsiung had sidled close to the front of the cliff, blocking Hornets' Nest's route of escape. Then he, too, knelt on the fire-scorched ground, conscious that twenty of his picked bodyguard had done the same nearby.

Hornets' Nest examined the heads and necks presented. He bellowed, as he had when a young man, before compromise and cruelty misplaced his ideals: 'Red Turbans! Yueh Fei! My victory is complete and the enemy driven off! With the silver and gold I provide we shall rebuild this camp . . .' He fell silent, evidently unsure of further plans. 'As for brave Captain Hsiung,' he continued, 'who perished obeying my orders, let his body be found for an honourable burial. I shall weep over it! And any who do not weep shall be punished!'

This last word echoed round the crags and cliffs. Hsiung could stand the farce no more. Kneeling a moment longer would taint his honour forever. He rose to his full height and coughed loudly. Hornets' Nest turned; and when he saw his way to safety blocked, reached for his axes. At once P'ao was shouting, 'Aim! Await the order!'

Hornets' Nest's supporters on the cliff were exposed to scores of tensed arrows and crossbow bolts. All froze. For a long moment no one dared move.

'Do not loose!' commanded Hsiung. He stepped forward, one hand on his sword hilt. 'Hornets' Nest!' he shouted, for this was no private conversation. It was like the actors' performances he had watched during festivals as a boy. 'It is a vile lie to claim you won the battle! It was won despite you. You are a traitor to Yueh Fei!'

The older man, however, was not listening, looking instead at the crossbows pointing like cruel eyes.

'Hornets' Nest!' called Hsiung, impatiently. 'Are you deaf?'

Now the rebel chief fixed his attention on his opponent.

'Neither deaf nor dead, boy,' he replied.

Hsiung took a step closer. 'I strip you of your command,' he cried. 'You are a coward and have lost the Mandate of Heaven!'

This last phrase had been planted by Liu Shui, quite insistent he should use it as often as possible. Hornets' Nest merely glowered.

'You may leave now with whatever clothes and weapons you carry,' said Hsiung. 'Or face justice.'

This last word seemed to energise the rebel chief. 'Justice?' he roared. 'That will only come when we face each other man to man!'

'No, sir! Hsiung!' pleaded P'ao. 'Let me order the archers . . .'

Too late, for Hsiung had drawn his sword and strode from the safety of his bodyguard. 'Let's settle this then,' he said.

Two men circling each other on ground blasted by fire, ground already sown with corpses. If one of them joined the dead, those failed seeds, did it matter? Both had been hailed and obeyed. Did the fall of leaders count more than lowly footsoldiers?

High above, monsoon clouds advanced towards the limestone country, ready to wash away all trace of battle, joy or loss. Ready to make the mountain streams delight in splash and motion.

Hsiung realised his breath was too quick. Why was he nervous? He had killed many men in combat and here was another. He longed for the dark lights to dance. Then his sword would be guided straight to Hornets' Nest's throat.

'You're afraid, boy,' taunted the rebel chief. 'You know I'm your master. Always will be.'

Hsiung resisted an urge to launch himself. That was what his enemy wanted.

'You daren't attack me,' said Hornets' Nest. 'You are the coward here.'

Still Hsiung did not reply. He was noting the patterns his enemy made with his axes. Far beyond the realms of conscious thought, he sensed moments in the pattern when the axes were less poised, more unwieldy. Hsiung edged forward.

'Come on, boy!' cried Hornets' Nest, breath coming out in gasps. There was fear in his voice now. 'What are you afraid of?'

Hsiung positioned himself a footstep closer.

'I will share my command with you,' said Hornets' Nest. 'Yes! That was always my intention. To adopt you as my heir! To be the father you lack! It is not too late.'

A flaw appeared in the circling, defensive pattern of Hornets' Nest's two battleaxes, Hsiung was sure of it. In that gap one might knock them aside with a single blow.

Around them Yueh Fei rebels shouted encouragement to General Hsiung, *Take his head! Take his head!* Hornets' Nest's few supporters either stayed rooted on the cliff path, watching the fight below with fearful expectancy, or had fled back to the cave. If their chief fell, no one doubted their fate.

Hornets' Nest's breath was coming harder now. Too much fine living had not prepared him for duelling. He must strike soon or lose all initiative.

'You puppy,' he grunted, feinting with his axes. Then, like a ghost of the furious young man who had earned the nickname 'Hornets' Nest', he leaped forward and aimed a blow. If it had connected, Hsiung's skull would have split open like a melon. It never did. He dodged in time to feel the wind of the blade. His sword passed through the axes' guard, finding Hornets' Nest's exposed throat. A momentary resistance of skin, a spurt of blood.

Hsiung playfully knocked aside flailing axes as his enemy staggered, one hand trying to stem the flow from his throat. With an easy forward slide of his foot, Hsiung swung back the sword and launched a blow, half-severing his enemy's head at the nape. Hornets' Nest's face still wore an expression of astonishment as Hsiung hacked again and again to make sure. He was surrounded by roaring, chanting voices. When the cheering subsided he raised Hornets' Nest's head aloft by its greasy hair.

Liu Shui appeared by his side, whispering in his ear: 'Tell them you will renew the Yueh Fei army,' he muttered.

'First we shall renew our army!' bellowed Hsiung.

'And bring justice to the whole of Lingling,' suggested his prompter.

'We shall seize Lingling County for our just cause!' shouted Hsiung.

The rest of his intentions were drowned in drums and shouts, a cacophony of excitement. Hsiung scarcely heard. He stared round the dense circle of frantic faces, mouths opening and closing like fishes, a shoal hundreds strong. He remembered Liu Shui's poem about hungry fish and felt himself drowning in air.

sixteen

天命

'Perhaps Lady Serenity might sound her chime less stridently?'

The request – and unwarranted title – came from Teng. Yun Shu considered it sensible to ignore all three. *Tinkle*. Ten more steps. *Tinkle*. By this means one showed respect to local gods and spirits, thus progressing in the Great Work. *Tinkle*.

'Perhaps my Lady of Jade Perfection did not hear me?'

Yun Shu sighed. The Sixth Precept was 'always maintain an even and harmonious disposition.' She had no intention of giving Teng the satisfaction of appearing ruffled by anything he did, said or mocked.

Tinkle.

'Perhaps the Honourable Teng is over-sensitive?' she suggested. 'Strictly speaking, I should click my fingers every three steps, as well as sound my chime.'

'You have a handsome chime,' he conceded, 'it is just I prefer nature's music. The sweet song of the birds! The wind's gentle sigh! The croak of frogs.'

Tinkle.

'Really?'

'Yes. And I am sure our companions feel the same. Don't you, Shensi?'

However, the old tomb-finder and their two Yulai guides seemed more amused than irritated. Lacking allies, Teng subsided and after a while Yun Shu tired of her spiritual practice.

They were moving through a landscape of exceptional loveliness. Spiralling peaks overhung with mossy creepers on every side and, between them, lush bamboo groves bright with purple, azure and yellow flowers. Insects droned. A gentle patter of warm rain on leaves lulled the travellers' spirits. After their recent dangers Yun Shu could only consider it a blessing. Yet even now they had reason to be afraid, though not of rebels. The Yulai hunters had informed her they were in tiger country.

'Look at this!' exclaimed the younger of the pair, lifting his shirt to reveal a back corded with muscle and scored by parallel claw marks. 'A striped demon did this to me last year! And not more than six *li* from the path we walk.'

Teng, who was listening in as usual, felt obliged to intervene. 'I'm sure it is not necessary to frighten a lady!' he exclaimed. 'Or display yourself.'

She detected discomfort in his voice.

'By all means tell the story,' she begged the tall, handsome Yulai. 'I would love to hear the details.'

He boasted of his narrow escape while Teng listened uneasily. Yun Shu even requested to examine the scars again.

For all that, it was still dangerous country, and the Yulai sharpened bamboo spears using the knife stolen from the dead soldier. When offered one of the makeshift weapons, Teng at first seemed inclined to refuse. Catching her disdainful look, he leaned nonchalantly on his spear.

'In times like these,' he opined, 'even a scholar of high purpose must bend like bamboo.'

'Yours certainly seems a little bendy,' she said.

He straightened, plucking at his chin. 'I have been assured otherwise, Lady Purity,' he replied. 'Many times! How tedious this journey is turning out to be!'

He kept an anxious eye out for movement in the undergrowth

and grew tense whenever a beast roared at night. One evening by the campfire she remarked on it to Shensi after Teng sneaked into the bushes to relieve himself.

'We all have secret fears,' replied the tomb-finder. 'Haven't you?'

Ashamed, Yun Shu glanced at her feet and resolved to be more compassionate in her thoughts. Until the next morning that is, when Teng referred loudly to her as 'Aunty Sour Tongue' while she was in the bushes. He also speculated to Shensi whether he was 'for it from that damn nun again today'. She interpreted *it* as an insult to her entire Order and found nothing more to say to him, especially when he attempted a jocular conversation about several sausage shaped rocks.

They arrived at Mirror Lake towards sunset and Yun Shu wept silently to see Sitting-and-Whistling Pavilion. A steady drizzle fell as they hopped over the stepping-stones to the small island where the shrine stood. Yun Shu was overjoyed to find someone waiting: Mother Muxing.

'Aieee!' shrieked the Yulai woman, rushing to embrace her two sons. 'How thin you are! What did they do to you, the devils?'

Word had not yet reached Ou-Fang Village of Hornets' Nest's death; the small group of refugees were similarly unaware.

'Are they after you?' she demanded. 'You must hide.'

'We have not been pursued,' said her eldest son.

Mother Muxing noticed Shensi and Teng.

'These men are Hornets' Nest's spies!' she cried.

Teng felt it opportune to intervene. 'Madam,' he began, with a trace of condescension, for she was a peasant, after all, 'you are quite mistaken! True, my companion and I were formerly in the employ of Hornets' Nest – quite unwittingly, I assure you – but subsequently . . .'

'No!' cried Mother Muxing, covering her ears. 'Honey words! You mean to cast a charm!'

It took a while for her sons and Yun Shu to reassure her that they would not have escaped without Shensi's assistance. Once this point was settled, Shensi voiced all their thoughts: 'Food?' he grunted. 'Where, please?'

They had an hour's wait before a dozen Yulai men and women from the village appeared with baskets of rice, vegetables, even a small chicken and pig's kidneys for frying with fiery Sichuan pepper. There were also salt fish wafers, Yun Shu's favourite, which she ate guiltily, aware that Perfected Ones dined on seeds, wild herbs and sunlight. There was wine, too, and Teng drank urgently.

After the feast, the villagers settled to sleep in the shrine and cells at the back. Teng, however, stared into the placid waters of the lake.

The night had cleared, revealing stars beyond count. Yun Shu watched him glance upwards, thoughts unreadable except for a sad, mournful demeanour. She cleared her throat. Swaying slightly, he turned.

'So you cannot sleep either,' he said, his voice thick with wine. 'What a night it has been! One to remember forever. Good, generous people after so many foul, cruel ones. So many!' He shook his head. The whites of his large, dark eyes caught glimmers of star and moon. 'Of course I learned how your parents treated you,' he continued, 'and about your marriage. I was very glad to hear from Lady Lu Si you have found a safe, honourable place among the Nuns.'

Somewhere in the distant hills a tiger roared. Teng flinched.

'It will not trouble us here,' she said. 'I, too, have fears at night.' Yun Shu lapsed into silent confusion.

He glanced at her. 'Oh, I'm not afraid. Not with you to scare off tigers.'

'Do you take me for a new Mulan?' she asked.

'Not exactly. But you have grown ... yes, *strong* since

we were children. Perhaps sorrow taught you to be strong.'

Really they should not talk like this. He had drunk too much wine to be decorous. Yet she wanted to hear more of his thoughts, especially the indiscreet ones.

'Tomorrow Shensi and I will re-visit a house of the dead,' he said, 'the prince's tomb. You are welcome to join us.' He hesitated. 'Yet I have a misgiving it may have consequences for us all. They say the past is dead, but I'm not so sure. Well, we shall see.'

He bowed and entered the shrine. Yun Shu stayed a while longer, looking towards Holy Mount Chang capped by its crown of stars. She imagined floating from its peak as an Immortal to fly among bright points of light in a sea of emptiness.

As usual, her thoughts soon descended to earth. Mostly she marvelled to be in Teng's company. Of course, she had every reason to hate and distrust him. Had he not betrayed her? Had he not condemned her to years of drudgery and scorn? There could be no forgiving that.

Yun Shu squinted up at the silhouette of Mount Chang. The new Teng was different from the gloomy, prickly boy she remembered. Though still pompous, he had aquired a knack for irony that amused her. And it was hypocrisy not to acknowledge he'd turned out handsome. At least, in a shallow, worldly way some women might find attractive. Foolish women, admittedly.

Maybe she had been too harsh on him. After all, exploring the dead prince's tomb demanded unusual courage. Oh, that would be a story to tell the Nuns! Teng had described the tomb's wonders on their journey to Mirror Lake until she felt an urge to see for herself.

天命

The next morning Yun Shu wondered what folly persuaded her

to join Teng and Shensi on their mission. Yet after the villagers left she slipped on her shoes and ran to catch up. They were following the lakeshore, burdened with sacks and lanterns 'borrowed' from Sitting-and-Whistling Pavilion. If they felt any trepidation at purloining Lord Lao's property they gave no sign.

Shensi glanced quizzically at Teng as she arrived.

'I invited her,' explained the scholar.

'Perhaps,' he added, addressing Yun Shu, 'you will glimpse the true nature of the Immortality you crave.'

An hour later they stood in the entrance of the tomb, soaked by the relentless monsoon, Shensi stubbornly sparking tinder and flint until lanterns were lit. Yun Shu hesitated, then followed the tomb-hunters into a tunnel reeking of earth and decay.

The time that came after was not measured by neat divisions of minutes, but by sensations, smells, sudden alarms. Though Shensi and Teng appeared confident she found herself trembling. At a crossroads in the darkness they encountered piles of jumbled bones, men and animals mingled together without regard for their souls. She cried out, panting fearfully. Shensi watched her but did not offer to lead her back to the surface.

'Do not be afraid,' said Teng. He turned to his companion. 'Go on, Shensi, we'll catch up.'

Shensi nodded and waded into the black wall surrounding them, parting it with his upraised lantern. As his light vanished into a huge chamber, Teng laid his own on the floor and crouched beside her, where she knelt before a mound of bones.

'This is Hornets' Nest's work,' he said. 'Piling them up, I mean. Long ago they were sacrificed to serve their dead Prince in his eternal life, as the old histories explain. Like all poor folk they were allowed nothing but tedious toil – even in death. Yet I'm sure their ghosts are at peace now, Yun Shu. They are resting from their labours forever. And so they defied His Highness.'

She barely controlled an urge to clutch his arm.

'Do you remember the bones in the watchtower?' he asked. 'And the wild dog Hsiung killed? How long ago it seems! Shensi says bones are everywhere.'

His earnest voice echoed in the empty darkness. A furtive glitter was revealed in his eyes and she recalled his betrayal. In this fearful place, she grew certain he would hurt her again. Like all the men she had known – Father, husband, Dear Uncle – he would hurt her. But only if she was foolish enough to trust him. Yun Shu rose. The thread between them, frayed by ten troubled years, snapped back in their faces.

'Let us find Shensi,' she whispered, 'I don't like it here.'

He nodded. 'Let us find him.'

He raised his lantern and led her into a large echoing cavern. More bones on the floor. Shards of broken pottery like fallen leaves. Yun Shu longed to cling to Teng's dirty robes as they advanced towards another glow-worm in the endless night. When they joined Shensi his expression was grim.

'Nothing valuable left!' he spat. 'Nothing at all!' Nevertheless he continued to sift methodically through the broken pottery. Teng hurried past him into a smaller chamber and emerged some time later with two heavy sacks.

'You've found something?' asked Shensi, eagerly. 'Show me.'

His partner held open the sacks and Shensi leaned forward. Yun Shu also peered curiously over his shoulder. The bags bulged with bamboo strips inscribed with ancient characters; also bones, tortoise shells, ox pelvises and shoulder blades, similarly inscribed.

'Are you mad?' asked Shensi. 'Who will buy *that*?'

Teng laughed with an edge of hysteria that echoed round the huge cavern like a warning – or challenge.

'No one alive!' he cried. 'Only the dead will buy! And me! Just us Dengs!'

Yun Shu gasped at such inauspicious words in so dreadful a place. She felt her store of *ch'i* energy, her life force, so diligently accumulated by meditation and the Great Work, diminish within her. They were sucking her essence! They were like hungry ghosts. What a fool she had been to come here! But the tomb-finder merely laughed at his companion's folly.

'The dead don't pay in any currency I know,' he said.

After they emerged into daylight and walked through the drizzle back to Mirror Lake, Yun Shu avoided Teng's touch or breath lest he taint her Inner Pearl. Suddenly it seemed as precious as her chastity when Dear Uncle forced her legs apart, crushing her face with the flat of his hot palm, grunting in satisfaction. This recollection strengthened her resolve. Yun Shu's expression was implacable by the time they reached Sitting-and-Whistling Pavilion.

天命

'I can allow you no further,' she said, blocking their way onto the stepping-stones that led to Sitting-and-Whistling Pavilion. She was hugging herself, fists clenched, afraid her slender presence would not deter them.

Shensi and Teng watched in astonishment but Yun Shu was determined not to weaken. The Great Work of her existence depended on it; all she had suffered would be lost, and with it her worth in this world, her future! What did offending Teng and Shensi matter compared to that?

'You are tainted!' she cried, fear swelling into hysteria. 'Both of you! I cannot allow you near Lord Lao's shrine until you have been purified. You are infected by death.'

'We are all touched by that sickness,' said Teng. 'We catch it with our first breath. Didn't you know?'

'Not all of us are cursed!' she said, something softer entering her voice, perhaps an appeal for understanding.

'Lady Serenity has had a fright,' Teng confided to Shensi, as though she was not present – the arrogance of a man towards a foolish woman. 'Not that I blame her.'

Shensi, however, was less tolerant. 'Does no one in these damned hills honour their debts?' he growled. 'I call her an ungrateful bitch.'

That word cancelled the possibility of retreat.

'I shall give you all the food and *cash* I possess,' she said, haughtily. 'Then you must go.'

A flush tinged Teng's high cheek-boned face. His eyes narrowed. 'As you wish, Aunty High Hat.'

Shensi spat into the lake and turned to his companion.

'Never mind her. I'll make those enquiries we talked about. And get our share if I can.'

'Do not risk your life for it,' said Teng. 'As for me, I'll return to Hou-ming. Join me there when you are able. There'll always be a welcome for you in Deng Mansions.'

Yun Shu, for all her previous certainty, felt an urge to change her mind. Perhaps Teng was right. Fear motivated her conduct and fear was an enemy of balance. It was too late now.

'If I get paid anything, my friend, so shall you,' Shensi promised.

With that, the two comrades embraced. After Yun Shu had handed over the food and *cash*, they went their separate ways, Teng towards Port Yulan and Shensi back into the hills. Teng paused before he left, as though about to speak. Then he shrugged, picked up his sacks of bamboo strips and bones, and departed.

Yun Shu prayed to images of demon-officials and Immortals appointed by the Heavenly Court. Of course her motivations were pure. Why not preserve her Immortal treasure, little enough as it was, earned through meditation and breathing exercises, chants and prayers, hour after hour, day after day? Teng was wrong to say only the poor were forced to toil.

Inner voices argued back. How unreasonable to hold a grudge! They had been children. How did that satisfy the Third Precept? And what would happen to Teng now? She could imagine him plodding through the limestone hills, easy prey for just about anyone. If he became meat for tigers, how could she explain it to Abbess Lu Si, who had doted on Teng as a boy and still regarded the Deng clan as the legitimate rulers of Hou-ming? These were worrying prospects.

She pictured him arriving in Port Yulan. His troubles would hardly end there. He had no money for the passage-fee back to Hou-ming. And while he was at home with the most obscure scroll, she suspected the dockside loiterers would fleece him like a village idiot.

Yun Shu chanted and burned incense until, weary of disquiet, she curled up on a prayer mat while the monsoon spilled from a warm, swirling grey sky.

'Are you sure you left her here?'

Even in the fogged state between sleep and consciousness, the voice was familiar. Joy quickened into wakefulness. Yun Shu threw aside her blanket and cried out: 'Bo-Bai! Is it you?'

Outside, she did indeed find Cloud Abode Monastery's eunuch servant, wearing travel clothes and accompanied by porters. It was his other companion who provoked her frown. There, smiling sardonically, stood Teng.

Weeks earlier word had reached the monastery of a battle near Port Yulan. Then Governor Jebe Khoja himself sailed off with an army to punish the Yueh Fei rebels. 'We were all afraid for your safety,' said Bo-Bai. 'And though Abbess Lu Si petitioned Worthy Master Jian for permission to send me to find you, he refused, ordering all Daoist clergy to stay clear of rebel areas lest we be tainted.'

'*Tainted?*' interrupted Teng, glancing significantly at Yun Shu. 'You Daoists seem to like that word. It's a shame you're not so pure yourselves. Worthy Master Jian, for instance, never protests when the peasants starve.'

Yun Shu remembered the Worthy Master from her ceremony

221

of acceptance as an Acolyte, a handsome, active man with shining silver hair, watching her closely as he stroked his wispy beard.

'Go on,' she told Bo-Bai.

'Abbess Lu Si decided to send me in secret,' said the eunuch. 'Before she did, Honourable Deng Nan-shi visited her with a request. He, too, had heard of the battle in Lingling County. He begged that I conduct his son, Honourable Teng, back to Hou-ming.'

Yun Shu felt a blush coming on and folded her arms. 'And what was Abbess Lu Si's response?' she asked, already guessing the answer.

'*Yes*, of course! What else?' broke in Teng. 'Lady Lu Si was like a stepmother to me after Mother died. She, at least, has a sense of generosity.'

Bo-Bai nodded solemnly. 'A very strong sense.'

'How foolish of me,' muttered Yun Shu.

The eunuch glanced sharply between them then continued his tale.

Upon arrival at Port Yulan, he found the hill country restless with rumours: Hornets' Nest had been overthrown by his deputy and Jebe Khoja's army slaughtered almost to a man. Recruits were flooding to the Yueh Fei cause. In short, it was advisable to return to Hou-ming while one still could.

Yun Shu, however, had other plans. 'I am afraid that I cannot return just yet,' she said. 'I swore an oath to walk upon Holy Mount Chang and cannot leave until it is accomplished.'

'*Cannot* is a debatable term,' said Teng. 'You mean *will not*. A simple removal of *not* solves the problem.'

Yun Shu ignored him. When it became clear she had no intention of relenting, even Bo-Bai agreed. He needed little encouragement. The eunuch had long desired to offer a sacrifice on the Holy Mountain to ensure he was reborn in his next re-incarnation as a complete man. He even kept the shrivelled member he parted with as a boy in a jar of vinegar in case a miracle occurred in this life. Everyone knew miracles were commonplace on Mount Chang.

Only Teng protested, but as no one paid the slightest attention he adopted a brooding silence, punctuated by observations of an acerbic nature.

seventeen

天命

Yun Shu left Sitting-and-Whistling Pavilion, turning her back on Mirror Lake, unaware she would never see the hills and limestone crags with their brocade of green again. Not in this life, at least. Even as she climbed through the woods, Yun Shu knew the map of her soul would forever include Mirror Lake.

At Ou-Fang Village they were met by Mother Muxing and her sons. Other villagers soon joined them, bowing to the young Nun of Serene Perfection and her entourage. While Yun Shu blessed the villagers with a fortune-bringing spell, Bo-Bai entered into deep conversation with Muxing, glancing often between the nun and Teng. When it was time to leave, Yun Shu was surprised by tears in her eyes as she waved farewell.

They comprised an unusual party on the dirt road through the hills. Bo-Bai led, accompanied by Teng using his bamboo spear as a walking stick. Next came Yun Shu, slightly apart lest she inhale impure breaths or brush her sleeve against someone lewd. At the rear were the porters; thin, gangrelly fellows dressed in threadbare hemp clothes, recruited from the stews of Hou-ming for the price of their feed.

Deeper into the foothills of Mount Chang they climbed, the Holy Mountain rising before them, its peaks and power enveloped by clouds. Yun Shu noticed these things and contemplated the intertwining flow of *yin* and *yang*.

Teng, however, incessantly disturbed her meditation.

'See that,' he muttered, turning to address her, 'how does *that* embody the Dao?'

They were passing through a village where a mournful, wailing crowd had gathered. Not for a funeral but a different kind of dying. The peasants' landlord – a petite man in silks surrounded by armed relatives and retainers – was evicting late rent payers, dumping whole households onto the road like buckets of slops. Already a straggle of grandparents, children, mothers and fathers thin as weasels, were leaving their ancestral village. Teng glowered at the landlord, quickening his pace until he joined the drifting cloud of evicted peasants.

'What is he doing now?' asked Yun Shu, in exasperation. 'I hope he does not get us into trouble.'

Bo-Bai's fleshy features were impassive. They watched Teng greet an old man and enter into conversation. Yun Shu noticed how the headman bowed to the youthful scholar, despite Teng's stained rags. She wondered at his natural authority; unless, of course, it flowed from mere arrogance, an assumption of superiority.

After a while Teng joined Yun Shu and Bo-Bai. To her surprise, he was more conciliatory than usual.

'Lady Yun Shu,' he said, 'please ensure the temple authorities in Lingling feed this unfortunate clan. It appears they have been evicted to satisfy the landlord's spite rather than through failings of their own.'

Wondering how he could be so sure, Yun Shu bowed. 'I will do what I can.'

She did not add that the Daoist leaders in Hou-ming Province had ordered all clergy to avoid the slightest contention with the authorities; and it was certain a wealthy landlord like this would smell sweet to local officials, as would his bribes.

'I have learned other things,' Teng mused. 'Hornets' Nest's replacement has sworn to make Lingling his capital and raises an army as we speak. The old man told me he has sent his sons to join the Yueh Fei rebels. That is his only hope of justice.'

'This new Hornets' Nest is more ambitious than his predecessor,' said Yun Shu. 'What is his name?'

Teng shook his head. 'A common name yet one that makes me melancholy. He would be my trusted servant if things had not turned out as they did. Poor Hsiung!'

Yun Shu glanced at him curiously. They walked in silence. Then Teng said: 'There is more. The mighty Jebe Khoja has been carried in a litter to Port Yulan and shipped to Hou-ming like a dying tiger. The authorities of Lingling County are in a panic.'

'Are you not a direct descendent of Yueh Fei?' she asked, softly.

He glanced at her. 'How do you know that?'

'Abbess Lu Si speaks of you Dengs often. Besides, it is common knowledge.'

'Better not remind our enemies. We are never safe.'

'Then you better not attract official attention,' she said. 'Why not masquerade as my servant?'

Deep offence darkened his brows. He laughed uncertainly: 'How droll! Very good!'

Yun Shu was about to retort she had never been more serious, for all their sakes, when his pain and humiliation stopped her.

He bowed and strode ahead to catch up with Bo-Bai, who had quickened his pace, displaying the instinctive tact of a palace eunuch.

天命

Later that day they caught their first glimpse of Lingling Town. It was a typical county capital, large enough to maintain a governor's residence and bureaux. There were four streets of importance, the rest being lanes winding around a hill. The markets sold necessities and little more. A military camp next to the governor's compound contained barracks for five hundred troops – all, save for a few scattered survivors, currently decomposing at the foot of Hornets' Nest's cavern. Yet Lingling had one advantage not shared by similar towns. Holy Mount Chang and its many shrines towered over its red-tiled rooftops, attracting pilgrims from all over the province and beyond.

A warm, fierce wind was blowing up from the valley as they arrived. Peculiarly, the city gates were unguarded.

'Where are the Great Khan's soldiers?' she whispered. 'Are no officials left alive in this County?'

'Even the toll collectors have fled,' said Teng, in surprise.

Once through, it became clear a host of other wolves lay in wait for pilgrims. Soothsayers and magicians lined the wide, dusty thoroughfare, along with stalls selling spells and amulets. Cold food and wine sellers cried out their wares. Others offered steaming tea and fresh rice or noodles flavoured with salt fish. At the sight of a genuine Serene One in her blue robes and yellow neckerchief, the boldest amulet sellers ran forward, urging her to bless their stock. Some even had the effrontery – or desperate need for *cash* – to suggest she buy.

There was a tense atmosphere in the street. Everyone seemed to be expecting something. Unwittingly, Yun Shu gave the sign by raising a hand to straighten her glossy, 'whirlwind clouds' hair. At once a hot wind blew. Paper windows rattled. Grit swirled in the air. To Yun Shu's amazement, tall dust eddies spiralled, swayed, danced in the roadway. Cries of astonishment and joy rose from a group of pilgrims beside a shrine dedicated to the Mother of Numinous Radiance.

'It is her!' cried a bald merchant with a pockmarked face.

Others took up the cry. Soon a crowd had gathered and, as Bo-Bai led them towards Sweet Dew Temple, the pilgrims followed, chanting prayers and the Numinous Mother's name. Yun Shu covered her head with her kerchief, jostled by elbows and sweating bodies, exposed to hungry, staring eyes. It excited

227

her to be treated with such reverence. Teng was less sanguine.

'Did you hear what they are saying?' he whispered in her ear.

Yun Shu wished he would not press so close.

'Apparently there have been miracles here ever since Jebe Khoja's army was destroyed,' he shouted above the hubbub. 'Odd clouds, magic snow . . . I'll find out what I can.'

'The Numinous Mother!' bellowed one man over and over, clapping three times with each repetition of the name. 'The Numinous Mother!'

Yun Shu was swept past shops and houses, up the hill to Sweet Dew Temple, amazed by the clamour. She felt certain it would shift to a more senior member of the clergy as soon as one appeared.

At the entrance to the temple compound she was met by just such a man. He had donned his finest yellow and black robes and seven-brimmed hat as the crowd approached. Blocks of incense had been freshly lit in ancient bronze censers. A dozen lesser priests and acolytes stood behind the cloud of scented, benign smoke, bowing and chanting. Yun Shu also abased herself before the chief priest and many in the crowd followed her example. Gongs boomed behind gilded pillars and frescoes.

Yun Shu felt herself swept forward into the ancient building. Only once did she glance back, to see hundreds of red, excited faces shouting and calling, all seeking advantage for themselves and their families. One face, however, frowned. It belonged to Honourable Deng Teng.

天命

Yun Shu was confined to the inner shrine room of Sweet Dew Temple. No punishment was intended, only honour, yet she struggled to comprehend how she deserved it. High Priest Dongxuan explained the matter, an eager glint in his eye:

'A miracle occurred when you arrived in the town, do you not recollect? Of course not, for you were in a transcendental state! Witnesses have explained how you floated through the gates, dust swirling beneath your feet. When you raised your hand a great wind blew! Furthermore, there have been reports of miracles all over the district. Divine birds carrying arrows in their beaks, spirit dragons dancing as they did when you arrived, trees suddenly sweating dew!'

He leaned forward and sniffed at her.

'Ah!' he gloated, as though it settled all possible doubt. 'A wondrous fragrance!'

Yun Shu felt a terrible urge to test the aroma of her own breasts and armpits but restrained herself.

'What does it mean?' she demanded.

Now the High Priest was less certain. He confided that, having consulted with an excellent local astrologer, he advised her not to step upon the Holy Mountain for two days and a night. In the meantime she must pursue the Great Work, all the while encouraging devout followers of the Dao to make offerings at the Temple. So saying, he sniffed deeply, ecstasy once more transfiguring his thin face.

Yun Shu's ongoing fast deepened her sense of dislocation. Meditation, breathing exercises, chanting and prayer merged into a blur of hours, all the while observed through window and door by excited crowds. A market established itself in the Temple courtyard, dominated by amulet sellers and a troupe of actors. Gongs sounded. Voices recited in unison. Even as Yun Shu slept she felt her spirit gaining *ch'i* energy. There were no dreams, just visions.

On the evening before her ascent to Precious Forest Temple on the Holy Mountain, Yun Shu received a visitor other than Bo-Bai or High Priest Dongxuan. Yun Shu regarded him through a haze of incense. Familiar as he was, he did not seem entirely substantial. Perhaps she was already half spirit and so detected a luminosity in people that turned flesh transparent.

She had been in the lotus position for hours without a

twinge, but as she recognised the visitor her legs felt suddenly stiff and uncomfortable.

'Yun Shu,' whispered Teng, 'they only let me in because I claimed to be your secretary. Bo-Bai arranged it. So you see, I did end up posing as your servant!'

She blinked at him drowsily.

'We are concerned you might be unwell,' he said. 'People say you have not eaten or drunk for days.'

His face reminded her of a glimmering image in a bronze mirror.

'I no longer need food,' she whispered back. 'Oh, Teng, when we were children who could have imagined this?'

He shook his head. 'Only a madman.'

'I will become Immortal!' she cried, greedily, 'I shall attain Bodhisattva and leave the husk of this body. Then all who have wronged me will . . . but no, it's not for that, not at all.'

'What's it for, then?' he asked.

She detected harshness in his tone, envy perhaps. To mollify him, she said, 'If that is too much, I shall become the Abbess of Cloud Abode Monastery!'

Still his face remained stiff. 'You have not answered my question.' He waved away a dense curl of bitter, pungent incense. 'What is this for? To prove yourself better than every-one else?'

'You are jealous,' she said, softly.

Teng bit his lip and stared at the ground. 'Yun Shu, I came to tell you something important. I have begun to understand small sections of the bamboo strips. They mention, among other things, the attainment of Immortality. You must be careful,' he warned, 'they speak of terrible danger.'

'You are jealous,' she repeated.

'Please listen a moment . . .'

'You believe that only you Dengs should be honoured,' she said.

'How foolish!'

'You do!'

'Actually I came here to beg. Though it hurts my abominable Deng pride! The family we met on the road, evicted unjustly, are here in Lingling and starving. Can you help them, Yun Shu? Will you speak to the High Priest on their behalf?'

Her eyelids closed with a flutter and she swayed to the rhythm of a fresh chant outside.

He rose scornfully. 'I suppose poor people do not matter to you,' he said. 'Only your Immortality matters.' He bowed with elaborate courtesy. 'I wish you joy of the mountain.'

Yun Shu no longer heard. The lotus position felt delightfully comfortable again. She imagined her body as a mountain criss-crossed by pathways and valleys and caverns, all humming with *ch'i* energy. An energy she directed to her womb where it coalesced as a glowing, brilliant pearl.

Above Lingling storm clouds gathered in the darkening sky. Lightning danced across the distant horizon. In Sweet Dew Temple, High Priest Dongxuan began to prepare silken robes for Yun Shu to wear during her ascent up the Holy Slope at dawn.

eighteen

天命

Memorandum to Worthy Master Jian, President of Hou-ming Provincial Daoist Council, 17ᵗʰ Day, 8ᵗʰ Month, Year of the Tiger, concerning the miraculous events on Holy Changshan involving the Nun of Serene Perfection, Yun Shu of Cloud Abode Monastery, Hou-ming, and the subsequent miracles denoting an extension of the Jade Emperor's favour.

Worthy Master Jian, it is with joy I write to share a great pleasure in the Dao that I witnessed with my own eyes. If you do not trust those eyes (for surely any man may see wrongly), I urge you to consult one of the hundreds who witnessed the miraculous doings I here describe.

It began thus: in the hour before dawn, the Nun of Serene Perfection, Yun Shu, emboldened by earlier manifestations of divine interest (described in my last letter to your Worthiness), donned robes of purple to represent a heightened dimension of yellow. So she demonstrated her ambition towards the Dao; moreover, she was encouraged to wear a wide girdle of black silk and scarlet silk, thus combining great yin and great yang, the ways of yellow and the ways of red.

May it be explained that throughout these preparations the gong beat as a warning to hostile spirits, for there was a turbulence over Lingling that early morning. Many attributed

232

it to a malicious dragon long resident in these parts. Suffice to say, Worthy Master, that dragon is the same monster who helped the rebels defeat the forces of His Highness Jebe Khoja, much to the dismay of all the Great Khan's loyal subjects.

Thunder echoed around the Holy Mountain and lightning danced around the peaks. 'Oh ho!' exclaimed some foolish persons. 'Now we will see whether this young Nun of Serene Perfection is all people make her out to be!' By that they meant: is her power sufficient to subdue the dragon cavorting spitefully over the Holy Places and preventing the offering of gifts and *cash* by honest pilgrims eager to pursue their own Immortality and Perfection through the Dao.

As the Serene One stepped from Sweet Dew Temple a great thunderclap echoed round the hills, signalling that the White Dragon had taken notice of her challenge and wished to give battle. At this many of the hundreds praying in the temple courtyard fell to their knees. But the Serene One was entirely unperturbed and seemed to float across the courtyard (though I did not witness this myself, other clergy were granted proof in that no footprints were afterwards discernible to mark her route).

At once the White Dragon began a succession of thunderclaps and lightning flashes so the very air tingled with energy. All to the benefit of Yun Shu! That lady opened her arms wide as she climbed the Holy Slope to the Sacred Peak, much as one embraces a friend or beloved rushing towards one, and scooped up vast effulgences of sheer *ch'i* energy each time the lightning flashed! The White Dragon merely added to her power even when seeking to abash the Serene One!

As she neared the Sacred Peak our foe deployed a fresh weapon. Rain lashed down from the sky like fierce whips. At once the earth ran with streams and trickles and many of the crowd lost their footing in the sticky mud, casting aside shoes and offerings. Sensing his advantage, the White Dragon renewed thunder and lightning, striking a huge rock near the

Serene One so that the stone glowed and smelt of strange essences. Though entirely drenched, she did not falter. Two thirds of the crowd had fled back to the safety of the town and the remainder cowered on the slope, yet she climbed on top of this very rock that had been scorched by lightning. Raising her arms, she remonstrated with the White Dragon, defying his worst.

Master, that was a sight to see! A final thunder crack louder than I have ever heard echoed round the mountain, rain beating down and bouncing off the rocks, until, by perceptible degrees, it slackened. Black, frowning clouds began to clear. Still the Serene One maintained her station, praying and commanding the White Dragon to be gone. At last, that perfidious spirit withdrew and the sky was the pure empyrean of summer!

Our jubilation can be imagined. Those who had not fled back to Lingling carried the Serene One up to Precious Forest Temple in a state of joyous piety.

Later I received reports that longstanding ghosts had fled the district along with the White Dragon. Also, there have been no miscarriages in Lingling since the miracle occurred, though they were frequent before. So I commend this Nun of Serene Perfection to you, Worthy Master Jian.

Chief Priest Dongxuan, Sweet Dew Temple.

The following was added in a secret code known only to the recipient.

Though the White Dragon was defeated, not so the rebels. I urge you to be cautious, Master, for they have acquired a new leader far more dangerous than Hornets' Nest. This Hsiung is said to be advised by a cunning master of strategy well known to the authorities (a certain Liu Shui).

As the clouds cleared, a bright sun came out over the hill country. The Holy Mountain's slopes shimmered and sweated in the glare. Groups of dazed witnesses to Yun Shu's miracle climbed to Precious Forest Temple, chanting hymns. Here and there, the pathway was littered with shoes and garments, rice boxes and water gourds, abandoned by those who fled the dragon's lightning and fury.

Also littering the path was a young man in a scholar's shabby blue robes, utterly sodden. He shook his cap so that droplets fell from its tattered earflaps and brushed wet hair from his forehead. Then he scratched itchy armpits. Glancing up the mountain, he watched hundreds of people carry a dwindling figure in purple robes onto the marble steps of Precious Forest Temple. Yun Shu, holding onto her hat with one hand as she was borne out of sight. Needless to say it was a far superior item of headgear to his own. The watching young man might have smiled, perhaps remembering how he had called her Aunty High Hat, except the joke tasted bitter.

Had Yun Shu really defeated a dragon? Little Yun Shu from Monkey Hat Hill? Certainly there had been black clouds and a violent wind, as if from a dragon's beating wings; also a downpour fierce enough to resemble a magical attack. And what of the lightning, a favourite weapon of dragons? One could argue the mere fact that so many pilgrims believed a miraculous battle had been fought – and won – proved the matter beyond doubt.

Teng shielded his eyes and stared at the black clouds drifting west, away from Lingling. Distant flashes indicated more lightning, as though the dragon was venting its spleen. He also detected far away echoes of thunder. If the creature could still roar and hurl lightning perhaps it had not been vanquished at all. For a moment he contemplated the bizarre notion that, rather than a dragon, he was witnessing a severe thunderstorm – one that had been building up for days. Then prudence prevailed: such thoughts were dangerous; too novel to pursue to their conclusion.

Perhaps Yun Shu was right and his doubts flowed from a green gush of jealousy. Certainly he was struggling not to envy the former servant-boy, Hsiung, now hailed as a leader of men. Worse, a leader of rebels bearing the name of Yueh Fei, his own ancestor! So mystifying a reversal to the natural order was better ignored.

Teng dreaded to think how his father would react, how he would inevitably compare his son's failure to a mere upstart's success. That was bad enough. Now to find Yun Shu – a girl – applauded as half-Immortal, a heroine of the Dao! What did it say about Teng's inability to satisfy the expectations of his ancestors?

How scornfully they must regard this wretch in threadbare clothes, alone without a single servant or underling, the last of a noble lineage.

He squeezed the sleeve of his robe so that a trickle fell to the ground. The itch in his sodden underwear and trousers intensified. He noticed a large, corked gourd-bottle beside the path, dropped in the stampede back to Lingling. Teng looked around for witnesses. No one. He approached the bottle and tested its weight. Liquid sloshed about. Glancing from side to side, he unstopped the cork and sniffed. Exactly as he had suspected!

Concealing this booty under his robe, Teng hurried along a path that led round the mountain to a small, long-abandoned shrine wreathed with small yellow flowers. As the sun beat down, he stripped off his trousers, stretching them out on a rock to dry. Wearing only his loincloth like a mad hermit, he sat gloomily, noting the shrine was a memorial to some Imperial official from long ago. Tombs, graves, bones everywhere he went! How wearisome it was to contemplate death. Yun Shu had been right to call him tainted. What she did not understand was how little choice he had in the matter.

Teng uncorked the gourd-bottle and drank. Belched defiantly. No doubt the green wine had been intended as an offering to Lord Lao. Stealing it could only deepen his bad luck, but so what? At least he'd confront karma in a blur.

The wine burned his throat, suffusing him with an inner heat that rapidly circulated through his veins. Likewise the sun warmed his skin. The wine went down in a series of gulps. It occurred to Teng he really should get drunk more often.

He remembered an obscure reference to cinnabar buds in the bamboo strips stolen from the dead prince's tomb. Abruptly, as insight will often poke through the soil of the mind like stealthy shoots, he understood the cinnabar buds' significance.

He stood up, clutching the gourd to his chest. Of course! Why had he not seen it before!

Teng paced before the shrine. With this understanding came a possibility of wealth and power almost as intoxicating as the raw country wine. At last he possessed something to sell in this sordid world! Something men would trade for heaps of jade and silk and gold! The collection of bamboo strips, lovingly buried with the dead prince's other treasures, was no less than an ancient treatise how to gain Immortality.

Chuckling oddly – by now he was quite drunk – Teng stared across the peaks and green-clad valleys of the limestone country. Blue lakes winked up at Heaven. Clouds roamed. Teng longed to ride them all the way to Hou-ming, no longer a wretched failure in the world's eyes and his own.

Not once did it occur to him, despite his father's stern lectures on how to be a proper, virtuous gentleman, who might bear the cost of his discovery.

Part Three

Worthy Masters

*Six-hundred-*li *Lake, Central China.*
Winter, 1320

nineteen

天命

Snow spilled from a drab, slate sky, driven in flurries by the icy wind. It was late afternoon, that hour when travellers hurry to find shelter before dark. Fortunately for the two merchants and their servants plodding through drifts of dry, packed snow, their destination lay only a few *li* distant.

They quickened their pace, urging the pack donkeys onwards with sharp blows, for the servants had learned their masters' style.

'Lingling Town!' announced the first of these, a wiry, diminutive man of around thirty years, dressed in garish silks that had browned and curled at the edges like old chrysanthemum petals.

His companion laughed coarsely. 'You mean the Noble Count's *noble* capital.'

This traveller was tall and muscular, his own silks more suitable for a medium-class flower house than a blizzard. Although he spoke slowly, there was a gleam of cunning intelligence in his sideways glance.

Waves of snow clouds covered more than Lingling County. Across lands south of the Yangtze to the North China Plain, thick flakes fell and settled, frozen into place by remorseless blasts from the Mongolian wastes. In many districts of the Empire a famine was entering its second year, provoked partly by heartless weather, more urgently by the demands of land-lords and tax-farmers, by unmanageable debts and by the sheaves of worthless paper bank notes printed in vast numbers by the Great Khan.

Even the Imperial Court was divided. Most Mongols sought to maintain the ancient ways of steppe and *yasa*, the all-conquering ways of Genghis Khan. Yet a growing number conceded that China, so wide and various, would never be ruled from the back of a shaggy steppe pony and sought to involve their Chinese subjects in official roles. So profound a division, ebbing back and forth across the royal dynasty's collective mind, stifled the possibility of consistent rule.

Little wonder rebels threatened government forces and officials all over the Empire. Most were little better than bandits exploiting the uncertainty of the times. A few, however, clung to higher ideals – and among these, to a degree generally described as quite remarkable, if not eccentric, was the self-styled Noble Count of Lingling.

The travellers initially received a suspicious reception at Lingling Town's city gates, but were waved through after the production of letters. They followed winding streets to what had been the Governor's Dwelling, now known as the Count's Palace. Here they were met in the courtyard by soldiers bearing pine torches that hissed when snow met flame. Darkness had come early and the travellers hurried indoors, rubbing their hands for warmth.

Deep in the palace lay a large chamber. In the centre stood a lacquered throne that had once graced a treasure room in a huge, limestone cavern. Yet the throne's current owner, the Noble Count of Lingling, ignored his splendid seat; he perched on a stool before a brazier, staring into the glowing charcoal as though its heat and light could banish dark thoughts. For a long moment he did not notice the servant bowing at the door.

'Sire!' cried the messenger. 'The visitors you asked about have arrived.'

The young man on the stool nodded curtly. He was in his late twenties and broad-chested as a young bull, his arms and legs thick-sinewed.

'Sire,' continued the servant, 'should I inform Chancellor Liu Shui of their arrival?'

Again the Noble Count seemed inclined to nod. Then he shook his head.

'Not yet. Tell the visitors I will see them in private tomorrow.'

Once the servant had gone, Hsiung resumed his examination of the brazier's hot, pulsing heart.

天命

The next morning Hsiung rose early, a habit retained from his days as a scullery boy to the Deng clan, except now it satisfied restlessness rather than duty. He was pacing Far Vista Terrace, with its famous view of Holy Mount Chang, when his chancellor joined him. The sky remained grey and laden, stray flakes fluttering down. The rising sun cast an eerie mountain-glow across the limestone hills, a country Hsiung had come to know well since defeating Hornets' Nest. The sun reminded him of last night's glowing charcoal; his dangerous thoughts as it reduced to ash.

Liu Shui bowed solemnly. Six years had scarcely altered the older man's appearance: still absurdly fat, still smiling like a jovial, serene Buddha.

'Noble Count,' he said, breath steaming in the frozen air, 'will you commence your morning audience?'

Hsiung was inclined to say no, tired of audiences and appeals for justice where neither side was obviously guilty. Baffling decisions about this and that – questions that always seemed to have been decided in advance by Liu Shui. But the Chancellor insisted: 'A daily audience is how the Song Emperors conducted the Empire's business. Are we to neglect their example?' As Hsiung could think of no argument to refute such precedents, he usually agreed. Only later did it occur to him that, despite elaborate audiences and rites, the Song had been overthrown by barbarians.

That morning Hsiung would have preferred to meet the two travellers from last night, but as their presence in Lingling was not known to his Chancellor he yawned and followed the older man to the chamber containing his lacquered throne.

Officials, all appointed by Liu Shui, waited with plans for extending the defences of Port Yulan and Lingling Town. The Chancellor nodded approvingly while they expounded their proposals, his hands buried in thick, trailing silk sleeves. When the officials knelt to proffer a memorandum and drawings, Hsiung took up the scrolls impatiently. Pretending to read them, he alternately grunted and glared at the officials. No one questioned the necessity of this charade, though everyone in Lingling knew the Noble Count was effectively illiterate. After all, the outer must denote the inner, even when the inner is a lie.

'And may I add,' said Liu Shui, smoothly, 'the proposed works will not only make your domains more secure, but create much needed employment for those peasants going hungry.'

Then an unheard of thing occurred. The Noble Count cast down the scrolls so they tangled at his feet. The room went silent.

'Why do we waste our revenues on defence?' he demanded. 'What of attack? Order a parade of all my regiments in one hour!' With that he stalked off to his private chamber and a breakfast of peppered kidneys. Liu Shui stayed behind, his brow furrowed.

The parade turned out to be a disappointment, especially as Liu Shui insisted on accompanying him, protected from the quickening snow by cloaks and a huge, gaudy umbrella carried by two servants. Hsiung felt like he was being shielded by a gigantic butterfly.

Only the Guards put on an impressive show, heavily armoured and helmeted, halberd pennants stiff with varnish. But they were just five hundred strong; the rest of his army, or at least those regulars under arms in Lingling Town, numbered barely twice that number. When Hsiung remarked upon it to his chancellor, Liu Shui bowed. 'I believe the majority of the army are preparing flood defences,' he said. 'One must anticipate floods when the snow melts.'

'What if we are attacked?' asked Hsiung, wistfully. 'We are surrounded by hostile forces.'

The Chancellor nodded. 'Forgive me, Noble Count,' he said. Then he examined hillsides deep with snow and Hsiung felt suitably reproached. No sudden enemy invasion was possible in conditions like these. Yet Hsiung would not relinquish his point.

'I need more regiments,' he said, 'all trained for attack! Our weapons are old and rusty. We are falling behind!'

Liu Shui bowed once more.

'As you say, Noble Count. But you will recollect that crowds cheer you as you ride by. That is because the people of Lingling County, though pinched, are not afflicted by the same famine as the rest of Hou-ming Province. That is because you spend more on their welfare than on conquest.'

Liu Shui withdrew after delicately asking permission on the grounds of ill health.

天命

After the Noble Count had dined, he summoned last night's secret guests to a private chamber adjoining his quarters. Liu Shui's subtle reproaches echoed in his mind and he was eager to avoid more.

The two men came and Hsiung examined them as they knelt, recollecting Liu Shui's warning they should not be trusted too deeply. But other men's faces most often shine with the character one hopes to find in them; so it was for Hsiung. He looked for loyal obedience and promptly discovered it.

'Well, Hua,' he said, 'what news do you have? And you, Chao?'

Chao and Hua had changed more than just their allegiance since Hornets' Nest's fall. Both now sported goatee beards and sideburns requiring frequent attention, as well as quantities of lemon-scented beeswax. Both had set themselves up as successful merchants trading rare woods and precious stones provided free by Hsiung in order to maintain their cover as spies. The sale of these goods led to sheer profit – Chao and Hua drove hard bargains, especially when it came to reimbursing *cash* to the Noble Count's treasury in Lingling. In this way they successfully acted as Hsiung's eyes and ears the entire length of Six-Hundred-*li* Lake, and particularly in the city of Hou-ming.

'Noble Count,' said Hua, 'first to military matters ...'

Hsiung listened as the spy told an interesting tale, aided by interjections from Chao, concerning Prince Arslan's continued absence. It seemed the ruler of Hou-ming Province, an area vast enough to form an entire kingdom, rarely strayed from court except to hunt, feasting day and night with his cousin the Emperor. Meanwhile, hundreds of thousands around the lake starved.

'What of Jebe Khoja?' asked Hsiung. 'Is he still Prince Arslan's right hand?'

Hua related how Jebe Khoja, despite lingering infirmities from his wounds, was kept busy suppressing bandits of every description. Yet as soon as one rebel was defeated another arose.

'He never tests his strength in Lingling County,' mused the Noble Count. 'I wonder why.'

It was a puzzle Liu Shui had already explained: Jebe Khoja knew the Yueh Fei rebels in Lingling were disinclined to extend their rule through conquest. If anything, Hsiung's strength ensured other rebel chiefs on this side of Six-Hundred-*li* Lake could not expand. There was another, less politic reason for Jebe Khoja's temporary blind eye: the fact he *possessed* eyes stemmed from Hsiung's merciful decision not to execute him at Fourth Hell Mouth, six years earlier. Chao and Hua, however, had another theory.

'He's afraid of you, Your Worship!' cried Chao.

'Frightened,' echoed his friend.

Hsiung tugged gently at his beard. 'Do you think so?'

'Of course, Your Highness.'

'There is no other reason,' protested Hua. 'People in Hou-ming talk of nothing else.'

'And *further* than Hou-ming,' added Chao, not to be outdone.

'Hmmm,' mused Hsiung, ordering wine for himself and his companions.

Once settled over their refreshments, he glanced imperiously out of the window at the ceaseless snow. Chao and Hua met each other's eye while he was not looking.

'What other news from Hou-ming?' he asked. 'Is the city as poor as ever?'

'Of course, sire!' said Chao.

'If only you were the ruler there,' declared Hua, sadly. 'The people will rejoice on the day you enter the Gate of Ten Thousand Victories clad in glory!'

This sentiment was a little too fine for his companion, who had drunk more than his share of the wine. Chao looked puzzled for a moment then added sagely: 'Ah, you'll need to wear your finest silks then, that is for sure!'

Hsiung might reasonably have detected flattery; certainly he frowned and turned the conversation to more relevant concerns.

'What of the dispute between the Daoists and Buddhists? Does it continue?'

Hua's tone mirrored the seriousness of his master when he answered: 'Ah, a pertinent question, if I may so!'

'Very persistent,' agreed Chao. 'Most persistent.'

Hsiung examined the taller of the spies in surprise.

'My partner means to say the dispute between Buddhist and Daoist is very persistent,' said Hua, smoothly. 'Furthermore, it is rumoured Prince Arslan has followed the fashion at Court and is besotted with the Buddhists from Tibet. It is said he wants to assign them the noblest monastery available in Hou-ming.'

'I see,' said Hsiung. 'But aren't all the monasteries occupied?'

'Not if you chuck out the monks and nuns,' said Chao, with a wink.

'If that's the case,' said Hsiung, ruffled, 'what of the new Abbess of Cloud Abode Monastery?'

'A holy lady?' asked Hua, curiously. 'Does she cast spells on your behalf?'

Hsiung did not answer; his face had taken on a brooding shadow.

'What of the Deng clan?' he asked. 'Poor old Deng Nan-shi? Does he go hungry? And what of his son, Teng? Do you know anything of *them*?'

Teng's name had a strange effect on Chao and Hua. For once they seemed uneasy.

'Teng?' mused Chao.

'Does the Noble Count have a connection with this Teng?' continued Hua, unctuously. 'Because, sire, I have heard he lives a very shocking life.'

'Very,' agreed Chao. 'Nothing but floating orioles and peony palaces!' He emphasised his point by jabbing a grubby finger in and out of a cupped hand. 'You shouldn't pay attention to anything *he* says about honest men.'

Meanwhile Hua was gesturing at his companion to shut up. To their surprise, Hsiung rose and paced before the window.

'Everything you say leads me to believe Hou-ming is ripe for plucking!' he cried. 'If only my army was large enough!'

The two spies watched coldly, calculating how the Noble Count's mood might affect them. All three were disturbed by a knock at the door, followed by the entry of an exceedingly rotund man. Chancellor Liu Shui had tracked down Hsiung and his secret visitors.

For a long moment he filled the doorway, looking from face to face with such innate dignity and authority they shifted uncomfortably in their seats.

'Noble Count,' he said, 'have these agents from Hou-ming provided useful news?'

There was irony in his tone: Hsiung suspected his wise chancellor already knew everything Chao and Hua had told him, and rather more.

'Very useful information,' he said, 'I am satisfied.'

'Good,' said Liu Shui, surveying the faces of the spies as a judge examines miscreants while deciding what sentence to impose. Though Chao became uncomfortable under this scrutiny, Hua stared back, smiling slightly so that his yellow front teeth showed.

'I'm glad you've come,' said Hsiung. 'I was just saying that Hou-ming is ripe for conquest! Apparently Jebe Khoja is frightened to death of me – and well he might be, since I've already trounced him once.'

'That's true,' agreed Chao.

Liu Shui's reply was to bury his hands in broad sleeves.

'I know you will not approve,' said Hsiung, addressing his Chancellor directly, 'but I have decided it is time to expand our armies, whatever the cost. We need warships, stores of gunpowder and naphtha, weapons of every kind!'

Chao and Hua nodded fervently.

'Once our army is large enough the justice of Yueh Fei will spread from district to district, county to county! The barbarians will run like hares, I'm sure of it.'

Still Liu Shui did not answer. His gaze flickered contemptuously over the empty flasks and wine bowls.

'Noble Count,' he said, 'this is a moment I have long feared and anticipated. Before you rush into this policy please consider the following. At present your position is secure precisely because you justify the Mandate of Heaven, in that you aid the people in times of hunger. Any attempt to challenge Prince Arslan is doomed. His army is too large and he is the Emperor's dear cousin. Even if you defeated Arslan's forces, more and more would be dispatched to Hou-ming Province. Your best attack against them is stealthy waiting. Every year their dynasty's grip on the Empire decays. I urge you, consolidate your reputation as a moderate and benevolent ruler. The rest of your ambitions will follow quite naturally.'

For long moments Hsiung did not reply. Tension grew in the room. Thick snowflakes swirled and danced outside. When Hsiung looked up, his expression was both determined and conciliatory.

'Old adviser, I believe that now is the time to build our army and fleet,' he said. 'For the sake of the tens, no, the hundreds of thousands who are starving because of the barbarians' misrule. That is my decision. But old friend,' he said, addressing Liu Shui in a pleading voice, 'do not desert me! I need your wisdom more than ever.'

Liu Shui nodded, his usually bland face gaunt with worry. 'As you wish. I will stand by you always. For all our sakes let us hope ambition has not blinded you.'

Chao and Hua were about to protest at such outrageous insolence when the frank integrity of the gaze between ruler and adviser silenced them. They sidled out of the room, leaving Hsiung and Liu Shui to debate the Yueh Fei rebels' next move on the great chequerboard of the Mongol Empire.

twenty

天命

Teng knew he had entered the theatre district from countless sodden posters glued over each other like faded fish scales. Every available wall was covered: the snow had been blowing horizontally for so many weeks that the posters' coloured inks had run and blurred.

He gathered his cloak and hat, pressing onwards until he reached a broad street lined with a dozen rival establishments. At each door touts harangued the drifting crowd: *No admittance for late-comers! Only the best acting here! Cho sings today! Better than the rest! Cho here!*

Teng ignored them and approached a large theatre hung with a hundred coloured banners. Though everyone else paid over a string of *cash*, Teng was waved through by the doormen to join the queue on a steep wooden ramp. He emerged halfway up tiers of seats occupied by young and old, male and female, people of all classes and professions seeking a temporary relief from Hou-ming, a time other than their own.

A stage protruded into more rows of chairs. At the side perched a dozen musicians on stools, as well as actresses and singing girls with sky blue skirts tight round their buttocks and black silk scarves accentuating the length of their foreheads. All fluttered butterfly fans, scanning the crowd for customers. Teng looked eagerly across vivid red mouths and faces painted white, his heart beating swiftly. But the one he sought was nowhere in evidence – that told him all he feared to know.

He sat down heavily on an end-of-aisle seat, jostling a flabby man protected by tin amulets sewn across his chest. Teng's clumsiness stemmed from cheap rice wine; he fell into a doze as the performance began, half-listening to the clash of cymbals and falsetto singing of the hero.

The theatre was illuminated by flickering lamps and thin winter light seeping from a dome above. The audience's breath steamed as Chen Song's *The Ancestors' Revenge In Han Palace* – a great favourite, even among Mongols who did not sense the play's hidden message – acted out murder and retribution, the brutal violation of a younger sister's chastity, then yet more retribution. Eventually every villain lay in a pile on the stage except the hero's hapless sister who had failed to commit honourable suicide and had to be helped along by her brother.

Many ladies dabbed their eyes as she recited a long, pathetic speech urging him to execute her as painlessly as possible. Meanwhile, the one lady Teng sought did not join the other actresses clustered round the stage. He left during the final applause, ignoring enquiries about when his own new play would be completed.

Teng found himself outside. The snow's purity and whiteness after the gloom of the theatre came as a relief. At twenty-seven he cut an eye-catching figure. Though still youthful he was no longer boyish, his sensitive dark eyes observing the world with a mournful, yet ironic intensity that could not fail to intrigue ladies of a certain taste.

An ache of loneliness almost sent him hurrying in search of the singing girl, Ying-ge, who he had hoped to find in the theatre. Was not her voice a lotus unfurled beside dancing autumn waters? And he might have obeyed the impulse and tasted the humiliation of being advised by her maid that she was 'entertaining a gentleman', had not a young lad in plain hemp clothes tugged his sleeve. Teng stepped back in surprise. The boy's expression was earnest.

'Honourable Teng,' said the boy, 'your father sent me. He commands you to return to Deng Mansions at once. He requires your assistance.'

Whatever a father requires, Teng had been taught to obey. Yet he hesitated, glancing up the side street where Ying-ge conducted her transactions. He was all too aware that, given his poverty and her need to live in an opulent style, she was obliged to fan her peony when a spring wind blew. He could hardly blame her.

It took nearly an hour to pick a way through snow-clogged streets to Deng Mansions. Its many roofs and pillars were crusted with wind-blown ice, none of which stopped Deng Nan-shi from opening his academy as usual. Thus one demonstrated a haughty attitude to adversity.

Teng hurried to the ancient audience chamber of the Dengs, long converted into a classroom. Over fifty – half the normal class – sat on the floor, listening as a slender young woman in blue and yellow taught a clapping song about Pan Gu. Teng's heart sank further. Not only must he contend with Father in a grim, duty-driven mood, but also Her Perfect Sereneness, Yun Shu – and he had no doubt she was feeling very serene indeed. She gave no sign of noticing his arrival. Teng used the opportunity to sneak off to the library.

As he feared, Deng Nan-shi lay on his divan, covered in blankets smelling of mould. Instead of issuing reproaches to his wayward son, the old scholar lay in a deep sleep. For a long moment Teng stared down at his father's gaunt, parchment-yellow face. Kneeling, he straightened the blankets then gently inserted a pillow beneath the scholar's balding head.

He remembered days when that hair had grown thick and long, when he and Hsiung would help Deng Nan-shi take his Tenth Day Bath, as prescribed by the Song Regulations for

Scholar Officials of All Grades. They would empty pitcher after pitcher of cold water over his head. Even then, drenched as an otter, his forehead a waterfall, Deng Nan-shi would maintain a dignified expression. After all, a scholar's bath was a rite and all rites must be conducted in the proper spirit . . .

Teng brushed the few remaining greasy locks from his Father's hot, perspiring forehead. A familiar enemy was advancing across the provinces of Father's body, a foe the doctor had declared beyond the reach of any medicine other than magic.

Brushing tears from his eyes, Teng strode to the classroom and bowed to the young nun wearing an Abbess's silver head-piece on her 'whirlwind clouds' hair. She seemed relieved by his arrival.

'Your Honoured Father?' she enquired, though a hundred little ears were straining to overhear.

'Asleep,' muttered Teng, wondering if the scent of wine lingered on his breath. Her own smelt clean, like willow.

'He sent for you yesterday as well, but no one could find you.'

That would have been hard, seeing Teng was exploring a manual entitled *A Hundred Ways To Make The Plum Tree Bloom* with Ying-ge, both of them fuelled by wine and delicacies costing the entire earnings from his last play – not that it had amounted to much. Only when those resources were nearly exhausted had he emerged to clear her from his mind with a final drinking bout.

'I was studying in the city,' he said.

The Abbess raised an eyebrow. 'Your field of study is well known,' she said, primly. 'To the great regret of many.'

'If one possesses a field, one should not neglect to plough,' he said.

'Unless that neglect is the way one avoids one's obligations.'

They became aware of the listening children.

'Well, Abbess Yun Shu,' he said, 'I am here now and shall

finish my father's work for the day like an obliging son.'

She bowed stiffly. 'I'm glad your duty extends so far.'

He was about to quip it extended farther than she could imagine but thought better of it.

'I shall tend to your father and send for food and medicine from Cloud Abode Monastery,' she said.

This offer was so great a relief to Teng, who lacked the *cash* for either, that tears touched his eyes. 'Then I thank you deeply,' he said, 'and sincerely, for it is a kindness I shall not forget.'

She was already on her way, shushing the unsettled children with a finger across her plump lips.

Perhaps that was why Teng gave his best to conducting a history lesson on the dreadful fate of Emperor Ming Huang and his betrayal by a beloved concubine, Yang Kuei-fei. Inspired by the theatre he had just left, Teng took on the various roles of those involved: the rebel An Lu-shan and besotted Emperor, finally the mincing, self-serving vanity of Yang Kuei-fei herself. Rows of guileless faces stared in wonder and alarm as he described the Emperor's agony when his own soldiers forced him to order the execution of his dear love. Though she had destroyed a once exemplary reign, still he could see no fault in her.

'The Emperor's tears fell like melting drops of ice,' declared Teng, finally. 'And let that be a lesson to all those who place pleasure before duty.'

The children chattered as they packed away their sand writing trays and Teng realised he had enjoyed the role of teacher more than he cared to admit. A slender figure watched from a doorway behind him.

'Ah, Lady Serenity,' he said, ruffled by her cool gaze. 'How is Father?'

'We ordered a doctor to visit and he diagnosed an excess of *yin* forming spores in the stomach. Also that it would be fatal if those spores spread. Food and medicine have been provided, as well as new blankets. I will address prayers to Chenghuang, the City God, reminding Him of the great services tended to Hou-ming over the centuries by the Deng Clan. But I fear the Honourable Deng Nan-shi is far from well.'

Teng nodded miserably. This was nothing new, making his absence from home all the more despicable.

'Yun Shu,' he said, after a pause. 'I will escort you back to Cloud Abode Monastery. There is no other way I can demonstrate my deep gratitude.'

At first they climbed the Hundred Stairs in silence. Teng sensed her mood was weighed down by other burdens than Deng Nan-shi's illness.

'It was good of you to take Father's class,' he said.

'I like the children.' Yun Shu wrapped her shawl tight against the cold. 'You forget that a Nun of Serene Perfection can never have children of her own.'

'No doubt there are compensations?'

'You refer to embroidered robes and influence. Oh yes, and the fact people beseech my blessing when I pass? True, there are compensations. Yet I have little choice in the matter.'

They climbed through frozen woods where bamboo cracked, laden with ice. Packed snow made each stone stair perilous.

'You have the choice to change your position,' he pointed out.

She paused, met his gaze. 'That is not a choice I choose to make!'

Her face softened and he saw that she understood his question was well intentioned. That he merely advised her as an older brother might.

'Teng, you know better than anyone how my family disowned me,' she said. 'How could I, a woman, maintain myself? How eat? Find shelter? Who would protect me?'

Her earnestness made Teng uncomfortable. He was used to females like Ying-ge, pouting and petting without any need for difficult questions. He laughed uncertainly. 'Are there no mirrors in Cloud Abode Monastery? You are hardly un-attractive. A husband could be found.'

Even as he spoke, Teng regretted so pointless and crass a remark. No respectable family wanted an outcast for a daughter-in-law. The only dowry she could offer was love: a treasure of small value to a marriage-broker.

Yun Shu did not reply. She carried on up the icy steps.

'To be a concubine is not dishonourable,' he mused, 'Lady Lu Si was my Grandfather's concubine and she . . .'

'Teng!' Again Yun Shu halted. 'Your concern is well meant but this subject is unwelcome.'

Her reversion to the role of Lady Serenity was deserved. He bowed, clasping one hand over the other and moving it up and down to indicate sincere respect. 'Forgive me if I am too frank, too quick to talk. Remember, I have never learned to sit cross-legged in silence for months and years at a time!'

Yun Shu could not help smiling. Their feet tramped regularly on the packed snow. Plumes of breath rose as they panted from the climb.

'You think like a man, that is all,' she said, 'with a man's freedom of choice. I am a woman. The fact that destiny appointed me Abbess of Cloud Abode Monastery was a miracle. My choices must always depend upon the choices of others.'

With a crack, her shoe slipped on an uneven clod of ice. Crying out, she fell backward, arms flailing. Teng was beside her. He grabbed her wrist as she toppled. Pulling her close, they wobbled together on the icy step for a precarious moment. The steep stairs yawned like a hungry throat behind them. Slowly, deliberately, he knelt, firmly lowering them both until they gained a steady purchase on the ice. Breaths steaming, they regained balance. She shot him a grateful look. Her cheeks were flushed.

'Thank you, Elder Brother,' she murmured.

'My pleasure, Little Sister!'

Laughing uncertainly, they struggled to their feet, brushing powdery snow off thick winter clothes. Then they realised Yun Shu's fall had a witness. Bo-Bai waited by the brassbound doors of Cloud Abode Monastery. Instantly laughter ceased. Yun Shu assumed an expression of stern piety appropriate to a senior Nun of Serene Perfection.

'Ah, Bo-Bai,' exclaimed Teng, upon reaching the top, 'how do the holy ladies treat you, my friend?'

A cold, formal bow was his reply. After a stiff and faultlessly decorous farewell on both sides, the gates closed behind Yun Shu with a clang.

天命

Deng Mansions contained as many rooms and courtyards as its grand name implied. All Teng's life the wooden buildings had been in a state of decline. Now some roofs were positively unsafe. He found his old companion, Shensi, peering up at a rafter creaking under a drift of snow.

In the era of the Deng clan's greatness, renting rooms to a dubious tomb-finder and antiques merchant would have been unthinkable. These days it seemed natural. An extra armed man in one's household added greatly to its security.

'You seem troubled,' said Teng, taking a seat in Shensi's cold, dusty apartment. It was cluttered with old pots and bronzes he had failed to sell.

'Just hungry,' grunted his friend.

'A common problem,' said Teng. 'I hear that in some remote districts there are arrangements between neighbours to swap unwanted children rather than allow the entire family to perish.'

Shensi wrapped a cloak made of dog furs round himself. It crossed Teng's mind he hadn't heard many dogs barking lately on Monkey Hat Hill.

He slapped his hands together and paced up and down to keep warm.

'I've come here for a reason, you know,' he said. 'If we do not get some *cash* soon we won't last the winter. Curse the snow! Will it ever stop? And I'm dreadfully worried, Shensi, not for myself but Honourable Deng Nan-shi. He urgently needs food and medicine. I can't even rely on picking up extra pupils: nearly all are in arrears with their fees, not that Father keeps proper accounts. A horrid mess!'

It was not Shensi's way to answer in haste, yet today he spoke at once.

'Bend your stiff scholar's pride and we could eat and drink soon enough!'

He referred to an old debate between them. A year earlier, to fulfil a drunken boast, Teng had taken up some ancient parchment from Deng Library and laboriously painted a landscape in the exact style of the Tang Dynasty master, Chang Tsao, even contriving to make the paint seem suitably faded. More astonishing had been his recreation of ancient seals denoting the artist and previous owners, gleaned from woodcut prints in the library. Once the family collection had included many original paintings of this kind – all traded over the years for food and clothes. Even Deng Nan-shi had praised Teng for his remarkable mimicry. But copying a greater talent was a bittersweet triumph. Teng longed for his own paintings to be regarded as masterpieces.

Shensi's proposal was to use his contacts among antique-loving connoisseurs and sell the forgery for a high price. Teng laughed nervously in reply. Oh, he was tempted! Horribly tempted! But such a venture threatened more than just criminal charges – and the punishment would be dreadful if their fraud was discovered – it betrayed all Father had taught him. Misusing higher knowledge and skills compromised the Deng clan's honour. Maybe even their natural right to rule Hou-ming Province on a just dynasty's behalf when the Imperial

Examinations were re-instated. It threatened the best part of his soul.

Teng considered Father lying on the divan in the library. Also his own hunger – and not just for food. Why should vulgar merchants parade their wealth? He could buy new silks, wine, precious hours of pleasure with Ying-ge and her delightful fragrances.

'Perhaps,' he said, remembering a phrase of Yun Shu's, 'I have no choice. Perhaps I must lower myself. But just this once. And never ask me again.'

Shensi chuckled coarsely. 'Leave the low stuff to me.'

Teng seemed not to hear.

'I might even turn vulgar merchant myself,' he announced. 'Do you remember the bamboo strips from the prince's tomb I spent so long translating?'

'You won't sell those,' predicted Shensi, 'except for firewood.'

'We'll see,' said Teng. 'From what I have heard . . . We'll see. And, of course, you would get half, for we found them together. But I fear those old bamboo books contain a great capacity for harm. I mean, in the wrong hands.'

'The only wrong hands are empty ones,' said Shensi.

Teng felt depressed all that day. He had surrendered to instincts of a deplorable kind. Meanwhile Shensi roamed the city in the best clothes they could gather, seeking the highest price for a recently discovered painting of the Lake by Master Chang Tsao. Finally he struck a deal with a new collector said to be acting as a broker to connoisseurs in the Court itself, a high official of unimpeachable standing in the Salt Bureau, called Gui.

天命

Clouds that covered much of the Middle Kingdom dispersed, leaving in their wake a pale, bright winter sky. The re-emergence of the sun warmed more than the earth: hearts lost to gloom remembered hope. Plans were moved forward.

Teng walked from Monkey Hat Hill to Golden Bright Temple, the largest Daoist temple in the province. He wore a fine new pair of boots and a quilted jacket of more than respectable cut, the fruit of Shensi's profitable transaction with Salt Minister Gui. Today, however, Teng had a very different customer in mind.

Golden Bright Temple, like most of Hou-ming, had known better days during the former dynasty; nevertheless it still attracted thousands of worshippers and idlers each month. A triple-storied gatehouse painted in many colours greeted followers of the Dao. Once beyond, they walked between two glazed pagodas into a huge square surrounded by cloisters and a temple complex six storeys high with fine, ornate roofs. One could survey the entire city and far vistas from the gilded balconies of Golden Bright Temple.

A large five-day fair had been established in the courtyard. Booths and canopies formed small streets where one could buy mats of fine bamboo and rushes, bows and swords (despite the restrictions on Chinese possessing weapons), dried fruits and meats, pet songbirds and hunting dogs, inks, brushes, honey preserves, artificial flowers and hats, ribbons, books, curios and pictures. There were fortune-tellers, conjurers, portrait artists and musicians vying to draw a crowd. In a time where so many went hungry, a few sales determined whether whole families ate that evening.

Now the sun had re-emerged, however feebly, people followed its example. Teng was forced to push to the temple through knots of bargain-seekers. On the steps he paused and frowned. Was that his mistress, Ying-ge, hurrying down one of the cloisters towards an entrance guarded by soldiers? But the girl had gone in a moment and he could not be sure. Inside the temple porch he hailed an acolyte, addressing him with his best Deng hauteur.

'I have an appointment with Worthy Master Jian,' he said.

The young priest looked at Teng doubtfully. Even in new clothes he did not appear the kind of notable who normally consorted with the leader of all the Daoists in Hou-ming Province. Especially as he was carrying a large, heavy sack rather than assigning the task to a lackey.

'Inform him Honourable Deng Teng is here,' added Teng.

Now the acolyte was more amenable and bowed slightly. The name of Deng still opened some hearts and doors in Hou-ming.

For an hour he waited in the temple porch. An hour of disquiet. It was not too late to return home with the sack of bamboo strips. He could bury them in Deng Library and risk no harm to anyone. If the ancient words were as potent as he believed, dare he unleash such knowledge on the world? That dilemma tormented him.

Years of slow, careful study had revealed the strips mapped a magical route to Immortality. One that had passed beyond the knowledge of humanity for fifteen centuries. Yet that route required no virtue from anyone pursuing its tortuous path. Instead one needed the morality of a rapacious ghost. Immortality could only be gained by sucking the life force, the very *ch'i*, from ripe, fertile victims, right down to the lining of their wombs. Its logic was remorseless. Teng feared it deeply.

There was another reason. Worthy Master Jian was distrusted by his father – and Teng had learned to heed Deng Nan-shi's judgements about people.

Of course, the old scholar might be blinded by history. The Deng and Jian clans had been bitter contenders for leadership in Hou-ming under the last dynasty. The Jians, at least, tacked with the wind and served Mongol masters. Did that make them villains? The mere act of living tainted one with compromises . . . Further speculation was cut short by the acolyte's return.

Teng was led up winding flights of stairs to the topmost storey of Golden Bright Temple. Here he found a large balcony with fine views of the lake and distant snow-clad mountains. A place where pure winds aided the contemplation of ineffable mysteries.

A small table had been set up in the centre of the balcony. Behind it, on a simple chair, sat a man in the gold, purple and black robes of a Daoist Worthy Master. It was the first time Teng had observed Master Jian close up.

He saw a handsome, sleek man, trim round waist and jaw, with well-balanced features and a habitually sensitive expression, as though he made it his business to feel deeply for all the Ten Thousand Creatures, whether they wanted it or not. He possessed a moist, yet strong mouth that could be relied upon to say what was judicious, wise and proper.

Worthy Master Jian's iron grey hair was neat as a statue's, yet his large angular eyebrows were black as the hair of youth, denoting exceptional character. In short, he was a man who immediately attracted goodwill, especially among women; a bringer of relief; a visionary; a speaker who could urge confidentially or roar like a ram; a holy gentleman of considerable property, ever distant yet near – or, at least, near enough to suit his benevolent purposes. All this Teng glimpsed in a flash.

'Ah, Honourable Deng Teng,' said Worthy Master Jian, leaning forward slightly to greet his guest then settling back again. 'Come before me! You are doubly welcome. First, for the sake of your honourable ancestors and father – I trust the excellent Deng Nan-shi is in good health, by the way, please do pass him my respects – and secondly because you sent the most intriguing letter I have received all winter. Come closer, tell me all about it.'

Teng did as instructed, placing the sack of bamboo strips on the floor. Though he was not customarily nervous with men of authority, his mouth tasted dry.

'I do have something unusual to bring to your attention, Master,' he said, 'a treatise, let us call it, that has taken me years to decipher.'

Impatience flickered across the Worthy Master's angular face. 'A treatise?'

'It expounds ancient wisdom and knowledge,' said Teng, hurriedly, 'I have come here to offer it to you.'

'Ah,' exclaimed Worthy Master Jian, 'an offer!'

He stared past Teng as if in profound contemplation of the distant mountains. The silence on the balcony gathered weight. Teng could hear a babble of excited voices from the market in the courtyard below, the sounds of a quarrel about prices, laughter, all the tawdry, vulgar noises of commerce. Suddenly he felt an overwhelming desire to disturb the Worthy Master's stillness.

'The treatise teaches one how to become an Immortal,' he blurted out. 'It instructs followers of the Dao how to acquire the Pearl of Immortality.'

Still the Worthy Jian meditated. He turned to Teng, as though dragged back reluctantly to temporal affairs.

'So your letter promised,' he said.

'Yes,' continued Teng, 'it sets out a clear, proven method.'

'Ah!' said Worthy Master Jian. 'You are now an Immortal, I take it?'

Teng blushed with confusion. 'No, I did not say that, sir, with respect . . .'

'You call it proven. How can it be *proven* without proof? Are you that proof?'

'As I say, Master. . .'

'Let me see this book,' interrupted the Worthy Jian.

Reluctantly Teng handed over one of the round bundles of bamboo strips tied with leather thongs. Worthy Master Jian cast him a resigned look and unrolled the book. Yet his gaze was intense as he read the characters.

'This,' he said, reading slowly, 'this is old. Where did you find it?'

For a long while he listened as Teng described the prince's tomb. When the scholar fell silent Worthy Master Jian tapped the volume with his forefinger.

'So, Honourable Deng Teng, you found these texts – all the natural property of the Dao – and wish to restore them to me. Your illustrious family was ever a friend of the Dao. I believe Cloud Abode Monastery, in particular, benefited greatly from your Grandfather's generosity. Very well, I accept. And more than that, offer my thanks.'

Worthy Master Jian sat back in his chair, smiling amiably. It took a moment for Teng to comprehend what had been said. 'Worthy Master, in my letter I mentioned the *sale* of this relic. I am hoping for a large reward in *cash*, so I might help my Honoured Father in his illness.'

Again there was a long silence. Only now Jian's handsome face wore a look of surprise, perhaps even sorrow. '*Cash?*'

'Yes,' repeated Teng, doggedly. 'Sir, you cannot conceive the dangers I suffered to win these holy texts and the hours spent setting them in order and translating obscure characters . . .'

'*Cash?*' broke in Worthy Master Jian, as though thinking aloud. 'A son of Deng Nan-shi asks me for *cash*. These are new times, I suppose, and all things decay and renew themselves, even once noble families.' His voice fell into a bemused whisper. 'Yet when a Deng tries to haggle like a petty merchant . . . Ha! Of course! Your father set you up for it! He once criticised the markets I hold each month before the temple and this joke is his revenge. How witty!'

'You do not understand,' said Teng, desperately. 'You see . . .'

'*Cash!*' repeated the Worthy Master. 'How amusing of your father! Please inform him I was suitably taken in. I grant him a complete victory.'

For a moment Teng felt inclined to argue further. Then his resolve collapsed. The Worthy Master's jibe about merchants filled him with deep shame. Unbearable for the Dengs to descend to the level of mere peddlers! Teng attempted a chuckle. 'My Honoured Father will be . . . amused.'

'And I accept his kind offering,' said Worthy Master Jian, reaching out for the rest of the bamboo scrolls. 'Though what use it may be I cannot guess. Yes, and the other books in your bags, I might as well unburden you of those as well. And I do believe you mentioned a translation?'

Soon afterwards, Teng found himself back in the market of grasping voices and eyes and flushed faces. His dignity as a Deng had suffered no compromise. Only now his sack was as flat as his purse. He felt nauseous and his forehead ached. He gazed up at the topmost balcony of Golden Bright Temple, catching a glimpse of priests clustered round a seated figure at a table. Teng had the peculiar feeling Worthy Master Jian was already evaluating the books of bamboo strips – and with more than casual interest.

twenty-one

天命

Eunuch Bo-Bai hurried towards the Temple of Celestial Teachers, his bamboo staff scraping the cracked, moss-stained flagstones of the courtyard. He paused at a steep flight of limestone steps to catch his breath, glancing back the way he had come. The bronze-bound gates of Cloud Abode Monastery remained firmly closed.

He could hear the low, monotonous drone of chanting within the temple and caught scraps of words: *The Dao that is bright seems dull . . . The great square has no corners . . . The Dao conceals itself in namelessness . . .*

They had only reached the forty-first sutra! Yet he dared not wait until the chant had fully unfurled like a gauze banner floating around the incense-filled temple. The steady beat of gongs and handbells signalled preparations for the next sutra. Bo-Bai slid apart the painted doors and bowed his way into the Temple of Celestial Teachers.

Within lay a complex pattern of brightness and shadow. Dozens of tall candles on bronze holders flickered around a life-size clay statue of a pot-bellied, grinning god in the lotus position. The worshippers stood in precise geometric positions before this ancient image of Chenghuang, the City God. All were female and dressed in gaudy robes denoting their status as Nuns of Serene Perfection. The lesser nuns wore yellow outfits that had once been golden; their superiors wore purple and blue silks, similarly faded and frayed at sleeve and hem.

Bo-Bai sidled over to a young woman in purple at the apex of the geometric pattern of worshippers before the altar. As he whispered in her ear she did not change her expression other than to blink rapidly.

At once Yun Shu retreated backward, bowing herself out of the Temple, all the while reciting a charm to avert misfortune for abandoning a rite. Another of the nuns, older and more care-worn, gave her departing superior a curious glance then occupied the vacant space at the head of the pattern. The forty-second sutra began: *The Dao breeds one; one breeds two; two breeds three; three breeds the ten thousand creatures . . .*

Yun Shu joined Bo-Bai on the limestone steps. The old man struggled to lower himself to his knees in apology for interrupting her, until she laid a gentle hand on his arm. There was something incongruous, even unnatural, about a venerable man deferring to a woman whose smooth complexion implied little worthy knowledge of this world – or the next.

'What is it, Bo-Bai?' she asked, in a distracted voice.

Her eyes widened. She sniffed the air, peering at the twilit sky. Distant plumes were billowing up from the city to the south of Cloud Abode Monastery.

'What is burning?' she asked.

'Lady Yun Shu,' said Bo-Bai, 'people have built bonfires all over the city to celebrate a great event. The Buddhist Holy Men from Tibet have brought a relic to Hou-ming.'

She fidgeted with her sleeve, plucking at a loose strand of silk. 'You interrupted the rite for *that*?'

'No, no,' he said, impatiently, 'the Buddhists claim the relic has spoken to them. It requires a suitable place to be venerated now it resides in Hou-ming. They say it wishes to live beside Chenghuang himself. *Here*,' he added, forcefully.

'I do not understand. What is this chattering relic?'

'The Buddha's knucklebone.'

Yun Shu laughed at his earnestness. 'Nonsense, Bo-Bai! Cloud Abode Monastery will always be Daoist.'

'People in the city are enthused by the relic. See how many fires burn!'

'Then I shall urge Chenghuang to teach the people better sense,' she said. 'We may be sure He will listen.'

Bo-Bai looked less certain. The Mongols were adept at playing off Daoist against Buddhist as a means of diverting opposition to their rule. With this in mind, sects of Tibetan Buddhists had been encouraged to seek followers in the Middle Kingdom. Sects that owed their prosperity and safety to the Great Khan.

Taking off a headscarf woven with divine symbols to reveal glossy, black hair, Yun Shu hurried back to the Temple. She felt uncomfortable when Lady Lu Si led the rite in her absence, fearful the nuns would draw unfavourable comparisons with her own conduct.

'See what else you can learn, Bo-Bai,' she called over her shoulder. 'When the sutras are completed I shall inform the *sanren* of your news.'

天命

The Temple of Celestial Teachers was the heart of Cloud Abode Monastery – and, in a spiritual sense, of Hou-ming itself. For hundreds of years the statue of the City God, Chenghuang Shen, had resided there, flattered and pampered by generations of Nuns.

The Temple consisted of a large rectangular hall with painted pillars on all sides depicting the constellations. Between the pillars were statues, paintings, shrines to demon-officials and numerous useful deities. Wooden doors could be slid open so worshippers in the Temple Courtyard might glimpse the rituals within, but the Temple was usually dark and shadowy, dense with *yin*.

Yun Shu hesitated before choosing it as a meeting place: recently the senior nuns' conferences had been marred by unseemly rancour. Today would surely be different. Not only was a threat to the monastery's existence certain to unite the *sanren*, Chenghuang's presence would moderate hot tongues.

Her appointment as Abbess had occurred six years earlier, following the miracle on Holy Mount Chang. The tale of her victory over the wicked spirit-dragon preceded her return to Hou-ming and, on landing at the harbour, she found herself surrounded by chanting priests and a sizable crowd. Even Worthy Master Jian had noticed her existence, summoning her to Golden Bright Temple and indicating she should tell the story of her victory to the Provincial Daoist Council. She had been carried in triumph through streets lined with curious faces, back to Cloud Abode Monastery and joyous congratulations from Abbess Lu Si and the other senior nuns.

Looking back, it was the last time they greeted her so warmly. Yun Shu sometimes wondered if they would ever view her with fondness again. None of it was her fault. Blame fate, the inscrutable workings of the Dao.

Abbess Lu Si had proudly accompanied her young protégé to the Provincial Daoist Council – and she had every reason for pride. Yun Shu's triumph would not only bring fresh worshippers but reflected well on the wise Abbess who had taken up Yun Shu when she was a divorced pauper, rejected by husband and family, a starving outcast whose potential only Lady Lu Si had recognised. Now that faith had been repaid gloriously.

The members of the Council, all men in middle or old age, had found Yun Shu interesting. Worthy Master Jian asked many gentle questions, expressing concern that the wicked dragon would cast a spiteful, vengeful curse on her. He promised to respond with potent spells on her behalf, pinning a silver and jade amulet to her chest that guaranteed protection. Yun Shu's blushes deepened to a crimson of

mortification when Worthy Master Jian made his next pro-
nouncement in a voice both firm and touched by regret.

'As for you, Lady Lu Si,' he said. 'I also have a gift. The
entire Council is agreed upon it. You are henceforth to be
relieved of a great burden.'

Yun Shu and Abbess Lu Si had exchanged confused glances.

'In short,' said the Worthy Master, 'you are freed of your
onerous responsibilities as Abbess of Cloud Abode Monastery.
Given the great favour shown by the Dao to Lady Yun Shu, she
is to be the new Abbess.'

For a terrible moment Lady Lu Si had tottered, on the edge
of fainting. Aghast, Yun Shu remembered Teng telling her how
the Mongols abused her abominably when Hou-ming fell.
Now, it seemed, she must endure another violation. One that
threatened all the success she had wrung from a troubled life.
Instead of fainting, the older woman cast Yun Shu a sad glance.

'I see you prefer someone more amenable to your policies,'
she said, with quiet dignity. 'Someone less loyal to the ancient
ways of the Serene Ones. Someone you can mould and shape.
If it is the will of the Dao, so be it.' She had bowed perfunctorily to the Council and left the room.

'Inestimable lady!' declared Worthy Master Jian, smiling at
the door.

Perhaps Yun Shu should have declined so vast an elevation,
except it is hard to deny what one secretly desires.

Since then Lady Lu Si would only speak to Yun Shu on
matters of ritual or practical affairs. Though the younger
woman tried hard to involve her predecessor in important
decisions, these efforts had been met – always quietly, never
angrily – with an insistence such burdens lay with Abbess Yun
Shu now. She, Lady Lu Si, was no longer worthy.

'Well, Honoured *Sanren*,' began Yun Shu, 'I thank you for your
presence.'

Five other senior nuns were present: Lady Lu Si, doddery old

Earth Peace, nervous, fidgeting Gold Immortal and Jade Perfected with her benevolent gaze. The fifth, Three Simplicities, younger than the rest by many grey hairs, smiled sweetly: 'What can we do but obey?' she asked.

Half an hour later it seemed obedience was the last thing on anyone's mind.

'They want to take away our Chenghuang?' asked old Earth Peace, utterly baffled. 'Where else would he go?'

'It is preposterous!' moaned Gold Immortal. 'Oh, we must pray every hour of every day. I will enter a spirit trance at once.'

'What is the Daoist Council doing on our behalf?' asked Jade Perfected. 'I have no doubt they are as concerned as ourselves.'

'Hah!' remarked Three Simplicities. 'As long as Worthy Master Jian is snug in Golden Bright Temple he won't remember *us*.'

Finally Lady Lu Si spoke. 'My question is similar to Jade Perfected's,' she said. 'How does our Abbess propose to avert this disaster?'

All eyes turned to Yun Shu. She picked at the loose threads of her sleeve, her heart pounding. 'I don't know,' she said. 'Not yet.'

At once Three Simplicities was upon her. 'You are our Mother.' Her tone was wheedling. 'We beg you to show us the way.'

Silent attention from five watchful faces.

'I must meditate and pray,' said Yun Shu.

'As must we all!' insisted Gold Immortal. 'Every hour of every day!'

'My fear,' said Lady Lu Si, quietly, 'is that faulty practise of the rites has led to this. Perhaps Chenghuang himself is angry with us. Such a thing has never happened in all the years the Nuns of Serene Perfection have tended his needs. Let us look to our own impurity.'

At this reproach Yun Shu glanced at the grinning, staring

face of Chenghuang. Could Lady Lu Si be right? Had she brought disaster upon the monastery through laxity and poor judgement? The old, secret fear sent by demons to taunt her dreams, the old icy doubts, returned with new force: that she had not truly defeated the spirit-dragon on Mount Chang. That she was not really favoured by the Dao at all.

'I will meditate,' she said, rising. 'Meditate and discover the truth.'

With that Yun Shu hurried from the Temple of Celesitial Teachers, conscious of the *sanrens*' eyes on her back – and of Chenghuang's stare, ready to punish her failures in this incarnation or the next.

天命

Despite numerous prayers, spirit-writing sessions, meditations and an attempted spirit voyage to consult the Weaver Maid in the Seven Primes, Yun Shu was no nearer a state of cosmic unfolding. Let alone a course of action. When the question remains obscure, how may one recognise the answer?

She decided to seek revelation closer to home – but not too close. Cloud Abode Monastery had become a place of droning, mournful chants ever since news of the Buddha's knucklebone spread through the city. Every nun except Lady Lu Si and the venerable Earth Peace – who was too lost in years to retain what was going on from one hour to the next – moved round the monastery in a state of tension, muttering in groups that went quiet when the Abbess approached. Loyal supporters of the Dao came to visit the City God and offer assistance. Unfortunately Yun Shu had no idea what to do if Prince Arslan upheld the Tibetan Buddhists' outrageous claims.

One foggy morning she donned simple robes and sturdy boots, leaving through the back entrance of the monastery, mindful of watchful eyes. Eunuch Bo-Bai, in particular, seemed to be observing her movements from dawn until dusk. Really, she would suffocate without a little fresh air – and Three Simplicities was welcome to complain about it as much as she liked.

The gate opened directly onto the woods and bamboo groves crowning Monkey Hat Hill. The trees were hung with beads of moisture and she could hear the music of busy little streams. Yun Shu took a winding path through the woods, aware the way was familiar. After a while her pace slowed, weighed down by the insinuating tongue of Three Simplicities.

'Abbess Yun Shu,' the nun had said, 'my niece has told me news that may save the Monastery.' Such an introduction provoked eager attention. The 'news' concerned Salt Minister Gui, who had amassed a large fortune and was using the money to establish his two sons in Dadu, the Great Khan's capital. This information shook Yun Shu profoundly. She had not seen her brothers since they were children. Now they consorted and rode with barbarian princes!

'So you see,' Three Simplicities concluded, 'perhaps your father will use his influence to help us.' She had coughed. How delicate her coughs could be, like a spider's nipping mandibles! 'For his dear daughter's sake.'

Yun Shu bit back a hasty retort, replying with dignity, 'Three Simplicities has forgotten what everyone knows. I am sadly estranged from my father.'

As Yun Shu followed the path through the woods she realised why the way was familiar. It led to the ruined watchtower on the cliff, discovered by Teng all those years ago. Memories quickened her step until she came to the rectangle of broken walls overgrown with dense thickets. It was smaller than childhood had perceived it, the brambles tamer, more ordinary; yet recalling the pain of Father's rejection made Yun Shu pull her headscarf tight.

She stood for a long moment, lost to anger and distress; then she noticed a young man with his back to her, seated on a pile of fallen stones, staring out at the lake. Yun Shu took a step back, snapping a twig. Startled, he reached for a sword at his belt. His hand fell and he bowed.

'I wondered whether you ever came here,' he said, nodding at the watchtower. 'I felt sure you would.'

Yun Shu shivered in the dank air. 'You are mistaken, Teng,' she said, 'chance not choice led me here. It is not a place I would seek out.'

'I thought you Daoists were blown around by destiny like seeds in the breeze,' he said, with a slight smile.

'Which sensible person is not?' she countered. 'But I believe, on this occasion, destiny did not direct me here. Neither did a wish for witty conversation.'

'Most likely you are right. Still, I believe three destinies did begin at this watchtower when we were children. Yours, mine and Hsiung's. Why shouldn't those destinies be happy?'

She examined his pensive face. Her eyes itched with tears she could not explain. 'Why not,' she said, quietly, 'why not.'

For a long moment both examined the ruined watchtower.

'I have never seen you with a sword before,' she said. 'Isn't that illegal for scholars?'

'Most things are. But even a scholar may wish to defend himself. Let us just say, it is prudent for me right now.'

'How oddly you talk!'

'No more oddly than you nuns.' He laughed dryly. 'And perhaps less obscurely than the revelations of the Mysterious Dao.'

She came a little closer to his seat. From the pile of stones one could look out across the lake, though not far today. Thick mists swirled over the placid waters. A dangerous perch. The cliff edge was a mere stumble away and falling on the limestone boulders below guaranteed a broken spine. She peered at the rolling wall of fog and pulled back.

'How is your father?' she asked.

'Better. Thanks largely to you.'

She hesitated. The cold air had brought colour to his cheeks and the whites of his eyes were bright. She recalled how he had caught her when she slipped on the Hundred Stairs, both of them tangled in a precarious embrace. Colour warmed her own cheeks at the memory. He had felt solid and strong then. Yun Shu realised she should not be alone with him here. It was improper.

'I shall leave you to your meditations,' she said.

Again he laughed, and she sensed nervousness. 'I never meditate, you know,' he said, 'I am too beguiled by the passing moment.'

'Then I shall leave you to your passing moment.'

Instead of resuming his seat he came over to join her. 'There are worse vagabonds than me loose on Monkey Hat Hill these days. Let me accompany you at a decorous distance to ensure your safety.'

So Yun Shu gained an escort. Though he stayed six feet behind, she felt conscious of his gaze on her back and allowed him to draw level.

'Your clothes are far more creditable than when we last met,' she said. 'You look every inch a prosperous Deng!'

'Appearances can lie,' he said. 'Even masterpieces by great painters can become lies.'

'Oh, you're all paradoxes today! Where, to put it plainly, has your *cash* come from? Or is that a vulgar question to ask an illustrious Deng.'

'The answer is vulgar, not the question. It has come from selling paintings like a petty merchant. I'm not proud of it, but it keeps Father fed and medicined.' He frowned. 'There was one sale – or attempted sale, for I didn't get a single *cash* coin – that worries me. It concerns one of your holy colleagues.'

'Indeed?'

'Do you,' he asked, cautiously, 'have dealings with Worthy Master Jian?'

'Of course,' replied Yun Shu, 'he is our Provincial Master. In fact he has asked me to help officiate at the Ceremony of

Fortunate Weather in a few weeks' time. A great honour.'

She was surprised by Teng's frown.

'Has he ever asked it of an Abbess before?'

'No.'

'Just you, eh?'

'We believe he wishes to warn the Buddhists how dearly Cloud Abode Monastery is regarded by officials of the Dao.'

They walked in silence for a while.

'Do not trust him,' he said.

'Who?'

'Worthy Master Jian.'

'Why ever not?' she asked. 'Why should I not trust a gentleman of proven kindness? A man who is respected by all?'

'Because . . . Call it a foolish suspicion, if you like, perhaps even bitterness that he cheated me. Yet I fear he is without scruples . . . Oh, never mind. Enjoy your great honour at the Ceremony.'

She wondered if he was mocking her in a way so subtle it sounded like sincerity. Unless, of course, he was drunk. Either explanation would have suited her opinion of his character. Yet whenever Yun Shu met Teng she invariably detected more than her prejudices. If nothing else, he made her smile.

She would have liked to ask his advice concerning the Tibetan Buddhists, for the Dengs were notoriously astute on political questions, but his behaviour was off-putting.

'Tell me,' she said, to change the subject. 'Are your plays still being performed in the city's theatres?'

'Where else! Actually, I'm writing a new one. Perhaps . . .' He cast her a searching glance. 'No, I'm sure you would rather not.'

'Rather not?'

'See my play when it is first performed. If you did, you could accompany Father and me as our honoured guest. Father would need to travel by palanquin, of course. I believe you would find the *subject* of my little drama highly diverting.'

Yun Shu pondered the propriety of this. Nuns and priest often attended festivals and theatres. The difficulty might be associating herself too publicly with a disgraced scholar like Deng Nan-shi.

'I shall consider it,' she said.

Near the back entrance of Cloud Abode Monastery a loud crack disturbed them. It came from the woods. No one appeared.

'A monkey,' said Teng, uneasily, who had again reached for his sword.

Yun Shu was less certain. She sensed spying eyes. Being seen with a handsome young man who bore a rake's reputation would feed gossip in the monastery. Yet she bowed and received his own bows of farewell, saying in a loud, clear voice, 'Thank you for acting as my chaperone, Honourable Deng Teng. Please assure your excellent father of our prayers for his health. I shall consider attending your play. Be at peace with the Dao!'

'Oh, I will,' he said, wryly. Seeing the concern in her face, he added, 'At least, I'll try very hard.'

天命

Not far from the entrance to Hou-ming harbour, like a ship of stone floating in the lake, rose the oval shape of Eye Rock. The island was lined on one side by low cliffs facing the city; on the other by a small shingle beach. A humble island, no bigger than a sizable garden, topped by shrubs and an ancient shrine.

For most of the year no one visited Eye Rock other than fishermen seeking birds' eggs or sacrificing at the shrine. Its weatherworn altar was dedicated to the protector of all waterfarers, Goddess Tien-Hou. Yet on one evening towards the end of winter, when sudden storms were common, the fishermen of Hou-ming and lake villages for a hundred *li* around held a raucous festival to invoke Tien-Hou's protection. Everyone in

Hou-ming took part, whether their livelihood depended on water or not, principally to dispel the winter gloom.

That year the Ceremony of Fortunate Weather was worthy of its name: a pure blue-black sky filled the twilit horizon, staging intricate wisps of cloud and patterns of stars. People looking down from the cliffs of Monkey Hat Hill saw hundreds of boats crammed with revellers, each a blaze of lanterns, so the dark lake glittered in mimicry of the night sky. Heaven's constellations are ordained and predictable in their movements, but the boats jostled with no discernible order, driven by raucous drumbeats and clashing cymbals to scare water demons.

Yun Shu observed this scene as she descended a narrow flight of steps cut into the cliff where Cloud Abode Monastery perched. Bo-Bai went before her with a bright lantern for the path was dangerous.

'Can you not go more quickly, Bo-Bai? See! The Worthy Master's barge is waiting at the jetty.'

Bo-Bai grunted irritably. 'My Lady can jump down to him if she wants.'

Yun Shu was attired like an Imperial Princess on her wedding day – the finest gold and purple silks and coral-crusted silver hairpieces, all loaned by Worthy Master Jian from the treasure room of Golden Bright Temple. Although, like any diligent Nun of Serene Perfection, Yun Shu avoided cosmetics, tonight she wore the white rice powder and pink rouge of a noble bride. In the highest possible sense that was her role in tonight's ceremony: and her spirit-groom was the Worthy Master himself.

At the foot of the steps was a short, stone jetty. Yun Shu hurried to reach the splendid barge covered with ornate carvings of dragons, phoenixes and holy toads. Its painted hull shone dully beneath moon and starlight.

She found the Worthy Master in the stern of the barge, his

robes as costly and splendid as her own. His forehead wore a crease of annoyance.

'You are late,' he began, as she took a seat beside him. He seemed to recollect something and laughed in a tinkling way. 'Never mind! I'm sure the Goddess will forgive you! As will Chenghuang. Let us hope so, at least.'

Yun Shu, who had been troubled by nerves for days preceding the Ceremony, felt more inadequate than ever.

At a gesture from the Worthy Master the barge shoved off, twenty oarsmen bending and straightening, while Bo-Bai watched from the jetty. Soon the cliffs of Monkey Hat Hill and silhouettes of Cloud Abode Monastery fell away. Yun Shu's heart fluttered with pride as the barge approached Eye Rock, dozens of smaller craft hastily moving aside to let them pass. In the midst of the crashing cymbals and drums she felt an urge to cover her ears and laugh with delight at the people's enthusiasm. But the Worthy Master's haughty, detached expression set the tone. Dense crowds had gathered on the shore, holding hands and swaying as they chanted Tien-Hou's titles, led by the usual spirit-mediums in loincloths and short cloaks.

In a moment, it seemed, she was following the Worthy Master down a gangplank onto the shingle beach of Eye Rock. Countless lanterns had been scattered and hung over the island; many hundreds more surrounded it. In a daze she was led to the foot of a rough staircase cut into the rock. Now, away from the attendant priests, he turned to her: 'I have chosen you out of all the priests and nuns and holy ones at my disposal,' he murmured.

She lowered her head. 'I am honoured, Master.'

'Good,' he said, in the same low tone, 'that was my intention. Also, so the entire city – and especially the Buddhists from Tibet – witness the importance we Daoists attach to Cloud Abode Monastery.'

'Thank you, Master,' she said, risking a glance at his delicate, narrow face. Never had he seemed more powerful, replete with dignity and wisdom.

'Come with me, Yun Shu,' he murmured. 'Do not fear what the Dao has in store for you.'

And truly all her fears vanished as she climbed the rough steps behind him, noting the tight sway of his hips as he ascended. At the top they found the shrine decked with dried flowers, food, wine, bronze bowls of smouldering incense. Facing one another over the ancient sacrificial altar, they chanted and bowed, repeating sutras to please the Goddess, matching each other like noise and echo. While they prayed, a ritual boat loaded with offerings was set alight on the shore.

When the sutras were spoken they watched the burning boat. Smoke billowed, flames roared and danced, sparks and ash drifted upward and across the lapping waters.

'Yun Shu,' said Worthy Master Jian, 'I have recently gained a marvellous, secret knowledge that offers me the means to join the Heavenly Host on Penglai itself. The blessed means to unite myself with the Dao.'

His voice rose in volume and intensity.

'A wonderful revelation has been offered to me by the ancient sages! That I might attain the diamond body of pure *yang* and take my rightful place among the Immortals!'

She shrank back. Never had she imagined such passion in the suave priest, usually so detached and restrained.

'Yun Shu,' he whispered, 'I need the assistance of a *yin*-source rich in *ch'i* energy. For the sake of Cloud Abode Monastery, I urge you to join my Great Work! I swear that as long as you are my helper I shall protect all you hold dear. Think how many will be converted to the Dao when I ascend on a cloud to Immortality!'

Her head span at these predictions. Had he gone mad? But he was the same good, handsome, earnest man as ever.

'How?' she whispered. 'Tell me how I can help.'

In a voice low and urgent, he explained how ancient books

had revealed secret rites. That they might be partners in a Great Work. When he explained what he required she blushed deeply.

'There is nothing improper in it, nothing at all,' he concluded. 'Will you do exactly as I ask? Become my spiritual spouse? I dearly hope you will.'

She found it hard to look at his face. For all his certainty, the rites sounded shockingly improper! Her heart beat quickly and tempting sensations stole through her body. She could not dispel a doubt struggling to find plain, intelligible words. Then Yun Shu dismissed it, imagining only her triumph in saving Cloud Abode Monastery, the honour and respect she would earn. Even Lady Lu Si and spiteful Three Simplicities would acknowledge she was worthy to be Abbess!

'Yes,' she murmured. 'Yes, Master Jian, I will.'

twenty-two

天命

Perhaps the Ceremony of Fortunate Weather pleased the goddess, for the months leading up to New Year were unusually free of storms. Hsiung had every reason to thank Tien-Hou: New Year's Eve found him at the prow of a two-masted merchant junk converted into a warship, the largest vessel in a small fleet of thirty craft crammed with Yueh Fei rebels.

Many commanders leading such a flotilla would have paced with worry, mindful of how few men could be deployed for an action promising either triumph or utter defeat. But Hsiung's heart sang like the wind in the stiff bamboo sails. Their progress was so steady that the square prow of the junk dipped and rose, casting up spray. New Year stars glittered, enticing him towards a future courage might construct – if he was bold and fortunate. His limbs itched for the release of battle, to prove himself so the grandees of Hou-ming Province took note, just as tigers in the forest assess a young challenger's roar.

He was joined at the prow by an old comrade, Captain P'ao, once a mere sergeant-at-arms and now perfectly willing to assume the title of general if destiny – or Hsiung – saw fit. The grizzled soldier cast a thoughtful glance at the deck covered with lolling men.

'Noble Count, I suppose it is too late to suggest we

283

send scouts before landing the whole force?' he said, quietly.

Hsiung frowned into the darkness ahead.

'That would involve changing my plan. Besides, there will not be enough time.'

Captain P'ao tugged his luxuriantly fierce whiskers. 'Still, it might be sensible,' he said, even more quietly than before.

'You trouble me unnecessarily,' said Hsiung.

'Perhaps, Noble Count, perhaps. But you will recollect from our days together in Hou-ming that I never staked all my *cash* on one throw when gambling.'

Hsiung chuckled. 'Think of the prize, P'ao!'

Certainly it was huge. Spies reported that a convoy of a hundred freighters and warships had moored at the port of Chenglingji to celebrate the New Year Festival. All the merchant junks were laden with blocks of pure salt from the Salt Pans a hundred *li* to the south – a treasure of immense value in a province still gnawed by famine. Four-tenths of the Great Khan's revenues flowed from salt taxes. Losing several months' production from a source like Hou-ming Province would be a blow to the profligate Mongol Court in far off Dadu, as well as a barterable resource for the Yueh Fei rebels.

Just as crucially for Hsiung's ambitions, he could capture a sizable fleet for conversion into his navy. No one truly ruled Hou-ming Province without controlling Six-Hundred-*li* Lake and that required many ships. Finally, by seizing Chenglingji – miserable hole as it was reputed to be – Hsiung could demonstrate that his power extended West and East, to the great benefit of his standing.

Even cautious Liu Shui had encouraged the raid, saying the soldiers and sailors of the Salt Fleet would be too drunk to resist. When the old chancellor learned the names of the two spies upon whom the whole venture depended his enthusiasm waned. So much so, he insisted on accompanying the expedition and was presently snoring in a cabin padded and draped with silks, a copy of Sun-tzu's *Art of War* laid across his chest.

'Ah, the prize,' murmured Captain P'ao. Then he brightened. 'Why shouldn't it be ours?'

This was the style Hsiung preferred.

'Unless,' said P'ao, 'your spies prove unreliable.'

'Chao and Hua won't let me down,' said Hsiung. 'You'll all learn to trust my judgement. Even Liu Shui!'

P'ao bowed, his grin revealing more gaps than teeth. 'As you say. But the Chancellor's counselled you well for six long years.' P'ao puffed out his broad chest. 'And some of us have been saving you from yourself for three times six!'

天命

Soon the lights of Chenglingji appeared on the eastern horizon and Hsiung grunted with pleasure. All was progressing in line with a plan that relied upon exactly timed arrivals and departures. The lanterns had been extinguished on the Yueh Fei vessels, despite the risk of ships colliding – for the next hour they must trust in starlight glowing on wave and foam to guide them.

'Captain P'ao!' he called. 'Signal to the other ships. Form the line!'

A single, blue lantern flashed in the darkness and any drunken New Year reveller gazing at the lake from Chenglingji might have wondered if a water dragon was winking. Gradually the Yueh Fei fleet closed up and turned north, drawing nearer to the shore. Hsiung stared into the darkness for a signal. Time passed agonisingly. Had they missed the landing point? Turning the fleet round would take an hour in the darkness, assuming they did not run aground. He peered to the east. Could that be a glimmer of dawn?

'Look!' cried P'ao beside him. 'Over there! Three fires alongside each other!'

'Helmsman,' called Hsiung, 'light the rear lantern and make no mistakes as you approach the shore.'

There was a loud creak as the sailors scurried to adjust the rigid sails of the long junk, then a rattle as oars were run out.

'Quickly!' ordered Hsiung. 'Why are they so slow?'

'Best let the sailors manage it,' murmured P'ao and Hsiung fell silent.

Soon the fleet had clustered round a shore of fetid mud and shingle. Lightly armoured men waded ashore while Guards in heavy lamellar armour were ferried from the larger junks in dozens of small boats. A breeze carried the bitter tang of reeds and the sweetness of decaying vegetation.

Hsiung stood beside the three fires as their flames cracked and waved with the wind. Chao and Hua knelt in the mud before him, foreheads pressed to the earth.

'Look around you!' he roared. 'Do you think we came here to wet our boots then go home again?'

Hua lifted his head. 'Noble Count, we cannot be blamed! When we sent messages to say the guards had been bought, we referred to *different* guards. All have been transferred unexpectedly!'

Hsiung tried to make sense of this. His entire plan rested on a gate through the city walls being left open by guards bribed at considerable expense. 'How can we gain entry to the town?' he demanded.

Now Chao looked up. 'The walls are lower than you might expect, Noble Count,' he said, 'and the ditches are in disrepair. You see, the family who rule Chenglingji – the Zhongs – steal all the public funds for their own use. Perhaps you can storm the walls?'

Hua scowled at his partner and interjected, 'Nevertheless these Zhongs are a most trustworthy clan, sire! If they divert funds it is because they hate the Mongols and long for a just ruler like yourself.'

Hsiung turned to examine the fleet. He could not care less about the Zhongs. Dawn was only three hours away by his calculation; one of those precious hours would be wasted in finishing the disembarkation, another in marching the men to Chenglingji. Storming the walls would squander any chance of surprise. But if the ramparts were as low as Chao seemed to think, perhaps his original plan might still work . . .

'Draw me a map of the ramparts,' he ordered.

After Chao and Hua had scratched it in the mud with a stick, Hsiung paced up and down. He could almost hear the dark lights whispering in his soul. How those swirling voices longed to rule him! One sweep of his sword would behead the wretched Chao and Hua and let the dark lights free.

Hsiung glanced guiltily at the ship where Liu Shui waited in his cabin. Instead of beheading the luckless spies he reached down, grabbing their shoulders.

'Up!' he said. 'Prove yourselves to me now and I'll forgive your failure.'

He hauled them to their feet.

'Captain P'ao,' he said, 'as soon as the column is ready, take the road to Chenglingji. You'll either find the gate open or the corpses of our friends here blocking your way.'

Hsiung took P'ao aside to whisper more confidential instructions. When he had finished the old soldier bowed low. 'I'll be following you soon enough, Noble Count,' he said. 'We're nearly disembarked.'

'The gate will be open,' promised Hsiung.

It only took moments for him to gather his 'bravest and best' and join the road toward the winking lights of the town, a road travelled ten years earlier by Yun Shu fleeing in the opposite direction.

Near the ramparts Hsiung waved his men to take cover. They examined the town from a flooded ditch choked with dead reed stems. He felt a small fish or rat brush his leg but did not shift his gaze from the gatehouse – a low and feeble defence by Hou-ming's standards yet formidable if one's army consisted of twenty men armed with halberds, bows and crossbows, as well as two mud-stained spies. The latter seemed his most useful weapon. Hsiung whispered in their ears and both nodded. He led his soldiers along the ditch, away from the gatehouse, while Chao and Hua took the opposite direction to re-join the road.

The next few moments would decide everything – whether he returned to Lingling a lesser or greater man; and whether he must endure, yet again, Liu Shui's courteous superiority. Hsiung's grip on his halberd tightened as Chao and Hua staggered towards the town, apparently supporting each other and hopelessly drunk on New Year wine. Outside the closed gates they stood swaying, calling up to the guards, most of whom were either asleep or in a nearby tavern, defying the Mongol curfew they were employed to enforce. Chao's voice drifted across the fields, bellowing for admittance.

'Now!' whispered Hsiung. One by one the rebels slipped across the open ground to gather at the base of the walls. The ditch was shallow in places, layered with decades of rubbish from the town. Clearly the inhabitants of Chenglingji feared no assault.

'Quickly!' hissed Hsiung.

Grappling irons padded with strips torn from cloaks were cast up until the rope grew taut.

'Up! Up!'

Hsiung led the way, using the rope to scramble up the brick-lined wall, his arms and shoulders aching from the weight of his armour. Fortunately the wall was as low as Chao had promised and he hauled himself over, gasping for air. A long sword appeared in his hand.

Laughter drifted along the walkway from the gatehouse.

'Get lost, you sots!' called a guard.

'Sleep it off in a ditch!' taunted another.

Other shapes crouched beside Hsiung. He pointed and half a dozen men crept along the walkway, keeping low. Snatches of song still drifted from the town below, for the sailors and soldiers of the Salt Fleet were seeking their pleasures all over Chenglingji, determined to drink the miserable place dry. The rebels paused on the battlements as the sound of a woman's moaning pleasure reached them through an open window. Hsiung felt his own lust stir and glanced at the field of rooftops below.

'Quick,' he whispered, as much to himself as his men.

They padded into the gatehouse as Chao and Hua called out a fresh entreaty to the guards enjoying a little raillery. It was their last enjoyment in this life. Hsiung led the attack, choosing a man nearest the warning bell's rope. A hot surge filled him as his sword connected, cutting short a startled shriek . . .

Hsiung wiped his blade on the headless torso of an unusually young and puny fellow for a soldier. Meanwhile his men secured the gates.

'Show the signal to Captain P'ao,' he ordered, his mouth uncomfortably dry. The dark lights were dimming in his soul, leaving a shrivelled desire he feared and longed to appease.

Three lanterns were soon hung above the gate. Somewhere in the town a cock crowed and Hsiung looked to the east in alarm. Dawn was almost upon them. Where was P'ao? Then he saw the main column, attracted by the three swinging lanterns like moths to the flame. Captain P'ao strode at their side, ordering his lieutenants to unfurl the banner of Moon-Beside-Mountain, the symbol of Yueh Fei.

天命

The next hour was necessary, perhaps. Hsiung had just over fifteen hundred men whereas the Salt Fleet carried twice that number. One might also mention the hundreds of government troops garrisoned in Chenglingji.

Hsiung watched the Yueh Fei soldiers pour through the gatehouse. His heart beat rapidly and he was impatient for the attack to commence. Lesser men must not be allowed to steal the glory this time! A triumph like Fourth Hell Gorge could be his again.

He leaned out of the battlements and shouted commands that would haunt him on restless nights when the wind blew west to Lingling: 'Followers of Yueh Fei!' Hundreds of faces turned up to him, swords, axes, spears and halberds bristling in the soft, rosy glow of dawn. 'All but the Guards are ordered into this town!' he bellowed. 'Not a single enemy shall live to defy us! Captain P'ao, the Guards must stay for my personal command.'

A great cheer greeted these orders. The whole town – by no means a large place – seemed to pause between breaths. Songs of celebration and the murmured endearments of lovers; infants wailing for milk and the yawns of servants lighting dawn fires; all were frozen momentarily by the rebels' collective roar. Then time flowed again and companies of Yueh Fei rebels surged down the narrow streets, seeking anyone capable of opposition. In a short time screams and wails rose into the brightening sky.

Hsiung clattered down the stairs of the gatehouse to join Captain P'ao at the head of five hundred heavily armoured, disciplined Guardsmen. P'ao whispered in his ear: 'You meant to order that not a single enemy shall live?' he asked.

'Of course,' said Hsiung, wondering what part of it had been unclear.

Now P'ao bowed with a trace of fear.

'You are right, sire!' he said. 'We have been too soft! Best make them dread your name!'

'Except for those who surrender,' added Hsiung, but P'ao had already hurried off to check the ranks.

Chao and Hua hovered nearby, holding looted weapons.

'You'll need those, my friends,' said Hsiung. 'Show us the quickest way to the harbour.'

'Yes, Noble Count!' declared Chao.

The next hour blurred in Hsiung's memory: marching at the head of the Guards, cutting down any who crossed their path with extravagant lunges of his halberd. Everyone was a potential enemy now. The Guards swept down the central street of the town to the harbour, surprising a force of sailors and soldiers forming up on the long quay for a counter-attack. Most were still drunk, many barely dressed. At the sight of the dense column chanting *Yueh Fei! Yueh Fei!* half scattered like rats – leaping into ships and desperately trying to cast off, hiding in alleyways or buildings. The rebel column rushed onto the quay and a pitiless fight followed. The ground and wooden jetties were soon littered with corpses; everywhere terrified men were hunted and hacked, pleading for mercy or striking back until courage or strength failed them.

Hsiung and his bodyguard rapidly dispatched a huddle of Mongol officers and he stood regaining his breath, an unnatural grin on his face. He had proved his strength! No less than two of the officers had fallen to his halberd strokes. How much simpler to fight than hear tiresome petitions and windy speeches! Then Hsiung's joy subsided. His precious Guards were spread all over the harbour, oblivious to the commands of their officers. One man tore the silks off a dead military official, entering into a fierce tug of war with a comrade until the garment ripped in two.

'P'ao!' he called. 'Jin! Reform the companies!'

Even P'ao had disappeared up a side street. Several of his picked bodyguard were missing – and he could not assume they had succumbed to anything more deadly than looting.

'You!' he shouted. 'Hey! You over there! Form up beside me!'

With the helpless panic of a parent who has lost his small child in a crush, Hsiung realised he had lost control of his men. Wheeling, he faced the town. Shrieks filled the air like the crying of gulls. Heaven alone knew what cruelties were being enacted in the name of Yueh Fei. Worse was his own urge to discard the restraints of command and stalk into town himself, sword drawn. An imagined face – or remembered, it did not matter, nothing mattered – a face like Overseer Pi-tou's loomed in his mind, pleading as Hsiung's thumbs found eyeballs and pushed into the softness, pushing and reaching in behind . . . 'No,' he told himself, looking round at the shabby wooden buildings of Chenglingji.

Hsiung turned towards the fleet tethered all over the harbour, hundreds of masts and as many hulls weighed down with precious salt. If he did not regain command soon they might slip their moorings and escape. Already boats had cast off, manned by the remnants of their crews.

'To me, Guards! Line up!' He seized any rebel soldiers who came near, shoving them into a ragged line. 'Sergeant, gather those men over there!'

Meanwhile the screams from the town continued as dawn became broad morning. Hsiung watched the first plumes of smoke rise. Burning down houses exceeded orders! Victory like this felt oddly like misrule, absurdly like defeat. So much so, that the sight of Chao and Hua hurrying towards him through the scattered bodies came as a relief.

'Noble Count,' called out Hua, 'we have managed to save the worthy Zhong family I told you about. They wish to offer you their eternal homage and submission!'

天命

At noon the rebel fleet sailed into Chenglingji harbour. It met a dismal sight. Although scores of vessels floated at anchor, a ship without its crew resembles an abandoned house. In the chaos of the massacre thirty valuable vessels had escaped, mainly of the lighter sort requiring fewer hands to tend oars or sails. As for the rest, their crews and attendant soldiers lay singly or in piles all over Chenglingji, wherever they had been cut down. Hundreds of women's corpses lay alongside them.

Nearly every house had been forced open and ransacked, its most intimate treasures violated.

When Chancellor Liu Shui of Lingling County stepped onto the quayside he glowered at a dismembered hand near his shoe.

'I seek the Noble Count,' he informed a Guards officer, none other than Lieutenant Jin.

'Up at the compound of the Zhongs, sir,' said Jin, his eyes oddly glazed.

'I have heard a great deal about that clan,' replied Liu Shui, stiffly. 'Lieutenant, ensure honourable burials commence as soon as possible.'

Jin watched the fat man enter the town, followed by a retinue of clerks and officials.

At the Zhongs' mansion Hsiung occupied their biggest chair, staring down at a dozen kneeling men in silk robes. All were suitably terrified, as well they might be after the dreadful storm that had swept away everything they once believed strong. Chao and Hua stood behind Hsiung's temporary throne, in the role of chief advisers.

'Let me understand this correctly,' said Hsiung, 'these people are the Zhong clan and accustomed to ruling Chenglingji?'

'They have all the contacts you'll need to squeeze the district dry, Noble Count,' whispered Chao. 'Offer them better terms than the Mongols and they'll eat from your hand.'

Hsiung was in a mood for clemency. Walking through the corpse-littered town had shaken his confidence as ruler. None of this had been his intention. Although Hua claimed the Noble Count had personally ordered the massacre while leaning out of the gatehouse at dawn, Hsiung had no recollection of such a command. Yet it was hard to deny the charge amidst so much grotesque evidence. Now he must decide the fate of these frightened men prostrating themselves before him.

'Sire,' whispered Hua, 'the head of the Zhong clan is so

beloved by the common people of Chenglingji he is known as *Dear Uncle.*'

'I see,' said Hsiung for want of a probing question that might test Dear Uncle's worthiness. He was about to order the Zhongs to administer the town on his behalf as Hua suggested when the doorway filled with a large, frowning figure. Hsiung glanced away uneasily. Conscious of many eyes upon him he rose.

'Ah, Liu Shui! You have disembarked.'

The Chancellor entered the room, hands buried in his sleeves. Kneeling Zhongs crawled out of his way as he advanced seemingly oblivious to their existence.

'Nearly seventy-five ships have been captured,' said Hsiung. 'Better still, a whole flotilla of paddlewheel destroyers, fully-armed with catapults, naphtha, thunderclap bombs, everything we hoped for, Liu Shui!'

'A great victory!' crowed Chao behind him.

'The Noble Count has triumphed again!' echoed Hua.

'No doubt,' said Liu Shui, gravely. 'Yet I hear the town was taken entirely by surprise and a general execution of the populace ordered. The Noble Count must now triumph in peace as he has triumphed in battle.'

Liu Shui examined the Zhongs at his feet, his frown deepening.

'Are these our new allies, Noble Count?' he asked.

A question Hsiung was unsure how to answer.

Hua was more forthcoming. 'The worthy Zhong clan beg to offer the entire revenue of this district to the Noble Count,' he said. Turning to Hsiung he added: 'A most benevolent family, loved by the common people, as I have informed Your Highness.'

Liu Shui continued to survey the Zhongs.

'That is not my information,' he said. 'Noble Count, I urge you to appoint new, more trustworthy administrators than these Zhongs, so highly esteemed by the Mongols and their lackeys. You may well ask yourself why the famine has been more severe in Chenglingji under their benevolent rule than in neighbouring districts. As you know, I have trained suitable men, all loyal to you. They should ensure justice and that the, ahem, unfortunate excesses of our victory do not linger in the minds of the people. Thus, deep bonds of loyalty to your rule, based upon love as well as fear, will be established here.'

For a moment Hsiung wavered.

'Always remember,' added Liu Shui, gently, 'a just ruler earns the Mandate of Heaven by aiding his people. Conquest is just a means to that end.'

'Noble Count,' said Hua, 'consider the revenue you will lose! Wealth that will build your armies! The Zhongs are good people, sir.'

Then Hsiung saw a way out of his dilemma, one that would please everyone. The Noble Count was so delighted with his own wisdom he beamed.

'I hereby appoint anyone chosen by the Excellent Liu Shui as governor of this town,' he said, 'but his officials shall be the Zhong clan, whose homage I accept. Under my rule peace shall triumph in Chenglingji.'

Liu Shui bowed low and left to make sure no further slaughter sullied the ideals of their cause. Hua, however, met the eye of a retreating member of the Zhong clan, a man Yun Shu had known a decade before as Dear Uncle, and silent understandings passed between them.

twenty-three

天命

When Teng considered the matter – which wasn't often – he suspected spring was his favourite season. As he emerged from his bedchamber in Deng Mansions, the same room he had occupied since boyhood, he listened to birds wooing all over Monkey Hat Hill. Out in the courtyard he paused, slipping the bone buttons of his tunic into their loops. Two pigeons puffed and cooed. The complexity of their feathers fascinated the painter in him.

He felt an inexplicable pang at their courtship and clapped his hands, driving them into flight. In a moment they were back, this time on the roof.

Of course the urgency of their dance was to produce a new generation. He remembered Yun Shu telling him how she liked the company of children. Perhaps that was natural.

Teng watched the cock pigeon mount its mate. An excited fluttering followed. It occurred to him, and by no means for the first time, that at his age he should be producing heirs for the Deng clan. After all, he and Father were the only Dengs left.

Oddly, the old scholar never reproached him. Perhaps his silence was a test whether Teng would do the right thing without prompting. A test he failed.

Oh, there were excellent reasons. The only families in

Hou-ming that Deng Nan-shi considered worthy of an alliance were desperate to avoid the honour. As for Teng, he shared his father's aversion to a demeaning match. Better to consort with Ying-ge than become a poor relation.

Teng had just drawn a bucket of water from the well when he heard women chanting. Smoothing back long black hair, he wandered over to the gatehouse in time to witness a procession descending the Hundred Stairs.

Eunuch Bo-Bai strode in front, holding aloft a long yellow banner decorated with black tassels. He ignored Teng as he passed. Then came a dozen Nuns of Serene Perfection with eyes modestly downcast. In their midst walked Abbess Yun Shu, who acknowledged him with a sideways flicker of her eyes, a greeting he returned with a flamboyant bow. When he looked up a faint furrow ruffled her brow. Teng wondered why he always tried to provoke her.

A dozen servants followed the nuns, carrying giant cauldrons, boxes, firewood and two large sacks. He watched them disappear down the hill, curious what Yun Shu was up to.

Recently she had taken to leaving Cloud Abode Monastery in a closed carriage at strange hours of the night. While they shared a class in Deng Nan-shi's school, he had enquired where she went. 'I ask,' he had said, 'as your concerned Elder Brother.' Her answer was a muttered remark about 'attaining Sublime Formlessness'. A phrase he didn't like to associate with Yun Shu. It featured often in the bamboo books from the dead prince's tomb.

Another time, sat in the garden with his lute for a little drunken moon gazing, he observed a barge approach the private jetty belonging to Cloud Abode Monastery. Even in the pale light of a full moon he recognised Yun Shu's slender figure. Wrapped in a suspiciously dark cloak, she hopped aboard as though accustomed to midnight boat trips. It was baffling and alarming. Her naive character was ill suited to intrigue. She was sure to paddle out of her depth.

*   *   *

That morning Teng planned to sell his latest drama, *I Weep for Su Lin*, to the highest bidder. A lengthy process obliging him to sip wine and tea as a succession of theatre proprietors examined the play. After that, pockets crammed with strings of *cash*, he would entertain Ying-ge in her boudoir – and be suitably entertained in his turn. So Teng dressed with special care in his best new silks and strode out of Deng Mansions before Father could persuade him to tutor the brighter pupils in calligraphy.

At the foot of Monkey Hat Hill, beside the Ward Gate, Teng learned the reason for the Nuns' procession. An outdoor kitchen had been established in the old market place and crowds of thin, raggedly dressed people were milling and jostling to bring their bowls closer to cauldrons of rice and vegetables. Yun Shu stood in front of the makeshift kitchen, urging patience, her voice drowned by the clamour of the hungry crowd. Teng wondered why no soldiers were present to maintain order.

He noticed a boy with a satchel wriggling between legs to escape the press, one of Deng Nan-shi's pupils. As the lad skipped up the lane Teng intercepted him.

'Hey! Chan-su!' The boy recognised Teacher's Son and stopped. 'Tell my father what is happening here,' said Teng. 'Say Abbess Yun Shu needs assistance.'

The lad sprinted up the hill and Teng was forced to consider a new threat to the Nuns. Twenty Buddhist monks in bright orange robes had pushed through the Ward Gate, followed by a small mob of excited supporters. Teng hurried down to join Yun Shu, who was still encouraging the hungry people to form a line. As he arrived, the monks reached her. Now Daoists and Buddhists faced each other before the steaming cauldrons. A restless crowd observed the confrontation.

'We received a vision!' roared a bellicose young monk, his shaven head shaped like an anvil. His accent marked him out as one of the fox-smell foreigners connected to the Tibetan sect of Makhala favoured by the Mongol court. 'The Buddha's knucklebone has sent a vision!'

At once many in the crowd rejoiced. The knucklebone was more revered in Hou-ming than Prince Arslan himself. A scurrilous joke claimed that it saved one from hell in the next life, whereas the Prince guaranteed hell in this.

'The Buddha commands those who desire bodhisattva,' continued the monk, 'do not eat Daoist food! They put a secret poison into the rice!'

Teng snorted at this bizarre claim; he also noticed some of the Buddhist monk's supporters carried clubs. Their intention was obvious. Anything likely to encourage loyalty to the Dao, and especially the Nuns of Serene Perfection, must be disrupted. It was well known the Buddhists petitioned constantly to gain possession of Cloud Abode Monastery.

'My dear monk,' he began, stepping forward with hands concealed in his sleeves like a noble Confucian scholar from the old prints in Deng Library. 'These delightful ladies are not murderers! As you see, our city is full of starving people. For the sake of the Holy Buddha, allow a few of them to eat!'

He was met by an unheeding, blank stare. 'Poison food!' shouted the Tibetan monk. 'Poison rice! Do not let the people be poisoned! That is our vision!'

His supporters edged forward, evidently planning to kick over the cauldrons. A gong resounded in the market square, echoing off abandoned buildings consigned to rot and decay since the Mongol victory. Again the gong sounded and people looked round fearfully. Even the anvil-headed monk shrank back.

A procession trooped into the market square. Only Teng was unsurprised by the old man leading a disciplined column of scholars three abreast, for he had recognised the gong's voice as a relic of the Deng clan, so precious to their ancestors his father had preferred to endure an empty belly on numerous occasions rather than sell it. Now the gong declared the authority of a Deng once more – and Teng's pride stirred.

For all his frailty, Deng Nan-shi cut a fine figure in his scholar's plain gown and black hat with stiff, slanting ear-flaps. In his hand was a fly-whisk.

Again the gong resounded, carried on poles by six youths, and he joined his son to stand between Yun Shu and the Buddhist monk. So natural was the old man's dignity the crowd went quiet apart from people muttering his name. All older folk remembered the days when Dengs ruled Hou-ming on the Emperor's behalf. Better days for most. Several fell loyally to their knees.

'What is this disturbance?' demanded Deng Nan-shi in the high-pitched, querulous tone of a high official.

At first the monk seemed abashed, but soon cried out with fresh vigour: 'Poison food! The Daoists mean to poison the hungry people!'

Deng Nan-shi held the young man's eye until the latter looked away. The old scholar turned to address the crowd.

'You all know my ancestors,' he said. 'I speak on their behalf. And I see the real poison here. Unscrupulous men seeking to baffle the people! Form a decorous line behind me. Enjoy the Great Dao's generosity! There is nothing to fear from the Nuns who protect the image of Chenghuang, our beloved City God. I shall eat the first bowl!'

Teng took Deng Nan-shi's arm and helped him over to the cauldrons where Bo-Bai waited with a huge wooden ladle. An old fellow who had kneeled earlier hobbled away from the crowd, bowl in hand, calling over his shoulder to his assembled clan, 'Obey the Honourable Dengs before all the food has gone!' Another clan followed suit, then another. Soon a long line grew, marshalled by Teng and other well-wishers of the Dao. Bowl after bowl filled from the cauldrons while Yun Shu and the Nuns chanted sutras and prayers petitioning the Jade

Emperor for a fertile spring. The bellicose monk watched sourly then led his comrades away.

'They'll be back,' Teng muttered to his father.

But the old man did not reply and Teng realised that only a great effort of will kept him upright at all.

Two hours later the procession of Nuns retraced their steps up Monkey Hat Hill, having shared all their food. Yun Shu and Lady Lu Si stepped aside to call at Deng Mansions.

Both were received in Deng Nan-shi's library where the old scholar lay on a mouldy divan. Afterwards, while Lady Lu Si prepared cordials for the invalid, Teng led Yun Shu outside.

'My father is quite exhausted,' he burst out. 'What folly to distribute food in starving Hou-ming without an escort of troops! Thank Heaven that Tibetan fool distracted everyone. If he had not, the crowd would have surged forward and overwhelmed you, then a riot would have broken out!'

Yun Shu's blush contained pale spots that were far from serene. 'Yet again you wilfully misunderstand. Really, I wonder how you did not inherit your noble father's wisdom.'

A bitter retort formed until the obviousness of her distress silenced him.

'You must learn from this,' he said, more gently. 'You are too cavalier with your own safety. Think of the distress if you were harmed! What possessed you to take such a risk?' He fell silent, as though too much had been said.

'Duty towards less fortunate creatures than one's self,' she said, 'that is what. But I have learned from today, Teng! And I mean to set up my cauldrons every morning. Worthy Master Jian has offered two sacks of rice a day for the purpose. He is a good, kind, generous man.'

At this Teng grew cooler. 'I'm glad you find him so,' he said. 'You realise he hopes to counter the Buddhists' distribution of free grain, don't you?'

Her guileless, naïve expression answered that question.

'Why you of all people?' he mused. Then he glanced at her sharply. 'Do such good works increase your inner store of *ch'i* energy, swell your life force?'

'Of course. Concern for all living creatures mirrors the kindness of the Dao itself.'

'I see,' he said. 'And is this something to do with your *journeys* in covered carriages and barges at night?'

It was a wild shot. Yet it hit the very centre, for her blush became one of alarm.

'You must not refer to that,' she whispered, 'it is a great secret!'

'If I notice, others will. It's almost like you have regular assignations.'

The extent of her distress surprised him. As did the realisation he was absurdly jealous.

'Will you ever stop taunting me?' she cried. 'Once I hoped you would be a sensible friend. The Elder Brother I lack! I have so much need of kindly advice!'

This cut his next witticism short. 'I apologise, Yun Shu,' he said. 'Of course your charity is worthwhile. A hundred hungry families will sleep better for your work.'

Lady Lu Si emerged from the library. She examined the Abbess's flushed, animated face.

'Thank you for your assistance today, Honourable Deng Teng,' said Yun Shu in a brittle voice that strove for detachment.

Teng watched as she marched off to the gatehouse, her shoulders slightly hunched, pursued by a curious Lady Lu Si.

天命

That night, a hot wind ruffled the lake, blowing from the lustful south. Teng found himself in Ying-ge's boudoir in a large merchant's house and compound turned over to peach-red women. Her suite of rooms overlooked a small inner courtyard with a pond of water lilies and indolent carp.

The door had been slid open to let in the night breeze and he lounged on a wide, low bed, looking at the pond. Though he had hoped for gaiety and pleasure, his union with Ying-ge had disappointed them both. She lay naked beside him, watching his expression. Then she yawned and rolled over, revealing smooth breasts and skin, the fragrant moss beneath her flat stomach. Still he did not notice her. Now she rolled onto her front, propping her chin in cupped hands.

'You usually have pretty things to say to me,' she complained.

He looked at her in surprise. 'Do I?'

'Yes. And you usually love to hear *me* talk.'

'But I still do.'

She pursed her lips and yawned again. Once more they were silent. When it became uncomfortable he said: 'What is it you want to talk about?'

Now Ying-ge was less sure. They had already gossiped about the theatre, already praised her new silk dress, a present from another admirer, and one she clearly expected him to match, if not surpass.

'You seem to have so much *cash* these days,' she said, wistfully. 'Where do you get it all?'

That was one topic of conversation he was reluctant to explore, though she pressed him for an answer by remarking how clever he must be and then how everyone was curious. Finally her eyes widened at a novel idea.

'You scholars are all poets,' she said. 'Well then, praise my beauty!'

She rolled over and rested her cheek on one hand, the other playfully adjusting a lock of her hair.

'Your beauty?' he said, in a distant voice, distracted by recollections of Yun Shu's foolish bravery that morning. Ying-ge's coquettish expression hardened.

'You don't notice me,' she said, pouting.

'Not at all!' protested Teng, reaching out to touch her hand. She sullenly pulled it away. 'It's just that I'm thinking,' he said, 'that the valley between your jade mountains would entice any traveller.'

She considered this for a moment, examining her own chest.

'What of my face?' she demanded, angling it towards him.

'Oh, oval as a phoenix egg.'

The compliment seemed to mollify her slightly.

'And my eyebrows?'

'I see willow leaves . . . and your mouth is as small as a fish's'

'What kind of fish?'

'Oh, a carp, for you are always seeking profit wherever you can find it.'

'Ah!' Now she tapped him playfully on the arm. 'I like that!'

'I thought you would.'

'And my lips?'

'Cherries – and as for your teeth, pomegranate seeds.'

Here he was lying, as no doubt a woman possessing as many bronze mirrors as Ying-ge knew well. Her teeth were small, pointed and uneven.

'I like you now,' she said, invitingly.

But Teng had risen. Pulling a dressing gown over his naked body he went over to the wine flasks and poured a bowl. Behind him Ying-ge's willow eyebrows rose in scorn: pouring wine was her work. But he had ceased to consider Ying-ge. Her vanity, though natural in a woman, bored him. Again he thought of Yun Shu and wondered if the curtained carriage had called for her tonight.

'A strange thing happened at the foot of Monkey Hat Hill today,' he said.

'Horrid, overgrown place full of ghosts!' she retorted, for Ying-ge didn't like her lover living in an unfashionable part of town in case it reflected badly on herself.

He told the tale of the cauldrons and starving people, concluding with his fears that a hungry crowd would mob Abbess
Yun Shu if she was not careful.

'It is disgraceful,' he continued. 'Merchants manipulate the
market for grain so their profits are bloated. They bribe
officials to turn a blind eye who, in turn, bribe princes and
court nobles. Thus the price of rice doubles and millet trebles!'

A loud yawn interrupted him.

'Who cares what happens to miserable poor people and their
ugly old Aunty,' said Ying-ge. Suddenly she became suspicious.
'Of course! I have heard of this Abbess. She is young and
pretty!'

Now Teng felt uncomfortable and wished he hadn't
mentioned Yun Shu. Another bowl of wine went down quickly.

'I knew her when we were both children, that is all,' he said.
'She was a kind of sister to me for a while. Then there was a
great misunderstanding between us.'

Ying-ge's icy laugh tinkled.

'Just a sister?' she asked, archly. 'I didn't think that was your
style.'

'Actually, I honour that lady a great deal. Though, at times,
she is the most vexing creature in the world.'

He poured and downed another cup. It was strong rice wine
and his head span a little. Then he chuckled. 'She is the most
quick-witted woman of my acquaintance – not that the sharp-
ness of her tongue isn't provoking.'

Even in his drunken state Teng became aware Ying-ge was
sobbing. Or appeared to be.

'I can see you do not love me at all!' said the girl, dabbing
her eyes with a handkerchief. 'It is this ugly Aunty you love!'

Teng suddenly wished himself back in Deng Mansions. Her
words disturbed him in a way he blamed on the wine. What
nonsense filled women's heads! Sitting down heavily beside
Ying-ge, he took her hands and kissed them.

'You fill my eyes!' he protested.

'I don't,' she sniffed, 'it's her, that horrid Nun who fills your eyes.'

Eventually he soothed her. Between them the cock phoenix danced and the hen flew loudly for a long while.

Teng was woken at dawn by a persistent tapping on the door. A maid finally gained his attention and led him to Ying-ge's tiny reception room where a male visitor waited on a low, padded chair. He examined Teng's half-dressed state and grunted.

'Chasing quails who sell their feathers again,' remarked Shensi.

Teng sat down opposite his friend.

'What is it, Shensi? Has Father's illness worsened?'

The tomb-finder pursed his lips. 'Good news for a change.'

He told an interesting story. First he reminded Teng that their chief customer, Salt Minister Gui, believed he was acting as a broker for an old, impoverished noble family, so desperate they were parting with their greatest treasures. Abruptly, Shensi went quiet and looked round the small room.

'Don't worry,' said Teng, 'it's safe to talk freely. Ying-ge can't hear.'

'Then I will. Last night our friend Gui summoned me with an offer. It seems he has customers at the court who will pay a fortune for paintings of horses. And he needs lots of *cash* to send to his sons in the capital. The Mongol princes are vying for the best horse paintings, especially by Han Kan and Li Lung-mien. Of course I told him we could provide both.'

'Was that wise?' asked Teng. 'Gui isn't a complete fool.'

'Ah, but he's greedy, said Shensi, 'that can make the cleverest man foolish.'

Still Teng doubted. The same might be said of themselves.

'So I'm to produce a painting by Han Kun – not too hard, by the way – and one by Li Lung-mien, which is a far greater challenge. When by?'

'I said a week.'

'A week!'

'Maybe two.'

Teng scratched his legs through the bed robe, picturing prints and copies of Han Kun in the Deng library. They were in poor condition but usable.

'Very well, but these are the last forgeries I will undertake. Never ask me again. This time I mean it.'

Was it Father's willingness to risk anything for the public good, as he had yesterday? Or did Yun Shu's purity lurk behind his vow? Teng could not be sure, but the decision brought an inner calm that had eluded him for months.

'You won't need to do it again,' said Shensi, wolfishly. 'Our good friend the Salt Minister is offering thousands, which can only mean he stands to make thousands more by selling them.'

When Teng returned to Ying-ge's boudoir he found her yawning extravagantly as though she had woken that very moment. Yet he caught an oddly alert glitter in her eyes and wondered, quite unworthily, whether she had spied on his conversation with Shensi.

天命

As Teng commenced his work he realised any art – music, words, brush strokes – was a story of stages . . .

First the flow of an inspired hand, copying ancient models in accordance to the Sixth Principle of Hsieh Ho. One must learn by example, revere the Great Masters . . .

Mid-morning light pooled in the centre of Teng's shabby studio, illuminating examples by Han Kun studied and rehearsed in small parts – that flying hoof twenty times over and flaring nostril a dozen times. So often he no longer referred to them. He became Han Kun, revelling in the master's glory, always mourning his own inferiority . . .

Even as he executed the boldest strokes, Teng sensed *ch'i* energy running as ink-sap through his hand, breathing out forms on paper . . .

Standing back, examining the painting for its adherence to Hsieh Ho's Third Principle. But if the horse lacked fidelity then surely he, Teng, could not be blamed when the depiction so closely – no, he could flatter himself, *exactly* – mirrored Han Kun's own.

With Li Lung-mien's horse the transformation required a great letting go of self, a drive to nullity. Teng remembered how a Daoist told the painter that if he continued painting so many horses he would become one himself. Teng spent days watching horses in the city and dreaming about the quiver of their sweating flanks, twitching tails, wind-stirred manes, the expressive emptiness of their eyes . . .

False starts and trials! Always Li Lung-mien's genius fled before him like a ghost, held momentarily then slipping through the hairs of his brush. Hsieh Ho's Second Principle spoke of a painter's bone, the strength of his brush stroke, and through this Teng gained the key. As afternoon light glowed and faded he painted a dappled tribute horse on faded brown paper, exactly matching Li Lung-mien's precisely broad style. Finally, tentatively, almost fearfully lest he mar so perfect a replica, Teng applied the seals and colophons in red ink he had created by carving on wax. Each was exact. How fine a mimic he had become!

A flask of wine. More pacing round his mockery of Li Lung-mien. In disgust at his persistent dishonesty, Teng altered the final seal of ownership so it attested the painting once belonged to the rebel hero Yueh Fei, aware such an ownership clashed with dates set out in the other seals. No matter. The Mongols were too stupid to notice subtleties. All they would see was a horse.

Chuckling at his petty act of protest, Teng sent one of

Father's pupils to buy another jug of double-brewed rice wine.

天命

As soon as he entered the packed theatre – its murmuring, speculation, hundreds of darting eyes – Teng feared a grave error of judgement. Too late now. An usher cleared a path to seats reserved specially. 'Make way! Make way!'

Four people followed the bustling man: Teng supporting Deng Nan-shi's arm; behind them, Abbess Yun Shu in the regal attire of a Serene One and, huffing in the rear, Eunuch Bo-Bai with a basket of cushions, flasks and refreshments.

'You will be pleased by our seats, Father,' murmured Teng.

The old scholar glanced at his son. As ever, a look midway between approval, query and unspoken criticism.

The arrival of their party did not go unnoticed. People rose to get a better view of the last surviving Dengs. Some bowed low. Others muttered amongst themselves. Just as visible was Abbess Yun Shu. Everyone noticed her public association with disloyal scholars. Hence Teng's fear of a grave error. Unscrupulous Buddhists might use the Deng clan's dubious reputation in their campaign to gain possession of Cloud Abode Monastery.

He glanced at Yun Shu to see if she had noticed. A flush of animation coloured her plump cheeks: the flutter of a smile touched the corners of her mouth. She was as excited as a child to be in the theatre. As ever, her naivety filled him with conflicting emotions. Alarm on her behalf, of course. More strongly, a protective warmth he could not explain. A desire to understand her better.

'Lady Yun Shu,' he said, 'please sit on Father's right side. It offers a better view of the stage, I think.'

The stage, jutting out into the tiers of seats, was bare apart from a backdrop depicting mountains and a gentleman's mansion that climbed a hillside in three distinct stages.

Once she was settled, he said, 'Notice the backdrop. I painted it myself. You might recognise the house from your famous ancestor's poems, perhaps?' To address her Teng was forced to lean a little over his father, who sat between them. The old scholar's glance passed from one animated face to the other. Whatever he thought did not reach his tongue.

'Can that be,' she began, 'yes, it must be! Three-Step-House in Wei Valley! Yun Cai's poems mention it often.'

Teng laughed with self-satisfaction. 'Did I not promise my new drama would interest you greatly?'

Perhaps too greatly. For Yun Shu had ignored Lady Lu Si's counsel not to attend the first performance of *I weep for Su Lin*. Principally because Teng had used the life of her ancestor, Yun Cai, as a loose model for his play.

It was a popular story. And a subtly provocative one. Despite telling how Yun Cai proved himself a hero by his loyalty to the Emperor, everyone in the audience knew that Emperor had belonged to the previous dynasty. In addition, Yun Cai's father had saved the life of the barbarian-baiting rebel, Yueh Fei, nearly two hundred years earlier. As two hundred years is but a wing beat of time, the implications were obvious. Accordingly, the theatre was packed.

'My play is not *exactly* based on Yun Cai's career,' Teng admitted to Yun Shu. 'I have made certain improvements.'

Her enthusiasm faltered a little. 'How can one improve on a life already lived?' she asked. 'One may question another person's decisions but not alter them.'

A slight smile crossed Deng Nan-shi's impassive face. Teng knew his father was thinking *she's got you there*. He decided to accept defeat gracefully. 'A wise thought,' he conceded, 'yes, very wise.'

Out of the corner of his eye, Teng spotted another party hurrying to their seats before the play began. The orchestra of pi-pa and lute, drum, clappers, flute and ch'in commenced the overture. Teng stiffened.

The latecomers were as notorious in Hou-ming as the Dengs. They wore glittering silks and hairpieces, shuffling on tiny lotus feet. A dozen male courtesans from Prince Arslan's palace, quite as well regarded as females of the same profession. In their midst, older than his companions, Golden Lotus, the concubine-spouse of Salt Minister Gui – the very man who had purchased Teng's forgeries for an exorbitant price.

Perhaps lingering guilt caused Teng's discomfort. Or a memory of placing the seal of Yueh Fei on one of the paintings. Mostly he feared Golden Lotus's presence would distress Yun Shu. When he glanced at her, it was obvious she had not noticed the newcomers. Delight at the orchestra made her beam. She revelled in every sensation of her release from the repetitive chanting and endless prayers in Cloud Abode Monastery. Relieved, Teng settled back as the play began.

'I am Yun Cai,' declared the male lead, a broad-chested singer with plenty of swagger. 'In my youth I was exiled to my estate of Three-Step-House in far off Wei Valley . . .'

The play unfolded for two tense hours. Yun Shu leaned forward in her seat, dabbing her eyes when the poet's great love, Su Lin, betrayed him to satisfy the ambitions of the father, who had been suborned by a corrupt minister called Lord Xiao afraid Yun Cai would expose his misdeeds. The plot was made yet more complex by the intrigues of the poet's faithful friend, P'ei Ti.

Ying-ge played the part of Su Lin. Her voice as she half-sobbed and sang was wonderfully pure:

The wine in my bowl
Is watered with tears,
Let me assure you,
The dregs of my heart!

Handkerchiefs wiping away tears fluttered like butterfly wings.

When Su Lin took poison, rushing back and forth upon the stage like a trapped moth, before subsiding gracefully into an

311

artful heap of silks, make-up, jewellery and silver hairpieces, many in the audience rose to protest. So extreme was their anguish on her behalf. Prominent among them was the Salt Minister's aging concubine, Golden Lotus.

Teng's own eyes filled with tears. How talented and beautiful was Ying-ge! How exquisite and graceful! No woman could compare with her for that. Yet in the midst of his admiration he recalled her pettiness and spite when crossed; her devotion to fashion and gossip. Ying-ge's sole topic of conversation was Ying-ge – a topic of which she never tired.

At last the Jade Emperor sent a Heavenly Official down to the Middle Kingdom. This Immortal's face was painted a shiny white. He rode a hobbyhorse in the form of a gigantic goose onto the stage, to the great delight of the audience. His speech in praise of loyalty and duty was almost as prolonged as the crowd's applause.

Teng turned to Yun Shu. She wept freely while Deng Nan-shi murmured soothing words. Teng's heart filled with pleasure. How natural they seemed together! Like father and daughter-in-law!

'Oh, Teng!' she cried, 'what a wonderful play! How it honoured Yun Cai! I enjoyed it very much! So very much!'

Then Teng understood. All along he had written *I weep for Su Lin* to please Yun Shu. She had watched from a shadowy corner of his mind through the long hours of composition, just as he sometimes imagined his dead mother's presence. Except Yun Shu was real, her breath warm. Her unique fragrance touched his nostrils: a combination of incense and sandalwood, the willow-scent aromas of hair and body.

As he led his party to the exit, acknowledging acquaintances and friends, Teng took a circuitous route to avoid Golden Lotus. Fortunately, deep in conversation with Deng Nan-shi, Yun Shu had not spotted him.

With a final backward glance into the theatre before following Bo-Bai and the others outside, Teng noticed Ying-ge addressing the Salt Minister's concubine, bowing and whispering. What about, Teng could not imagine. Then both looked straight at him. Their expressions were cold. A horrible suspicion took root in his gut.

twenty-four

天命

Yun Shu rattled and bumped in a heavily curtained wooden box. It was dark in the carriage. Only echoes of the world reached her: rain drumming on the roof; the coachman abusing someone who blocked their way; snatches of drunken laughter. Yun Shu closed her eyes and attempted the mantra Worthy Master Jian had taught her: *om mani padme . . . om mani padme . . .* wishing she understood the words. But then, she wasn't meant to.

Yun Shu recognised the toll of a bell. It belonged to Golden Bright Temple. She squeezed her amulets to suppress fear. What use would she be if less than serene? As ever, Yun Shu doubted her fitness for the test to come. Every seventh day of the month she participated in Worthy Master Jian's magical rites. The seventh day was when the divine and human worlds touched – briefly, tantalisingly. Worthy Master had explained it all. Yet for all the pain and inner sickness she suffered, his handsome, dignified face showed no sign of regeneration. If anything, his silver hair had whitened, not darkened.

The carriage came to a sudden halt and the curtain was flung open. Her face veiled, Yun Shu stepped out into humid air, glimpsing a temple courtyard wet with rain. A thick, round pagoda rose into the night sky. Its topmost storey bulged and red lights glowed behind shrouded windows.

A nameless priest escorted her to the closed door of the pagoda. He rapped out a secret pattern and was rewarded with a tinkling bell. Having received this sign, he waved her inside.

It took a moment for Yun Shu's eyes to adjust after the darkness of the carriage. The walls and roof were painted black and decorated with constellations and deities. The lacquered floor shone with images of rivers, mountains, lakes, cities. A single piece of furniture stood in the centre: a reading stand carved to represent Mount Kunlun, home of the Immortals, on which an ancient book of bamboo strips rested. A pale lantern cast a silvery light.

In this crucible of inner preparation and meditation Worthy Master Jian sat cross-legged and perfectly still. Yet she sensed his frustration.

'Yun Shu! Sit beside me. We shall clarify our intentions.'

She timidly took up the lotus position. They both stared forward into the Infinite. For a long while neither moved and Yun Shu's heart beat slowed: she was accustomed to silence, stillness, the creation of spirit-rooms. It startled her when he spoke again: 'Yun Shu, are you receptive tonight?'

His voice was kindly, patient. Again fear flickered. 'I have prepared myself, Worthy Master.'

'Good.' His eyes narrowed. 'Yun Shu, it is now six months since we began this Great Work. A noble, lofty work, do you not agree?' She bowed submissively. 'Yet our progress is slow. We have still not progressed from the Stage of *Ch'i*.'

'Yes,' she said, guiltily.

Why did her voice tremble? She should be proud, exalted.

'Yun Shu,' he said, 'you are aware that I am from an impeccable family?'

Again she nodded.

'My family was second in this province only to the Dengs and they have almost passed away. Old Deng Nan-shi is sick and his son a foolish wastrel. All my life I have been accustomed to obedience, power. The Dao sends me whatever

I desire. And now I approach my fiftieth year, despite all my piety, all my mastery of the Dao's secrets!'

She ducked her head at the imbalance in his voice. He was rumoured to drink elixirs of mercury to prevent aging.

'Yun Shu, if anyone is destined to join the Immortals it is me. But can I rely on you?'

Was there pleading in his voice? The stone of fear in her heart softened a little. 'Worthy Master,' she said, 'if you . . . I am ready. Let us ascend now if you wish.'

She sensed his breath quicken. He rose, bowed to the effigy of Mount Kunlun, and led her towards the stairs.

For the next few hours he used her in the Seven Places of the Seven Primes. All as specified in the bamboo strips. At first there was pleasure for her but that soon passed as the rite progressed. Soreness and pain forced her to gasp. Gasps she stifled lest he grow angry. He had struck her once for ruining the rite. All the while he held back his *jing*, his precious seed, as he had for twenty years.

For long hours he harvested her life force, projecting it up his spine to swell the pearl of light that would one day make him Immortal. At intervals he forced her to drink a bitter, foul elixir that sent her head spinning, before gulping deeply himself.

Worthy Master Jian rose and re-tied his gown. Bowing to the Five Directions, he departed quietly, leaving Yun Shu alone on the bed, her body and breasts shining with perspiration in the lantern light, her inner places bruised. The worst ache of all swelled in her spirit like an ugly toadstool releasing venomous spores.

天命

For days after the ceremony Yun Shu withdrew to her chamber, sick in soul and body. She suspected Worthy Master Jian had encouraged her to drink more of the bitter elixir than before.

Each time a little more. She would have feared poison except he drank so much of the metallic, green sludge himself.

Lady Lu Si attended her frequently, tight-lipped with anger. Yun Shu knew very well what the older nun thought of Worthy Master Jian: a distrust she was beginning to share. But when she voiced her fears, Lady Lu Si cut the subject short. 'Abbess Yun Shu,' she said, genuinely distressed, 'it is for *you* to decide what is best, not I! There can not be two Abbesses.'

Yun Shu regarded her predecessor through bloodshot eyes. The bags beneath them hung like bruises. Her once shiny black hair, so thick and strong, was thinning. 'I need good counsel,' she whispered.

She was surprised to see tears in the old nun's eyes. 'That is why I will remain silent. Remember, silence is thunder.'

The next day she brought an unexpected visitor. Yun Shu had risen finally and was resting on a marble bench over-looking the lake. The monsoon rolled west, leaving a flawless blue sky. Despite sunshine on her face she felt cold inside.

Yun Shu looked away uneasily as Lady Lu Si led her guest over, ashamed what he would make of her wan face and trembling hands.

'I was told you are unwell,' said Teng, examining her closely. 'May I join you?'

She nodded, indicating a marble bench beside her own. For a long while he seemed reluctant to talk. Yun Shu noticed Lady Lu Si had withdrawn, leaving them alone. Finally, he looked up. 'Tell me,' he said with unexpected passion, 'have your *meetings* with Worthy Master Jian continued?'

She blinked at him. Teng rose and began to pace the meditation platform.

'No need to reply! I see the mischief. That rogue! No, I am to blame. It was I who gave him those accursed bamboo strips. I who translated their obscurities!'

'I do not understand,' she said.

'Of course you do! Or, at least, should. Don't you see that

Jian is following slavishly, quite slavishly, the ancient method for gaining Immortality! Stage by stage, leap by hop! He is mad!'

'It is a great honour,' she mumbled. 'He promised to ensure Cloud Abode Monastery does not pass to the Buddhists if I help him.'

'The rogue!' repeated Teng. 'The Jian clan always lacked principle.'

She might have mentioned what the Deng clan's high principles had cost the populace of Hou-ming. 'As ever, I have no choice in the matter,' she protested.

'Even so, I beg you not to drink the elixirs,' he said. 'Do not look so surprised I know about them! Remember I translated the infernal list of ingredients he is using. Utterly irresponsible to spend so much *cash* on dubious potions when half the city longs for a bowl of broth! Mad, I say!'

Despite her pale cheeks, Yun Shu managed a feeble blush. 'Then you must know about . . .'

'Of course!' he waved her embarrassment away. 'Such practises are well known. But I worry about the elixirs. They contain, let us say, *unnatural* things.' Teng laughed harshly. 'Jian is a fool to be so credulous! If the bamboo books spoke truly we would hardly have found a pile of bones in the dead prince's coffin.'

Both fell silent. Again he settled on the marble bench. 'Do you remember Mirror Lake, Yun Shu? How innocent we both were. Sometimes I dream of the limestone hills.'

She watched him closely. 'As do I,' she said.

Side by side they stared out across glittering Six-Hundred-*Li* Lake. Fishing boats and flocks of white birds floated between tree-clad islands.

'You must take care,' he said. 'I need not mention Lady Lu Si's concern for you.'

'There, at least, you are mistaken,' she said. 'Lady Lu Si will never forgive me for becoming Abbess.'

He looked at her in surprise. 'Is that what you believe?'

'How could I believe anything else?'

'I see. Yes, I see.' Again he brooded. 'Yun Shu, you need a little *fun*. A diversion from your duties and burdens. Just like Lady Lu Si herself at this time of year.' He rose with a business-like air as though something had been settled. 'Yes, that's it.'

'What is?'

'I take it you are at leisure, Yun Shu, in two days' time?'

'I am, but . . .'

'Then consider the matter decided.'

With that he bowed and departed. Yun Shu was left to ponder the significance of two days' time. Yet she made no alternative appointments, just in case.

The mound stood near the Gate of Ten Thousand Victories, higher than the decaying city ramparts, more hillock than mound. Those still dwelling in Hou-ming called it The Grave. No more was necessary.

It wore robes of grass and ferns. Hundreds of flowers planted by mourners. Petals of every shade and shape, blue to vermilion to white then back to blue. Why should not The Grave sustain colour and beauty? So much colour and beauty lay within it.

On this exact day, forty-four years earlier, the mound had been constructed, layer by layer. Nearly two hundred thousand corpses, as well as countless dogs and cats. Even, absurdly, caged songbirds and parrots. Proof Prince Arslan's vows were cast in stone. His dead brother's grave mound cast a long, cold shadow over Hou-ming.

Teng and Yun Shu stood to one side as Lady Lu Si knelt at the foot of the mound. Tears glinted on her once lovely cheeks. Her spirit was far away, mingling again with the companions of her youth. All banished too early. Too senselessly. Each day she woke to the insoluble guilt of survival and escape. If being used by dozens of Mongol braves and abandoned as dead, bleeding from every orifice, can be called escape.

Yun Shu glanced at Teng. He was watching the old nun carefully as she knelt and wept. She felt an urge to take his arm and lean against him. Buttress his pity with her warmth.

Lady Lu Si had told her how Teng, when just a boy, noticed her distress on an anniversary of the Great Sacrifice. 'Aunty Lu,' he'd said, 'we shall go to The Grave and tell all those people they are not forgotten. Then I'll cheer you up with a treat!' His treat had been a picnic of wild fruit picked on Monkey Hat Hill. It had given Lady Lu Si heart to face another year. Every year since, he had taken her to visit the ghosts before arranging the best treat he could afford. A tale that moved Yun Shu deeply.

After half an hour, Lady Lu Si rose and dusted down her skirts. When she joined the younger folk they bowed.

'Well,' she said, dabbing her eyes, 'it is done for another year.'

'Not quite,' said Teng.

He led the two nuns in their blue and yellow robes back into the city. Although whole wards and districts still lay abandoned, home to vagrants and creeping vegetation, the area round prince Arslan's palace was busy and populated. Before they entered a fashionable teahouse, Yun Shu cried out, 'Look! Isn't that the actress who was Su Lin in your play? Her voice is sweeter than a nightingale's!'

Teng followed her pointing finger. 'I wonder what business she has in Prince Arslan's palace,' he said. His anxious expression made Yun Shu ask what troubled him. A question he brushed aside.

Yet delightful hours followed. For once Teng had plenty of *cash*. Fine teas were served along with pastries and cakes, sweets and savouries. He drank wine, the ladies more sober refreshments. Yun Shu was presented with a health-giving cordial to counter her sickness.

All the while, he exercised his considerable wit, sharing tales of actors vain as peacocks and theatre-owners miserly as squirrels. Towards the end of the long meal he grew serious.

'Yun Shu,' he said, 'I have a confession. I invited you along not just for your pleasant company. No, it was to play matchmaker. Is that not so, Lady Lu Si?'

The old nun smiled. 'Teng told me,' she said, 'you believe I am angry with you for becoming Abbess. For stealing my position.'

Yun Shu turned accusingly to Teng. 'How could you? I told you in confidence!'

He waved away her upset with a wine cup. 'Hear Lady Lu Si out!'

In a quiet yet firm voice the former Abbess explained the extent of Yun Shu's mistake. 'At first, when you asked for my advice, I always held back. Out of pride, perhaps, and hurt. But it is a long time since that has been my motive. I dread factions among the Serene Ones. I am afraid to weaken your authority as Abbess.'

Yun Shu reached over the table and took the older woman's hand. 'Well I insist on your advice from now on! Let there be no more misunderstandings between us.'

The nuns talked earnestly as they walked back to Monkey Hat Hill, debating how best to avert the Buddhists' claims. Teng followed behind, lost in thought.

Before they parted at the foot of the Hundred Stairs, he said quietly to Yun Shu. 'Come to Deng Mansions at noon tomorrow. There is something I must give you. While I still may.'

She smiled at him. Never had he seemed so handsome. She felt reluctant to leave his company. 'Your treat and your matchmaking have quite restored my health! Thank you.'

'At noon,' he said. 'Time is pressing hard.'

天命

Noon the next day found Yun Shu outside Deng Mansions. A mournful bell tolled across the once great city of Hou-ming.

Teng appeared promptly in the gatehouse, his bow of greeting low. She sensed he was nervous. Not to be outdone, her own bow exceeded his in gravity.

'We are all politeness today,' she remarked, adjusting her robes as she straightened. He watched her closely.

'Surely politeness toward a guest is proper,' he said. Dark shadows ringed his eyes. Under one arm he carried an ox bone scroll case capped at either end with carved jade stoppers. His clothes were creased as though recently slept in.

'Are you unwell?' she said.

'Why do you ask?'

'You don't seem yourself.'

'Come with me. We must talk frankly before Father discovers you. Then you'll *really* see some politeness. You know how he dotes on you.'

He led her across the courtyard to a door hanging on one hinge. Beyond lay a long corridor reeking of mould that terminated in a section of collapsed wall. Beetles and woodlice feasted on the wet wood.

'The last big storm severely damaged this part of the house,' he said, 'and there is no money for rebuilding.'

He led her to the rear gardens of Deng Mansions and the mound sculpted to represent Holy Mount Chang. Teng pointed at the moon-gazing pavilion on top of the false mountain. 'We can talk privately there.'

She nodded and climbed the short flight of steps, taking a seat on a cracked marble bench beneath the domed roof of the pavilion. Moss and creepers covered the floor. Teng leaned against a pillar, tapping the ox bone case against his leg. Yun Shu gazed across the lake at distant mountains.

'Aren't you going to ask why I brought you here?' he said.

'You will tell me eventually. All I need do is wait.'

His laugh was uneasy. 'Do you remember this toy mountain

when we were children? My illustrious grandfather built it. I often think it is like the previous dynasty, faithful to a mountain's appearance but not its essence, namely, strength and power. Also,' he added, wryly, 'there is no dragon on this Mount Chang for you to subdue. Except myself, of course.'

'I remember playing here,' she said, 'but I'm not sure you were ever a wicked dragon. Besides, some dragons are friendly.'

He glanced toward the house as though for unwelcome visitors.

'It was never just the two of us,' he said, 'Hsiung was the third corner of our triangle. Now there's a strange thing! Then I was superior to Hsiung in every way except muscles. His master's son, no less! Now he is the Noble Count of Lingling. Yet I hear his rule was harsh in the port of Chenglingji.'

Yun Shu started at the name. 'Chenglingji? Really?'

'Not only was there a massacre, Hsiung has retained a most disreputable family as the town's rulers. Some refugees report they are more rapacious than when they served the Mongols.'

Her gaze returned to the distant mountains. Images of Dear Uncle's face and tongue required banishment. Always there were dragons to drive away. She could never escape them.

'That is not the reason I asked you to come,' he said, offering the ox bone scroll case, 'it was for this.'

Yun Shu removed the stoppers and pulled out a tightly rolled scroll painted on yellowed silk. Some of the characters were unfamiliar to her.

'Perhaps you can translate it?' she asked.

After he had done so, illuminating the finer legal points, Yun Shu looked at him in puzzlement. 'I'm sure I should thank you,' she said, 'but what use are claims on an estate I shall never see, let alone possess? Especially as you tell me this Wei Valley lies hundreds and hundreds of *li* to the West. Has not the very law that gave this document force been set aside by the Mongols?'

'One day the ancient laws will be restored,' he said, 'and some claims are moral, not legal. You, or a member of your family, might find this document useful. You could use it to reclaim Wei Valley for the Yun clan, for the noble poet Yun Cai's ancestors. Therefore, take good care of it.'

She bowed. 'I am grateful for your kind intention.' Yun Shu met his eyes. 'There was more, Teng, wasn't there?'

She dearly wanted there to be. Over the last year she had come to regard Teng as her closest friend. No, her dearest. His voice seemed always tuneful to her; his words worth hearing. The play of his sensitive eyes like light on a busy stream.

'How well you read my mind!' he said, fidgeting a little. 'You see, I have been foolish and indiscreet. Worse, not entirely honest – though I had my reasons. I meant to make fools of our Mongol friends and their toads.'

'You are in trouble? You must take care!'

'Shensi believes we should flee Hou-ming,' he said. 'He has heard rumours. But it's all right for him! I cannot leave Father. I must stay and hope for the best.'

Yun Shu watched his familiar, proud face and wanted to touch his shoulder, comfort him with the warmth of her hand. So strong was the urge, so improper, she blushed. 'I will help if I can,' she said.

He smiled at her offer. 'Do you never wonder how burdensome great ancestors can be? You are a descendent of Yun Cai, whereas I boast no less a hero than Yueh Fei! And my only benefit is the constant sense of being a disappointment! Yet I suspect Yun Cai would applaud your loveliness of soul.'

At this praise her blush deepened.

'When you blink like that it makes me think of moth wings,' he said, quietly. 'Forgive me, I'm talking nonsense. Yet again, living for the moment. You, Yun Shu, live with eternity in mind. No doubt that is better.'

'No, no.' Yun Shu struggled to reply. 'I had a strange thought yesterday, at the grave mound. Nearly two hundred thousand bodies beneath that robe of earth. I thought, are our bodies to be despised so that one only considers Immortality? Oh, Teng, it is a doubt no Nun of Serene Perfection should have! Yet I feel it here.' She laid a hand across her breast. 'There is a great joy in a simple, natural life.'

He listened with close attention. 'Please explain.'

'I am a woman, Teng. And while Immortality seems as cold and distant as the stars, this woman's body . . .You know what a woman's body can do. Why should I not love? And be loved in return? Why not?'

She feared he would despise her for not mentioning duty. Then it came, a flash of comprehension. Yun Shu understood her daring words. That if Teng offered to marry her, poor though he was and utterly without prospects, she would surrender the position of Abbess. She would descend the Hundred Stairs and dwell in the rotting carcase of Deng Mansions, bringing fresh life to sweep away the decay, raising gardens of happy days, flowers of contented nights.

She understood, as well, that never more would she risk her happiness by assisting Worthy Master Jian. Whatever the consequences, she would drink his elixirs no more, suffer his practises on her body no more.

Yun Shu knew she should rise, thank him decorously for the ox bone scroll and leave. Somehow she could not.

To her surprise he laughed. More a chuckle of relief. 'So that is how you feel.' Again he chuckled. '*Those* are your innermost feelings! I thought you cared only for your duty as Abbess! Dearest Yun Shu, I must tell you that I share . . .'

'Teng! What is this?'

They turned in surprise. At the foot of the miniature mountain stood Deng Nan-shi, leaning on his stick. The old man peered up at them. 'Teng, why do you entertain our Honoured Guest alone?' he demanded. 'Did you not think of telling me she is here?'

Teng almost ground his teeth with vexation and frustration. He shot her an imploring glance. She smiled in reply.

It did not matter their conversation had been delayed.

Nothing mattered now. She felt sure of him. Of his intentions. His own innermost feelings. Her doubts and anxieties resolved by the simple word *share*.

'Come, Yun Shu,' commanded Deng Nan-shi, 'I insist you take tea with me in the library.'

Wearing an expression of filial resignation, Teng followed her down the steps of the mound. They returned to the house, Yun Shu speaking gaily of inconsequential things that seemed to her, somehow, more profound than a thousand sutras or obscure prayers or mantras. Just as a puddle may reflect enormities of cloud and sun and sky.

twenty-five

天命

The next day, summer's languor and waves of monsoon changed suddenly to autumn. Or so it seemed to Teng. Yet he feared change. For decades he and Father had dodged the threats around them, defying the Mongols' authority by clinging to Deng Mansions. The old scholar's insistence on teaching the Five Classics was a subtle rebellion. Now their luck had drained away, except Teng could not really blame misfortune, just his own poor judgement – and vanity.

He had believed Ying-ge was too besotted with him to ever betray his secrets. Yet it was a long time since he had patronised her boudoir. According to Shensi, she had been seen entering Salt Minister Gui's private residence: a fact that darkened his suspicions.

That morning, a hot breeze arose on Six-Hundred-*li* Lake, making loose shutters rattle and leaves flurry. All afternoon Teng loitered in the gatehouse or paced before the library where Deng Nan-shi rested on his divan, having dismissed his classes early. The old scholar rarely ate these days, nourishing himself upon tea and memories.

Teng hoped Yun Shu might find an excuse to conclude their conversation. His mind swirled with little else. He felt sure Deng Nan-shi would approve and commission a suitable matchmaker. Yet he hesitated before mentioning his plan to the old man. After all, such decisions belonged to parents not children.

Towards dusk Teng entered the library and found his father awake, peering at fading light through the window. Teng bowed low then adjusted the old man's blankets. Deng Nan-shi watched him closely.

'I was remembering your dear mother,' he said. 'The dimming light often summons her to my mind. Even though she came from a more shadowy family than us Dengs, she shone with inner brightness.'

Teng wondered if his father had guessed his intentions towards Yun Shu.

'Are you comfortable now?' asked Teng.

'Yes.'

Nervously rubbing forefinger and thumb, Teng listened to the wind. The trees of Monkey Hat Hill swayed and whispered like a sea of leaves.

'You're afraid of something,' remarked Deng Nan-shi. 'What is it?'

Teng laughed uneasily. 'Just your reproaches, Father! As ever.'

'Does First Son deserve reproaches?'

'I fear my actions may have put you in danger.'

Deng Nan-shi's gaunt forehead puckered into a maze of lines.

'Do not fear for my sake,' he said, 'I do not matter. You are the last Deng, the final hope of our ancestors. Who else will carry the family rites into the future? If you are in danger, look to your own safety, not mine.' Deng Nan-shi's expression hardened. 'I do not care about . . .'

Teng never learned what his father did not care about. At that moment the doors of the library were thrown open. Shensi entered in travelling clothes and boots, a sack on his back, sword at his side. Ignoring Deng Nan-shi, he gestured impatiently to his friend: 'Quickly! We must talk.'

In the courtyard wind moaned and clouds scudded across a red sunset. Waves broke at the foot of the cliff.

'What is it?' asked Teng.

'No more time,' said Shensi. 'We must go at once.'

For a moment Teng hesitated. He could soon gather what remained of his *cash*, a few clothes . . . His glance crept back to the library.

'You go, Shensi,' he said, 'you know why I must stay.'

The tomb-finder nodded. 'I have no such obligations. Goodbye then.'

With that he hurried across the courtyard to the gatehouse and disappeared. Teng watched him leave with a burdened heart. Though he and Shensi were opposites in every way, for years adversity had bound them together. And Teng detected more wisdom in Shensi's prolonged silences than hours of garrulous talk from his actor-friends in the theatre district. More loyalty, as well. Now they might never meet again.

A moment later Shensi was back, only this time running. 'They're waiting outside!' he shouted, charging down a colonnade to the gardens. Teng wondered whether to fetch his sword. Before he could decide a dozen soldiers rushed into the courtyard, just in time to see Shensi vanishing.

'After him!' bellowed an officer. A squad pursued the fugitive, swords drawn.

More soldiers entered the weed-choked courtyard, followed by two ornately carved palanquins carried by barefoot servants. Torches were lit and passed round the troops as Teng waited on the library steps. He did not doubt the identity of the men concealed in the palanquins. Childhood fears returned with new force – along with the image of three puppies hurled off a cliff, spinning and scrabbling as they fell. Salt Minister Gui and Golden Lotus stepped out.

The concubine wore a red, green and turquoise huntress's outfit, complete with shiny boots and a short whip. Golden Lotus's femininity had scarcely declined since Teng first saw him sixteen years earlier. Above all, his tiny lotus feet and bustling little steps remained the same. One could not tell his *yin* from his *yang*.

Salt Minister Gui struggled out of the narrow palanquin like a clumsy bear confined in a box. He seemed distracted, an abacus in his large hands. He glanced round sleepily until he caught sight of Teng on the library steps. Then he frowned and pointed: 'That one!' Teng offered no resistance as two soldiers seized his arms.

'Search every room,' ordered the Salt Minister. 'Fetch anything valuable.'

Teng stirred. 'There is no need for that,' he said, 'I surrender willingly. Take me to the judge.'

By now Gui had approached. He pointed at him with an odd jabbing motion. A vein on his forehead bulged. He breathed heavily.

'Hit this one!' he managed. 'Yes! Hit!'

Teng's stomach took the blow. He doubled over, tottered, gasped for air.

'The library!' commanded Gui. 'Into there with him.'

The Salt Minister followed his soldiers into the long room lined with cases and shelves. Here he appeared to forget Teng's existence, let alone that of Deng Nan-shi who had struggled up from the divan and stood shivering, blankets round his ankles. 'Ah!' chuckled Gui, 'just as I thought.' Teng watched the broad, awkward man amble to the nearest shelf, muttering as he inspected its contents: 'G-get the secretary, I must have an inventory . . . Oldest first, yes, then according to value.' Gui produced his abacus and clicked the beads with astonishing rapidity.

Teng noticed a disconcerting reminder of Yun Shu in her father's face – for his eyelashes fluttered as he worked the abacus.

'Your Honour!' broke in Deng Nan-shi, having mastered a coughing fit. 'This is an unusual way to enter my house.'

If Gui heard he gave no sign. Shoving past the hunchbacked scholar he picked up a musty old volume of poetry. Deciding it was valueless he tossed it to the floor.

'Where are the pictures?' he asked. 'Scrolls, pictures? Statues of horses or holy b-books of the B-buddha?'

Deng Nan-shi raised a contemptuous eyebrow. 'Are you robbing us?'

At this the Salt Minister froze. His thick finger raised to jab again, only this time at the old man. Gui turned to the nearest soldier and muttered: 'Hit!' Just as the soldier's burly arm swung Teng rushed forward. The blow knocked him sideways. Blood dripped from his torn lip. The library span wildly.

'Enough!' said Gui. 'Do not call *me* a robber, you old b-brigand! Your son has treated me . . . cheated me . . . Hit!' he cried.

Another blow. Teng staggered comically, keening and clutching his chest. Golden Lotus's rouged lips twitched.

'This Yueh Fei dog, this *rebel* has tricked me out of thousands,' continued Gui. 'I'll have every *cash* coin b-back!'

Deng Nan-shi glanced at Teng in alarm. His son lay crumpled on the floor, breath whooping. 'Can you be sure?' he asked. 'There must be a trial before punishment. Where is the judge?'

'Hah!' exclaimed Golden Lotus. 'No need for a trial! Your son's concubine, Ying-ge, told us everything! A fraud to trick the Excellent Gui's noble friends!'

To Deng Nan-shi's surprise the Salt Minister grew distracted again and muttered as he flicked through a large volume of old paintings depicting fishermen on mountain lakes: 'How odd that people think me g-greedy!' he mumbled. 'How absurd people are! My sons are b-both at the Great Khan's court! Of course they need gold, silver. People do not try to understand. Yet I am more honest than other officials.'

'If you have been wronged, we shall recompense you,' interrupted Deng Nan-shi. 'We shall pay twice your losses.

No, three times! Then you can send plenty to your sons.'

The Salt Minister did not listen. His abacus clicked furiously. It was Golden Lotus who replied: 'Honourable Gui has already decided how to be paid. All this!' Golden Lotus's arms swept wide in a gesture encompassing the entire library. 'All this now belongs to Gui!'

For a long moment Teng and Deng Nan-shi stared aghast. To his son's amazement, the old scholar nodded. 'Yes, take it! Take it all! Only set my son free.'

'Oh, we will take it,' said Golden Lotus in his singsong voice, producing a long ivory fan that opened with a click. Daintily he wafted, stirring a stray lock of hair. Outside a greater wind shook the ancient trees of Monkey Hat Hill.

Meanwhile Gui continued to assess his gains, issuing precise instructions to clerks who had entered with writing materials and ledgers. Golden Lotus came over to Deng Nan-shi so he could whisper in his ear unheard.

'We cannot free your son,' he murmured. 'What if he told our customers that the paintings they paid so much for are forgeries?'

Before Deng Nan-shi could protest, the library doors opened. Lanterns flickered. The soldiers sent to pursue Shensi had returned.

'The other rebel escaped,' reported one. 'We think he fled over the cliff.'

The officer in charge glanced nervously at the Salt Minister. Fortunately the abacus was still calculating profit and loss, too busy for Shensi.

'He is dead,' declared the officer. 'Good work.' He turned to his superior. 'Your Excellency, shall I also arrest the old . . .' But Gui had already begun to leave, followed by Golden Lotus on his shuffling little feet. The officer shrugged. 'Take this rebel but leave the old man.'

Though Deng Nan-shi remonstrated, it was no use. Teng was dragged into the courtyard and stripped of his new silk clothes.

Meanwhile, servants collected every scrap of paper, scroll and ancient volume in the library, every painting and print, filling wooden crates under the direction of the clerks. A large cart hauled by oxen had been driven into the courtyard, overseen by a Salt Bureau official. What ensued was efficient and swift. Within two hours Teng was prodded down Monkey Hat Hill, his neck weighed by a huge wooden yoke and chain, stumbling behind the ox cart. It carried three centuries of the Deng clan's elegant taste, passion, wisdom, acquisitiveness and – in the end – frailty.

天命

What followed may have been an accident. Perhaps a soldier cast aside his burning torch as he left. Perhaps secret orders had been issued by the Salt Minister. Or even by Golden Lotus. Perhaps it was fate, insisting the past, however glorious, was dead. A space must be cleared for something new that would, in its turn, be replaced. Yet as Deng Nan-shi examined the empty shelves of Deng Library, tears running down his grizzled cheeks, desperate with plans to bribe the judge when Teng came to trial, he caught a scent of smoke. His old ears detected an unfamiliar rumble.

An entire wing of Deng Mansions was ablaze. A loud crash was followed by swarms of angry sparks as roof beams collapsed. The old man stumbled towards the well for a bucket of water. Then the wind changed direction and enveloped him in smoke. Flames danced and skipped like gleeful devils, leaping from roof to roof. Empty family apartments that once echoed with voices and gossip and ambition crumbled in on themselves. Kitchens where servants cooked three centuries' harvests became giant ovens preparing a last banquet of ruin. Corridors raced with fire rather than heedless, running children. Everything burned, even Deng Mansions' looted heart, the ancient library building where generations of scholars had come to study and learn. Finally the great reception hall converted into a classroom.

The ancient complex of buildings blazed on Monkey Hat Hill, visible from the city below. Some pointed in alarm. Others laughed to see the Dengs destroyed at long last. A crowd from nearby wards and Cloud Abode Monastery hurried to put out the fire but were too late. Two of Deng Nan-shi's grown-up pupils braved the flames, wet scarves tied round their mouths, emerging from the smoke with the scholar's limp body.

Deng Mansions burned through the night. Only rectangles of blackened, smouldering beams and ash remained, over-looked by a peculiar mound shaped like Holy Mount Chang. A battered moon-gazing pavilion perched on it, unscathed by the inferno.

twenty-six

天命

Months later, two men – the first short, with an affable smile, the other broad as a village bully – bowed themselves out of the Noble Count of Lingling's audience chamber.

'Ensure refreshments are provided for these gentlemen,' ordered Hsiung from his throne.

Chao and Hua, their silks gaudier than ever since the fall of Chenglingji, looked suitably grateful for this mark of favour. Once they had gone, Hsiung instructed the other servants to follow, so only Chancellor Liu Shui remained. Both sat in silence, considering the spies' news.

It was noon and the broad window shutters were wide open, revealing all the glory of Holy Mount Chang, its slopes and many shrines bright in the crisp winter light. Within the audience chamber, lesser symbols of power – bronze offering tripods and carved friezes depicting Yueh Fei's immortal deeds – also caught the pale sun.

Hsiung sighed heavily and removed a black scholar's hat with long earflaps in the style of the previous dynasty. 'I should have expected it,' he muttered. 'I should have offered them my protection here.'

Liu Shui pursed his wet, red lips. 'They would not have come,' he said. 'It was their fate, perhaps. But to perish in such a way, that was unexpected.'

Rising from the chair, Hsiung threw down the hat and paced before the window. 'I suspect murder,' he said. 'And when the time comes, those responsible shall pay with their lives. And the lives of their families to the third generation!'

'Robbery certainly occurred,' mused Liu Shui. 'How else are we to explain the confiscation of Deng Library, a most valuable collection? Not least because it contains many unique papers relating to our great inspiration, Yueh Fei. I shall make enquiries about the whereabouts of those documents. Such artefacts must not remain in the hands of Salt Minister Gui.'

'I say it was murder!' exclaimed Hsiung.

Again Liu Shui pursed his lips. 'Possibly. Probably. One must not jump to conclusions. That is how injustices occur that rob the wise ruler of his integrity before Heaven.'

'How else can Teng's death be explained?'

'You heard the spies, Your Highness, he perished in the fire. The question is, was it started deliberately? Accidents are not murder.'

As usual Hsiung felt his rage deflate under the scrutiny of Liu Shui's arguments.

'At least my old master escaped,' he said. 'Hua believes he is treated well at Cloud Abode Monastery. I shall send a box of silver for his maintenance.'

Liu Shui nodded. 'It shall be arranged, Your Highness. Now to the other matter they raised.'

Picking up his hat, Hsiung resumed his seat on the throne. 'You refer to the transfer of troops?'

'Yes, Noble Count.'

Chao and Hua reported the Mongols had halved their garrison in the Salt Pans. Instantly Hsiung had realised that revenge, complete and perfect revenge, lay within his grasp. Imagining such a possibility, he forgot the Dengs. There were enough bitter reasons of his own to seize the Salt Pans without using their fate as a pretext.

'With my new fleet I could fall on them like a hawk! Then

the Salt Pans would be ours and, with them, such revenue! Ah, that would be power, Liu Shui. The Mongols would fear me then! And any who have mistreated the slaves there will feel the harsh cut of their own whips.'

The Noble Count's chancellor nodded: 'They appear to have made a foolish blunder.'

'Oh yes,' said Hsiung, 'according to the Zhongs in Chenglingji, the Salt Pans have not been so poorly defended since the last dynasty fell.'

'Which is all very strange.' Liu Shui shifted huge buttocks in his chair, a lower, plainer seat than the Count's. 'It seems rather too tempting, rather too convenient. Perhaps it is a trap.'

'There is such a thing as good fortune,' protested Hsiung. 'One must not always be suspicious.'

'Perhaps. Assuming you capture the Salt Pans, Noble Count, what then? For the first time the Imperial authorities in the capital would really take note of us. They would be forced to send a large force to crush you. The salt monopoly is vital to them.'

Hsiung put the hat back on his head, adjusting the earflaps so they pointed defiantly upwards. 'Good! Then we can test my new fleet.'

'A fleet, Noble Count, that is untrained and lacks experienced officers. What would be the consequence of its loss?'

Now Liu Shui had his ruler's full attention.

'Surprise is a powerful weapon in war,' Hsiung countered, 'as is courage. But do not be alarmed, Liu Shui, I will take to heart your wise warnings.'

'Please do,' said the Chancellor, blandly. 'And, Your Highness, please ensure your bodyguard are always close. Your exploits at Chenglingji have earned you many enemies.'

'You are like a hen fretting for its chick,' said Hsiung.

'Hens are known to drive away evil spirits,' pointed out Liu Shui. Then he, too, bowed himself out of the audience chamber, leaving the Noble Count alone.

Shadows shifted. Hsiung remembered Teng as a boy, their games, alliances, quarrels. It seemed he had possessed no other friend since, at least, not of his own age or who shared so deep a bond. The audience chamber pooled with dark corners. Clouds advanced over the winter sun. Hsiung recollected Chao and Hua's more pleasant piece of information – and how it might offer a temporary cure for loneliness.

天命

All day, a chamber in the Noble Count of Lingling's palace was prepared for a special entertainment. It involved a private performance by a notable actress from Hou-ming who happened to be in Lingling to visit the shrines. She also happened to have travelled under the protection of two merchants named Chao and Hua.

The lady in question applied much energy and enthusiasm to her preparations. Musicians were summoned from the town and auditioned. Several were rejected before she declared herself satisfied. Then came the matter of a suitable banquet while the entertainments unfolded, including those of the 'looking at flowers and buying willows' variety. In short, a delightful evening was planned for the Noble Count's pleasure.

Once the many preparations were complete – not least the lady's make-up and tantalising outfits – she sprawled on a divan, fanning herself with a vacant expression on her pretty young face. In this pose Chao and Hua found her, having slipped past while the maids arranged their own hair.

'Ying-ge!' called a knowing voice. 'Idling, are we?'

She sat upright with a start. Her long-lashed eyes narrowed and her mouth – described by a recent admirer as resembling a carp's – pouted angrily.

'It is just you!' she said, fanning herself with extra vigour. 'What do you want?'

'To see all is in readiness for the Noble Count,' said Hua. 'What else?'

'With you, it could be anything.'

The understanding between them was revealed by the way she glanced sideways at him. Chao, who knew all about it, chuckled coarsely.

'Now, you two!' he warned. 'Hands to the oars.'

Ying-ge rolled her pretty eyes. 'Is it a large oar?' she asked, sweetly.

'You can tell me later,' said Hua. 'Now remember what we discussed.'

She hid a yawn behind her fan.

'How can I forget when you say it so often?'

Hua grinned without mirth.

'Well, that's good then,' he declared, stealing a sugared plum meant for the Noble Count on his way out.

Hsiung's gloom persisted over the afternoon. He tried to dispel it through intense sword practise with a local master and four hundred arrows discharged at targets dragged on wheels. At least his exertions provoked an appetite. Hsiung donned fresh silks then proceeded to the Chamber of Willow Music – as he was begged to refer to it by a demure maid who accosted him on the way.

On entering he frowned. The plain room had been transformed by rolls of hanging gauze, especially round a large bed at the rear. A cushioned chair and low tables laden with fine bowls stood before it – everything necessary for a banquet. A space had been cleared at the foot of the table, marked out by silk curtains. Behind these, musicians waited on stools, watched by Hsiung's bodyguards – evidently placed there by Liu Shui. As the Noble Count entered they struck up a stirring, yet subtle tune on pi-pa, ch'in, flute and drum. A girl in neat red and green silks appeared, fluttering on tiny lotus feet. She bowed deeply to her guest.

'I am Ying-ge,' she said, smiling as her face turned gently from side to side like a flower in a gentle breeze. 'Will you dine, Noble Count, until I perform for your pleasure?'

Hsiung could think of no other response than a graceless grunt. As soon as he was seated, a line of servants appeared with dishes – a hot soup of pork and pickles, omelette with meat sauce, duck and slivers of toasted almonds, beef shredded with dried mushrooms, bamboo shoots and fried frog legs. Finally his favourite: flower kidneys with hot sauce. As he dined Hsiung remembered the simple meals he and Teng enjoyed in Deng Mansions. A bowl of millet had been a feast to them. And now Teng would eat no more. Hsiung had seen too many fire-shrivelled corpses not to know what must remain of his old friend. Between each dish he drank bowls of fine wine to suppress melancholy. Finally he belched and looked up, for the music had stopped. Ying-ge knelt before him, her forehead touching the floor while her back remained perfectly straight.

'The Noble Count appears sad,' she said, glancing up at him with a concerned expression. 'Is His Highness displeased with my arrangements?'

'No. It is just that I learned of a friend's death today.' Hsiung frowned, surprised by himself. The revelation emerged so easily. At first he was afraid to have shared so much. But her face was kindly, so he added: 'A friend from when I was a boy.'

'Ah,' said Ying-ge. She brightened tentatively. 'Shall I sing happy songs to make you happy?'

His expression offered no encouragement either way.

'Yes, I *shall*,' she said. 'With your permission. But only after I have performed very sad songs to honour your dear friend.'

Her first was from the popular play, *The Soul of Chen-nu Flees Her Body*:

> *Pictures of spring stir my feelings,*
> *Spray upon spray of green willows,*

The briefest brush of wooing swallows,
Bees in pairs, golden orioles,
Each longs one for the other.
I know the Jade Emperor commends
Twoness – as a model for all mankind.

It was a shock for Hsiung to realise he was weeping. He, who never cried! Never showed weakness! No, he must stop now, this would not do. Ying-ge realised the effect of her song and, after hurried instructions to the musicians, began another:

One stroke and the world's glories are gone:
Leaves of autumn in a cloud of dust.
Spring, summer, autumn, winter revolving:
Leaves of autumn in a cloud of dust.

Hsiung brushed away a last tear.

'My friend once recited a verse like that. Perhaps it was the same one. Even as a boy he was a scholar, you see, whereas I . . .' Hsiung drained a full cup. 'Now play your happy songs,' he commanded. 'I want to smile! To laugh!'

But he looked at her with a sense of wonder. She had brought him tears, stirred emotions he thought dead in his soul. He would always be grateful to her for that. And her graceful beauty fascinated him.

Towards midnight they lay on silken sheets, entwined in each other's limbs. Everything about Ying-ge delighted him. She seemed so curious about his life and all he longed to become.

'So you will sacrifice at the altars on Holy Mount Chang in a fortnight's time?' she asked, admiringly. 'Why, you are like an emperor!'

Hsiung chuckled and pulled her closer. He was blissfully drunk, his body glowing. 'You sound like Liu Shui! Oh, he has many rites planned. Even an hour praying by myself in the

341

Buddha Maitreya's sacred caves. Afterwards I will emerge reborn.'

Prompted by her steady interest, he told her of the ritual, all the while resting his head on her soft, yet firm, mounds. How fine it was to be the Noble Count of Lingling! Would so fine and beautiful a lady have anything to do with him otherwise?

Before they fell asleep she asked, as though moved by a sudden thought: 'What was the name of your friend?'

'Which friend?' he replied, dreamily.

'The dead scholar you told me about.'

'Oh, Teng. Deng Teng. Poor fellow.'

He began to snore. Beside him, Ying-ge's limbs stiffened and she stared intently into the darkness.

天命

Hsiung had heard this particular lesson many times before. If not from Liu Shui then, long ago, from his old master Deng Nan-shi in distant Hou-ming. Now, standing in Precious Forest Temple on Mount Chang, Hsiung stifled a yawn.

'Thus,' concluded Liu Shui, 'the Sons of Heaven regulate Time and Space through the Proper Rites. Without this service the seas would boil and mountains crumble.'

'I am not the Son of Heaven,' pointed out Hsiung.

'True, but you have been granted the Mandate of Heaven in Lingling County – and other places besides. It is surely significant your palace overlooks one of the sacred mountains upon which Heaven itself rests?'

Hsiung was holding a large hat with seven tassels upon which heavy jade charms hung. Liu Shui wished him to wear this outlandish headgear for a whole night, calling it a Hat of Communication with Heaven.'

'There is one reason I agreed to this,' grumbled Hsiung, 'and that reason still holds. After so many years of poor harvests I must do everything in my power to aid the people.'

This answer pleased Liu Shui deeply, for his Buddha-like smile – so often absent of late – returned wider than ever. The Chancellor bowed very low.

'Thus speaks one worthy of the Mandate of Heaven,' he said. 'Maintain yourself in purity all night and you shall be called upon at dawn.'

It was a long night in the shrine room of Precious Forest Temple, slumped in front of the statues on a coarse hemp mat. Dozens of Hsiung's 'bravest and best' patrolled the courtyard and walls, for Liu Shui was alarmed by reports from his spies that the Mongol court wished to assassinate the Noble Count in revenge for the loss of their Salt Fleet. Neither food nor wine were permitted. Nor was company of any kind and this lack troubled Hsiung more than an empty stomach. His hunger was very specific.

In the weeks since Actress Ying-ge's arrival he had summoned her more and more frequently; likewise his presents to her had increased in generosity, for he hoped to persuade her to remain in Lingling as his concubine after her pilgrimage to Holy Mount Chang was complete. Maddeningly, she would only pout in reply and pretend to look serious, saying: 'Noble Count, that was not why I came here!' or 'What of my dear parents in Hou-ming? I must return and ask their permission.' The more she resisted his suggestions, the more he wanted her.

Towards dawn a loud gong resounded through Precious Forest Temple and Hsiung rose reluctantly. Now he must place himself on display. Straightening his Hat of Communication with Heaven, he strode to the entrance and slid open the doors.

The courtyard beyond was crammed with people: priests, monks, soldiers and officials from Liu Shui's growing secretariat. Behind them came lines of townsfolk from Lingling and peasants drawn to the luck-bringing festival from hamlets and villages. At the sight of the Noble Count, the front ranks fell to their knees, followed by those behind. Hsiung surveyed the people in the aloof manner Liu Shui had advised. A deep silence reigned in the courtyard.

Then the Noble Count descended to the group of priests, who rose, bowing and chanting continuously. They cleared a path through the crowd, out of the temple complex and onto the Holy Mount itself. Here a newly-built road climbed to a specially constructed altar above the temple. Soldiers from the Guards lined the way with flaring pine torches. Hundreds of lights danced on the dark hillside, mirroring the apparent jumble of constellations above. Glancing back, Hsiung saw a red dawn behind the eastern hills.

With Liu Shui at his side he climbed the cinder road. Still no one spoke or sang. The only noise was the steady chant of the priests, Daoist and Buddhist, and the wind against the mountain. At the top he found more priests sacrificing thrice-blessed cocks and hens on a side altar to deter demons. On the main altar, decorated with a carved relief of the Emperors of the Five Colours, Hsiung found a scroll designed to aid germination of all seeds presently sleeping in the earth. He picked it up and pretended to read. Liu Shui had taught him the supplication by rote yet Hsiung caught himself mumbling as whole phrases fled his mind. He felt light-headed from hunger. Giving up, he stood with his head bowed, apparently in profound communion with the Jade Emperor. A sumptuous breakfast filled his imagination.

When he turned, Hsiung found the hillside covered with silent, kneeling people, peering up at his silhouette and golden, silken robes, his immense many-brimmed hat. As Liu Shui had instructed, he prostrated himself one more time towards the west and retraced his steps. Cheering began. Hsiung suspected Liu Shui's influence, for the first to cheer were the officials in their uniforms, but soon hundreds of others joined in.

His heart and head grew dizzy at their enthusiasm. Hsiung floated down the hillside to the final part of the rite. He must now enter a series of caverns carved into a cliff by a Buddhist

Immortal's prayers, long ago in the Han Dynasty. Only when Hsiung had prayed there by himself for an hour could he proceed to breakfast.

Hsiung climbed the cliff and entered the low doorway of the shrine. The crowd milled expectantly on the slopes below. A door closed behind him, shutting out the dawn's feeble light. Yet the cavern was bright, illuminated by dozens of candles and lamps smoking faintly.

As Hsiung stepped deeper into the sacred network of caverns he felt an odd unease and glanced round. Liu Shui's intention had been for the people to see he prayed alone, thus convincing them of his sincerity and influence with Heaven. Hsiung sniffed the air suspiciously. Was that the echo of a footfall? Perhaps Liu Shui had instructed a priest to be at hand.

So Hsiung advanced deeper into the maze of caves, seeking the gigantic statue of the Buddha where he must pray. Candles became less frequent, shadows wider and deeper. Carved stone friezes depicted figures enduring the torments of hell, their mouths an eternal scream, the very sinews of their faces knotted in agony. Again Hsiung paused. A shuffle behind him? Or did it come from the cavern ahead? Everything was different here. Perhaps it had been his own footstep echoing. Hsiung examined the carved sinner in hell, wishing he had brought a sword, even a knife – though using edged weapons was a sin in itself. It was said killing a single fly cost a day of torment in hell.

Cautiously now, Hsiung advanced down a narrow corridor until he came to a large chamber hollowed from the rock. Here, too, were many candles clustered round a huge statue of the cross-legged Buddha, his smile beatific and hands raised palm upwards. The rest of the room was obscured by deep shadows. Hsiung felt his back prickle but did not look round. He was sure now. Someone far less sublime than the Buddha was in the caves. Maybe more than one.

He bowed deeply to the statue, as though gripped by piety, in the process removing the heavy Hat Of Communication With Heaven. His hands closed over two of the large, solid carved jade charms dangling from strings. He coughed loudly to mask the tearing sound as they came free. Now he held the hat in one hand and jade weights in the other.

Rising, Hsiung glanced round for other useful objects. There was a solid wooden reading stand near the Buddha's statue. Abandoning all pretence, he dashed over to this flimsy shield and stood behind it, looking around. If no one else was there, no one would witness his fear. For a long moment it seemed he had made a fool of himself before the Buddha's smiling face. Then a figure dressed in black stepped silently from the shadows, a long sword in his hand. On the other side of the cavern another appeared with a thick bamboo stabbing spear and an axe in his belt.

Hsiung turned to make a dash for the entrance but a third man blocked his way, a curved short sword in each hand. Their faces were covered by scarves to reveal only eyes and tousled hair. Hsiung licked his lips.

'If you tell me who hired you I shall spare you,' he said.

His voice rolled and echoed round the stone walls. The three men examined him. Hsiung noted that the spear was poised, balanced in the second assassin's hand as though ready to throw. He leaned closer to the reading stand so it covered his chest.

'If you attack me before the Buddha's statue you will suffer torments in hell,' he said. 'Tell me who hired you and I will permit you to leave unharmed.'

He hoped for signs of uncertainty, weakness; two of the men remained utterly impassive but the spearman crouched nervously – he must be the first target. The middle assassin waved a forefinger at his companions and they advanced, step by step, over the sand-covered floor of the cavern. Hsiung gripped the hat and, with a maniacal bellow, hurled one of the jade weights at the spearman's exposed face. So unexpected was his attack the assassins halted, instinctively raising their weapons to parry. The jade charm hit the spearman's face below the eye, instantly drawing blood. As Hsiung had hoped, the man reacted by reflex, throwing the spear. It struck the reading stand with an echoing thud and hung there quivering. Hsiung took possession of it.

The four men in the cave went still, assessing each other. Hsiung kept hold of the hat in one hand and gripped the short bamboo spear in the other, ready for thrusting. Its former owner produced a large, curved axe from his belt.

Hsiung's glance flickered casually over the swordsman. That was the weapon he wanted, the weapon he loved best. He had never liked spears. Hsiung felt the first dance of dark lights and laughed oddly. The noise echoed round the wide cavern. Of course, the chickens and cocks on the altar had not been enough to satisfy the thirsty earth! Always there must be sacrifices. He thought of Teng, screaming in agony, trapped in the burning buildings of Deng Mansions, the innocent world of boyhood melting like human flesh and fat in the flames . . . Oh, there must be a sacrifice to renew the seeds.

So strange was his laughter the assassins paused to glance round. A costly temerity. In that moment Hsiung leaped forward and thrust the spear into the swordsman's stomach, twisting it furiously as he raised the hat to fend off an impulsive blow from a short sword. Then he ducked round the toppling swordsman and seized his weapon, shoving the skewered man so he received an axe blow intended for Hsiung's head. It struck dead flesh, splitting open the skull. A useless blow, and one never repeated, for Hsiung felt a black joy grip his soul as the dark lights danced and skipped . . .

When he became aware of himself the axe man lay face down, his head attached to its neck by a fold of skin, a dark pool spreading over the sand-strewn floor. Hsiung's arm bore a gash that was dripping red.

Panting, he located his third opponent. The assassin was backing away, clutching a wound on his chest, appalled by the sudden calamity that had befallen his comrades. Hsiung followed, frowning to himself. He knew it was vital to keep this one alive. How else would he find out who had sent them to kill him? But he could feel his breath quicken, his frown becoming an angry glare. How confident they had been! How contemptuous! Three armed men against one with just bare hands for a weapon!

The assassin's nerve failed and he fled down the passage. Hsiung leaped after him with a bellow of triumph. His long sword slashed repeatedly at the man's legs so that he tumbled head over heels onto the carved stone frieze of Hell, tendons torn open. In the semi-darkness Hsiung kicked away the short swords. The assassin was cowering, shielding his head with an arm. Was he saying something? Hsiung could not tell, did not hear. As the dark lights directed, he hauled up the fallen man by his hair and began to rub his face against the rough surface of the frieze. 'Who sent you? How did you know I would be here? Who betrayed me? Who? Who?' His shouts echoed down the corridor and through caverns lit by countless candles. Hsiung ground the face back and forth, back and forth, grating it against the nose and brow of a stone sinner in Hell until his hands grew wet and slippery and snapping noises woke him from his black dream.

Hsiung shrank back in horror. A faint gleam from the cavern revealed the assassin's maimed, desecrated face, the holy frieze shiny with his blood. What had he done? And in the Buddha's shrine! What karma must fall upon him for such gross profanity? For a long while Hsiung stared at the carved sinner's tormented expression. Images of men he had killed on Hornets' Nest's behalf – women and children, too – assumed the carved sinner's features, before vanishing, only to be replaced by another. And another. Finally by a vision of his own screaming, contorted face.

* * *

When Liu Shui found him kneeling before the statue of the Buddha, Hsiung turned to his chancellor with a feverish expression.

'They have damned my soul! They attacked me here! I have nothing left to lose. Yet I had to defend myself, Liu Shui! I had no choice. I tell you, we shall seize the Salt Pans and make them suffer, too!'

Liu Shui bowed fearfully, afraid to look at the maimed corpses of the assassins, lest the taint infect his own rebirth.

Part Four

Salt Pans and Inner Cauldrons

Hou-ming City, Central China.
Spring, 1322

twenty-seven

天命

'Abbess Yun Shu! If there is no danger to Cloud Abode Monastery, why is the Worthy Master asking this of us?'

Lady Lu Si's question was far from serene. The other senior nuns murmured excitedly – all except for Earth Peace, who had nodded off in her special chair.

The rest knelt on the flagstones of a large, octagonal star observatory where generations of *sanren* had gathered each year to discuss the monastery's preparations for the *qingming* spring festival. From this high platform beside the cliffs of Monkey Hat Hill one could see far across the lake, as well as benefit from favourable breezes.

Yun Shu certainly needed a strong wind to guide her reply to Lady Lu Si's question. Worthy Master Jian had instructed her what to say if challenged by the other nuns. Those arguments, persuasive when uttered in his deep, confident voice, jumbled in Yun Shu's mind. Teng had warned her that the Worthy Master was not to be trusted. Right now, neither were thoughts of Teng. They almost always provoked tears.

'I can only repeat his assurances,' she mumbled, thinking of Teng despite her intention to concentrate on the matter at hand.

Jade Perfected frowned. 'This makes no sense, Abbess! Master Jian says we need fear nothing. Very well, I am reassured. Then he requires us to pack up everything of value in our dear, blessed monastery. Pack it up and have it carried to Golden Bright Temple so he can protect it.'

'Furthermore,' broke in Lady Lu Si, 'removing our valuables creates an impression the Daoist Council is preparing to surrender Cloud Abode Monastery to the Buddhists.'

'A most unfortunate impression!' echoed Gold Immortal in her high, fluty voice.

'An impression that we are weak,' added Lady Lu Si, 'that our resolve lacks a centre.'

'Yet is not weakness the ultimate strength?' ventured Jade Perfected.

Yun Shu recollected the final argument Worthy Master Jian had instructed her to use: 'That is why the Daoist Council is asking this of us,' she replied.

'How so?' asked Jade Perfected.

'Because,' said Yun Shu, 'removing our valuables shows Prince Arslan we will obey whatever he decrees.'

A lengthy silence followed. Yun Shu looked round the *sanren*. All were considering her words. She doubted any were satisfied, least of all herself. Doddery old Earth Peace began to snore.

'Will it not indicate to Prince Arslan that we anticipate he will transfer our beloved monastery to the foreign Buddhists?' asked Jade Perfected. 'That we are amenable to such a thing?'

'Worthy Master Jian believes it demonstrates our loyalty,' said Yun Shu. 'There is much I do not understand about his reasoning. But I am certain of one thing: he will never allow Cloud Abode Monastery to pass from the Nuns of Serene Perfection. It would be unthinkable.'

Faith must be their final assurance. Even to her it sounded feeble. The other nuns exchanged dubious glances. Three Simplicities cleared her throat.

'Abbess Yun Shu,' she said, 'no wonder you have such confidence in the Worthy Master. You participate so intimately in his rites. Only you know how deep he goes when conducting his ceremonies with you. I imagine it is all very satisfying. If only one could watch!'

Yun Shu's blush deepened. She rose angrily. 'This decision was not made by me but the entire Provincial Council!' She could not imagine an alternative to obedience. Since Teng's hideous death in the inferno of Deng Mansions she lacked the will to fight. At the thought of him her anger subsided. 'I have no choice,' she muttered. 'I must instruct Bo-Bai and the other servants to co-operate in this matter.'

The other *sanren* remained kneeling. But Lady Lu Si's expression was hard. 'Let us hope the Worthy Master uses our valuables worthily. The Nuns of Serene Perfection have dwelt in this holy place for over four hundred years. It is not for him to end that sacred bond.'

Earth Peace's snore developed into a whinny. All rose and bowed to the Abbess as she left the octagonal star observatory. Yun Shu was glad they had the decency to wait for her to leave before beginning their denunciations.

Over the next week, porters led by a nameless priest known only as 'Void' came and went between Monkey Hat Hill and the Worthy Master's treasury in Golden Bright Temple. Ancient bronzes, robes, gongs, statues, illuminated volumes of Daoist and Buddhist holy texts, all were gathered. Centuries of gifts to the Nuns of Serene Perfection were carried away. Yun Shu insisted a strict inventory must be taken by Lady Lu Si and Jade Perfected – to Void's evident displeasure – but it was impossible to keep track.

Her thoughts were haunted by other lost treasures. Alone at night or when she visited the ruined watchtower for a little solitude, Teng crept back to her, a ghost of many ages. Sometimes a pedantic boy, her earnest *xia*. Then a young man, still half boy, teasing her as they stumbled through the limestone hills near Lingling. Or a handsome rake, his profligacy driven by disappointment and sorrow, risking everything to protect his father. *Dear Teng*, she thought, *how would you advise me to save Cloud Abode Monastery?*

Yun Shu watched the last line of porters descend the Hundred Stairs with a terrible sense of desolation. It seemed to her they were stealing her memories of Teng, one by one.

天命

Yun Shu's duties as Abbess of Cloud Abode Monastery left little time for her own affairs, particularly during the *qingming* spring festival. Then the image of the City God, Chenghuang, was paraded through important avenues and streets in Hou-ming, the God grinning this way and that. Thousands followed, beating drums and lighting firecrackers, at times linking arms, petitioning Chenghuang to shower prosperity upon a people who had suffered so grievously through war and famine.

Yun Shu walked beside the statue, chanting favourable sutras, her splendid robes a hundred years old, glittering with semi-precious stones and embroidered magical symbols. Many admired the young Abbess who had defeated a wicked dragon on Holy Mount Chang. Just as many wondered if the Buddhists from Tibet would carry Chenghuang's image during the parade next year. For Prince Arslan's decision on the Nuns' future loomed.

At midnight Yun Shu was granted a respite from ritual. Lady Lu Si led the chanting in the shrine room to honour Chenghuang, so the God would feel welcome after His journey through the city.

Yun Shu returned to her sparsely furnished chamber. The night was warm and she removed all her heavy silk clothes, stretching this way and that, naked apart from a thin cotton shift.

She fanned herself with a blank sheet of paper. It was the day when letters must be sent to relatives alive and dead. First to her mother's *shen*, her spirit, and to Teng's. Then to one still living yet dead to her in every meaningful way.

The letter to Mother was soon composed. Yun Shu reported that her service to the Dao since last spring had brought honour to the Yuns. She concluded by hoping Honoured Mother's Ghost suffered no inconvenience and her daughter's monthly offerings were received favourably.

Yun Shu chanted her mother's name a hundred times to summon her ghost, then burned the letter so it would journey straight to the spirit world.

For a long while Yun Shu tried to picture Mother's face. Teng had once said that he, too, sometimes attempted the same voyage of recollection, always unsatisfactorily. And now Teng's own face could only be reclaimed through memory.

She repeated the ritual, except for a different ghost: *Teng, Teng*, she whispered a hundred times. The letter that she burned to ash, tears stinging her cheeks, consisted of nothing more than a poem. She knew Teng would comprehend all her heart through its words:

> *Autumn wind rises,*
>   *Plump clouds burn,*
> *Pine, bamboo, plum tree wither,*
>   *Geese fly south and north.*

Inspired by duty rather than affection, Yun Shu turned to her last letter. She wrote hurriedly without any expectation of a reply:

Honoured Father, I write as your dutiful daughter, mindful of your lingering displeasure. First, I pray that you and my honoured brothers prosper for a thousand autumns. Likewise, your chosen companion, Golden Lotus.

Next, I pray the rumours concerning the destruction of Deng Mansions are unfounded. People claim Deng Teng perished in a fire started by your men, at your command. Father, only you know the full cause of that tragedy.

Honoured Parent, it cannot be that you do not know how high I have risen through the Dao's favour. I cherish the hope you feel a little pride in your daughter. In obedience, Yun Shu.

This letter was not consigned to the flames but sent – as was a version of it every year – to Salt Minister Gui's residence in Prince Arslan's palace compound. Eunuch Bo-Bai carried the message, delivering it personally to Gui's secretary.

天命

A week later, a messenger arrived at Cloud Abode Monastery, asking for Abbess Yun Shu. He bowed deeply and presented a letter smelling faintly of sandalwood. Her nose twitched. With a suspicious glance at the messenger she opened it:

Yun Shu (sometimes called Abbess Yun Shu), you are summoned to Salt Minister Gui's residence in five days at the noon bell. Not presenting will be disobedient badness.

The letter was not signed. Yun Shu's emotions leapt between surprise, excitement, thankfulness and fear. Father had showed signs of forgiveness! Yet re-reading the letter stirred doubts. Not only was its style odd – indeed, vulgar – the characters were ill formed, suggesting a cheap, hired scribe. Then there was the scent of sandalwood.

For an hour she paced her apartments, leaving the messenger outside. Finally she summoned him: 'Inform my Honoured Father I shall obey all his instructions. But tell me, did the Salt Minister give you the letter himself?'

The messenger shrugged. 'A maid gave it to me.'

Yun Shu could learn no more from him.

* * *

She arrived at Prince Arslan's palace on the allotted day. Fourteen years earlier, before her marriage into the wretched Zhong clan, the palace compound occupied a third of its current size. Since then the Prince had decreed much of the area within Hou-ming's city walls should be cleared of houses. Not to create vegetable patches for hungry folk but parkland where deer could graze and be hunted by his entourage.

As Yun Shu arrived, a new boundary wall was being constructed by thousands of conscripted peasants. Dust drifted through the air, along with clouds of smoke. Many houses and other buildings – warehouses, temples, countless shops – had been either burned or dismantled. Their ash was shovelled over the soil to fertilise grass seeds specially imported from the north.

Everywhere, one heard beating hammers and saws. Teams of men pushed wheelbarrows of roof tiles and earth and timber from broken houses to create artificial hills. Other peasants laboured in the spring sunshine to dig a lake modelled on the great Khan's in the capital, Dadu.

Soldiers stopped her palanquin at the barrier. Bo-Bai explained the Salt Minister's invitation and they were waved through. Soon she entered an ornate gatehouse leading into the palace itself. Here the guards were more diligent. Yun Shu was forced to wave her letter, though none of the Prince's elite Mongol bodyguard could read.

Beyond the gate, Yun Shu lowered her head. When she had lived here – if one might call it living, rather dragging through day after day, year after year – she had slept among the servants, an outcast in her own family. Sensations flooded back: scrubbing, sweeping, a thousand petty humiliations. She pulled her Abbess's robe and shawl tight to hide her face.

They passed through lesser gates into a wide courtyard. Here she disembarked from the palanquin, leaving its sweating porters and Bo-Bai to await her return.

Someone familiar, a slender woman approaching her thirtieth year, had been sent to greet her.

'Pink Rose!' cried Yun Shu. 'You are still here!'

Her old friend among the family maids had hardly changed. Pink Rose bowed very low. 'Honoured Abbess,' she said, 'I beg you to follow.'

Yun Shu smiled. 'Call me by my proper name! Have you forgotten our whispered gossip while the house slept around us? I have not.'

The maid looked around fearfully.

'No,' she said, 'I have not forgotten.'

The two women – for neither were girls any longer – glanced sideways until Yun Shu spoke. 'Pink Rose, how are my family?'

Her old friend's expression clouded.

'I must not say, Yun Shu! It is not for me to say. Who knows if we are being watched?'

Yun Shu followed with a heavy heart. They passed courtyards bright with coloured flags and gilt carvings, not to mention crowds of idlers in silks maintained by taxes and government monopolies. Prince Arslan's court had gained flocks of lackeys and hangers-on. The palace was a maze of staring eyes.

They reached an area of houses allocated to high officials. Of all these, Salt Minister Gui possessed the grandest. Its familiar, low silhouette and ornate, upward-curving roof tiles filled Yun Shu's eyes with uncontrollable tears.

'This way,' murmured Pink Rose.

Yun Shu expected to be shown to the main audience room, there to prostrate herself before Father's chair. Terror gripped her at the thought of his reproaches – and excitement, too, for once he had finished chastising they might begin again.

Pink Rose gestured at a side door leading to a small courtyard garden.

'Are you sure?' asked Yun Shu.

'We are already late, I shall get into trouble,' urged Pink Rose.

Yun Shu followed down a clean, well-swept corridor to a

sliding door. Beyond lay a rectangular garden. Dozens of clay pots were laid out in patterns on the gravelled paths. Some contained fish, others miniature trees or blooming flowers. In the centre was a flagged area with a circular marble bench around a drooping willow. On the bench sat a beautiful lady in perfect make-up and silks, her silver hairpiece glinting in the sun. When Yun Shu looked more closely the illusion was dispelled.

'Where is my father?' Yun Shu said, looking round.

Golden Lotus produced a fan. It clicked open and began to waft. 'Please be seated.' His voice was high-pitched and mellifluous.

'Where is Honoured Father?' repeated Yun Shu.

Now the fan paused. 'I can't tell you until you sit beside me.'

Yun Shu obliged, keeping a distance from her host. The scent of sandalwood itched in her nose. 'Father is not here, is he?'

'What a bright girl you are! Very bright!'

Yun Shu watched him withdraw a packet of folded letters from his silk girdle bag. There were over a dozen and she recognised them at once.

'My annual letters!' she exclaimed. 'How do you have them? They were sent to Father!'

A faint smile played over Golden Lotus's rouged lips.

'I believe he never received them!' cried Yun Shu.

The fan wafted back and forth. 'Your father is away at the Salt Pans,' he said. 'Does it surprise you that I wish to see my stepdaughter?'

Yun Shu did not disguise her scorn. 'I was never *that*.'

'Oh, but you were. Your Father commanded it. Did you come here, even now, to disobey him?'

'No,' said Yun Shu, hating the tremor in her voice, 'of course not. But . . .'

'There can be no *buts*,' said Golden Lotus, mildly. 'One either obeys or one is disobedient. That is all.'

Yun Shu dabbed her eyes with a sleeve as Golden Lotus opened one of the letters.

'Look,' he said, 'written in your seventeenth year. It begs forgiveness.' He opened another. 'So does this, written only two years ago.'

Yun Shu's head was lowered, tears upon her cheeks. She glanced up. Golden Lotus had risen, his delicate, manicured hands clenched as he stepped uncertainly over the crunching gravel with his tiny, lotus feet, graceful as a dancer even in the midst of his agitation.

'No one thinks of me!' he exclaimed. 'How often I am unhappy! All people consider is themselves. Your Honoured Father is so very clever! His Excellency Jebe Khoja trusts him to write all his reports concerning taxes. Letters sealed with Prince Arslan's own seal that go straight to the Great Khan. But, oh, his moods! Only I know how to bring him peace. He would never have reached his exalted position without me.'

Yun Shu stared fearfully at Golden Lotus. His outburst reminded her of the time he had tried to bind her feet, nearly twenty years before.

'What has this to do with me?' she asked.

Golden Lotus subsided and resumed his seat on the bench. 'Do you really not know what has happened?'

'No.'

'Then I will tell you.'

Still he paused, once again fanning himself.

'Your two brothers are dead,' he murmured in his gentle falsetto, 'or so we believe. First Son got involved with a lesser prince in the court. We do not really know. It seems this prince had ambitions beyond his stature. Certainly, the prince has been banished. And so have your brothers, along with many of the prince's friends and followers. Only their banishment . . .' Golden Lotus's eyes filled with tears. 'It was the kind that lasts forever! Their handsome young bodies are lost to us! We do not know where they are buried. Yet we dare not mourn in public, in case Prince Arslan thinks dear Gui is disloyal to the Great Khan. Those poor, foolish boys!'

The fan grew agitated as it rose and dipped. Yun Shu knew she should wail, weep, lament so close a loss. She felt nothing. Perhaps even a secret gladness. Her brothers had always been strangers. Now, with their deaths, Father's attention became a possibility. Golden Lotus evidently sensed her reaction, for he nodded.

'Everything has changed. Your Father cannot bear to think of it. Not yet. So angry! So miserable! Nothing I do or say calms him.'

The scent of sandalwood in Yun Shu's nostrils intensified as Golden Lotus leaned forward, placing his hand on her knee. Her breath caught, paralysed by his touch.

'And that,' he said, 'is why I wanted to speak with you.'

Their faces were an arm's length apart. She exhaled slowly and shrank back. Still the pressure of his hand lay on her knee.

'Why?' she said. 'What can I do?'

'I have an offer,' Golden Lotus's hand withdrew and he grew businesslike. 'If you ceased to be Abbess, you could become a wife. I could arrange that, Yun Shu. You could live here with your husband – I have one in mind, young, strong, handsome, a minor official in your father's service who would do whatever you like – especially when it came to making grandsons for the Salt Minister. All disobedience would be forgotten. And my dear Gui would have a future for which to gather wealth, in the form of his grandsons.'

Yun Shu's mouth felt uncomfortably dry. She rose and bowed.

'I will mourn my brothers,' she said. 'And petition Heaven for their favourable rebirth.'

Golden Lotus fanned himself. 'I did not expect you to agree at once,' he said. 'But do not imagine you will always be Abbess of Cloud Abode Monastery. Think of the Buddhists from Tibet! If you lived here we could keep each other company while the Salt Minister is away. I suspect you, too, are lonely. How pleasant it would be for us both!'

Yun Shu wished to hear no more. She left with a hurried bow.

Yet Golden Lotus's suggestion of children touched longings that grew deeper each year, however hard she suppressed them. Inevitably she remembered her last meeting with Teng. It had seemed – for she knew he'd felt the same – he would have satisfied those longings.

Yun Shu wept silently in the palanquin all the way to Cloud Abode Monastery. Golden Lotus's sad, watchful eyes and insinuating singsong voice seemed to shadow her progress.

天命

'Your thoughts drift from the Great Work.'

Yun Shu glanced up guiltily at Worthy Master Jian. 'I apologise, Master.'

They were kneeling side by side in the lowest level of Wild Goose Pagoda, meditating upon the cosmic journey ahead. Even after his reproach, Yun Shu's focus dissolved as soon as it hardened. She glanced sideways through half-opened lids at the Worthy Master, cross-legged on the mat beside her, his eyes closed. An unfamiliar odour hung upon his breath, rank and metallic. He sighed and relaxed his posture.

'I see we will make no progress until you are emptied of speculation,' he said.

Lately the handsome Worthy Master had aged rather than attained the sheen and luminosity of an Immortal. His yellowish skin and thinning grey hair reminded her of the priest called Void: as did a new intensity in the Worthy Master's gaze.

'I can tell from your sniff you have detected the scent of the Great Reverted Cinnabar within me,' he said, not without pride.

'Worthy Master,' said Yun Shu, 'please explain.'

For once he seemed happy to share his secrets. Even inclined to provoke a little admiration and wonder.

'I know you are not insensitive to the Dao,' he said. 'You must sense my progress in the Immortal Work. And the reason for my success? Ha! Here I may well garner a little credit.' His voice slurred as though tipsy.

'You would not believe the care one must take. And the expense! Pearls ground to powder, mica, sulphur, mercury and essence of gold! Then again, what of those apparently simple ingredients that turn out to be as rare as a prince's treasure? Silver-grey mushrooms with seven spots in exactly the same shape as the Seven Primes! Apricot kernels ground to dust and salted with powdered mother-of-pearl! You see, the bamboo strips revealed several paths to Immortality. Oh, the care one must take when heating one's cauldron!'

Yun Shu listened with a growing sense of dismay. Were the ancient treasures of Cloud Abode Monastery being squandered on *this*? Were the donations of the faithful being frittered on bizarre concoctions? Wealth that could purchase food and shelter for the hungry! Oh, she knew very well how Teng would have judged the Worthy Master's priorities.

'Sometimes there are errors,' he continued, 'terribly expensive waste. How could there not be? I confess freely to nights of vomiting and loose bowels. Yet each reverse brings me nearer . . . You look unhappy! You feel concern for my health!' The Worthy Master frowned. 'Your concern does not interest me,' he said, coldly. 'You disappoint me.'

She could contain herself no longer. 'Forgive me, but I *am* afraid! Your skin is grainy as old parchment. I fear the bamboo books are false. False counsellors. After all, did their original owner gain Immortality? Or did he turn to dust?'

Worthy Master Jian rose angrily, pacing before the lectern where the ancient books rested. 'This is how you repay my trust in you!' he cried. 'Of course there is trial and error, you foolish, deluded woman.' Unhealthy blotches streaked his pale face. 'You have no idea,' he continued, 'how I protect you. Even now the Buddhists from Tibet are offering me a sliver of the Buddha's knucklebone for my elixir. All they want in return is Cloud Abode Monastery. Do not tempt me by betraying my trust, Yun Shu!'

She was sobbing now, dabbing at her tears with a prayer shawl. His tall, thin body leaned over her like a shadow.

'Why shouldn't I trade a mere building for the greatest prize! Why shouldn't I?' Yun Shu shrank in horror. 'Do not tempt me!' he cried. 'Do not!'

Then, staring down at her weeping figure, he shook his head as though clearing his mind. Still her sobs continued.

'Yun Shu,' he said, in a calm voice. 'I have distressed you.' She sniffed, trying to master her tears. 'I regret my lack of balance. I was at fault. You are no use to our rites unless you are serene.'

As her weeping subsided, he sat beside her on the mat, gentle and wise once more. A faint desperation in his eyes softened Yun Shu's fear to reluctant pity.

'You see,' he said, 'life has taught me a perfect horror of death. No doubt you think that unbalanced? Impious, even. Yet consider how we die a little each day in a thousand ways. Our thoughts arise then vanish. Our breaths come and go. We glimpse a swallow flitting over a twilit sky, hear its song, then it has gone. Friends of one's youth decay and change until barely recognisable. Father, Mother, Brother, Sister, all share their moment until – like glints of sunshine on a pool obscured by cloud – their light vanishes.'

She listened closely.

'Yun Shu, how I have meditated upon these things! Over and over! Compare the coarsening of my hair and teeth and skin with that enjoyed heedlessly, thoughtlessly by foolish youth! And death itself, the pain and humiliation as one's spirit shudders from the body to beg before the Infernal Judges in hell. Who knows what reincarnation and birth one must endure next time? What dreadful lives one has already endured. The tedium of starting yet again, learning and re-learning all life's lessons only to have that knowledge snuffed in a cruel instant!'

He paused, rubbing his hands, a smile of dreamy elation on his face.

'But to become an Immortal, Yun Shu! To attain full realisation! Then life and death flow and weave together. Always happy, whether loitering in Heaven or wandering the world. Eternally poised to act for the good of all creatures! What demons I would exorcise, how many sick people I would heal! Yun Shu, is that not worth a little suffering? To control the rivers and mountains! Anything at all! Playful as a child, sage as Lao Tzu! Yet we have not even attained the Stage of Shen.'

He stopped and she stared up at his flushed face. Then her heart hardened.

'If we attain the Stage of Shen,' she said, 'you must promise to save Cloud Abode Monastery.'

'Yes,' he said, 'that I can promise.'

He drew a silver box from his robes. Inside were pills of crushed dates mingled with secret essences and autumn minerals.

'Eat seven of these and so shall I,' he whispered. 'Meditate all the while upon the Weaver Maid and her union with the Cosmic Herdboy.'

They chewed and swallowed together until the pills were gone. Soon his eyes were unnaturally glazed and bright, as she sensed her own must be. Warmth glowed in her deepest cinnabar chambers and her breath quickened uncomfortably. Her heart beat too fast.

He led her up a staircase round the circular walls of the pagoda to the second storey. Her palms felt hot and each step brought a deeper haze.

twenty-eight

天命

Sometimes, to distract himself from the pain infecting every limb and muscle, Teng imagined he was a long-legged crane. In this guise, while he hacked at sticky wet soil, his spirit soared free. Up he flew, flapping round the huge wooden derrick – an ungainly pyramid fifteen men high, in the midst of which a great vertical drill rose and fell to batter bedrock deep below the earth's surface. Up he flew, until he was circling on currents of warm, clean air, untainted by the swamp below.

Aloft the world gained colourful, tempting horizons. North lay the body of Six-hundred-*li* Lake, dotted with islands like green stepping stones he might follow all the way home. To the west blue mountains rose, wreathed in mysterious cloud. Among them was Holy Mount Chang and Lingling County, the possibility of help and friends. But as he circled in his imagination, Teng could think of no way to get there. So he looked east, following the shore of the lake north a full hundred *li* to Chenglingji Port and a civilized road to Hou-ming. That, too, was a way he could not take. Then he looked south, across endless reed beds and salt marsh, treacherous mud and barren hills where only thorns and stubborn scrub found a roothold. A dangerous, harsh, circuitous route home; a way almost too fearful to be attempted.

Frustrated in every direction, the circling spirit-crane looked downward. Then the Salt Pans' pitiless grandeur overwhelmed Teng's imagination. Daunted, he resumed whatever backbreaking task he had been assigned . . .

'Put more into it, Teng! Remember what I told you.'

The quiet but insistent voice belonged to Foreman Wu Mao, a grizzled, thin young man with muscles hard as bamboo. His words pierced the fog of exhaustion in Teng's brain. What must he remember? What must he remember? Yes! That if they did not reach bedrock by sunset their whole work gang would be punished. That meant no food . . . He dug his spade into the wet, crumbly soil and feverishly filled a bucket.

'That's it, Teng! Only dig with a slow, steady rhythm.' Foreman Wu Mao's voice floated. Vanished. Still he dug and dug until each spade load of earth weighed as much as Monkey Hat Hill. They were lucky that day. The work gang exceeded the target set by Chief Overseer Pi-tou. That night they ate . . .

Now he had been promoted. No longer digging the hole that surrounded the borehole into the bedrock, he had been assigned one handle of a two-man pump. Up, down, up, down . . . Thick, milky brine spurted from a bamboo pipe into a huge, cast iron pan already coated with a crust of precious crystals. Flames roared beneath the pan, fed by gas charged with the sun's essence that burned ceaselessly, piped up from the earth and distributed along snaking tangles of bamboo tubes. Sometimes there were explosions. Eruptions of back-drafting flame would set a dozen men ablaze. Today the flame burned submissively and Teng pumped up, down, up, down, his spine and legs aching, hands raw on the wooden handle until the huge iron pan bubbled and frothed.

'You two! Drink!' urged Foreman Wu Mao, offering a bucket. 'No charge for water in my floating oriole house! It keeps your *yang* strong!'

Swaying with exhaustion oddly like nausea, Teng did as

instructed, gulping earthy water with more pleasure than he had many an exquisite wine . . .

'Lazy slaves! Do not wait for it to cool!'

With that barked command, Overseer Pi-tou strode off to the next work gang tending their garden of salt, to repeat the same bellowed order. Foreman Wu Mao was left with his forehead pressed into mud, alongside the dozen members of their gang. When he rose, his normally measured voice was edged with fear.

'You heard the Overseer! We should not wait for it to cool! Fetch wet rags!'

These he wrapped round his bare feet and hands. Using a ladder, he climbed the still scalding cast iron pan, making no complaint other than a grunt when his skin brushed the metal. Shovel load after shovel load of salt crystals were poured into buckets before Foreman Wu Mao could stand no more.

'Each must take a turn,' he gasped. 'We must finish this before he comes back.'

When Teng climbed the ladder he felt faint. Swirls of noxious fumes from the burning sun essence and steaming brine left him giddy. He tried to use the spade accurately but his face was melting like wax in the shimmering heat, his forehead blistering painfully. The first shovel load emptied into an upheld bucket, as did the second. The third missed entirely, landing on the muddy ground. Teng bent to scrape up a fourth when an angry roar stopped him.

'Get that fool down from there!'

Hands grabbed his ankles. He was dragged from the ladder until he knelt, whooping pure air on the wet ground.

'Why, it's the gentleman scholar!' crowed a harsh, self-satisfied voice. 'I've had orders about our gentleman scholar.'

Teng understood his bad luck. Overseer Pi-tou had happened to wander past their derrick and seen the salt wasted by his clumsiness.

'Hey, Wu Mao!' barked Pi-tou. 'For squandering salt your gang gets half rations tonight.'

If it had been prudent to moan, all Teng's comrades would have done so. As it was, they averted their eyes from Overseer Pi-tou's hawk-like face and shaven head.

'Well then, punish him for it! All of you!'

Teng's fellow slaves and indentured labourers were prodded into a line by Overseer Pi-tou's soldiers and, one by one, kicked or punched Teng as he knelt. A smirk crept across the Overseer's face.

'That's the way to do it! Eh, scholar?'

Even in the midst of the beating Teng realised his comrades' blows possessed more show than force. At the word *scholar*, Foreman Wu Mao cast him a quick, searching look.

That night Teng lay beneath a single blanket on the wet earth. It was drizzling. The southern end of the lake was famous for its rainfall and he had grown used to constantly grey skies. Even through the steam evaporating from hundreds of boiling, simmering iron pans, he had noted the way swells of light gilded the rain-clouds above, how they billowed in the wind like dragons puffing out their chests. Perhaps misery unlocked these insights. Certainly he had never noticed such things so deeply; insights that made him long for brush and ink and paper to capture a little of what he had learned.

Those were harsh lessons. Every moment of every hour haunted by pictures – Deng Mansions burning, roofs collapsing with sprays of sparks, smoke, roars of wind-fed flame . . . And the certainty his actions had brought disaster upon their ancestral home. Through his greed and vanity, believing he could make fools of their enemies. Clever Deng Teng! Now, for all he knew, his own father was dead, burned alive as he sought to extinguish the flames. At best, cast adrift without a home, sick and frail, in need of medicine to suppress the malign mushrooms detected in his wizened frame by the doctor. Teng knew no means to discover the truth. Asking questions in the Salt Pans would be madness, especially if Overseer Pi-tou found out – as he was sure to do.

Teng shivered beneath his blanket. Strength seeded by Deng Nan-shi's tales of the Deng clan's natural greatness and fitness to rule put out roots. Strange, perhaps, it should germinate in the mud of the Salt Pans. Yet Teng understood the only restitution he could offer his ancestors. He must restore the glorious name of Deng. At the very least, there must be sons. And surely that same rich, nutritious blood-broth would sustain him while lesser men perished. The blood that had run through Hero-general Yueh Fei: the curse and blessing of his destiny.

More than that, less filial but closer to his heart, he remembered Yun Shu's animated face as they talked in the moon-gazing pavilion. She had revealed her innermost feelings. Feelings he shared with all his heart. For both their sakes he would find a way back to Hou-ming. Of all the good he had ever known, she seemed best.

That night Deng Teng embraced a stark choice. Accept this hellish place until he escaped or deny reality and perish. His first act of acceptance was sleep.

He awoke at dawn to find Foreman Wu Mao looking down at him.

'Eat now since you had nothing last night,' he said.

Teng eagerly took the bowl and shovelled yesterday's cold rice into his mouth. When he dropped a few grains, he scooped them up and devoured them with a sauce of dirt. Running his finger round the wooden bowl, he licked until every dreg of starch and sustenance had been consumed.

'You're a scholar, eh?' asked Foreman Wu Mao.

Teng nodded, laughed hoarsely. 'Fully literate,' he said, 'with ink for blood.' Then he shrank back: the foreman might not know words like *literate* and punish Teng for his ignorance.

But Wu Mao seemed to savour the unfamiliar syllables.

'Lit-er-ate,' he said. Then more forcefully: '*Literate*. It means, I think, you read and write well.'

Teng nodded. 'You understand exactly.'

'We shall talk later,' promised the Foreman, rising to ensure the other labourers had been fed.

That day Teng was assigned the task of jumping on a wooden board to compress salt crystals into square bricks. An easier job than pumping or digging, yet one he could barely manage. His face and body were purple with bruises from the beating decreed by Overseer Pi-tou.

Later, as the work gang gathered for warmth round the gas flame, Foreman Wu Mao sat beside Teng. He seemed uneasy and Teng sensed why. It was a feeling he had learned as a boy when he wanted to ask Hsiung for a favour but feared to lose face.

'Foreman,' he said, softly, 'you are thinking I can be of service in some way.' Wu Mao looked at him suspiciously. 'Do you read minds, scholar?'

'No,' said Teng, remembering Ying-ge's betrayal, 'I wouldn't be here if I could.'

After Wu Mao had explained his difficulty, which was more his family's than his own, Teng nodded. 'Paper, ink, brush,' he said. 'That is all I need.'

Once these were produced he composed a letter on behalf of Foreman Wu Mao's First Brother, who also led a work gang in the Salt Pans, to negotiate a favourable dowry with a distant cousin in a village south of Chenglingji famous for its apricots. Teng, relishing the feel of the brush, took special care. By the time he had finished, the entire work gang surrounded him, whispering as though a rite was being enacted. So it was. The rite of all civilized men to create and record and share thoughts.

After Teng read the letter aloud – including a prolonged and passionate appeal to the bride's family for a large dowry –

Foreman Wu Mao whistled through his few remaining teeth.

'Strong!' he muttered. 'I'll take it to my brothers and uncles. With a letter like that they might throw in a bride for me!'

Married foremen were allowed huts in an enclosure of their own. However, the Salt Authorities insisted on taxation of the dowry to such a degree that many could not afford to marry. For this reason, younger brothers like Wu Mao often went without a bride.

Weeks later the reply arrived: Teng's letter had so impressed the local Sub-prefect (who had been paid a suitable fee for reading it) that he instructed the bride's family to agree the marriage terms without haggling. As a result, Wu Mao's First Brother moved into his own hut upon immediate receipt of wife and dowry.

'We will talk later,' said Foreman Wu Mao, his face flushed with satisfaction. Teng was left to wonder what about.

天命

Once enslaved or indentured in the Salt Pans a man's world dwindled. The past grew unreal, especially the consolation of happier times. Sixteen hours of toil each day, brief feeds, the discharge of bodily functions, all conducted in view of one's gang. Perhaps half an hour's muttered talk round the gas flame before exhausted sleep.

A man's vision dwindled, too, reduced to the tool in his hands or snatched glimpses of the sky. If one scaled the high wooden derrick with its drill for deepening the borehole that allowed access to the precious salt-brine, there was little to see. Countless similar derricks spread across the swamp for several *li* in all directions and hundreds of iron pans emitted wreaths of steam into the dank air. On the landward side, one could trace the extent of the boundary walls and towers protecting the Salt Pans and imprisoning its thousands of toiling ants. Or even examine the fortress compound where the Salt Minister's bureaux and warehouses were located, along with barracks of bored, restless soldiers. If one looked out across the lake, scores of small islands surrounded by rings of mud rose from the shallow waters to form a natural defensive barrier against marauding fleets. A desolate place unless one was a bird. White gulls, herons and cranes gathered in huge numbers to feast on tiny creatures in the mud and darken the sky at dusk and sunset.

Teng kept his eyes and ears open. He had been transported to the Salt Pans in chains at the beginning of autumn. Five months later, his body had hardened and grown tolerant of pains that, before his arrest, would have set him squealing. Only fools squealed in the Salt Pans. Weakness invited attempts by other slaves to steal your rations and clothes. In the case of pretty youths, more intimate treasures were looted.

Teng knew he was lucky to have gained the confidence of Foreman Wu Mao. Through him he heard rumours that Jebe Khoja had arrived at the Salt Pans shortly before New Year. When he left, half the garrison appeared to sail with him.

'It is a ruse,' revealed Foreman Wu Mao, as they sat beside the dancing blue flame one cold evening.

'How so?' asked Teng.

The younger man examined him. Then he seemed to decide. In that moment Teng knew he had gained a huge advantage against the fate Salt Minister Gui intended for him.

'Word has reached my friends that the Mongols merely gather in villages up the coast, ready to issue forth in fleets of small boats. They are waiting for something. Or someone.'

Teng nodded thoughtfully. 'The jaws of a trap,' he murmured.

Foreman Wu Mao held out his hands to the flame so they seemed to glow, but said no more. Teng wondered who these well-informed friends might be.

Another evening, Foreman Wu Mao's burly brothers and uncles arrived at their derrick and muttered in a close huddle, passing round leather wineskins. Teng tactfully withdrew to the shelter of the boiling pan and tried to sleep. He was awoken by a gentle tug on his shoulder.

'We need your services,' whispered Foreman Wu Mao.

Teng, who slept in damp clothes and rotting shoes, rose at once. He was led to the circle of Wu Mao's relatives, who assessed him coldly. Remembering he was a Deng and they – whatever the ironies of their current positions – mere labourers, Teng returned their gaze.

'Deng Teng,' said Foreman Wu Mao, holding out the same cheap paper, ink and brush he had used before. 'Write the following, if you please: *Separate must become together.*'

Teng looked at him curiously. But asking was dangerous in the Salt Pans. The question was, who would receive it, and why. 'Nothing more?' he asked.

Wu Mao nodded. It took little time to oblige. He was then dismissed to his blanket while the foreman's brothers and uncles disappeared into the night to rejoin their own work gangs, for their clan had toiled in the Salt Pans for three generations. This fact gave Teng a chance to extend his influence.

'Tell me, Wu Mao,' he said, a few days later, 'were the Salt Pans like this in the previous dynasty?'

The foreman granted him one of his sharp looks. 'Why do you ask, scholar? Are you going to write a history? I'll warn you now, no one cares about the likes of us. All they care about is how much salt we send.'

Teng threw caution aside, explaining the exalted rank of his Grandfather and all that the Dengs had lost by the change of dynasty.

Wu Mao replied with new respect: 'No wonder Overseer Pi-tou has been instructed to take special care of you.'

He answered Teng's original question: though life had been hungry under the Song Dynasty, conditions had been easier, wages higher and taxes lower. Above all, there had been no slaves to reduce the earnings of the salt workers and no omnipotent tyrants like Overseer Pi-tou with the power of instant life and death. Worse, many of the old salt-working families were being enslaved as a punishment for spurious debts invented by the Salt Bureau. It was well known these unfortunate wretches' wages – no longer payable because they had been re-classified as slaves – were stolen by Bureau officials. As a result, many salt workers had fled to join the Red Turbans.

'Perhaps the old conditions could be restored,' said Teng, 'if we were not ruled by foreign devils.'

Wu Mao looked round nervously. No one could overhear.

'Perhaps,' he replied.

When Deng Teng climbed the wooden derrick to inspect the Salt Pans, he always paid particular attention to the fortress compound. That walled rectangle crammed with buildings was the beating heart of power in this dismal place. And things were stirring in its hidden chambers.

One day he said to Foreman Wu Mao: 'I have noticed many soldiers on the walls of the fortress. This seems impossible when half the garrison so publicly sailed away.'

They were inspecting bamboo pipes for leakages.

'What goes away with great show can return in secret,' said the Foreman. 'Hold the pipe straight! Let us be thankful Overseer Pi-tou's men did not find this leak before us.'

When it had been sealed, Teng said: 'That is not all. I noticed lines of men with large packs on their backs, all tied together like a train of mules and whipped along by guards. They seemed to be taking a road through the marshes into the hills.'

'Of course,' said Wu Mao, 'the Salt Minister maintains an illicit trade with customers in the southern lands where hardly any officials dare go. Those men carry blocks of pure salt and are forbidden to untie them from their backs on pain of death. They even sleep with them on.'

Teng considered this as Wu Mao caulked another bamboo water pipe.

'How corrupt the Middle Kingdom has grown,' sighed Teng, unconsciously using a favourite phrase of his father's. 'The Mandate of Heaven must surely pass into worthier hands.'

Foreman Wu Mao straightened and examined him in his careful way.

'There are others who believe that,' he said, softly. 'My whole clan believe it and are ready to act. I tell you, the Buddha Maitreya is coming to cleanse the world! Then a new golden age shall begin, my friend. The Great Togetherness will unite all people! Look around you: famine, war, signs in the sky. Proofs are everywhere.'

'You are a Red Turban,' whispered the scholar. 'So was my father! So am I.'

Foreman Wu Mao nodded. 'I sensed you were a good man. Here's another leak. We will talk of this later.'

天命

Later, always later. Teng sometimes wondered if he would survive long enough to hear the foreman's revelations. He was ordered to haul timber for a neighbouring derrick, leaving Foreman Wu Mao to fulfil his quota with a reduced number of hands. Teng dragged bundles of bamboo logs over the mud, slipping and sliding when they stuck until, with a heave, he advanced a little further. Such agonies interested Chief Overseer Pi-tou. Teng sometimes noticed him watching avidly.

Perhaps this, and the certainty he could not endure such treatment, drove Teng to desperate intentions. He would be avenged, whatever the cost! As he lay beneath his blanket, Teng pondered the apparent withdrawal of Jebe Khoja's garrison. What prey did they hope to lure? He suspected it dwelt in Lingling County, proclaiming rebellion and the cause of Yueh Fei. In short, Jebe Khoja hoped to trap and destroy the Red

Turbans led by the Noble Count of Lingling, once and for all.

This realisation stirred uncomfortable memories. He had failed Hsiung when they were boys, neglecting the duty of a worthy master to protect his servant. Now he glimpsed a way to make amends.

He contrived to speak to Foreman Wu Mao alone. Spring was well advanced and vast flocks of birds that wintered in the marshes were gathering to return north. Among them were countless wild geese. Teng recollected that such creatures loved to bear good news.

'My friend,' he said, 'I cannot last much longer.'

Wu Mao nodded. That much was evident. 'Overseer Pi-tou has you very much in mind.'

'That is why I intend to attempt an escape, while I still possess the strength.'

'Foolish!' cautioned Wu Mao. 'No slave ever escapes the Pans except into mud and marsh – from which he never comes out.'

'At least it will be a better way to die. Only, Wu Mao, I beg a favour. And I must speak bluntly. Does your clan maintain contact with the Yueh Fei rebels?'

Wu Mao's face remained entirely expressionless.

'If so,' said Teng, 'warn the Noble Count of Lingling a trap has been prepared here.'

'Some of my clan and our friends believe that,' conceded Wu Mao. 'Messages have been written and sent.'

'Perhaps word of your suspicions has already reached the Noble Count?'

'I don't believe so,' said Wu Mao. 'Messengers were sent two months ago but none returned. Besides, our usual way of passing letters is ineffective. All boats in and out of the port are controlled more tightly than ever. Not a single sailor is allowed to disembark and all loading is carried out by Mongol guards who speak no Chinese.'

'Such precautions cannot be accidental,' said Teng. 'Still I beg you to try! A message must get through. I shall attempt to carry one myself.'

Foreman Wu Mao shook his head. 'If so, you won't come back. But I'll pass your request to those who have the power to act . . .'

They were interrupted by a glimpse of Chief Overseer Pi-tou in the distance. All the salt workers were extraordinarily sensitive to his presence. A dozen soldiers followed him.

'He's seen us together,' whispered Teng. 'Strike me! And do not forget my request!'

Foreman Wu Mao did as instructed, at least with regard to the blow, adding fake kicks for good measure. He was rewarded with an approving glance from the Chief Overseer. Whether he fulfilled his promise concerning the message Teng could not know. That night he launched a plan so unstable its only ballast was desperate hope.

天命

Slaves in the Salt Pans wore no chains. Why bother with the expense and inconvenience of fetters? The surest bondage was the belief that a better life lay forever beyond reach. Such invisible chains endure for generations.

Teng considered this as he passed boldly along walkways of earth raised above the marsh. Wooden derricks towered on all sides; he glimpsed the glow of countless gas flames surrounded by huddles of exhausted men. The sound of singing drifted from some work gangs, enough to give him heart.

A moonless midnight, the stars obscured by clouds spilling their burdens of rain, filling the darkness with slanting, wind-blown showers and songs of water. On such nights lamps were trimmed and guards kept to their shelters. Yet Teng had a ready answer if challenged. Soon enough his chance came to test it.

His plan was simple: find an unobtrusive route to the eastern side of the Salt Pans, where he had spied a gate through the ramparts leading to the marsh beyond. There might also be a chance of sneaking over the earthen ramparts. He had stolen a coil of rope used to lash pipes for that very purpose. Another possibility was to follow the line of battlements to the shore where a long pier jutted far out into the lake. Here cargo vessels moored to load blocks of salt and unload supplies. He could stow away or, failing that, steal a rowing boat.

Before he got halfway to the ramparts, a shout rose above the whisper and splash of the rain: 'You! Halt!'

Teng sensed hundreds of slaves and indentured labourers stir as they drowsed. He obeyed at once. A hue and cry would have a single result: he was too weak to run.

Two Chinese mercenaries strolled over from a small, thatched guard post by the side of the earthen walkway.

'What you doing here?' demanded the first. His accent was from the far north.

Teng deployed the answer he had prepared. 'I have been sent to seek Chief Overseer Pi-tou. My foreman fears a great loss of salt.'

The men exchanged glances.

'Who is your foreman?' demanded the guard.

'Xin-qun,' said Teng.

'Never heard of him,' said the guard.

'He's been appointed recently.' Now Teng tried to appear anxious – an easy enough pretence. 'Let me pass! If the salt is lost I shall not take responsibility!'

This seemed to satisfy them.

'Go your way,' ordered the guard. 'Though we have not seen the Overseer all night.'

Teng hurried on until the land rose a little and the marsh grew drier. A black line of earthen ramparts appeared through the darkness. Compared to the great walls surrounding Hou-ming the defences were flimsy. For Teng, they were merely the first of countless obstacles before he could reach Red Turban territory.

Muddy paths led past yet more derricks, a few rotting in the dank air, having exhausted the underground pools of brine beneath their boreholes. He paused in the shadow of one. The gatehouse before him seemed deserted; the guards on this section of the ramparts were either called away or neglecting their duty. Now was his chance, perhaps his only chance. Teng left the shelter of the fallen derrick and scuttled towards steps leading up to the battlements. The crumbling, earthern stairs were lit by a swinging lamp suspended from a chain. A voice called from the shadows: 'Going somewhere?'

Teng did not move. His interrogator remained invisible.

'I'm seeking Chief Overseer Pi-tou!' he blurted. 'I must find him!'

A tall man in armour stepped out of a doorway concealed by a thick curtain. Other faces peered behind him. The drizzle fell constantly, illuminated as specks of light by the guttering lamp. Teng recognised the armoured man as one of the Overseer's bodyguard. His luck had failed.

In the hour before dawn he was led from the guard post. He had crouched there all night while the soldiers played cards or exchanged gossip. Most were Chinese and scarcely better fed than the labourers they coerced; a few among them, like the tall man from the Overseer's bodyguard, displayed small signs of wealth. Most were grumbling about unpaid wages. As he listened, Teng realised how thin their threads of loyalty must stretch.

A small escort armed with crossbows took him along the walkway of the ramparts. Life stirred in the Salt Pans below; nests of ants commencing their day's unvarying routines. It was a long walk and, in different circumstances, he might have found the reed-covered marshes beautiful, as a red dawn lit channels of water and fields of swaying stems.

He entered the large fortress compound. It, too, was stirring. Teng was shoved through a parade ground. The number of troops garrisoned in so confined a space amazed him. Barracks had been established anywhere offering a little shelter, and not just for ill-disciplined conscripts: there were native Mongol guardsmen, as well as Turks and Uighurs from the Great Khan's western possessions.

He was prodded into a courtyard surrounded on three sides by tall warehouses with red-tiled roofs. The fourth side framed a tall doorway in the fortress wall, presumably leading out to the marsh. The courtyard contained scores of wooden carrying frames and piles of heavy, rectangular salt blocks.

The guards led him into a warehouse. Before his eyes could accustom themselves to the gloom he was thrust to his knees. When Teng glanced up, two familiar faces looked down at him. As usual, Overseer Pi-tou was grinning slightly. His companion seemed less sanguine. Salt Minister Gui applied a silk kerchief to his perspiring forehead. Everywhere were stacks of spears and fire-lances, bundles of arrows and crossbow bolts. The Overseer looked to his superior.

'He was caught trying to escape, Your Excellency,' he said. 'You'll recollect I suggested we drown him, sir. I know just the place, a good-sized pool with somewhere dry and sheltered for His Honour to sit. You could watch me at work, sir, if you have time to spare before breakfast.'

Gui's expression was that of a vexed, sulking child. He withdrew his abacus from his belt and clicked the beads with fierce intensity. Overseer Pi-tou shifted uneasily.

'You heard the Salt Minister!' he barked at the kneeling Teng. 'Explain yourself!'

For a moment Teng was about to speak; after all, it was his nature to speak, however indiscreetly or recklessly. Yet he suspected silence might annoy them more.

'Good!' chuckled the Overseer. 'I like it when they're difficult. What do you want me to do with him, Your Honour?'

Still Gui clicked the beads like a weaver with his shuttle. When he stopped a peevish look crossed his face. He yawned extravagantly.

'I want him to disappear,' he said.

At this Teng raised his head higher. His fate was revealed. He had nothing left to lose. 'If I'm charged with a capital crime let me come before a fitting judge!' he cried. 'You, Gui, are not such a person. You are a corrupt official who barely possesses the normal attributes of a man. Heaven's Mandate does not extend to *you*!'

Gui's attention wandered for a moment. He frowned down at Teng. 'None of that matters here,' he said in a puzzled voice. 'You are an intelligent man, Deng Teng. Surely you see that?'

'Take me before Jebe Khoja!' demanded Teng. 'He is concealed here, is he not?'

'Not in this warehouse, no,' said the Salt Minister, 'he has far b-better quarters.'

Now Overseer Pi-tou half-rose. 'Let me teach the gentleman scholar something, Your Worship!' He turned to Teng. 'I've taught scholars like you before! I'll teach you to read and write, my friend!'

Teng did not flinch. Instead he stared at the Salt Minister.

'Tell me,' he said, 'did my Honoured Father survive the burning of Deng Mansions? You have sons of your own who love you. Well then, you must know how I need the truth before I die.'

The mention of sons had a bizarre effect on Gui. The older man shrank back, blinking rapidly as Yun Shu did when agitated. His shoulders stiffened like an enraged peacock's.

'No more talk from you! So you t-taunt me with *that*! You cheated me! Yes, your Father is alive. He, too, shall f-find out what it is to lose . . . Overseer Pi-tou! Hit him!' he cried, shrilly. 'Then s-send him far, far away!'

Overseer Pi-tou was glad to oblige. An hour with the Salt Minister tested all his restraint so he wasted none on Teng.

'Stop!' shouted Gui.

Reluctantly, Pi-tou halted the beating.

'He must be able to walk,' pointed out the Salt Minister, resuming some private calculation on his abacus.

Teng was dragged into the courtyard. Twenty barefoot men in rags were gathered, thin and pale as bean sprouts.

'Load them!' ordered the Overseer.

Groggily, Teng watched the first semi-naked porter being strapped into his load. Overseer Pi-tou gestured. 'This one next,' he ordered. 'See it's done properly. If you need further commands I'll be at breakfast. I've worked up an appetite.'

天命

Twenty departed, led by an old man to manage the food and water. Each porter carried a third of his weight in pure salt, strapped to a wooden frame on his back and secured with bolts. No bending was possible. No lying down unless someone helped you or you never wanted to rise. Sleep only possible by propping your weight on a forked stick – and Heaven help you if the stick broke.

The mule-train of slaves was bound for a town ten days' march to the South. That much Teng learned. The prospect tormented him all their first day on the sticky, squelching path through the marshes, up into arid hills where streams trickled over algae-coloured rocks and hawks wheeled. With half-closed eyes he stumbled forward. Oh, it was simple enough! First one foot, then the other. Every sway set his heart lurching. He had already seen how the old man leading them struggled to help a fallen porter to his feet: it was a miracle he succeeded.

On and on, passing the skeletons of men who had been driven the same way, the soil around them bare of grass from the salt that formed their shroud. Teng glimpsed grinning skulls and remembered the ruined watchtower on Monkey Hat Hill. So many bones. All his life, so many. On he went, passing tiny villages where people turned away from the caravan of misery and bitter salt, perhaps to ignore their own shame they did not help, dared not help men so badly used and judged so worthless as to be driven to death like beasts. But that was unfair. Beasts had value, if only for their hides, grease and meat.

Onwards, climbing into foothills that would become mountain trails all too soon. There, the old man at the front ordered a halt, using wordless gestures and grunts to instruct the porters to form semi-circular rings round a waterfall, propped up on their forked sticks.

The cliff was covered with lichen and ferns. The old man ladled water into the wooden bowl chained to each man's waist. They watched hungrily as he struggled to light a fire and boiled millet in a blackened iron bowl. He served them one by one, muttering to himself. At Teng he hesitated, ignoring the proffered bowl. The old man eagerly bolted down Teng's ration.

So that was the way of it. Instructions concerning the gentleman scholar had been issued. Teng knew how short a distance he was expected to travel – and how very far, the farthest a living thing may go, into eternity. Tears clouded his vision. Already he felt half-invisible.

At dawn he stumbled on like the rest, using the forked stick for balance as the path climbed round huge, squat boulders, up towards a distant pass. They were one and a half days from the Salt Pans now. At noon their guide ordered a halt and the mules propped themselves upright, snatching a little exhausted sleep. Teng's was dark and deep. Perhaps that was why he did not wake when the rest of the caravan set off, opening his eyes to find the last man a *li* ahead. Yet Teng was not alone. Their thin, starved guide had stayed behind. For long moments the old man scratched his lice, mumbling incoherently.

'Have you been ordered to kill me?' asked Teng.

The old man did not reply. Perhaps he was simple and could not understand.

'That would not be hard,' said Teng, 'I am helpless enough. But I have wealthy friends who will reward you if you set me free from this salt block.'

It seemed the old man might be considering his offer, for his leathery, lined face was puckered as if in thought. Then, with a sudden cry, he lunged forward and snatched Teng's forked stick. Teng reached out to retrieve it, almost toppling. Flailing, he balanced just in time. The old man backed away and Teng understood.

'No!' he cried. 'Do not kill me that way! Do it quickly, if you must!'

But the old man was hurrying up the path after the salt caravan, Teng's stick in his hands, glancing back occasionally to see if he was pursued. And so he was, for a while.

Finally Teng gave up. He was marooned as effectively as any shipwrecked sailor cast upon a spit of sand exposed to the tide.

It took half a day. At first he struggled back the way he had come, hoping to reach the waterfall that had slaked their thirst last night. The way was so slippery, the angle of the path so steep in places that he made agonising progress without the aid of a prop. Many times he swayed back and forth, certain the end had arrived. Each time he steadied and advanced a little further . . .

What were a man's legs but stilts carrying his soul? What his arms but branches sprouting greedy twigs? What his lungs but bellows sucking in air, then discharging it into a sky utterly indifferent? What was a man's back, the same spine that grew from jelly in his mother's womb to rings of hard, cushioned bone? Oh, one might feel proud of one's precious spine. So strong! So flexible! Until it weakened – slither of foot on ground, uncertain, tottering steps, frailty never imagined when a boy green and growing . . . Until legs and arms and lungs and spine declared themselves spent.

A moment of sorrowful fear! To wobble at the centre of the Eight Directions. He might fall this way or that. Face forward with the salt block pressing his nose into the damp earth, filling his nostrils with peaty earth-tangs, grave reeks. Or he could fall backward, arching to land on the salt block, rest on the salt block like a grave slab, helpless as a beetle or a tortoise on its back, waving futile limbs. At least, facing up, stars and wheeling birds might be glimpsed.

Perhaps that was why Teng toppled back rather than forward. Because of the stars . . .

For hours he struggled to rise. Oh, he was the last of the Dengs! If he did not have sons . . . Every combination of arms and legs pushing in unison had no effect. He tried rolling onto his side for a better purchase. No success. Then he lay panting, staring up at the sky. Dusk soon. Darkness would follow. He prayed for a clear night. Never before had the patterns of swirling clouds seemed so beautiful or precious, even when rain tumbled down at him like tiny beads of glass melting on his cracked lips and tongue . . .

As he lay, eagerly drinking in the patterns of the constellations, their divine shapes and brightness, Teng found himself mouthing half-forgotten words . . . Father's favourite, composed by the Emperor Wu:

> *Autumn wind rises,*
> *Plump clouds burn,*
> *Pine, bamboo and plum tree wither,*
> *Geese fly south and north.*

When he finished, a shudder passed through Teng's exhausted body. Feebly his bowels discharged what little they possessed. He felt giddy; the constant ache in his body numb. Relief crept over tortured limbs like fresh, water-scented mist.

With it came awareness of dawn's possibilities in the changing light. Was that a long-necked goose skimming at the edge of his vision? In his mind he urged it to fly across Six-hundred-*li* Lake to Monkey Hat Hill.

The folly of his numerous unhappinesses struck Teng like a kind of wonder. How foolish to have been so unhappy! For all his learning, he had understood nothing. Nothing of value. Now his studies approached their end. Here, unexpectedly, was the examination he had prepared for since boyhood. Not the Emperor's test of worthiness for high office as Deng Nan-shi had hoped. Not some test to determine one's fitness to be granted the Mandate of Heaven, in however petty a capacity, as official or judge.

Hard to learn so much so late. That all he cared for now was not the name of Deng, or a moment's fame, or wealth, or the praise of strangers. He longed for the touch of his mother's hand and Father's ambiguous presence, looking between him and Hsiung as they played in the overgrown courtyard.

And there was another discovery: deeper than all others. He longed to touch Yun Shu's hands, defying every decorum or restraint, and use his own to bring himself close to her so their lips brushed. Gently at first, then with urgency. How sick he had grown of propriety! Sick of misconceived denials! Of all the regrets in his life she seemed the greatest.

Teng's thoughts fell away into dark places where memory and speculation sweated feverishly.

twenty-nine

天命

The Noble Count of Lingling paced the mud and shingle beach, seemingly oblivious to rain slanting from a warm, overcast sky. It was dusk; dull fires glowed to the west. The sun sank behind distant mountains, barely discernible in the murky air. His heavy boots left patterns in the mud. Servants with umbrellas hovered a little way off, ready to shelter him, but he waved them away. Perhaps the rain would clear his intentions.

These were best expressed by a fleet of eighty junks and warships at anchor near the small island where he had landed to get a little solid earth beneath his feet. This fleet, carrying over three thousand of his best troops, all veterans of harsh encounters with the Mongols, was a like a quiver of arrows waiting to be loosed. And his target, the Salt Pans, lay only a few hours to the south.

Hsiung's lips tightened as he imagined their attack. The monsoon was gradually raising the water level of the lake, as it did every year between spring and autumn. High waters meant increased manoeuvrability for his ships. A perfect time to assault the Salt Pans, protected as they were in winter and autumn by a maze of small islands and treacherous shallows.

Even now, after months of reports that the Mongols were withdrawing, leaving only a skeleton garrison, Hsiung grappled with familiar doubts. Perhaps Chancellor Liu Shui was to blame for his uncomfortable feelings. From the outset, the fat man had questioned every scattered piece of intelligence, always smiling his Buddha-like smile as he advised caution and delay.

It had been the spymasters, Chao and Hua, who were most bellicose. As he walked back and forth across the sticky, squelching mud their voices echoed in his mind: 'Noble Count! We are assured by your servants in Chenglingji, the noble Zhong clan, that now is the time of the Salt Pans' greatest weakness. We must not squander it, Your Highness!'

Liu Shui, still smiling, had shaken his head slightly and Hsiung had sensed different counsel would prevail. Ever since his old friend and adviser had found him weeping and distraught in the Buddha's caverns, cradling him in his arms until tears diminished into silence, he had possessed an unspoken power over Hsiung.

'Noble Count,' the fat man said, once Chao and Hua finished, 'I advise the following bold actions. First, that you deploy only a third of your forces when you attack the Salt Pans.'

'Sire!' broke in Chao. 'Is that wise? A total victory would secure mastery of Six-hundred-*li* Lake forever! Let every soldier be deployed.'

'Ahem,' replied Liu Shui, 'a most interesting observation, but foolish. If nothing else, defeating one small force will not secure mastery of a large province – and certainly not *forever*, as Master Chao suggests. I counsel leaving the bulk of your forces in reserve. If the Mongols have stripped their garrison bare, as the Honoured Spymasters believe, a few thousand will be more than adequate.'

'I shall consider it,' said Hsiung, gloomily. His mood was often subdued since the Buddha's caves.

When the audience was over and they sat alone over tea, Liu Shui had sighed. 'Will you follow my advice, Noble Count?'

'Yes,' said Hsiung, 'it is sensible. Three thousand picked men should easily crush a garrison a third that number. More would simply create problems in ferrying and feeding them.'

Liu Shui had nodded thoughtfully. 'Will you follow this counsel as well? Let Chao and Hua stay with me until your attack is successful. Above all, tell no one of the date you intend to sail. Not even your concubine.'

This had been a harder concession. Ying-ge was all the pleasure he took from a grey world.

'Very well,' he said.

'And one final thing, Your Highness,' said Liu Shui, his eyes flashing. 'May a new servant of mine accompany your entourage? His name is Shensi and I have instructed him to locate a certain slave in the Salt Pans . . . assuming the poor fellow still lives. For I have learned it is by no means likely Deng Teng perished when his ancestral home burned to the ground.'

At this Hsiung gasped. 'Then he is suffering as I did! A slave in the Salt Pans! Of course this Shensi must seek out Teng. Of course!'

So exciting had been this news that Hsiung could not help sharing it with Ying-ge, reminding her how she had won his heart by comforting him when he was grieving for an old friend. 'Well, it seems he may not be dead after all and that I may have the power to save him!'

Naturally, he had resisted her curious exclamations and questions for a little while. Had he not promised to reveal nothing? But Ying-ge was an exception. He hated to disappoint her. Never before had a lady, and so captivating a lady at that, cared for him deeply, with no advantage to herself – for she often longed to return to Hou-ming where her family dwelt. It was a notable sacrifice on her part, a proof of love that she condescended to remain in a dull hole like Lingling . . .

Those conversations had taken place weeks before. Now Hsiung ceased pacing on the muddy shore and turned to his servants.

'Order the senior officers to assemble on my ship in an hour,' he commanded.

After the conference where the plan of battle was agreed, he lay on a narrow cot, awaiting dawn.

It was odd to feel afraid. Not that he feared a stray blow or arrow might end all he had won, Hsiung derided such threats, even welcomed them in a way he could not explain. No, it was a Salt Pans long gone that frightened him, as an adult recalls his childish terror of bogeymen like Big Voice Yang or shadows on a wall at night. A Salt Pans where demons wore human forms, their faces contorted with a cruelty he had found unimaginable after the kindness and urbanity of his boyhood in Deng Mansions. Foremost among those demons was Overseer Pi-tou, his pock-marked features smiling as he raised the whip, smiling when angry, always angry, even when he dragged Hsiung into the deep ditch where the abandoned brine hole bubbled like a foul well and he had been ordered to remove his clothes and kneel. A repulsion akin to nausea gripped Hsiung and he rose from his cot, startling the bodyguard outside.

Returning to his blankets, the Noble Count curled like a dry leaf, hugging himself. All that was gone! Perhaps it never really happened. Yet as he repeated that old mantra of denial a realisation grew, one so simple it amazed him he had never glimpsed it before. There had been no dark lights until Overseer Pi-tou. Pi-tou was their monstrous father. Then Hsiung remembered the tortured faces of the sinners in hell and sensed the possibility of a terrible revenge.

He fell into an uneasy slumber. It was fortunate that, when he woke, he could recall nothing of his dreams – or what he did in them – except a vague, uneasy excitement.

天命

Not content with shedding more rain, the clouds darkened,

threatening a storm. Still Hsiung ordered the fleet forward, led by sailors with experience of this coastline. An hour later, their progress slowed by a slack breeze, warning cries arose from lookouts stationed on mastheads.

'Small boats ahead! A line of them!'

Hsiung, who stood with General P'ao – the former sergeant having gained yet another promotion – waited expectantly.

'They've seen us!' shouted the lookout. 'Some are heading east, others west. Some flee back to the Salt Pans.'

Hsiung turned to his old friend. 'What does this mean?'

'That they're looking out for us,' replied P'ao. 'Perhaps we're expected.'

'Perhaps,' muttered Hsiung. 'It is a chance we must take.'

Soon low-lying islands of mud, rock and water-loving plants rose on the horizon. None were bigger than a large field, most much smaller. Between them flowed channels lined by reeds: a perfect place to conceal small boats for an ambush. The rain fell ceaselessly so that the muddy brown water shimmered and danced.

'Go cautiously now!' urged the captain to the tillerman. There was no other way to advance unless one risked being stuck on a mud-bank. But the main channels were deep and wide enough for their largest vessels to sail two abreast. Still they saw no trace of the enemy, just occasional flocks of birds startled by the creak of bamboo masts and sails.

'The Salt Pans!' cried General P'ao from the prow. 'Noble Count, I see them!'

Hsiung also peered through the rain, his heartbeat quickening. The same dismal place of his nightmares, only smaller than he remembered. Then it had seemed to cover the earth. Hundreds of pagoda-shaped wooden derricks rose above the level of the vast marsh, each denoting a borehole. A thousand angry demon eyes from the gas flames. Over there the squat lines of the ramparts and menacing ugliness of the fortress.

Where was the opposition he expected? The fleet of small

boats he knew were stationed here had not issued out to delay them, though they must have received warning of the attack.

'Make straight for the piers and jetties!' he commanded. 'While they're still napping!'

Even here their luck held. Only a few hundred of the enemy gathered to contest their landing. Flights of arrows and small thunderclap bombs hurled by whirling tiger catapults from the warships' decks soon sent them scurrying back towards dry land and the safety of their fortress. Steam billowed up from hundreds of boiling pans, obscuring the scores of guards who ran to and fro on the fortress battlements.

Hsiung understood why it was so easy. The spymasters' reports were entirely correct! The Mongols had diminished their garrison to a size where it was only capable of oppressing the slaves and indentured labourers working the Salt Pans. Yet this realisation brought no exultation. Hsiung could not forget his first glimpse of this hell when he arrived as a boy.

Still the rain fell, turning the ground to mud. He stepped onto the wooden pier, a hand on his sword hilt. All around him armoured men climbed ashore, streaming down the wooden planks of the jetties to take up position on the foreshore. It was a manoeuvre they had practised many times on the wharfs of Port Yulan. Hsiung turned to General P'ao, whose expression was thoughtful. Perhaps he, too, experienced unpleasant recollections of this dismal place.

'I want it done quickly,' said Hsiung.

General P'ao bowed. 'As you say, Noble Count! The sooner we're home in Lingling the better.'

He strode off to form the troops into a phalanx, ready to attack.

天命

A no man's land of about three *li* climbed from the jetties and piers to the fortress, a wide strip of dry ground rising from the marsh. To the left of this strip lay the channels and walkways and tiny islands of the salt workings, a maze of boiling pans and derricks: no place for heavily armoured men unless they wished to sink up to their waists in mud. To the right of the strip rose earthen ramparts, leading all the way to the fortress.

Hsiung realised he must enter trapped ground: marsh on one side, high walls on the other. General P'ao evidently shared his misgivings, for he whispered: 'What do you think?'

Hsiung glowered up at the battlements of the fortress: the defences had collapsed in places and there wasn't even a proper ditch. Few troops seemed to be manning the place.

'We have come too far to hesitate,' he said. 'Order the attack.'

Flags waved. Drums echoed. The three thousand strong columns of rebels advanced across the sticky ground, weaving around thatched huts. Behind them came special teams with a hundred siege ladders. Hsiung's disquiet increased: the terrain reminded him of somewhere else, though he could not think where.

Then they were through the huts and were only two *li* from the fortress gates. At once the echo of huge kettledrums rose from behind the battlements. Hsiung raised his hand and flags fluttered to order a halt.

As though in response to his signal the wide doors of the fortress opened and a column, a dozen men wide, poured out. Hsiung peered at them through the rain: banners, signal drums, above all they wore the armour of trained guardsmen. The hole in his stomach became a pit. Doorways high up in the fortress walls that led onto the earthen ramparts of the Salt Pans had also opened, emitting a stream of archers. Their intention was obvious, to pour arrows down on the dense ranks of Yueh Fei rebels.

Hsiung reacted instantly.

'Captain Jin! Clear those ramparts, whatever the cost. General P'ao, forward at double speed! We must drive them back into the fortress before they deploy their full force!'

A terrible urge to charge forward at the head of his men had to be mastered. Liu Shui had cautioned him against risking his life – if he perished in battle their army would become leaderless and thousands would die unnecessarily. So he hung back as the rebels surged forward, clashing with the Mongol forces. Arrows and crossbow bolts arched down from the fortress, blending with the rain.

'Your Highness!' shouted his standard bearer. 'Look to our left!'

Hsiung turned, just as an arrow rushed at his helmet, bouncing off the wet metal. He did not need the help of his standard bearer's pointing finger. Hundreds of lightly armoured troops had appeared from hidden places amidst the derricks and boiling pans, some attacking from the raised earthen walkways, others in small boats. Their aim was obvious: to harry the rebel flank. Hsiung realised they now faced enemies on three sides: and already the casualties from the flights of arrows were severe. As he watched, more and more of the heavily armoured Uighur guardsmen jogged out of the fortress gates.

'It is a trap!' he shouted, turning to his standard bearer. But the man was on his knees, an arrow in his chest, eyes bulging as he struggled to keep the flag showing. Others seized it as he fell face forward into the mud. 'Drummers!' bellowed Hsiung. 'Order a retreat to the ships! No, halt! Do not sound a retreat, damn you!'

He had realised the extent of the Mongols' cunning. An examination of his fleet revealed scores of small enemy boats packed with marines, appearing from hiding places in the maze of islands out on the lake. It would take all his navy's strength to repulse them, let alone sail in and out of the jetties for an orderly embarkation of the rebel troops. Meanwhile the assault against them could only intensify.

A sudden stillness entered Hsiung's soul: the din and roar of battle seemed to die away. He noticed Jebe Khoja watching from the battlements of the fortress and, quite dispassionately, Hsiung comprehended the Mongol general's revenge. The sweet, delicious irony of it all. For Jebe Khoja had merely tempted and trapped him, as he had tricked the Mongol to advance too far into Fourth Hell Gorge eight years before. In that moment of stillness he saw more enemy troops gathering, an endless supply, and realised the Red Turbans were not only trapped but outnumbered. Hsiung felt no grief at this realisation. Or despair. He possessed a single ambition: not to fall with dishonour. Ignoring all Liu Shui's admonishments, Hsiung swept out his long sword.

'Beat the drums for a new attack!' he ordered.

Followed by his bodyguard, Hsiung strode to the front rank of the rebel Guards where his men were wavering.

'Yueh Fei!' he bellowed. 'For justice and the Buddha Maitreya!'

With this rallying cry the rebels renewed their assault, hacking and trampling scores of Mongol infantry. Always there were more, always another hundred to replace those killed. And though Captain Jin had succeeded in clearing the ramparts to their right of archers, still arrows and crossbow bolts fell from the fortress walls in front of the rebel army.

Hsiung cut a way through to General P'ao who had come within a *li* of the gates and could advance no nearer.

'Hsiung!' he called. 'We must retreat in an orderly way while we still can!' But the Noble Count raged with pride at the three Mongol warriors he had dispatched. 'We must retreat to the jetties!' repeated P'ao. 'With luck we might hold them off until our ships are ready to start embarking the men. That way at least some of us might escape.'

Hsiung's joy died away. Jebe Khoja remained visible on the battlements, tantalisingly near.

'Damn you!' he said, bitterly. 'Order it then!'

Soon the rebel signal drums were beating and they withdrew, somehow still fighting and in good order, back towards the piers. Halfway there, Hsiung squinted up at the sky in surprise. Something had changed. He laughed. For the first time in days the rain had stopped. In that new silence another noise arose, one that forced all those on the battlefield, rebel or warrior loyal to the Great Khan, to look round in alarm.

天命

Perhaps the name of Yueh Fei inspired the new noise. Perhaps long-simmering outrage reached boiling point at the sight of the rebels – who were, after all, the salt workers' one hope of liberation. Perhaps it was the desperation of men driven to any fate rather than famine and perpetual abuse.

It began in a small way. A group of Uighur footsoldiers, beaten back from the rebel flanks, chanced upon a work gang hiding near a derrick. Frustrated by their retreat from the battle, the Uighurs found easier meat, cutting down a dozen slaves and indentured labourers. The surprise came when the barefoot, dirt-encrusted wretches fought back. After the Uighurs had been overwhelmed by sheer numbers, the foreman, terrified of reprisals, seized a metal hammer and began to beat the side of the bubbling iron pan. Six feet across, it resounded like an enormous gong. *Deng . . . deng . . . deng.* The sound drifted across marsh and borehole and bamboo derrick. *Deng . . . deng . . . deng.* Now another work gang joined in, catching the rhythm. Like a hot wind the clanging spread from work gang to work gang, stirring memories of failed revolts. Only this time they were not alone against the Mongol troops.

That was the moment when the entire battlefield drew breath to listen. Even Jebe Khoja, surveying his inevitable triumph from the fortress's battlements felt a stab of doubt.

First singly, then in small groups, semi-naked men appeared on the spider's web of raised earth walkways linking the hundreds of brine holes. They carried improvised weapons:

hammers and spades, lengths of chain and long staves of bamboo. Others wielded hatchets or knives. Pitiful weapons compared to those possessed by the thousands of heavily-armoured Mongol troops and their allies. But in ankle-deep mud the swift, barefoot man often has the advantage, and few were more accustomed to keeping their balance in slime than the salt workers.

Deng . . . deng . . . deng. Thirty thousand men toiled in the Salt Pans. When half that number roused themselves and streamed to join the battle, forming long, bellowing mobs on the walkways, it became clear that the Mongols – who had out-numbered Hsiung's rebels two-to-one – were outmatched in their turn.

The ancient military sages all agreed: men willing to die always defeat those fearful of death. The slaves and labourers of the Salt Pans were already under a death sentence. Those who knew hopeless awakenings in the drab light of dawn, day after day, season through season, each year futureless and featureless because destined to be exactly like the one that gave it birth – only those knew what little worth life can possess. How small a purchase on this illusory earth. Here was a possibility of revenge.

Men willing to die always defeat those fearful of death. So it proved.

For a long, terrible hour the battle advanced back and forth until, finally, the Mongols – already wearied by slipping in the mire – discovered their way back to the fortress had been blocked by thousands of slaves. To their front the Yueh Fei rebels took heart, driving deep into the packed Mongol ranks. Fallen men lay in piles across the mud. Scores tried to escape across the walkways or took last stands around towering wooden derricks. There they were hunted and pulled down. Neither side took prisoners.

Yet only a few *li* away, a little distance beyond the ramparts, marsh birds still dipped their long, curved beaks into a sediment composed of irrepressible life and death, millennia of rotted plants and diverse bodies. The birds gorged on fleas, insects and leeches, oblivious to the thousands of men tasting their last hour on this earth. Clouds drifted west to reveal a pale, blue spring sky.

By dusk the fighting was over. Hsiung set up his headquarters in a port official's bureau at the head of the main pier. In this hall thatched with reeds he took stock. The Mongol fleet had finally withdrawn, having suffered a mauling. The rebels' own losses had been severe: a third of the fleet either sunk or burned, including some valuable warships. Though the Yueh Fei rebels might claim victory on both land and water, the gaps in their ranks made it a sour one. Faithful Captain Jin was gone, even old P'ao, who could survive any calamity, had taken a chest wound.

Hsiung stepped outside and stared up at the fortress. Its battlements were lit by many lamps; despite the slaughter, hundreds of defenders remained within its brick-lined earth walls. Until they were dislodged he could not claim victory. And any siege when he had not only his troops but thirty thousand hungry salt workers to feed would not last long. Hsiung summoned an adjutant.

'Take three ships and fly to Lingling!' he commanded. 'Tell Chancellor Liu Shui he is required at once. Tell him I need reinforcements and as much grain as he can gather.'

The officer bowed, pressing both fists together, and hurried off to find undamaged ships. At that moment Hsiung became aware of a delegation approaching, escorted by his picked bodyguard. Ever since the calamity in the Buddha's caves he had detected the threat of assassination everywhere.

Hsiung sat regally on a stool taken from the thatched hall, legs spread wide, back straight, hands resting on thick upper thighs. Half a dozen men wearing paltry hemp clothes abased themselves before him, awaiting his command to speak. Hsiung's glance flickered over their heads to the dark line of the fortress. He had no siege engines other than ladders; any spirited defence by Jebe Khoja's surviving men – and they were sure to fight to the last arrow – would cost hundreds, perhaps thousands, of his best troops.

'Well,' he said, irritably, lowering his gaze to the supplicants before him. He fully expected requests for food he was unable to satisfy.

At this cue a grizzled face lifted. Hsiung found himself being frankly examined by an elderly man with bird-like brown eyes.

'I am Wu Chen of the Clan Wu,' announced the man. 'Our ancestors came to the Salt Pans from Wu Village a hundred years ago. We offer pledges of loyalty.'

'I accept them,' said Hsiung, his attention already drifting back to the fortress and calculations about siege ladders.

Old Wu did not withdraw. 'Noble Count!' said the salt worker. 'Your victory is incomplete. Therefore, so is our own. As long as the foreign demons hide in their den none of us are safe.'

'So I fear,' said Hsiung, leaning forward. 'Do you have a suggestion?'

At this Wu glanced at his friends for support.

'There are ways in,' he said, quietly. 'Ways that don't involve storming the gate. And another thing, Noble Count: after days of rain there is often a thick fog the next morning.'

It took only a moment for the significance of this to sink in.

'Fetch all the Captains,' ordered Hsiung. 'As for you, Wu, say exactly what's on your mind and I'll reward your clan all the more.'

That was encouragement enough for Wu to point at particular sections of the fortress and mutter words intended for the Noble Count's ears alone.

天命

At dawn, dense fog rolled in from the lake, beading with glistening droplets every plant stem and hard surface. Hsiung ordered extra water to be boiled in the gigantic salt cauldrons to swell the cloaks of vapour wrapped around his men. They moved silently, guided by members of the Wu clan and other Yueh Fei rebels, each leading a column fifty strong. Cocks could be heard crowing within the fortress. No one on the walls noticed the group carrying large clay gourds wrapped in cloth from which cords trailed. Gingerly, each man piled his heavy container against a thick, iron-studded door cut into a hidden corner of the fortress ramparts; an entrance long disused, if the moss growing over it and mildew stains on the metal gave any clue.

When the mound of gourds resting against the door was as large as one might find in a melon market at harvest-time, an officer crept forward with a glowing fire-pot. Still no one stirred on the walls. With a flash the fuse lit. The officer scurried back, seeking any hole that might provide cover. Moments later the burning powder ignited with a huge roar like a thousand bellowing dragons. Before its echoes died away another explosion boomed round the Salt Pans from the far side of the fortress.

'Yueh Fei!' called an exultant voice in the mist. 'Yueh Fei! Yueh Fei!' replied thousands more. The hidden columns waiting in line rushed forward to the two breaches in the walls.

Naturally, the defence in the mist-shrouded alleys and streets of the fortress was resolute. It could hardly be otherwise. The Mongols were accustomed to victory plucked from disaster through the sheer force and courage of their arms. Outside the Salt Minister's residence, hundreds took a stand, determined to protect their tribal khan, Jebe Khoja. All were cut down, their corpses despoiled and beheaded. Elsewhere, the rebels discovered cowering men: ill-paid Chinese mercenaries, quite willing to surrender without a single parry or blow.

By mid-morning, when the fog had begun to clear, Hsiung strode through the front gate of the fortress, surrounded by his bodyguard. As a boy-slave in the Salt Pans he had never entered this citadel. Now he looked around eagerly, not at the buildings – all ordinary enough – but for particular captives. In his determination to find them he almost fell victim to a Mongol archer hiding on a roof. But the arrow bounced off a lucky jade disk he had been given by Ying-ge as a love token and the assassin was hunted down with crossbow bolts.

Seated upon a throne dragged from the Salt Minister's residence into the parade ground, Hsiung surveyed the prisoners. The Mongol and Uighur warriors were easily dealt with. Once stripped of armour, boots and weapons, they were branded with their own slave irons on forehead and cheek, then driven off to toil in the Salt Pans, for Hsiung was determined the precious salt must keep flowing. Lesser officials and Chinese guards who refused to swear allegiance to the Noble Count went the same way. The group that remained was smaller and more select. Hsiung's pleasure as he surveyed them was almost like a flutter of fear.

For the second time, Prince Jebe Khoja was his prisoner. The Mongol noble had tried to die fighting but suffered an unlucky halberd blow to his legs that swept him to the floor. There he was disarmed and trussed like a peacock. Now, held upright by two nephews, he refused to bow to the rebel Count. Hsiung expected nothing less: had Jebe Khoja abased himself, he would have been revolted.

'Your Highness,' he said, using an interpreter though he knew the Mongol prince spoke Chinese, 'you had a good plan. Unfortunately for you the Mandate of Heaven is against you. That is your bad luck.'

Jebe Khoja laughed harshly, replying in Chinese with a thick accent.

'All luck runs out, Noble Count, even yours. As I have learned.'

It was Hsiung's turn to laugh, though less confidently.

'Having enjoyed so little luck in my youth,' he said, 'I've plenty left in store.' His Captains applauded their master's wit. 'Prince, you shall be given a ship so you can return to Hou-ming with a message for Prince Arslan,' said Hsiung. 'As for your officials and household, they may also accompany you.'

Jebe Khoja nodded in surprise at these generous terms. He had fully expected his head's removal. 'I am, regrettably, once more placed in your debt,' he said, with bitter dignity.

'I want nothing in return,' said Hsiung.

Yet he could not explain the real motive for his clemency: that he longed for Liu Shui's nod of approval as one might a father's affection; that he wished to set a little mercy against all the killing he had inspired when the Infernal Judges assessed the length of his torment.

Hsiung's eye fell upon a tall, familiar figure kneeling with Jebe Khoja's other high officials. His merciful mood vanished. He had recognised Salt Minister Gui, the very same man who had enslaved him when just a boy and burned Deng Mansions. For a long moment he considered rescinding his offer to allow Jebe Khoja's officials to sail with him, a dilemma settled, in the end, by vanity. He could not risk his honour by breaking a pledge so soon after it had been uttered.

'Halt!' he commanded, pointing at the Salt Minister as he followed Jebe Khoja out of the parade ground. All eyes turned, glancing between the tall, spindly official clutching his abacus and the thick-limbed soldier on his throne.

'Consider yourself lucky!' said Hsiung. 'Had I seen you earlier, you would not be leaving with dignity like your master. Remember his words, Gui! All luck runs out. If we meet again it will be the very end of yours.'

Hsiung glowered as the prisoners were led away towards the piers. There was still one enemy he longed to meet. So badly that he had issued a large reward for his capture. While he brooded on his borrowed throne a deep emptiness in his soul echoed with painful cries: his own when he was a boy and ten thousand since, memories of the indignities he had suffered, some so shameful he dared not acknowledge them even to himself.

He was stirred by the arrival in the parade ground of a large, jabbering group of salt workers. Most wore clothes looted from fallen enemies – boots, tunics, cloaks and weapons. In their midst was a single prisoner, his head shaven and face pockmarked. Hsiung stiffened, fists clenching as they rested on his legs. Yet he found it hard to look at the prisoner and flushed with distress, so that his captains, noticing his every gesture and mood like anxious lovers, exchanged looks.

Chief Overseer Pi-tou was thrown onto a patch of bare earth before Hsiung's throne. For a moment he grovelled, then fixed a sharp glance on the Noble Count of Lingling. Did he see only a feeble, lowly boy? Hsiung believed so, and quailed until the old anger asserted itself and his hand crept towards his sword. How simple it would be to sweep that hated head from its neck!

'Noble Count!' exclaimed Foreman Wu Mao of the Wu clan. 'We have captured this man as you decreed.'

Still Hsiung did not speak. The dark lights had issued forth from the black corners where they hid in his spirit, seeding a hundred fantasies of squashing the bald, pocked-marked head until the skull cracked and oozed pulp like a marrow; of boiling that gourd alive; severing nose and ears and eyelids with special implements, organ by organ. Those foul dreams – or desires – made him shiver and remember the frieze of the sinner he had desecrated in the Buddha's caves. Then an inner voice whispered to his soul, quieter than the first, urging moderation and calm; the ambiguous satisfaction of justice. It was this voice that lent him the courage to stare down at his old tormentor.

'What am I to do with you?' he asked.

Overseer Pi-tou remained silent. Hsiung turned to the

assembled Wu clan and other rebel leaders. He sensed he should offer them something – or someone.

'How is justice best served?' he asked. 'Does this man deserve mercy?'

These words, so hard to utter because he longed for his own fists and feet to deliver their verdict, never ceasing until his enemy shrieked and begged and implored, soiling his clothes with shameful essences, fawning with big eyes like a whipped bitch – these words, unimaginable when Overseer Pi-tou had entered the square, suddenly felt strong and good, pure as slanting sunlight.

Foreman Wu Mao bowed. 'He deserves no mercy,' he said, flatly.

Hsiung nodded. Still he hesitated before surrendering his prize.

'I shall give him,' he said, slowly, 'to whatever punishment you and your companions see fit, even if that means his release.' He stared up at a sky littered with puffy clouds. So he did not see his old abuser dragged away, or hear his curses. When he glanced down again a sallow, scowling fellow knelt before him, a man he recognised as an agent of Liu Shui.

'Noble Count,' said the man, 'that last prisoner confessed to sending someone dear to us all on a march to his death. I mean, the Honourable Deng Teng.'

Hsiung leaned forward. 'The Chancellor told me of your mission. You are Shensi, are you not? Find Teng! Take fifty swift men as guards.' He turned to General P'ao. 'Ensure this man is given every assistance!'

Hsiung rose heavily and withdrew to the Salt Minister's residence where he lay on a silk-strewn bed, unable to sleep or recover his strength. Would he have rested more easily had he known the penalty exacted on Chief Overseer Pi-tou by an assembly of the Salt Pans' foremen? But boiling a man alive in a huge iron cauldron while hundreds watch and jeer is rarely restful. Fortunately, he soothed himself with images of beautiful Ying-ge – and the knowledge that a jade disk given by her as a love token had warded off a Mongol arrow meant for his heart.

thirty

天命

Eyelids caked with their own brine, sticky from griefless weeping, would not open. Could not. A strain of muscles never before noticed prying those lids apart. Suddenly revealed: washes of light filtering through coated lashes. Golden light becoming blue, a realisation of sky . . .

Teng stirred into consciousness, aware of pain in every limb, his chest aching to draw breath. Worse was the itchy thirst, worse even than hunger – in itself a desperate kind of hunger– so his mind became a single lust: water. Suddenly he thought, *I am dying of thirst*, as small children declare their situation to the world in perplexed wonder. Then he had another thought: *Let it be soon.*

The blue sky contained wisps of cloud. He had seen that sky before! Exactly when, he was less sure. Once it had lain across his eyes as skies are reflected upon clear lakes. He had seen a special lake once. Where was it? A half-forgotten shrine where a young woman bathed in shimmering green water, her pure skin glowing . . . A painful gargle rose in his throat. By the time it subsided, he was spent. Oh, he thought, now is the time to commence my next incarnation. He waited, falling back into a dark, dry dream.

Something new penetrated the mist. Had he been conscious, he might have feared a fox taking a bite out of his nose or a bird probing with its beak before tugging out his eyeballs. Surely now he would meet the Infernal Judges! Be honoured by them as one of their exalted caste, a scholar-official, an Honourable Deng!

Something stroked his lips. They were solid as mud-baked bricks. And again. Unexpectedly, his tongue – heavy as a laden barge – tried to move forward. Again, a brush against his lips. His tongue stirred.

Now hearing returned, bringing messages from the darkness. Were those voices? He grew certain of it. Words were less clear.

The stroking moved to his eyes. He shivered. Felt the eyelids stir like slaves whose chains have been removed. A moment later they opened and a face filled the sky. Teng panicked. It was a ghost! Poor, faithful Shensi! He was waiting to greet him when he woke in Hell.

Now his lips were being moved by some outside force. Then the tip of his tongue melted into softness like a clod of dry earth watered gently. Swallow, Teng urged himself, *drink more . . .* that was his last thought for a while. His body took care of the drinking without a need for thought, until the first droplets trickled down the baked tunnel of his throat.

天命

For two weeks he lay on the foggy border dividing all things from their final destination. It turned out to be a far from lonely place. All manner of faces swam into view, some strangers, others remembered from his former life, albeit vaguely. There was Shensi, of course, ugly and scowling but no less welcome for that. And a big fat man's face topped with a high official's fancy, tasselled silk hat. But Teng could not recall his name, only that once he had met him when fleeing a dark, terrible cave.

Best of all was a face he recognised yet did not – or not quite.

Its shape was familiar, even some of its expressions, but it had changed too much for Teng to be convinced.

The first time it appeared he turned away in exhaustion and fell asleep. When it returned, Teng accepted with a sense of acute wonder it belonged to Hsiung. Oddly enough, this realisation was more unsettling than when he had been unsure.

As Teng grew aware of his surroundings he realised his bed stood in a chamber decorated with silk drapes and wall-paintings. Servants circulated constantly. Though he felt too feeble to rise or even sit up without help, every few hours water and pulped food were fed to him until, day by day, he regained a little appetite.

The time came when his vision recovered full clarity. He had been able to speak for some days and so he asked the servant crouching in a corner to raise the paper blinds. The man obeyed with an alacrity and respect that gave Teng new strength.

Up the blinds went, revealing a large garden filled with flowers and trees, floating insects and butterflies. For a moment Teng watched, lulled by soft colours in the sunshine, for it was late spring and the monsoon had paused, a delightful time of year. Then he peered more closely. He had detected an unusual garden ornament – no, a dozen of them – hanging from ropes on the high wall that surrounded the garden. He squinted to see more closely. His eyes opened wide.

A dozen men dangled from iron spikes. All were a purple-grey, no, mottled blue, rotting in the heat. A large crow landed on one of the sagging heads and pecked vigorously. Teng turned to stare at the wall.

'Who?' he croaked. Every word was still painful. 'Who are they?'

The servant looked around for someone passing by, but the garden was deserted. Finally he noticed the hanging men.

'My old masters,' he said without a trace of mourning.

'Every male in the Zhong clan hangs either there or in the market square, back to the third generation.'

'Why?' managed Teng.

'Because they betrayed the Noble Count,' explained the servant, fearfully. 'May he live a thousand years!'

A thousand years, echoed in Teng's mind. *A thousand years*. He connected Yun Shu to the corpses rotting on the wall. Her husband's family were no more. Then he was dreaming a fruitless search through the smouldering, smoke-blackened corridors of Deng Mansions. Finally he reached the miniature mountain constructed by Grandfather Deng in imitation of Holy Mount Chang. She turned to him as he climbed towards her. 'They have done to the Zhongs what the Mongols did to us Dengs!' he cried. 'We are free to marry!' His dream folded into darkness.

天命

Teng recovered sufficiently to receive formal visitors. He found that, with the aid of a stick, he could totter round the garden to a bench set before an oval pond. Averting his eyes from the dangling Zhongs allowed him to appreciate the flowerbeds, the gentle rustle of rare bamboos. Humming birds weaved over the still pond, yellow-crested and darting as they snatched droning insects.

One afternoon he returned to his room to find the servants in a fluster. Half a dozen had appeared from nowhere, scrubbing the floor and artfully strewing flower petals round precious, paper-thin porcelain bowls. Others lit tapering cones of subtle incense. Still more produced trays of wine and tea and covered bowls of delicacies.

When Teng asked the reason he was ignored. From this he deduced his visitor was not only feared, but his arrival was imminent. He took a seat upon the couch and awaited events.

A butler preceded His Highness to ensure that all was proper.

Satisfied, he withdrew, murmuring to someone further up the corridor. Feet scurried, followed by heavy, booted footfalls. Teng was confronted by the arrival of a tall, broad-limbed man. The servants fell to their knees, pressing their foreheads to the freshly scrubbed floor. Teng limited himself to a bow while remaining on the couch – it was doubtful he could have managed more. In any case, kowtowing to the family kitchen boy was a humiliation he could not contemplate.

It became apparent he was not the only one who was uneasy. The Noble Count of Lingling looked around the room as though seeking something to criticise. He stood awkwardly, tapping a large bunched fist with an impatient hand. His weathered face, though not unkindly, seemed melancholy to Teng. The exquisitely tailored silks he wore somehow did not fit. Teng thought it best to break the long silence.

'Noble Count,' he said, 'forgive me for not rising. You see how I am . . .'

As Teng had anticipated, reference to his weakness granted Hsiung enough superiority to feel at ease.

'I take it you have been well treated by my servants?' he said.

'Impeccably treated. I owe you my life.'

Now Hsiung relaxed further. He waved his hand nonchalantly as though such gifts were trifles. Still he hovered.

'It would be the greatest honour for me if you took the refreshments you have arranged,' suggested Teng, delicately.

'Yes, I have a little time. Why not?'

Hsiung took a seat swept first by a diligent servant with a gigantic fly-whisk. Wine was brought and delicate pastries stuffed with shredded swan's wings and strips of roasted bear paws flavoured with a rich, pungent spice. Both were medicinal and intended to aid Teng's recovery.

'You have grown since I last saw you!' exclaimed Teng, sipping his wine.

Hsiung shot him a suspicious look. 'Of course. We were just boys.'

'If only my honoured father could see us together,' said Teng, sadly. 'It would give him great joy. Yet I do not know for certain whether he is even still alive.'

'I have ordered spies to confirm that,' said Hsiung. 'But I believe he is safe. Be sure I'll do all I can to protect him. Such is the respect and gratitude I feel for Deng Nan-shi.'

He was interrupted by Teng clutching gratefully at his hands. So unusual was intimate contact with the Noble Count his attendants moaned excitedly.

The two boyhood friends – scholar and soldier, former master and kitchen boy, man of meagre means and rich, triumphant warlord – glanced up to find Chancellor Liu Shui beaming down at them, sheer delight on his fleshy face.

'At last!' he cried. 'A truly advantageous friendship for Your Highness!'

Teng felt Hsiung pull away his hand. The Noble Count laughed uneasily.

'How so, Liu Shui?' he asked.

'That is simple,' replied the Chancellor. 'As I have mentioned before, Confucius names three advantageous friendships. With the sincere, the upright and the man of perceptive observation. Surely Honourable Deng Teng possesses those qualities.'

Teng bowed modestly and replied: 'If I am to be pine, bamboo and plum tree, first I must recover a little sap.'

Chancellor Liu Shui grunted approvingly at this clever allusion.

'What is all this talk of trees?' asked Hsiung.

'They are symbols of friendship,' explained Teng, 'for neither pine, bamboo nor plum tree die in winter but remain constant and blossom before spring comes.'

'Aptly expressed!' said Liu Shui.

Teng detected a shadow of resentment in Hsiung's face as though the Noble Count wanted all his Chancellor's praise for himself. He would need to step carefully. Pleading exhaustion, he was glad to regain the relative safety of his sickbed.

*　　*　　*

The next day Hsiung returned, this time with servants bearing boxes of books, writing equipment and silken clothes. All the garments were used, there having been no time to measure and make so many splendid outfits. Teng expressed his appreciation in the warmest terms, yet could not help wondering if he would soon be wearing the clothes of men currently rotting outside. It seemed an ominous way to regain one's dignity.

Pleased by his own generosity, the Noble Count went so far as to mutter: 'Who'd have imagined it.' Though the exact nature of *it* was not explained.

After the presents, Hsiung insisted on taking Teng for a drive in his carriage 'to see something worth seeing'. During the journey through the small town of Chenglingji neither was sure what to say. Their past, shared and brutally severed, both connected and forced them apart. Perhaps, thought Teng, the Noble Count could not forgive the fact he had once played the role of inferior. When Teng considered the matter, perhaps he could not forgive it either, though for opposite – and quite justified – reasons. He asked Hsiung about the capture of Chenglingji and received a glowing account that avoided any reference to a massacre of innocent townsfolk.

Their destination turned out to be the harbour. They stepped onto the wharf and the Noble Count gestured at long lines of shipyards. A large fleet was being constructed by thousands of scurrying labourers, paid for by revenue from the Salt Pans.

'You will be surprised by my plans,' he said, 'perhaps even amazed.'

Teng waited for more. A calculating look crossed Hsiung's face.

'I cannot share those plans, even with you.' His tone suggested pleasure in being the guardian of so important a secret. 'After the trap that nearly destroyed us in the Salt Pans, only a tiny number share my intentions. It is better that way.' Hsiung laughed bitterly. 'I do not mind telling you, Liu Shui even wants me to say nothing to my own concubine! She will be joining us soon, along with two of my spymasters. Then you shall see a fine woman!'

Teng sensed Hsiung had more boasting in mind.

'From your tone, I divine she is a notable beauty,' he said, helpfully.

'Ha! Some might call her divine.'

'She, at least, cannot be a secret. Surely I have heard of her?'

'Perhaps,' chuckled Hsiung, 'she is an actress from Hou-ming. When she arrives I shall order her to perform for both our pleasures. Ah Teng, how she can sing! When I thought you had died she sang a song all about grief that won my heart.'

Teng had rarely seen Hsiung so voluble, even as a boy, and smiled at the softening of his old companion's character.

'That would be an honour,' he said, bowing. 'What is her name?'

'Ying-ge.'

Teng's expression froze. He struggled to maintain his smile.

'Ying-ge? An actress, you say?'

'Yes,' said Hsiung. 'Have you heard of her?'

'No . . . no . . .' said Teng, plucking at his chin. Habits of pride made him a poor liar; fortunately his host was too busy explaining the merits of his new navy to notice.

On the drive back, Hsiung was disappointed when Teng pleaded exhaustion and closed his eyes. The Noble Count even muttered: 'If I had undergone the same trials as you, Teng, I would have recovered weeks ago!' Still the feeble scholar did not stir.

Shielded by frailty, Teng's mind swirled. Ying-ge had betrayed him to Salt Minister Gui, no doubt for a substantial reward. Given Hsiung's infatuation with her, there were few limits to the mischief she might deploy. His one hope was that Ying-ge did not know the Salt Minister had revealed her treacherous actions. A hope as slender as her waist – and insinuating tongue.

天命

'That whore, coming here?' exclaimed Shensi.

'Speak more quietly,' urged Teng, 'I do not wish to join those poor wretches.'

They were on a bench beside the pond, their eyes drawn irresistibly to the bloated, maggot-infested and fly-bound corpses still dangling a little distance away. When the wind changed direction, Teng smelt them in his room and thought the sickly odour a warning to be cautious.

'The Noble Count serves a noble cause,' he muttered, 'but we must take care, Shensi, great care.'

The tomb-finder grunted.

'I'll pack everything necessary for a quick escape,' he said. 'A man with *cash* and supplies could hide in the hill country behind Chenglingji until his beard turned grey.'

With that he left, looking round to check he was not followed.

Later that day, Teng found himself picnicking with the Noble Count at a beauty spot inland from Chenglingji, where waterfalls converged to form a deep pool in a rocky valley. Blessed by every kind of natural beauty, it was the kind of place gentleman-scholars painted and praised in verse.

Their picnic consisted of forty separate dishes, many heated on charcoal braziers: spiced fish, shreds of peppered beef and snow peas, frogs legs sautéed in copper pans and served with sesame seed biscuits. A small orchestra provided fitting harmonies to complement the ceaseless, eternal music of the waterfalls. Though Teng's fingers were still stiff from labouring in the Salt Pans, he was persuaded by Liu Shui to play a patriotic tune from the former dynasty on the lute. Though unexceptional, his performance was applauded loudly by all present, especially the Noble Count.

'Ah,' he said, 'how I remember the hours you spent practising that damned instrument when we were boys! You did not know it, but I often slipped into the city to see what fun could be had for far less effort!'

His Highness was drunk enough for a little indiscretion. Chancellor Liu Shui bowed. 'I believe Honourable Deng Teng has a deep wish for you to show him the waterfalls,' he murmured.

Teng looked up in surprise. He had expressed no such wish.

'Why not!' declared Hsiung. 'I need to walk off that dinner. Follow me, Teng!'

They climbed into a grove of pines and followed a winding path littered with ancient, worked flints – proof that men long vanished had used this place. Summer's small birds were plentiful and inclined to sing. Trills and warbles echoed round the wood. Soon they reached the very brink of a waterfall where it fell to join the pond below, flowing between two breast-shaped boulders.

In the distance lay the rooftops and smoke plumes of Chenglingji, framed by the sparkling blue waters of the lake. Teng tried to stare beyond the horizon all the way to Hou-ming.

Reviving strength left him eager to return. Firstly to discover if his ailing father was still alive. If so, arrangements for his care must be set in motion without delay.

Just as urgently, he longed to meet Yun Shu and renew their last, lost conversation. Teng could no longer evade his desires. Yet returning to Hou-ming without knowledge of the situation in the city would most likely end in his arrest.

Thus it was uncanny when Hsiung answered his thoughts: 'I'm glad we have a chance to speak alone,' he said, 'I have firm news concerning your father.'

Teng stirred from his reveries.

'It is good news,' added Hsiung.

Agents had witnessed the old scholar being maintained as an

invalid in Cloud Abode Monastery and treated with great honour. 'You can thank our old playmate, Yun Shu, for that,' he said. 'Doesn't that seem strange? When I told Liu Shui he said that I was pine, you were bamboo, and she was the plum tree. Does that make sense to you?'

Teng nodded. 'I often think of those years when we three played together. Do you remember our old home fondly? I cannot believe it has been reduced to ashes.'

Was that a flicker of annoyance he detected in Hsiung's face? Or some other emotion? Perhaps now was the time to address the past with integrity. The alternative was endless evasion.

'Hsiung,' he said, 'you have grown into a great man who does much good for the people he rules. Maybe my father's influence helped in that. Despite the awkwardness of our previous stations in life, I hope you remember Deng Mansions fondly.'

Hsiung cast a sideways glance at Teng. 'You have no idea how fondly.' Tears started to his eyes. 'I remember Deng Nan-shi as the model of a learned gentleman.'

Teng, too, found himself weeping. As long held-back tears often will, they led to laughter and recollections of hilarious scrapes in the ruins of Monkey Hat Hill. By the time the two men returned to the pond for more wine, they were side by side, shoulders close together, a detail Liu Shui acknowledged with his broadest smile.

Later, as they rode back through the twilit countryside in a large carriage, accompanied by dozens of cavalry, Liu Shui spoke of the relics of Yueh Fei that had been stolen when the library of the Dengs was looted by Salt Minister Gui.

'How I regret not punishing that man when I had him in my power,' mused Hsiung. 'He should have burned alive, just as he burned Deng Mansions.'

'Not all the relics of my ancestor were lost,' said Teng from his corner of the carriage. 'Although it is a trifle, I gave a scroll written by my great ancestor to Abbess Yun Shu of Cloud Abode Monastery. It granted the ownership of a valley in the distant west to her own ancestors, the Yun clan. So something remains.'

Liu Shui grew thoughtful. 'The fact that it alone was preserved is surely significant.'

Near Chenglingji he resumed the topic. 'The cause of Yueh Fei would be strengthened if we recovered those documents and relics. Perhaps it is a duty for you, Honourable Deng Teng, as the great man's only youthful descendent. Besides, I am sure you are anxious to return to Hou-ming to help your father.'

'You read my wishes exactly,' said Teng.

He dared not add that part of his eagerness stemmed from Ying-ge's imminent arrival.

'I can offer you a bodyguard,' said Hsiung. 'Perhaps even the protection of my two Spymasters who are in and out of Hou-ming on my business.'

'Noble Count, I ask only for my friend Shensi,' said Teng.

The carriage passed through the town gates and as the gentlemen parted for the night, Hsiung said in a puzzled, wine-softened voice: 'Do you know, Teng, for years I feared you would grow into a foolish prig. You've proved me wrong. And I'm glad.'

With that he strode to his wing of the mansion.

天命

For the next two weeks Teng often found himself in the Noble Count's company. Not a day passed without a meeting over dinner or visit to a pleasure spot or merely to drink tea and wine in the cool of evening. Though long silences were common between them, they were of the companionable sort.

Teng grew accustomed to Hsiung's brooding and often wondered what was passing through his mind. He sensed dark thoughts, if the contraction of the Noble Count's brow and disturbingly intense expression were clues. Sometimes Hsiung would squeeze his bunched fists until the knuckles whitened, prompted by inner tensions he never shared with Teng. The latter gentleman was glad to be spared.

One hot, long afternoon in early summer while Hsiung was drilling his army before the walls of Chenglingji and practising attacks by siege towers, ladders, covered ramps-on-wheels, Teng sat in the garden of the Noble Count's residence. Only the Zhongs' skin and bones remained, still dangling, still objects of interest to flies. He found himself composing a song in his head and sent a servant for ink, paper and brush. Instead the boy returned with a rotund, huffing figure.

Teng's respectful bow to Chancellor Liu Shui was matched equally.

'Honourable Deng Teng,' said Liu Shui, 'may I claim an interview?'

Again Teng bowed. 'That would be an honour beyond my expectation.'

The fat man took a seat beside him on the stone bench. Both examined the floating water lilies for a while.

'We have been greatly pleased to note your companionship with His Highness,' remarked Liu Shui.

'The pleasure has been entirely my own,' said Teng, 'as has the honour.'

The Chancellor nodded gravely.

'As a scholarly gentleman you will realise, of course,' he said, 'that the Mandate of Heaven has already been lost by the Mongol Yuan Dynasty – assuming they ever really gained it.'

'Of course,' said Teng.

'This is the hour for righteous men, however humble, to be chosen by Heaven as saviours of the people.'

'There are countless examples,' agreed Teng. He went on to mention several from numerous dynasties.

'Yet no ruler, however strong in battle,' said the Chancellor, 'prospers without benign government for the people. Otherwise he is little better than a bandit.'

'Yes,' said Teng, more warily. The wily old scholar-official was clearly preparing for something.

'That is why,' said Liu Shui, 'we are greatly pleased by your influence on His Highness. My agents report that other influences – I may say, less favourable ones – are drawing near. For the sake of your noble father and the cause your entire family perished to defend, perhaps you might be persuaded to stay in Chenglingji until the autumn?'

Teng grew attentive.

'I fear that will not be possible.'

'Ah,' said Liu Shui. 'Please consider my proposal. When I have passed away His Highness will require a new adviser. Who better than a man of impeccable family, intentions and education?'

With that, Liu Shui rose and bowed. Teng did likewise, watching him waddle back into the Noble Count's residence. Oddly, Liu Shui had merely voiced a vague, stirring ambition of his own.

The next day Teng accompanied Hsiung to the wharfs of Chenglingji. Since their last visit the construction of warships had advanced hugely. Many were already on the water, their crews drilling and practising manoeuvres to the signal of flag and drum. It seemed much practice was necessary. Two, in particular, avoided colliding by a miracle, their captains screaming abuse and refusing to give way. Despite this interesting sight, Hsiung's attention kept drifting towards the main body of the lake. He shielded his eyes with a callused hand for a better view.

Recollecting his conversation with Liu Shui, Teng asked: 'Tell me, is this new fleet of yours for attack or defence?'

'Ah hah!' chuckled Hsiung. 'So you see how the wind blows. It is a great secret. Yet old Liu Shui told me you are worthy of our confidences.'

Teng waited expectantly as Hsiung leaned forward to ensure not even the passing breeze might overhear.

'We intend a blow the Mongols will never anticipate: to attack Hou-ming before autumn lowers the waters of the lake too deeply. My navy should be able to get in close while a land army causes a diversion by attacking the ramparts.'

Everything on the busy dockside seemed to freeze apart from the two whispering men. Teng's eyes widened at the audacity of the rebel scheme. In four months Hsiung might be lord of the very city where he had spent his childhood lighting fires, sweeping, cleaning, and emptying chamber pots! While he, Deng Teng, rightful heir to the leadership of Hou-ming, called his father's scullery boy *Noble Count*. What might Hsiung become next? Prince? Emperor? Such transformations were possible when dynasties lost the Mandate of Heaven. And what would Teng be when the storm clouds of war blew away? A superfluous man, forgotten even by his own heart, famous as neither painter nor scholar-official. Perhaps even a pitiful teacher, his ambition drained by fresher, more confident minds, until all hopes of success were futile.

His discomfort was answered by another version of his destiny. One without glory but happier. He imagined a long clean room lit by soft lamps where children played round their mother's skirts. He sat with a woodcut book of Yun Cai's poems, bowl of wine to hand. A vivid picture. The identity of the laughing mother was no surprise to Teng.

'What is your view of my plan?' asked Hsiung. 'Liu Shui believes I should seek your opinion. Do you think now is the time to capture Hou-ming?'

He was saved from replying by a cry and clang of bells.

'A flotilla! A flotilla approaches.'

Hsiung clasped Teng's arm with excited, heedless fingers. 'That will be Ying-ge and my two spymasters! They were delayed because she insisted on visiting her sick parents in Hou-ming. I respect her for that, though she did not ask my permission. I would hate to think she could be unfilial, though that would be impossible for one as loyal as Ying-ge.'

Teng watched curiously. The Noble Count was giddy as a puppy.

Within half an hour the flotilla had tied up at the wharfs. Teng found Shensi by his side.

'I've got everything in place if we need to run,' murmured Shensi.

'Good, we might . . .'

Teng fell silent. He sensed Shensi grow taut beside him. Two familiar figures – and despite the years since their last meeting at Hornets' Nest's camp, despite new silks and jade jewellery and plumpness, there was no mistaking them – rushed from the ship to abase themselves before the Noble Count. A third, also well known to Teng and Shensi, descended the gangplank with mincing little steps and shuffles, her fan working to hide shy blushes of joy.

The Noble Count of Lingling had eyes for no one else. He leaned over her as she fell to her knees and bowed on the dusty earth, apparently eager to kiss his boots. Whatever he whispered was heard only by her. She shot him a grateful, wondering look and rose with her head constantly bowed. Then he strode to his carriage and she followed as swiftly as tiny lotus feet allowed.

The two men in silks also rose, brushing dust from their knees, watching Ying-ge's progress closely. As she followed her master through a crowd held back by soldiers, all those present bowed. Except, that is, for two men with stiff, expressionless faces.

At the sight of Teng her eyes widened slightly but she gave no other sign of recognition. A moment later she had been handed into the Noble Count's carriage and they were on their way, accompanied by cavalry.

'Well,' said Teng to Shensi.

The latter grunted in reply.

Their attention shifted to the pair advancing up the wharf with satisfied faces, one tall and muscular, the other wiry and sly. When they reached Teng and Shensi, the newly-arrived men halted in surprise. For a long moment the four examined each other.

Hua smiled slightly. Chao's grin revealed more black teeth than white. Teng had gone pale apart from red spots on his cheeks, while Shensi studied every inch of his enemies from toe to scalp. Still Hua smiled until Teng met his eye with the kind of impassive gaze Grandfather Deng used as Prefect in the days of his glory; a gaze suitable for condemning malefactors to death. The smiles stopped. Without a word being exchanged, all four men understood each other's intentions exactly.

Part Five

Documents

The contents of a sealed case delivered by a secret courier into the hands of Abbess Yun Shu, Cloud Abode Monastery.

First, a hand scroll in a bamboo tube stopped at each end with moulded beeswax. Upon opening, the following was revealed:

A coloured ink painting on paper of a wide landscape. In the centre an old wooden pavilion with tiles missing from the roof, perched upon a mound shaped like Holy Mount Chang. Within the pavilion sits a lady wearing red and green silks, the colours of love, wealth and happy new life. She stares out across wide waters, empty save for blurred islands and rectangular sails on the horizon.

Behind the pavilion is a luxuriant stand of green bamboo; nearby grows a single, thick-trunked pine; beside that is a plum tree heavy with blossom – in short, The Three Friends.

A poem has been written in exquisite calligraphy above the trees:

> *No geese on the horizon, just sails.*
> *The Lady of Serene Perfection is patient.*
> *Amidst bamboo and pine, delicate blossom.*
> *Who knows when the plum will fruit?*

The picture itself does not bear the artist's seal, perhaps because he wishes to remain hidden or its recipient already knows his name.

Also enclosed, a small silken bag containing two plum stones, each painted with lucky characters. The first reading *blue plum*, the second *bamboo horse*, meaning a couple attached to each other in early youth.

Finally a sealed letter addressed to Honourable Deng Nan-shi:

Honoured Father, your son begs forgiveness for not kneeling before you. He begs you to overlook his failures, most especially, the loss of our ancestral home and bringing calamity upon our house through his foolishness.

Honoured Father, I now find myself in a safer place, the location of which I dare not mention. My companions are honourable and decent, though nearly all of low birth. Some would certainly meet with your approval.

Honoured Father, I have resolved to find honest employment to support you through diligent labour, however scanty the reward, so you may live in a little comfort and peace as you deserve. Therefore, I implore you to take good care of your health until I return. This I shall arrange as soon as I can.

It is my understanding you are housed and fed by the Nuns of Serene Perfection. Please offer them my thanks for fulfilling that duty until I return. Mention, I beg, my name to Abbess Yun Shu, and commend the painting I have sent. Assure her my intentions are sincere, honourable and unquenchable.

Your dutiful and ever repentant son, Teng.

天命

Report to Chancellor Liu Shui in Lingling Town from the High Commissioner for the Newly Adhered Navy.

Early summer, 1322

Excellency Liu Shui, I hereby make a just and true report. You urged me in your letter of instruction to spare no detail, however unfortunate, so you might be fully surmised of the situation here in Chenglingji. This I do reluctantly, for reasons Your Excellency shall shortly hear.

I begin by stating that much has been achieved. The Newly Adhered Fleet is, for the most part, afloat. That is to say, its hulls are watertight and sails or oars in position. A great many of the paddlewheel destroyers are now capable of rapid movement, despite the problem of poor workmanship.

Accordingly, I divided the fleet into five squadrons, each of thirty vessels, and appointed trustworthy commanders of proven worth to train the men.

Now, Your Excellency, I come to matters I quake to set forth. You urged me to frankness so I shall not fear punishment from yourself. However, I beg that this report does not reach those who might use it against me.

First to the question of command. It has pleased His Highness to heed the advice of certain people here in Chenglingji. Above all, his spymasters, now promoted to the rank of Lesser Ministers; also his concubine, Lady Ying-ge.

As a result, my five original squadrons have become one huge squadron led by Lady Ying-ge's cousin, Admiral Won-du, who has experience as a naval officer. To be more exact, as the captain of a two-masted junk charged with the apprehension of petty smugglers for the Salt Bureau. Admiral Won-du has in turn appointed a dozen old drinking cronies as his senior officers, dismissing my appointees and any captains who express disquiet or have superior naval experience.

Next to the matter of weapons and training. Although catapults and crossbows have been fitted at great expense, as well as naphtha spraying pumps, thunderclap bombs and noxious cloud bombs, I must report a disturbing lack of proficiency. The catapults, only effective if manned by experienced crews, lie idle even on those rare occasions when the fleet attempts manoeuvres. Vital rehearsals of boarding and disembarkation of marines are neglected.

Admiral Won-du's decision to abolish the squadrons means

that the fleet sails back and forth across the lake with drums pounding and a thousand flags flying, incapable of dividing into more flexible units if harried by enemies, hugely impressive in appearance but impractical in battle. No one dares mention this reality to the Noble Count, especially in the hearing of Lesser Ministers Chao and Hua or the Lady Ying-ge.

Will these difficulties be overcome by early autumn, as I am commanded? I would welcome a chance to discuss that question with Your Excellency as soon as you return to Chenglingji from Lingling.

Ma Fu, High Commissioner for the Newly Adhered Navy.

天命

Memorandum from the Chief Minister of the Right Hand Secretariat to His Highness Prince Arslan, Hou-ming City, Hou-ming Province.

Early summer, 1322

Your Highness, I have been commanded by His Imperial Majesty to express grave displeasure at your report concerning the loss of the Imperial Salt Pans in Hou-ming Province. The Imperial household requires every resource to maintain its necessary expenditure. Moreover, the success of bandits against an army comprising not just native troops but men of higher, governing races has caused much disquiet in the Royal Chambers. How, His Imperial Majesty asks, could such a reverse occur?

Hence, His Majesty commands the following actions:

One. The content of this memorandum shall be restricted to the smallest number possible. Any discovering it must be silenced.

Two. Your Highness is hereby informed that a fleet and army large enough to crush the Yueh Fei bandits has been gathered in the Yangtze Delta under the pretence of exterminating pirates. Its real purpose is to sail swiftly west and enter Six-hundred-*li* Lake prior to the rebel attack on Hou-ming planned for the autumn that your agents have learned about. Thus, the bandits shall find themselves like a ship driven onto merciless rocks by an irresistible wind.

Three. Your Highness is commended to raise and train as large a force as his domains may support, both land forces and naval forces, to assist the Army of Righteous Reprisal upon its arrival in Hou-ming Province.

Four. Traitorous elements amongst the population must be identified and harried, so that those wavering towards treason are dissuaded from throwing in their lot with the bandits. His Majesty states: 'Beware of corrupt or inept officials! Each is as bad as the other, as one rat is as bad as ten mice.'

Let it also be known that His Imperial Majesty entertains grave suspicions of the lower elements of the Daoist clergy and would encourage rigorous scrutiny of their activities. Let it similarly be known that those proclaiming the cause of the Buddha Maitreya are to be punished mercilessly, while those worshipping the Buddha Makhala shall have every benefit heaped upon their temples and monasteries, especially those clergy from Tibet spreading messages of peace and obedient harmony.

Six. Your Highness will understand the importance of tempting the bandits into a decisive engagement with our forces before winter. All policy must tend towards that objective, even at the risk of giving the Yueh Fei bandits temporary advantages.

On behalf of His Imperial Majesty, Hsieh-Ho, Chief Minister of the Right Hand Secretariat.

天命

The diary of Chancellor Liu Shui

(Written in a code decipherable only by those closely familiar with Yun Cai's 'Lotus Poem'.)

Early summer, 1322

14th Day, 4th Month, 1322

Arrived back in Chenglingji towards dusk. As our flotilla approached the land, I glanced back to the West and was amazed by the depth and complexity of the sunset: sunbeams slanting directly towards the Noble Count's palace. Surely a sign! But when I remarked upon it to the captain he said that midway between equinoxes the sun often went down at that angle. The implication is that Heaven is unsure whether to grant its favours to the Noble Count.

My mind was full of Navy Commissioner Ma Fu's report concerning the poor condition of our fleet upon which all our schemes depend.

Later, on arrival at the Temporary Palace, I received appalling news. Not only was His Highness indisposed and incapable of seeing me until the morrow, but the Bureau chiefs reported to me in whispers that Navy Commissioner Ma Fu had been accused of spying by Ministers Chao and Hua. A short trial that very day had led to his immediate execution, as demanded by Admiral Won-du. It is impossible Hsiung could have taken so severe a step without the clearest proofs. Yet if Ma Fu – with us since the very start of our rebellion – was a traitor, whom may we trust? I prepare for sleep with a heavy heart.

15th Day, 4th Month, 1322

A most dismal day. The monsoon returned with fresh force, making the roofs of our Temporary Palace resound like warning drums. Little light in the sky. Much grey.

I was finally admitted to the Noble Count in his quarters. I thought him ailing, his face bloated and pale. When I drew near, he reeked of strong spirits despite the early hour. Naturally, I begged to discover what evidence had condemned Ma Fu. At first he was reticent, then he said – remorsefully, I thought – that Minister Hua had reported his suspicions concerning the Navy Commissioner at the end of a long banquet. Although he could not remember it exactly, it seemed he had ordered Hua to execute poor Ma Fu at once and that Minister Hua, though terribly reluctant, had obeyed sooner than risk His Highness's wrath. As he spoke I noticed the Noble Count's hands shaking: never a good sign with him.

At that moment there was a most disturbing occurrence: the Lady Ying-ge appeared through a side door and stood watching us silently, her large brown eyes unwavering. Her beautiful face – and it is an exquisite ornament – turned towards His Highness. At the sight of her, he puffed out his chest like a pigeon in spring and frowned angrily. At me! At me! Then he ordered our audience was over. I left crestfallen.

16th Day, 4th Month, 1322

I spent the morning contemplating my retirement to a monastery. Towards noon the Noble Count called upon me in a very apologetic frame of mind. He said that he has been sick of late. So much so that a doctor specially summoned from Hou-ming by the Lady Ying-ge has prescribed medicines. Then he told me (for the hundredth time) how a gift of a jade disk from that lady saved his life after the Battle of the Salt Pans. Though I tried to turn the conversation to the condition of the navy and Admiral Won-du's fitness for command, the Noble Count seemed distracted. Few decisions were reached.

Tonight, as I write, a riotous banquet can be heard in the Noble Count's wing of the palace. It grieves me to hear such shameless echoes of excess.

18th Day, 4th Month, 1322

Yesterday His Highness was again too ill to receive me. At dawn I sought out Honourable Deng Teng and found him practising divine exercises to the rhythm of the rising sun, his legs and arms tensing and relaxing as one breathes in and out to the rhythms of Eternity. He is a most graceful, handsome gentleman. Yet as soon as he observed me, Deng Teng slumped upon a bench, apparently exhausted by his exertions. I believe his frailty is a matter of policy.

When I broached the subject of the Lady Ying-ge he became cold and suspicious. By these tokens I suspect he has some prior knowledge of her that he is afraid to reveal. Perhaps that knowledge might aid us all, however dangerous he seems to think it.

8th Day, 5th Month, 1322

Weeks have passed since my last entry. The reason: business of state. Above all, a journey to the Salt Pans to ensure the workers there are adequately fed and that the blocks of salt keep flowing. Both aims were achieved.

Today I returned to Chenglingji days before I had notified the Noble Count he could expect me. Perhaps that explains his surprise and annoyance that I had arrived to witness an event of importance.

At noon the Newly Adhered Navy conducted extensive manoeuvres on the lake, which we observed from a special platform built at the end of a long pier. The climax was to be a mock naval battle between different halves of our navy, in which countless missiles of finely ground flour (a lamentable waste when so many are hungry all over our domains) were thrown at the opposing vessels until many were ghostly white

– a most unpropitious omen, of course, white being the colour of mourning. The Noble Count seemed hardly to notice, his eyes oddly glazed and glance flickering frequently towards Lady Ying-ge. I detected every sign of a lovers' quarrel between them. I have never seen him like this, yet dare not enquire too deeply lest he enters one of his dark moods.

As the Newly Adhered Navy sailed clumsily back and forth I witnessed Honourable Deng Teng trying to approach His Highness, only to be rebuffed sarcastically in a way that greatly reduced our noble guest's dignity. Directly afterwards I noticed Hsiung glancing for approval – how well I know that look! – towards Lady Ying-ge, who seemed to be smiling behind her fan.

Does she, then, have some prior acquaintance with Honourable Deng Teng that makes her ill-disposed towards him? If so, I fear for his safety.

20th Day, 5th Month, 1322

Today I prepared a lengthy discourse on the virtues of the righteous, benevolent ruler for the edification of the Noble Count. Although Hsiung pretended to listen I could tell his thoughts were elsewhere. Would that had been true of his yawns! I left disappointed.

In the afternoon I interviewed our new Lesser Ministers, Chao and Hua, to learn the exact nature of their duties and divine their general intentions. They seem to have the title and rewards of a Minister without any burden of responsibility. Chao is certainly the stupider of the pair and more easily gulled – although his physical strength makes him more intimidating than his constant companion. Hua is a quick-witted fellow who hides his true thoughts behind suave pleasantries and flattery when in the company of superiors; with inferiors he is merciless. I am not so foolish that I do not realise they whisper ceaselessly against me to the Noble Count.

As he left, Hua remarked casually that even the highest can turn out to be cunning traitors and that, as His Highness's spymaster, he would never lower his vigilance. What disturbed me was his next enquiry – so innocent as to be positively menacing – concerning the state of Honourable Deng Teng's health. Clearly he is up to something that bodes ill for our noble guest.

天命

Letters to Salt Minister Gui from anonymous agents misfiled in a ledger designated *Extraordinary Duties*.

(All are written in code, hence, perhaps, the secretary's error. None of the usual copies of an official reply are attached to the letters, suggesting none were ever sent.)

Summer, 1322

20th Day, 5th Month, 1322
Salt Minister Gui, are you still the one our letters go to? Reply by the agreed way: red (yes), blue, (no). Tell the Prince: attack still planned for autumn, exact date to follow as soon as known. We shall report in person as soon as possible to discuss our reward. Ox and Snake.

2nd Day, 7th Month, 1322
Salt Minister Gui, did you receive our last letter? Red (yes), blue (no). Date of attack set for 9th Day, 9th Month. No reply received from previous message. Confirm our reward as agreed please! Red (yes), blue (no). Ox and Snake.

1st Day, 8th Month, 1322
Salt Minister Gui, did you receive previous message? Please confirm without delay. Red (yes), blue (no). Speak again, we beg Your Excellency, to your superiors regarding our agreed reward. We shall send another message nearer to the 9th Day, 9th Month if you do not reply to this. Ox and Snake.

天命

Police Report to Salt Minister Gui.

Late summer, 1322

Your Honour, the monthly report you requested some time ago concerning the registered scholar, Deng Nan-shi, is hereby attached. Does Your Honour still wish to receive these reports? I humbly beg forgiveness if this question is presumptuous, but it is many months since you asked for them and we have heard nothing from Your Honour. Inspector of Police, Er Dan.

Report: Our informant in Cloud Abode Monastery states the scholar Deng Nan-shi's health remains very grave: 'It is as though he is waiting for something before he allows himself to die. When not resting, he occupies himself in meditation or staring into space. Sometimes he writes poems. He receives neither visitors nor messages, but spends time with Abbess Yun Shu, for whom he demonstrates a great affection and respect.' Conclusion: no cause for arrest or interrogation at the present time.

天命

The diary of Chancellor Liu Shui

(Written in a code decipherable only by those closely familiar with Yun Cai's 'Lotus Poem'.)

Summer, 1322

10th Day, 8th Month, 1322
A most regrettable altercation occurred in the Noble Count's

morning audience. At least, one may call the outcome regrettable. As I write this in my quarters I fear spies peering over my shoulder for the first time since I gained the honourable station of Chancellor.

The dispute was provoked by Deng Teng in his role as Respected Friend to the Noble Count. This position gives him the right to voice what others dare only think. One can never fault his integrity or courage. The Noble Count had used the audience to instruct his officers about a new campaign that would commence in twenty days. A campaign larger than any ever attempted by the Yueh Fei rebels: in short, the capture of Hou-ming City.

The senior officers – many loyal to our cause since its birth – muttered anxiously and in great surprise, so the Noble Count was forced to silence them. It was obvious the majority do not consider our strength sufficient for so bold an offensive, yet feared to say so. There was an angry light in the Noble Count's eyes that made even me hesitate. Fear is the poison that has spread through our court since Lady Ying-ge and her circle gained influence over Hsiung's mind – as instanced by the summary execution of Naval Commisioner Ma Fu and others accused of treason.

Into this silence stepped Honourable Deng Teng. 'Your Highness,' he said, 'I would be failing in my obligations to you if I did not voice a deep concern. Though only a scholar, I have observed the manoeuvres of the Newly Adhered Navy with close attention. Your Highness, it does not seem ready for so essential a role.'

At this the officers nodded with relief and grunted their agreement. All that is, except Admiral Won-du. *He* protested they were ready to defeat a force twice their size. Yet I could see the doubt in my beloved Hsiung's eyes, for Deng Teng had merely voiced his own fear.

'Your Highness,' I murmured in his ear, 'your Respected Friend is certainly right.'

'Noble Count,' urged Teng in his forthright way, 'I beg you to be cautious! First sail with the fleet yourself and attack a town up the coast. That will reveal the Navy's true readiness.'

A fierce debate followed, but Deng Teng's point was so well argued even the scorn and insinuations of Ministers Chao and Hua had no effect and the Noble Count agreed to a trial of his navy's strength. Let me add that Teng's most vociferous supporter in this matter was the doughty General P'ao, a man whose loyalty to Hsiung can never be doubted.

11th Day, 8th Month, 1322

The Temporary Palace is full of rumours and whisperings; most concern the sincerity and trustworthiness of Honourable Deng Teng. No need to ask which well of malice they are drawn from. I have long noticed a deep tension between Teng and the circle clustering round Lady Ying-ge. She never leaves the Noble Count's side so it is a great struggle to speak with him alone. The piles of memoranda, petitions and needful decisions that must be authorised grow daily.

12th Day, 8th Month, 1322

His Highness led the Newly Adhered Navy out into the lake for their first taste of true action. They will assault a fortress on the coast north of Chenglingji and be gone some days.

Almost as soon as the Navy had vanished over the horizon a most distressing incident commenced in the gardens, where Honourable Deng Teng was exercising with his close companion, Shensi. Chao and Hua came with a contingent of armed men, seeking to arrest Deng Teng for high treason. They claimed to have intercepted letters proving this crime. By a lucky chance I happened to be taking my afternoon walk in the same section of the gardens and so intervened at the precise moment when weapons had been drawn.

My own bodyguard – each of whom is worth three of those employed by the Lesser Ministers – ensured violence was prevented. Nevertheless, Chao and Hua hurled many charges at Honourable Deng Teng, not just of treason, but that he had tried to seduce Lady Ying-ge in the Noble Count's absence, making improper suggestions of an amorous kind. Deng Teng's motive, they claimed, was base jealousy, for everyone knew of the Noble Count's humble beginnings in the Deng household.

So their plan is revealed! Not just to use forged documents but Ying-ge's undoubted power over Hsiung, his blindness and absurd devotion. In this way jealous madness might be unleashed. A plot, I fear, likely to succeed.

Such grave charges cannot be ignored and I have placed Deng Teng 'under arrest' in my own quarters while I think of a way to avert injustice.

18th Day, 8th Month, 1322

At dawn I took it upon my own authority as Chancellor to send Deng Teng and his companion Shensi away before Hsiung returns. Accordingly, I requisitioned one of two swift ships owned by Ministers Chao and Hua, bolstering their crews with picked men of my own. These men are fanatical in their devotion to the cause of Yueh Fei. I have instructed them that Deng Teng is the last descendent of our Great Hero capable of siring sons and that they must sacrifice their lives sooner than allow him to perish. All swore solemn oaths to never fail in that duty.

Luckily the ship was being maintained in a state of readiness for instant departure. It has been made quite clear to the captain that a failure to co-operate will lead to his immediate execution, followed by the death of his two sons who I have taken hostage.

These desperate measures are the only way I can see of preventing a crime that would damage Hsiung's equanimity forever – more deeply even than the sacrilege he committed in the Buddha's caves. At least he was defending himself there. If, in a jealous rage, he ordered the death of his boyhood companion, nay, the only son of the noble scholar who fed him when he was an abandoned child, how lamentable a fall from virtue that would be!

With luck, Chao and Hua will not discover the absence of their ship until tomorrow, by which time Teng will be beyond reach.

Word has arrived that the 'trial' of the Newly Adhered Navy was chaotic. I anticipate Hsiung's return with foreboding. His moods, darker and less manageable with each year that passes, will hardly be improved by the failure of his beloved fleet.

20th Day, 8th Month, 1322
The Noble Count has returned. I am still reeling from the harshness of his criticisms towards me. If it did not mean abandoning him to the mercies of Ying-ge and her circle, thereby condemning our noble cause to failure at the very time we are gaining in power, I would resign my Chancellorship. I can write no more tonight.

30th Day, 8th Month, 1322
Despite all evidence of the fleet's weakness in battle and all the advice, no, entreaties, of his trusted captains and officers and officials, the Noble Count has sailed off to attack Hou-ming. As for me, he avoids my presence. I suspect pride lies behind it – and the ceaseless flattery and whisperings of Ying-ge. She gave me a smile of malicious triumph as she waved a yellow handkerchief in farewell. In less than ten days they will be besieging Hou-ming, having disembarked our land army to surround the city as planned. At that point the Newly Adhered Navy will assault the harbour and wharfs using specially built ships with towering prows. I fear such an assault may prove inept. Worse, I begin to have misgivings we are sailing into a trap. Yet surely our agents would have reported any gathering of enemy forces?

2nd Day, 9th Month, 1322

We wait for news of the war. Nothing yet. However, an unexpected – and not entirely unwelcome event – has occurred. Ministers Chao and Hua sailed away without warning in the middle of the night. No one knows where or why. Lady Ying-ge seemed as surprised as anyone. All her valuables had been packed for days, as though she anticipated a sudden departure of her own. Spies in her quarters have reported that these treasures – jewellery, pearls, silks and *cash* given as presents by the Noble Count – vanished along with Ministers Chao and Hua. It is assumed a maid provided the thieves with access to Lady Ying-ge's not inconsiderable wealth.

Her anger and wailing shook the palace! She even sought me out, shrieking demands that I send ships and men in pursuit of her treacherous allies. That, I advised her, scarcely concealing my amusement, was impossible; all available men are needed to protect the Noble Count's belongings from thieves in his absence. The expression of mingled vexation, hatred and fear on her pretty little face was a joy to behold. If my suspicions prove correct her fear will be more than justified.

Part Six

Heaven's Judgements

thirty-one

天命

Hou-ming City, 8th Day, 9th Month, 1322

Yun Shu's palanquin slowed to a halt. The street was blocked by bare-chested penitents, some moaning in a trance, others chanting half-learned sutras. Their hysteria had been gathering for months, years. Passions simmering since the riots between the Buddhists and Daoists at the start of the summer. Now that cauldron, stoked by ambitious men, threatened to boil over.

'Bo-Bai!' she called, leaning out of the palanquin. 'Can we advance no further?'

It was dusk. Already she was late for her appointment with Worthy Master Jian at Golden Bright Temple. All day she had delayed her departure from Cloud Abode Monastery. Reports flew everywhere of crowds inflamed by holy men from Tibet. The city authorities were also much to blame. As soon as the huge rebel fleet had been sighted near Hou-ming, proclamations appeared on all ward gates stating the Yueh Fei bandits planned to massacre the entire population of the city.

Prince Arslan's intention had been obvious: dissuade malcontents from supporting the rebels when they attacked. Yet the people had reacted in surprising ways. Though it was over forty years since the Great Sacrifice in Hou-ming, terror was an abiding wound. The loss of entire generations haunted everyone. Sheer panic welled from the dark places of numerous souls. Crowds of the Buddha's most zealous followers gathered in the slave market, burning incense, chanting, praying and pleading for salvation. This mass of bodies blocked Yun Shu's way.

'Bo-Bai!' she called 'Should we go back?'

The tall old eunuch appeared at the window.

'Hide yourself!' he hissed. 'What if you are recognised?'

Yun Shu hesitated. Yet her robes were plain enough and her nun's 'whirlwind clouds' hair concealed beneath a shawl.

Certainly some fanatic might decide Abbess Yun Shu's presence was an affront to the Buddha Makhala. Around them penitents jostled and advanced slowly in the direction of the market square. Many were emaciated by hunger and labour; their naked torsos bore lesions caused by accidents, whips, disease. People with nothing to lose except their hope for a favourable rebirth.

'I dare not disappoint the Worthy Master,' she told Bo-Bai. 'If the palanquin can go no further, I shall walk.'

Though Bo-Bai protested, Yun Shu was accustomed to getting her way.

'You'll be no help to anyone dead,' he muttered as she stepped out of the palanquin and pushed into the crowd. 'He won't be able to suck you dry then.'

Yun Shu ignored both warnings. 'Golden Bright Temple is not far. Stay close to me, Bo-Bai.'

They came upon a clear alleyway that led in the direction of the temple. Yun Shu's ears echoed with droning voices and shuffling feet. Surely the authorities should not allow such a gathering, not with enemy forces approaching the city. Surely they would clear the streets.

'Over here!' she called.

'No! That is not the way!'

Too late. She had broken out of the shuffling procession and hurried into the dark alleyway. A moment later Bo-Bai appeared behind her.

'Yun Shu,' he said, 'we should go back.'

The alley had narrowed alarmingly. She saw a flickering glow of fires in the distance. 'See! We must be near the Temple now.'

At the end of the narrow passage her mistake become obvious. With the realisation came revulsion – more of spirit than body, for it seemed she had stepped from familiar Hou-ming, the stage she had known all her life, to a place not of this earth, to Di-yu itself, the Underworld Mansion, one of the Ten Courts of Hell. If so, it was a court without a wise or benevolent judge, or any law except the reasonless passions of distressed, misguided souls.

Large fires had been built all over the slave market. Smoke and waves of heat shimmered. The roar of flames joined loud chants and screams.

Yun Shu realised many of the men and women in the square were seeking instant salvation from the miseries of this world. Of course, she had heard of such desperate steps towards nirvana: *Relinquishing the Body* or *Mounting the Smoke of Glittering Colours*. Never had she imagined such practices in Hou-ming. As she watched, a man clad only in a loincloth, his skin shiny with oil, limbs bandy and thin, applied a burning torch. Instantly he was ablaze – standing quite still while the flames absorbed his sins until he slumped to his knees. Elsewhere in the square others tried different ways to Abandon the Body. Glimpses were revealed through drifting clouds of smoke then obscured. A man with a huge cleaver, hacking frantically at his own fingers, wrist, then arm. Another used hooks to gouge out his eyes, screaming the Buddha's blessed name over and over.

Yun Shu backed into the alleyway and buried her head in Bo-Bai's chest.

'We must stop them!' she cried. 'It is a blasphemy against the compassionate Lord Buddha! How can they do this in His name? It is an offence to the Dao!'

Amidst the chanting and shrieks drifting from the slave market, Yun Shu suddenly understood that true perfection could never be attained by senseless, self-centred acts like these. True union with the Dao meant entering its cosmic flow with kindness, hand in hand with the Ten Thousand Creatures.

She remembered Worthy Master Jian's lofty indifference to the people's suffering. The leaders of the Dao in Hou-ming must act to calm the people! Did she alone glimpse the truth? The people's fear was goading them to madness.

Her thoughts reverted to Teng. Ever since his painting and poem confirmed that he was alive, Yun Shu had speculated obsessively. First there had been deep, miraculous joy. Deep, tearful joy. Next, mobbing worries and questions. When would he return? Yet his painting had been almost sensual in its provocative symbolism, the poem charged with promises. She must wait for him, trust he would find a way back to Hou-ming. Still, anxieties gnawed. What if he decided, after all his trials, that she was unworthy, tainted by her intimacy with Worthy Master Jian?

Yun Shu knew how to prove herself. As Abbess of Cloud Abode Monastery she had a duty to help the people, whatever the risk to herself. That was what Teng would expect of her.

'Bo-Bai,' she said, 'take me to Golden Bright Temple! I shall persuade the Worthy Master to remonstrate with these deluded souls. They will surely listen to him. Especially if he rouses the Buddhist clergy and we speak as one.'

The old Eunuch's expression, already grave, darkened further. 'For one who is wise,' he said, 'you learn men's hearts far too slowly. But let us go.'

天命

By the time they reached Wild Goose Pavilion, dusk was almost night. Peals of brash trumpets and drums in the distance indicated that the city garrison was attempting to enforce a curfew.

Yun Shu stared at the high tower with its bulbous top storey. Lights were burning up there: also below, near the base. She hardly expected to find the Worthy Master still waiting, so it came as a surprise to discover him cross-legged before the reading stand shaped like Mount Kunlun. The books of bamboo strips maintained their place of honour on the stand.

A letter had been crumpled and cast away, as though in despair or anger. At the sight of his handsome face, gaunt and glazed, complex feelings tightened her breast. She had meant to reproach him, demand he lead a procession of priests onto the streets to curb the people's excesses, yet the words died in her throat. How thin he had become! Perhaps the elixirs and rites were making him a creature of spirit rather than flesh.

A noise startled her. Cold eyes watched from a dark corner. They belonged to the hairless priest, Void.

'Worthy Master,' she cried, bowing low, 'there is great hysteria in the city. I was delayed by the crowds.'

Worthy Master Jian nodded. A metallic smell confirmed he had been consuming another concoction.

'I cannot perform the rite tonight,' she said, 'I am too lacking in balance! Surely we should consider the welfare of the city on a night like this, not Immortality!'

He examined her. His eyes were glassy and swollen, rims red. At first Yun Shu quailed. Then words long suppressed tumbled out.

'Worthy Master, do you never fear the books are false? Oh, I will not carry on with this! You must find another spirit-partner!'

His expression hardened. 'It is too late for that, Yun Shu,' he said. 'We have ascended the Steps together. Tonight we must enter the final stage, that of Great Merging. It cannot be otherwise.'

'I beg you,' she said, tears starting to her eyes.

He glanced at the crumpled letter lying on the floor.

'Do you know what it says?' he asked.

'How could I?'

'Then read it.'

She smoothed out the paper and read its contents several times.

'Now you see my dilemma,' he said, in a far away voice. 'Look at me closely, Yun Shu!'

It was a struggle to obey.

'Do I look healthy to you? I fear that I am fading. If it weren't for the elixirs I would already have slipped into the Serene Darkness, there to be treated with honour, certainly, but also to be reborn yet again. I command your help, Yun Shu.'

'Rest!' she urged. 'Meditate! Send for doctors!'

He laughed hoarsely. 'Ah, my dear! It would not be enough. I need you to give me all your *ch'i* in the Stage of Great Merging, you must withhold nothing from me. Nothing! Not a drop of pure life! It is my only hope. Otherwise, though it is the last thing I want, I will accept the Buddhists' offer in that letter.'

'Master!' she cried, in distress.

'If I exchange Cloud Abode Monastery for a sliver of the Buddha's knucklebone I will have a chance. If you do not help me, I have no choice!'

'I . . . am not spiritually prepared,' she said.

A gentle smile crossed his face.

'You will be.' He turned to where Void waited in the shadows. 'Fetch the necessary things. Prepare Abbess Yun Shu and bring her to the Final Stage in an hour's time. I shall await you there after my own preparations.'

With that, the Worthy Master rose swiftly from his lotus position and mounted the staircase leading to the higher levels of Wild Goose Pagoda.

天命

Void coughed and held out a jade pillbox decorated with the symbols for *yin* and *yang*.

'No,' said Yun Shu, remembering the last time she took Void's magical pills charged with autumn essences.

'They are good,' insisted Void. 'The Worthy Master is relying on you.'

'They are poison!' she cried. 'I was sick for a week after . . .'

'Be quiet! Obey or betray the Nuns in your care!'

With an unsteady hand, Yun Shu picked out seven pills as directed, swallowing quickly to be rid of their bitter flavour. Nothing happened for a while. Then her vision blurred and she entered a shadowy state. Half aware of Void's gentle, droning chant, she followed him up the spiral staircase to the final destination of their rites.

As Yun Shu emerged from the doorway she was permitted to observe the top storey of the pagoda for the first time. The walls were decorated with glowing circles of candles to represent sun and moon. A round bed covered by a quilt stood in the centre of the circular room. Most surprising of all, a circular portion of the roof folded back to reveal the clear night sky. Propitiously, it was a warm night.

Void took up the ancient book of bamboo strips from a hidden pocket in his robes and began to recite in a nasal singsong – words that had not been heard for nearly two thousand years, a prayer haunted by the ghosts of long dead priests and princes, their fearful slaves and concubines, lost bodies and spirits, all, all reduced to words bubbling in time's ceaseless crucible.

Only then did the Worthy Master appear. His silken robes rustled, decorated with images of sun and moon.

'It is time, Yun Shu,' he said, triumphantly.

She nodded, trembling. Tears glistened in her eyes.

Yun Shu untied the sash of her long silken cloak and lay back on the sun-shaped bed, staring up at the night sky. Her eyelids fluttered and she heard herself pretend to moan as his touch used the intertwining shapes of *yin* and *yang* in the cosmic egg. With great solemnity, he opened his robe and pushed himself into her.

'A light shines through me!' he exclaimed, his breath quickening slightly. 'The golden flower blossoms! Ah,' he gasped, 'now the embryo is rising! I can feel it rising through me!'

'Please stop!' begged Yun Shu.

'The colour white is in my head!' he declared. 'Black . . . red . . . green . . . yellow . . . It is exactly as the bamboo scrolls promise!'

'No!' she pleaded, 'please stop for a moment!'

'The spirit embryo!' he cried. 'I can see it! I am clear as autumn rain. Soon the embryo will be born!'

The Worthy Master's breath was calm and rhythmical now. She felt him quicken his steps within her. The pain worsened, stung, bruised. It seemed to infect her very womb. A terrible realisation gripped her. In exchange for the birth of his Immortality, he would steal the fruitfulness from her womb! Teng would not want her then! What use would she be to him?

Feebly she tried to rise, push him off. But her head span. Void's pills left her too weak and sickened.

'It is now!' declared the Worthy Master. 'I am almost reborn! It is strong! So strong!'

But something happened. Instead of rising through his spine to form a divine embryo that would coalesce into his rebirth as an Immortal, his *jing*, his earthly seed, hoarded within him for twenty years and all his rites with Yun Shu, the *jing* he had swollen with her stolen life force, escaped. She felt pulsing within her, a warmth.

'No!' he cried, in horror. 'No!'

A hot rush between her legs as he desperately withdrew his cinnabar stem. He could not contain himself. The Dew of Pearl that had cost a prince's fortune in precious elixirs turned from pure spirit to common, worldly seed that scattered, warm and dripping, over her thighs.

Utter silence in the chamber apart from their laboured breath. Void's chanting had ceased in horror. A long shriek of despair emerged from the Worthy Master.

'It has gone!' he cried. 'The embryo! You have stolen it for yourself!'

Yun Shu lay still, staring up at him in amazement.

'You moved!' he said, with a bitterness she could not have believed possible. 'Everything is your fault! It will take years to regather a tenth of what I have lost. By then it will be too late. I shall have faded into dust!'

'Please,' she whispered, 'do not give Cloud Abode Monastery to . . . you promised!'

He leaped up and began to pace the pagoda. 'You led me to the final stage quite deliberately,' he ranted. 'Quite purposefully! You are in league with my enemies! All to steal my Pearl of Dew! You demon-bitch, you fox fairy!'

At this insult Yun Shu froze. Another man's voice from her girlhood echoed – Golden Lotus accusing, cursing: *Fox fairy! Fox fairy!* Then Worthy Master Jian rushed at her, punching her shoulders and face, so that she shielded herself with her slender arms.

'Get her away from me!' he screamed, tears of grief and rage and despair trickling down his cheeks. 'Oh, I will trade Cloud Abode Monastery for a piece of the Buddha's knucklebone! You have no one to blame but yourself!'

Too shocked even to weep, Yun Shu found herself hustled down through the various storeys of Wild Goose Pavilion.

Outside she fell to her knees. Void scowled with savage distain before slamming the door.

Her mind seemed without focus. She squinted stupidly. Void's magical pills were gaining in power, not lessening. She began to sob.

'Abbess Yun Shu!'

The voice came through a fog. She turned in confusion,

longing for it to be Teng, offering forgiveness. But she was defiled, tainted! Her womb was poisoned, drained of life! There could be no more affection. Never more would Teng send her paintings and poems. He would despise her forever as a demon-bitch, a fox fairy!

'Yun Shu!' called Bo-Bai.

'Take me home!' Her words tumbled between gasps for breath. 'I am worthless. Quite worthless! I have failed everyone! No one wants me now, Bo-Bai! Send a messenger to my father's house. Seek out Golden Lotus and tell him I accept! I accept his offer. Tell him to collect me from Cloud Abode Monastery and take me to my father's house. Tomorrow! Tell him that, Bo-Bai! Oh, I am unworthy to be Abbess!'

Maddened by Void's pills, she would not listen when he remonstrated – could not.

The grieving Abbess and faithful servant reached Monkey Hat Hill unchallenged. Prince Arslan had concentrated his soldiers around the palace, aware that the next day would bring a battle that would decide the fate of his entire province. On the Hundred Stairs they found a street urchin hiding from the curfew. Minutes later, having scrawled a hasty letter in the gatehouse of Cloud Abode Monastery, Yun Shu sent the lad slipping through the dark, deserted streets of Hou-ming to Golden Lotus.

Lamps burned late in Wild Goose Pavilion. For Worthy Master Jian was composing desperate letters of his own.

thirty-two

天命

Hou-ming City, 8th Day, 9th Month, 1322

Midnight on Monkey Hat Hill: the night warm and stars vivid; the woods and ruined mansions steeped with shadows. A gentle sound like sighing surf washed over the hill when a breeze arose from the lake. Stray, sapless leaves drifted down. Then the fitful silence of night resumed.

The city at the foot of Monkey Hat Hill was silent now, the authorities having succeeded in enforcing their curfew – temporarily, at least. People waited in the brooding night for what daylight must bring: war, battle, death for victor and loser alike. This balmy autumn night was the last many would ever know.

Not all the shadows on Monkey Hat Hill were motionless. Two folded themselves into the darkness beneath a pine tree as a boy ran down the Hundred Stairs, a letter in his hand. Barefoot and nimble, he leapt the worn stairs two at a time as Teng and Hsiung had done when lads. In a moment he vanished into the night.

'That same boy accompanied Abbess Yun Shu and Bo-Bai when they returned to the monastery not so long ago,' came a cultured voice from behind the pine trunk.

'He's carrying a message,' replied a gruff, low voice.

'Of course, and probably from the Abbess herself. The question is where. And to whom.' After a brooding pause the cultured voice broke out, 'Why did you stop me from speaking to her?'

The owner of the gruff voice stirred impatiently. 'It might get us killed.'

Teng and Shensi lapsed into their anxious vigil at the foot of the Hundred Stairs. From this vantage point they could spy upon anyone climbing Monkey Hat Hill, allowing plenty of time to take up position in a nearby garden. If Teng's predictions were correct they would not have to wait long – and that suited his feelings exactly. He found it painful to stand here, knowing Deng Mansions – reduced to a twisted, charred pile of beams and ash – no longer existed to shelter him or his clan's spirits in their ancestral shrine.

Further up the hill in Cloud Abode Monastery, Father would be asleep or meditating upon inner pictures. Since arriving back in Hou-ming, Teng had not dared make his presence known to anyone, not even Deng Nan-shi or Yun Shu, lest they were under observation by spies. Instead he had concealed himself in an old overgrown mansion recollected from childhood while Shensi entered the city, seeking reliable information.

There were other reasons for not risking a message to Yun Shu. Part of him feared her reply. What was he but an impoverished scholar, little better than a beggar? He could offer her nothing but fine words. Besides, no firm understanding existed between them. His imagination might be tricking him about her feelings.

'I wonder who that boy was taking the message to,' he mused aloud.

The destination Teng had in mind stirred old jealousies. He feared it was Worthy Master Jian. A love letter or tender message for the Daoist priest's welfare perhaps – a concern more physical than spiritual. Oh, he knew very well what 'exercises' were in the bamboo books.

Teng struggled to master such thoughts. 'Who do you think she was sending the message to, Shensi?'

The old tomb-finder grunted. 'Not important.'

'It is to me.'

'No more talk.'

Their original plan had been to find a means of using the small junk provided by Liu Shui to spirit Deng Nan-shi to the safety of rebel-held Lingling – an endeavour more easily imagined than accomplished. Government warships were every-where on the lake, stopping and searching merchant vessels. They had been forced to hole up for days in an estuary to avoid the attention of paddlewheel destroyers sailing back and forth.

Teng, however, had unexpected allies, for Liu Shui had assigned well-armed and reliable men to protect Yueh Fei's priceless descendents. These fanatical followers of the rebel cause had given Shensi the confidence to plan an ambush he could never have contemplated with just Teng by his side. For that reason he and the scholar waited in darkness, swords to hand, while three warriors lurked in a nearby garden – the same garden Yun Shu had played in as a little girl when her father and Golden Lotus lived on Monkey Hat Hill. Somewhere in the woods a wild dog barked.

'Are you sure they'll come tonight?' asked Shensi, gloomily.

'You must have a little faith,' replied Teng. 'Remember the letter. And, of course, their inordinate greed. Oh, they'll come.'

The letter in question had been found shortly after their flight from Chenglingji in Chao and Hua's private junk. The captain, an old intimate of the spymasters, claimed to have no knowledge of the letter's contents, just that he had been ordered to deliver it to a gentleman in Hou-ming. Conveniently, he didn't know the gentleman's name either. Dangling his head in the lake while Shensi held his ankles refreshed the captain's memory. 'Salt Minister Gui!' he spluttered. Another dipping revealed this was one of many letters delivered to that party.

Upon breaking the wax seal, Teng discovered the document was written in code. Ever since he was a boy, Teng had liked puzzles and ciphers and mental challenges that offered a chance to confirm his superior faculties. Common scum like Chao and Hua could never devise a code too difficult for a trained scholar. As their junk sailed towards Hou-ming, he had used every waking hour to unpick the code. Once deciphered, the letter surprised even him.

'*Salt Minister Gui*,' he had translated in a pedantic, triumphant voice to Shensi. '*We have had no confirmation you received our last message*. Mark that, Shensi! Their correspondence is no new thing. Clearly Chao and Hua are traitors. And no doubt Ying-ge is an accomplice. *Red (yes). Blue (no)*. A password or signal . . . *We will honour our offer to meet you at midnight of the 8th day, 9th month, in the house you once showed us. In case you do not arrive like last time, we mean the house below the ruins of Deng Mansions. We beg you to join us at the exact centre of the garden*. Note the preciseness of their instructions. They don't trust our dear Salt Minister and who can blame them? Clearly their business transactions have not been satisfactory! Now we come to it: *Do not forget the great reward you promised us. Think how we have earned it a hundred times over*. Ah, they really don't trust him! It is signed: *Ox and Snake*. Little difficulty guessing who is the ox and who the snake, eh? Tell me you aren't impressed, Shensi!'

Teng had beamed expectantly. The former tomb-finder scowled. 'We never got our share of the dead prince's treasure from Chao and Hua. Now they'll pay.'

'Do you mean to blackmail them?' asked Teng, in alarm. 'That is not possible. We must warn Hsiung! Prince Arslan knows all about his plans. He may be sailing into a trap. Surely he will postpone his attack on Hou-ming now.'

'No blackmail,' replied Shensi.

'What then?'

'I mean to kill them.'

* * *

That was why they waited on Monkey Hat Hill at midnight of the 8th Day of the 9th Month. To kill Chao and Hua. And why the junk intended to carry Deng Nan-shi to safety had been sent back to Chenglingji with a warning for Hsiung. Teng's hope was that it reached the rebel fleet before any trap set by the Mongols snapped shut.

天命

They took up position in a thicket of rhododendrons overhung by an ancient pawlonia tree. The gardens had reverted to young woodland in the twenty years since Salt Minister Gui and his household left for the security of Prince Arslan's compound. No one except wild animals and birds came there now.

As Teng had predicted, they did not wait long. One of the bodyguards assigned by Liu Shui appeared by their side.

'They're here,' he murmured. 'The two Ministers and four guards, that's all. They carry lots of bags as though they've just arrived in the city and come straight here. Ministers Chao and Hua are on their way to the gardens now with a lantern. They've left their men at the gatehouse.'

Teng's breath quickened. He felt an intense discomfort in his bowels. It had been one thing to threaten revenge: securing it was quite another, especially with a sword he had never used in anger. Luckily, their own bodyguards were formidable fighters.

'Are the Ministers armed?' he asked, ashamed of the squeak in his voice.

Shensi ignored him: 'You three surprise the guards they left by the gatehouse. Not one must escape.'

The rebel soldier nodded. Teng immediately detected a flaw in Shensi's plan. 'If our own men do that, who remains to subdue the Ministers?' he asked.

Again he was ignored.

'Don't attack the four guards until you hear fighting in the

461

garden,' said Shensi. 'That'll be us. Bring us their heads as proof.'

The soldier saluted with two fists pressed together. A rustle of leaves and he vanished into the darkness to find his comrades. Shensi quietly drew his long sword and Teng did likewise. Then they froze. A light had appeared at the entrance to the garden.

'Is he there?' called out Chao in a brash, thick voice. 'He'd better be this time!'

Teng had seen Chao drunk so many times he could not mistake the signs. Beside him, Shensi stirred with anticipation.

'Quieter, you fool!' That was Hua.

'Why?' jeered his partner. 'There's nothing but mice to be afraid of here. No one can hear us.'

'Even so,' replied Hua, 'we should be careful.'

'It's that damned lunatic Gui with his crazy little he-whore who should be careful. If he doesn't pay us what we agreed, I'll . . .'

'Shut up! You should never have drunk that brandy. What if he hears.'

They came into view, heading for the paved area in the garden's centre overlooked by the rhododendrons where Teng and Shensi lurked. Both spies were dressed in plain travelling clothes, Chao carrying a flickering oil lamp while Hua held a bag close to his chest as though afraid of dropping it. Close up, Teng was alarmed by Chao's broad-chested bulk. If it came to a fight he had little doubt who would triumph. At least Hua, though wiry, was small. In addition, he was out of breath from carrying the heavy bag. Teng wondered how he could arrange a brief trial of these two criminals – with himself in the role of judge, of course. He suspected Shensi had other notions of justice.

'Where is he?' demanded Chao. 'That abacus he's always clicking gives me the creeps. It's like he's counting dead souls.'

'He will come.'

'Why should he?' asked Chao. 'I told you not to give him the information before we got paid. This is your fault.'

'By tomorrow we'll be rich enough to set ourselves up as lords,' said Hua.

'So you say. Why hasn't Gui replied to your last few letters?'

'Because it was too dangerous. He chose not to take the risk.'

'I don't like it,' said Chao. 'There's another thing you haven't considered. What if the Noble Count wins his glorious battle tomorrow?'

'Then we leave Hou-ming Province with all we've got off him – and that's a lot – and set up elsewhere as wealthy merchants. So I, at least, have considered it.'

'Consider *this*!' The battlecry belonged to Shensi. He leaped out of the rhododendrons and brought down his sword on Chao's shoulder while the drunken man looked round in confusion. A bellow rose into the night. The lamp swung at Shensi, forcing him to dodge. Sparks and burning oil flared. Then Chao, clutching his wound, disappeared into the darkness, shouting for help.

'He's mine!' cried Shensi. 'You take the other.'

With that he was gone, leaping round a corner of the path towards the abandoned house. By now Hua had drawn his sword and stood looking for attackers. Aware all surprise had gone, Teng stepped from the concealment of the bushes.

'Lesser Minister Hua,' he said, 'I advise you to throw aside your weapon. I promise a fair hearing, though I suspect you wouldn't offer the same courtesy to me.'

If he expected Hua to obey this eminently reasonable command – and he did – Teng was instantly disappointed.

'Who else is with you?'

A question answered by shouting and clashing metal at the gatehouse. The bodyguard provided by Liu Shui had pounced.

'Who else is here?' demanded Hua, staring round into the darkness, his sword arm pulled back to thrust. Discovering no one, a puzzled look crossed his face.

'Just me,' said Teng. 'Now, drop your sword.'

Hua kept examining the undergrowth. 'Just you?' he asked, incredulously. 'Then I'd advise *you* to drop *your* sword. Do you expect me to surrender to a coward?'

He made a pretend tiger roar, just as he and Chao had amused themselves when seeking the dead prince's tomb all those years before. Ruffled, Teng said: 'I strongly advise . . .'

'Shut up!' said Hua. 'You're a weakling! It's that precious Deng blood of yours. Everyone knows your grandfather hung himself instead of fighting the Mongols like a man. Well then, give me your sword like a sensible . . .'

At that moment he leaped at Teng, sweeping his blade. The scholar cried out, managing to parry the blow at the last moment. Hua stepped back. With another bellow, he slashed again – a feeble stroke, inexpertly delivered. Teng's ripostes were similarly inept. Back and forth they swung and parried, clanging and uttering ferocious grunts until, finally, both were winded and backed away. Sounds of fighting still drifted from the gatehouse, including an agonised scream that Teng thought horribly like Shensi's voice.

'One of yours, I think,' said Hua.

'Perhaps.'

Teng wondered if Hua shared his desperation for help. The spy's earlier taunt had been correct: it was in his blood to expect others to do his fighting.

'I am going to pick up my bag and walk away,' said Hua. 'If you follow or interfere, I'll kill you.'

Uncertain of his enemy's intentions, Hua stepped cautiously over to his fat leather bag. Still Teng hesitated. It would be better to wait for one of the bodyguards. Hua laughed coarsely as he seized the bag with one hand, holding the sword in the other.

'It's like I say,' he said, 'you're a coward. Just like your grandfather.'

The insult, so often rehearsed by Teng's deepest fears and anguished pride, or sheer weariness of being scorned by men inferior in every way except guile and an absence of scruples, forced up his sword. Teng charged at Hua. 'Yueh Fei!' he cried. 'Yueh Fei!'

Back and forth they clashed, only this time in deadly earnest. Despite his enthusiasm, Teng was clumsier than Hua. First he took a gash on his left arm, then a cut on his scalp that began to trickle blood over his forehead.

'Had enough?' gasped Hua, crimson from his exertions.

Teng's chest burned for air. His body, still not fully healed from the misery of the Salt Pans, felt as though it would curl into a senseless ball and beg for mercy.

'Yueh Fei!' he called, desperately, as though his great ancestor might help him. And perhaps the Immortal Hero of the Empire did watch from the Jade Emperor's Cloud Terrace and approve his hapless descendant's foolish courage. Teng's next desperate sword stroke – for the first time in the entire fight – connected with an intimate part of Hua. Not his flesh, it was true, but a bulging purse attached to his broad girdle. The bag split and burst, spilling a tinkling rain of gems and pearls and gold objects onto the moss-covered paving stones.

Hua involuntarily tried to grab his precious treasure, lowering his guard for a moment. Long enough for Teng to level his sword and drive it deep into the small man's chest. Having delivered this blow, Teng let go of the hilt and staggered to one side, breath panting. His heart pulsed as though it would split and burst like Hua's bag of treasure.

'Y-you!' gurgled Hua, blood bubbling up from his punctured lung. He dropped his own sword and vainly attempted to grip Teng's. Slowly he toppled forwards, driving the hilt deeper in. After a last twitch he lay motionless.

At that moment Shensi arrived, followed by two of the body-guards assigned by Liu Shui. The old tomb-finder surveyed the scene coldly. Blood trickled from Teng's wounded scalp, dripping onto the ground where jewels and gold objects lay scattered.

天命

The corpses of the four guards and Minister Hua were thrown off the cliff into the lake below. The body of their own man – for one of the rebels had perished in the fight – required more honour. As the first beams of dawn filtered through the young woods surrounding the Salt Minister's old house, they dug a shallow grave and left him to rest.

Chao had managed to escape yet they did not think he would return soon.

'He'll wait for the end of the curfew,' said Shensi, 'it's too dangerous otherwise. Besides, he's badly wounded. We've time to set things in order.'

This included a thorough search of the bodies before throwing them over the cliff. Once opened, the baggage contained a fortune in *cash*, jewellery and silver ingots bearing the Imperial treasury's seal of authenticity.

Among the valuables, too, a gold and bronze leopard with red jewels for eyes. A treasure found in the dead prince's tomb a decade earlier and somehow filched from Hornets' Nest. Teng remembered Hua's deep fear of curses. Perhaps that curse had worked itself out.

For the first time in all the years he had known him, Teng saw tears on Shensi's grizzled cheeks. 'At last,' sniffed the tomb-finder, 'something! This time I'll not lose it!'

'We must go now to Cloud Abode Monastery,' said Teng. 'I must find my father before Chao informs Salt Minister Gui what has happened.'

With that, as dawn seeped a faint trace of light to the east, the four surviving rebels climbed the Hundred Stairs towards the monastery, bags of loot on their backs.

thirty-three

天命

6th Day, 9th Month, 1322

Dawn, three days before Teng was to attain the unlikely exploit of killing a man. Far out on the lake where the water was deep as forty people standing on each other's shoulders, down through drifting clouds of sediment and vegetation to the lake's bed, fish of many kinds were feeding. They had discovered a banquet.

The remains of a burned junk rested on the muddy, rock-strewn bottom, half-hidden by gently swaying weeds. Its mainmast had snapped and projected at an angle. The hull, split open by a gigantic crossbow bolt, showed signs of charring. Weapons lay within the wreck, as well as diverse objects to maintain a floating house. None were useful to the fish and crabs and eels. As dawn light filtered through the cloudy water, nocturnal feeders worked furiously, aware the coming of day would bring more powerful eyes and jaws.

The junk had been sunk the previous evening after a chase by paddlewheel destroyers from the government fleet. A few lucky hits by bomb-hurling catapults set her ablaze. She had drifted down slowly, along with her secrets.

The greatest of these had resided in the hearts and minds of the junk's crew: memories and flickering, earnest convictions

467

balanced by doubt. All gone, treasures uncountable. Now long-jawed fish sought what profit they could from flesh and bone and blood and sinew that had encased those treasures. Eels entered gaping mouths to find tongues that once laughed or cursed, told truth and lies. Soft, spongy meat, easily swallowed. Larger fish worried away at open wounds. The very smallest discovered an interest in eyeballs.

One of those lost treasures wore a scroll case on his belt. Within, already ruined by water, was a pulpy mass of documents: Chao and Hua's coded letter to Salt Minister Gui, as well as Teng's translation and a further note in which he warned Hsiung that he was leading the rebel fleet – and by extension, the noble cause of Yueh Fei – into a certain trap.

Its belly gorged, a pike broke from the feast and swam upward. It sensed a disturbance in the water: unusual currents and vibrations. Upward to a roof of shimmering brightness lit by the rising sun. Dark shapes surrounded by clouds of bubbles were disturbing the glimmering veil of the lake's surface. The unusual vibrations intensified, frightening the king-pike. Still it rose, drawn by impulse. Finally it broke through, hovering between worlds of water and air, glassy eyes staring. Images implanted themselves – high, threatening prows, painted hulls, sails, oars, shadows – incomprehensible to the fish. But it understood danger. With a flick of silvery tail, it swam back down towards the lake bed to lurk among reeds until its meal had been digested and another must be found.

天命

Just as the pike broke water and took fright, Hsiung emerged from a hatch in his paddlewheel battleship and climbed on deck. Like the fish he surveyed the horizon. What he saw made him glad.

Ships flying the vermilion flags of Yueh Fei and the Red Turban cause were advancing across the lake – nearly two hundred, each loaded with soldiers, marines and sailors. The autumn sky was blue and cloud-chased, the morning hopeful. The dawn's flush mirrored a return of colour to his own cheeks after months of dissipation and banquets, striving always for mirth, led by the moods of Ying-ge. Those moods were part of her fascination. Yet, somehow, away from her judging eye and subtly conveyed disapproval, away from her radiant expressions of affection, he felt a new energy. When a servant rushed up offering a bowl of breakfast wine he waved it away.

'Bring me pure lake water,' he commanded. 'Seeing the lake will bring us victory I wish to honour it!'

The officers clustered round him applauded this clever sentiment, so that Hsiung felt like a Noble Count indeed. Already he no longer required medicines. Though intended to renew his vigour, the draughts often left him listless and dull. No need for such potions now! After his victory he would never need them again.

'Fetch Admiral Won-du!' he commanded.

Coloured flags flew to summon the Admiral, who obligingly left the huge, rectangular floating castle used as his flagship. There were ten such monstrous vessels in the Yueh Fei fleet, each large enough to contain hundreds of marines. Their role was critical to Hsiung's plan of attack: sail up to the fortified harbour walls of Hou-ming, lower ramps and storm the defences. Then Hou-ming would lie beneath his knife like the throat of a panting, exhausted deer, its mouth frothing, eyes rolling helplessly . . . Hsiung felt the dark lights stir and gasped so loudly some of his officers exchanged curious glances. He must not think that way again! Had he learned nothing from the Buddha's Caves? How hard it was to be burdened with a foreknowledge of torment!

At that moment Admiral Won-du clambered aboard Hsiung's battleship; like his maternal cousin, Ying-ge, he was unusually handsome and rosy-cheeked. His cold, watchful eyes, however, suggested a calculating character. Won-du was known as a swordsman and Ying-ge had often implied – in the subtlest of terms, of course – he might even be a match for his master, the Noble Count. Perhaps that was why Hsiung frowned as the Admiral bowed, though there were more pressing reasons.

'Admiral, what is your report?' he demanded, taking a seat bolted onto the gently swaying deck. Again Won-du bowed.

'The enemy flee before us, sire!'

Although light ships shadowed the rebel fleet and occasionally disappeared over the horizon, none had dared to engage. Hsiung stirred in his chair. The danger lay in losing the element of surprise. Although Prince Arslan must know the rebels were displaying their strength, the Mongols could scarcely imagine they would be bold enough to assault Hou-ming itself. Even now, so late in the campaign, just a few picked officers were aware of Hsiung's exact intentions.

'Do we still have surprise?' asked Hsiung. 'That is what matters.'

'A hundred times over,' said Won-du.

'How far are we from Cape Fou?' asked Hsiung. 'When will we arrive?'

Now the Admiral tugged his perfectly trimmed beard. 'Soon, sire!'

'How soon, exactly?'

'I shall send forth scout ships to find that out, sire!'

'Do you mean you have not sent them already?' Hsiung detected a faint glitter of defiance or irony in the Admiral's eye. 'I require that information in an hour's time!'

Won-du bowed low and withdrew. The next few hours were critical to their plans. Already the Yueh Fei fleet was a day behind schedule. How slowly they advanced! Hsiung had even witnessed ships colliding as though captained by idiots, despite most of the fleet being spread out in a crescent several *li* wide.

Although Won-du assured him there was no need for a tight formation when no opponents of any account existed on the lake, Hsiung looked at the straggling disposition of his ships with growing unease. Until the land army disembarked at Cape Fou, a mere two days march from Hou-ming City, he could not rest easy. That should have occurred yesterday morning and now, it seemed, there was no certainty they would even reach the Cape today.

His mood of brightness dimmed and Hsiung remained in the chair fixed to the deck of the battleship. All around him sol-diers and sailors scurried, orders were shouted, the steady rhythms of cranking pedals and splashing waterwheels filled the air. Hsiung seemed not to notice, lost in thoughts or dreams glimpsed through half-closed eyes . . .

Twenty years had passed since his last sight of Hou-ming, a child's vision limited by everything he had not known or under-stood at that age. Now he dreamed of Hou-ming as he longed for it to become, ruled by a firm yet benign hand. A new palace would stand on Monkey Hat Hill, named . . . he didn't know what, the details would come later. Besides, Liu Shui always helped him find difficult words.

His palace! Hsiung did not imagine splendour or excessive pomp while those he ruled went hungry. Although Deng Nan-shi had taught him as a boy the outer must reflect the inner, Hsiung knew the match was often false. Not in his palace, though! Purposeful bureaux directed by Chancellor Liu Shui would spread prosperity as the planter of rice tenderly inserts his carefully nurtured shoots into muddy paddies. Bandits and scum would no longer plague the defenceless peasants. All would be taught that heads separated from necks cannot be rejoined – and that would be their fate if they persisted in wrongdoing! Then again, the streets of Hou-ming would benefit, too. No more beggars – why should anyone beg when they could be employed as soldiers or labourers or manufacture weapons destined to one day drive the Mongol usurpers back to their miserable steppes? Scholars, too, would regain their prominence, dutifully studying for the Imperial Examinations that Deng Nan-shi had told him should determine worth and merit. Why not, when Liu Shui could arrange it all ...

Hsiung stirred and opened apparently drowsing eyes. The officers and crew on the command deck began to bustle. Slowly his eyelids lowered.

Thoughts of scholars led, as always, to the Dengs, and especially Teng. Hsiung knew Liu Shui had helped his childhood companion escape Chenglingji. He also knew the Chancellor well enough to understand there must be an unimpeachable reason for so rash an act. And in this case it was obvious: he had not trusted Hsiung to behave well. Deep, hidden grief brought tears to his eyes. He rubbed as though at a speck of grit. Was Teng just a speck in his soul? Or the speck of grit that pearls form around?

Hsiung knew he would feel more secure with his old friend's sceptical intelligence by his side than a hundred bowing Admiral Won-du's. Or even – another thought laced with guilt – a hundred insinuating murmurs and caresses from the sinuous Ying-ge. Yet had not her gift of a jade disk saved his life?

Hsiung reached up unconsciously to check it still hung round his neck, then lapsed back into daydream, imagining the clean, prosperous streets of Hou-ming before the Mongols had slaughtered nineteen out of twenty, before ancient Wards had fallen into ruin and rotting piles of timber. When he became Prince all would be renewed!

Prince Hsiung of Hou-ming! Prince Hsiung, defender of the righteous cause of Yueh Fei! Prince Hsiung, Red Turban lord and beloved of the Buddha Maitreya! *Prince Hsiung.*

Had he not always been lucky when everything appeared lost? Unless, of course, there had been no luck at all, merely the working out of Heaven's will – of the Mandate of Heaven.

* * *

'Cape Fou, sire! We've arrived.'

Hsiung opened his eyes. Daylight and images of armed men, flags, masts, shifting patterns of ships replaced his dream. Rising abruptly, he laid a hand on the upward-angled hilt of his long, faithful sword.

'Fly the flags to prepare for landing!' he ordered.

天命

They arrived at mid-morning and at once delays mounted. Yet Cape Fou was a perfect place to disembark the army of eight thousand infantry led by General P'ao. A natural harbour existed where a broad, deep river joined the lake; all one need do was form an orderly line of ships, sail them in, unload their cargo of soldiers and supplies, then depart to rejoin the fleet.

The mischief, as always, stemmed from ineptitude. Captain vied with captain to discharge his share of the army until blockages formed. General P'ao paced on the shore bellowing angry orders. Admiral Won-du demoted officers associated with the disgraced Naval Commissioner Ma Fu, leaving his own men – who were the real culprits – in command of their vessels.

The chaos largely escaped the notice of the Noble Count. Still aflame from his vision of Hou-ming ruled by one worthy of Heaven's Mandate, he did not care to contemplate anything that might contradict it. Instead he led a sortie of paddlewheel destroyers out into the lake to drive off a dozen government vessels observing from a distance like wolves following a herd. At the rebel ships' approach the enemy withdrew until Hsiung decided to relinquish the chase. By the time he returned to Cape Fou the troop ships were slowly advancing in lines, a formation that had taken hours to accomplish. Admiral Won-du assured him any delays in disembarkation were the fault of General P'ao.

The landings continued late into the night. P'ao's scouts reported that the hinterland behind the Cape was oddly

473

deserted, as though the villages had been emptied deliberately; perhaps their inhabitants had merely fled.

天命

7th Day, 9th Month, 1322

The lookouts on the highest masts called out: *Hou-ming! Hou-ming!* Despite the demands of dignity, Hsiung hurried to the prow of his battleship and peered forward. The morning had been misty, but since noon yet another cloudless day cleared the horizon. At first he could not be sure if the dark smudge on the distant shore was Hou-ming. Yet his breath quickened as slowly – agonisingly slowly for a fleet seeking the advantage of surprise – the city landmarks became recognisable.

That elevated promontory surrounded by cliffs must be Monkey Hat Hill, crowned by Cloud Abode Monastery. Dark lines coalesced into ramparts and towers, said by his spies to be in a lamentable state of repair. Straggling, vertical threads above the city became recognisable as plumes of smoke and rumours swept the fleet that no battle would be necessary. The people, inspired by the rebels' approach, had risen as one, slaughtering the Mongols and their lackeys.

Hsiung listened coldly as Admiral Won-du related this tale with all the certainty of a triumphant hero.

'Let us concern ourselves with victory not rumours! We will advance to a position three *li* from the coast,' replied the Noble Count. 'Arrange for spies to land and report on the disposition of General P'ao's army. By now he should be approaching Hou-ming. When he arrives we will launch an assault to support him without delay.'

The Admiral bowed with a flourish.

'And Won-du,' said Hsiung, quietly, 'if you prove incompetent one more time in this campaign I shall relieve you of your command.'

A hot flush crept over Won-du's handsome face. It reminded Hsiung of Ying-ge's expression when angry.

'Do you understand?' barked the Noble Count.

The Admiral bowed low and withdrew. Yet when Hsiung looked round he was astounded by the disorderly formation of the fleet at the very time they should be most alert. At last he glimpsed his folly in allowing Ying-ge's relatives and their followers to gain such high positions in the Newly Adhered Navy. How often Liu Shui had warned him, at first through hints, then the bluntest of reproaches. Hsiung stirred uneasily, remembering Navy Commissioner Ma Fu's advice regarding the Five Squadrons. Had Ma Fu really been the traitor Chao and Hua claimed? He would ensure a large present of silver was sent to the Navy Commissioner's sons and family, in recognition of past services to Yueh Fei's cause.

Hsiung's one comfort was that the government forces had been taken entirely by surprise. Only a handful of vessels opposed the Newly Adhered Navy. Once again he detected Heaven's hand.

An hour later such reassuring thoughts were replaced by sheer alarm.

'Won-du! Signal for the fleet to gather in the shape of a fortress!'

Signal rockets rose and drums beat wildly. Everywhere flags fluttered, confusing the original command until a few captains decided they had been given full permission to flee back to Chenglingji.

'Tell Won-du to form a screen of our fastest ships! Damn him, I shall gather them myself.'

Dum dum dum beat the signal drums. Squadrons of enemy ships were approaching fast while the Newly Adhered Navy still struggled to assume a defensive stance. Though the rebels outnumbered the government fleet two to one, Hsiung sensed how swiftly disaster might fall on them. By now a fifth of the rebel battleships had formed a screen and the Noble Count ordered his ship to the front.

'How far off is dusk?' he asked the captain.

The old sailor peered to the west.

'Two hours at most, sire.'

'Then that's how long we shall deter them,' he said. 'See their flagship in the centre?'

The captain examined the line of advancing prows and nodded.

'Make straight for it at full speed. Order the other ships to form an arrowhead shape behind us. We shall be its point!'

Dum dum dum. Soon the rebel ships were in motion. As they gained speed Hsiung hid his anxiety. Courage was no cure for ignorance when it came to naval strategy. Yet once again Heaven's intervention disproved his fears. For as the rebels approached, the government ships turned aside, sailing away from the Newly Adhered Navy into deeper waters.

Dusk was settling quickly when Hsiung returned to the massed rebel fleet. Cheering greeted him as though he had gained a great victory. Yet Hsiung wondered why scout ships had not been deployed to give warning of any night attack on the dense square of rebel ships. Again Won-du was at fault. Hsiung decided a new Admiral would be appointed in the morning; but the purges of Navy Commissioner Ma Fu's experienced men had been so thorough it was difficult to identify a single officer of merit.

An uneasy night followed. Above the lake countless stars rotated in intricate patterns. Below, hundreds of lesser lights clustered on every horizon so that the Noble Count felt hemmed in wherever he turned. It was impossible, surely, that each light denoted an enemy ship. Still no word of General P'ao arrived.

天命

8th Day, 9th Month, 1322

At dawn Hsiung awoke with a start from his couch on the ship's deck. Mist drifted across the lake and his blanket was damp with dew. Throwing it off, he rose, calling out to his picked bodyguard.

'Any news of P'ao while I slept?'

The officer on duty bowed. 'No, sire!'

Hsiung squeezed his hands, recollecting he had intended to dismiss Won-du. There seemed no time for that now.

'Summon all my senior captains,' he commanded. 'Send at least three boats to land spies on the shore. I must know the exact moment our land army approaches Hou-ming . . .'

Before he could say more a loud bang echoed across the lake, its exact origin obscured by the rolling mist. Hsiung recognised it as a signal rocket – and not one of his own.

'To arms!' he bellowed. 'All men to arms!'

For the next few hours the fog thickened with screams and the echoing detonations of thunderclap bombs hurled blindly into the swirling air. Smoke thickened the mist as dozens of ships burned. Hsiung's own battleship collided with a large three-masted junk and fierce exchanges of arrows were resolved by a furious boarding led by the Noble Count himself.

By noon the fog began to melt away, revealing the extent of the losses on both sides. Scores of rebel ships had been captured or sunk; an equal number of government vessels suffered a similar fate. Unexpectedly, the mist had favoured the rebels, for in such conditions tenacity and courage counted more than manoeuvrability and skill. In that regard, the Yueh Fei soldiers, fanatical in their grievances against the foreign usurpers, had the advantage.

The Noble Count's elation at his capture of the enemy junk faded when he realised how close to the shore the Newly Adhered Navy had drifted over the course of the fighting. Equally alarming were the fresh squadrons of enemy ships

477

arriving from the west as though they had been awaiting the outcome of the battle in the fog. The rebels' advantage in numbers had already been reversed. With a shock, Hsiung realised they were almost trapped.

'They knew we were coming!' he exclaimed. 'To the exact day!'

Hsiung turned to examine Hou-ming in the distance. If a trap had been prepared for his fleet, how must P'ao be faring on land? And until the Red Turban land army arrived he dared not attack the harbour walls of Hou-ming by water.

Twilight found both fleets tending scorched wounds. More plumes of smoke rose from Hou-ming. Long, anxious hours passed without a single report of P'ao's advance.

thirty-four

天命

9th Day, 9th Month, 1322

Every melody, however harsh and unpleasing to the ear, floats upon some kind of harmony. That red autumn dawn, Hou-ming floated upon an insistent swell of disharmony. The first riots broke out in the Southern Suburbs where clans of fisher-folk and sailors loyal to the Red Turbans lived in filthy, impoverished villages reclaimed from swampland. The news that the Yueh Fei rebel fleet was engaging the enemy out on the lake and that a large land force had disembarked south of the city was enough to provoke their rebellion. Abused and oppressed for two generations, at last they could respond in kind. A force of two hundred reluctant Chinese mercenaries sent to pacify the fisher-villages was soon disarmed then recruited to the rebel cause. In alarm, Prince Arslan sent messengers to reserves of his own hiding in the hills north of Hou-ming and ordered the closing of the Southern Gates, despite a fixed plan to keep all the gates temptingly open. A company of Tipchak archers promptly used the confusion as a pretext to loot a dozen floating oriole houses in the entertainment district.

Panic spread through the slums and commercial districts of Hou-ming. It seemed a massacre would again descend on them like a ravaging typhoon. Everywhere people fled onto the

479

streets carrying bundles of possessions or pushing handcarts. Thousands besieged the Northern Gates, a stream seeking release from a simmering, tight-lidded cauldron. At first they were beaten back by Prince Arslan's men until the soldiers were almost overwhelmed. If the Yueh Fei rebels did establish a siege, the Mongol lord would need the co-operation of those he had ruled – and utterly despised – for so long. Besides, a reduced population meant fewer mouths to feed. Thus he ordered the opening of the Northern Gates and all day refugees flowed into the countryside. With them departed yet more of Prince Arslan's claim upon the Mandate of Heaven, for what manner of ruler abandons his people when they are threatened by a hostile fleet and army?

Rumours of the battle on the lake rushed back and forth. At first the Noble Count of Lingling was triumphant; his navy had smashed a force twice its size through sheer courage! Surely the Buddha Maitreya's manifestation on earth must follow such a portent! . . . An hour later . . . Heaven had chosen the Great Khan, the only true Emperor of the Middle Kingdom! Already the rebel fleet was reduced to firewood floating in the lake amidst the corpses of a hundred thousand Yueh Fei bandits . . . An hour after that . . . Flee the city! The rebels are triumphant and are attacking the Southern Suburbs, slaughtering man, woman and child as they advance! Even Prince Arslan has fled, taking whatever treasures he can carry!

So the day passed.

天命

At the very start of that terrible day, a messenger had rushed from Golden Bright Temple bearing a hastily penned letter to the head of the Buddhist clergy in Hou-ming. Strangely, it contained no reference to the disorder consuming the city and threatening so many of their faithful followers, Buddhist or Daoist. Instead, Worthy Master Jian offered, on behalf of the

Provincial Daoist Council, to exchange Cloud Abode Monastery for a generous portion of the Buddha's knuckle-bone. If the aforesaid holy relic was sent to Worthy Master Jian by dusk that same day, then the Buddhist authorities would be granted full possession of Cloud Abode Monastery from the very same hour, including the image of Chenghuang the City God. Finally, the letter stipulated the exact size and weight of the bone sliver.

The Buddhist Tibetan clergy wondered if the wily Worthy Master was attempting a ruse. Such a hasty offer, so contrary to Daoist interests and on such a desperate day, was incomprehensible. But they had long heard rumours of the Worthy Master's eccentricities and concluded that the Divine Buddha Makhala had afflicted him with madness. Accordingly, they rushed off messengers agreeing the exchange. Soon news of it was circulating all across the city, further proof – to some, at least – of the world's imminent end.

Those most affected by the Worthy Master's decision were among the last to learn of it. It was mid-morning before an embassy arrived at Cloud Abode Monastery with an Edict of Instruction signed by the President of the Provincial Daoist Council.

Yun Shu had risen very late, weak and unsteady from the effects of Void's magical pills charged with autumn minerals. Her most intimate place felt raw and bruised. More painful was the recollection of the Worthy Master's rituals, his anger and denunciations. The thought of it brought on wretched tears. The unfairness of his accusations!

Then there was her hasty, insane letter to Golden Lotus calling upon him to collect her from Cloud Abode Monastery. Yun Shu could only think Void's pills were laced with demonic promptings. How else might she explain her conduct? If only she had heeded Bo-Bai's warnings! Yun Shu had no idea what to do if Father appeared at the gates of Cloud Abode

Monastery and ordered her to accompany him back to Prince Arslan's compound. A father's word was law, especially after her hysterical request for his protection. The damage to her standing as Abbess would be fatal.

The one threat Yun Shu failed to anticipate that morning, as crowds of refugees gathered in the streets and two fleets clashed out on the lake, was the Worthy Master's desperation. Hence her surprise when messengers from Golden Bright Temple beat on the closed bronze doors of the monastery with the butts of bamboo clubs.

At that precise moment the Nuns of Serene Perfection were gathered in one place – before the grinning image of Chenghuang – beseeching the City God to avert a massacre. They had formed a shape with their bodies that imitated the Great Dipper constellation and had commenced a sutra. All fell silent as shouts of alarm and running footsteps crossed the courtyard to the Temple of Celestial Teachers. Fifteen Nuns were present, the rest having fled the monastery for the safety of their families. As many servants also remained, continuing their routines under the stern eye of Eunuch Bo-Bai.

Suddenly the painted wooden doors of the Temple slid open, revealing a pale autumn morning. Candles in the shrine room flickered and glowed. A few stray, brown leaves blew in past four men wearing the purple robes of Daoist priests. At their head stood Void. The assembled Nuns muttered prayers and fingered amulets to avert misfortune arising from the interruption of their rite.

'Where is Abbess Yun Shu?' drawled Void. His eyes were red-rimmed and unfocussed.

'Do you really not recognise me?' she asked, contemptuously.

The wind was rising in the trees of Monkey Hat Hill.

'Read this,' he instructed, holding out a sheet of parchment on which hastily composed characters snaked in ribbons. She recognised it as the Worthy Master's handwriting when in a divinely inspired condition.

Unfolding the thick paper – at least no expense had been spared for that – she read the letter with shock then anger.

'This is a foolish edict!' she exclaimed. 'I refuse to believe the Worthy Master wrote it!'

Void surveyed her laconically.

'Even if he *did*,' she added, 'I do not believe he possesses the necessary authority!'

'It is the Provincial Daoist Council that commands you,' said Void.

'How can they! The city is in chaos. They cannot have met to discuss such a matter.'

'The Council expects obedience from registered Nuns,' he said. 'Are you not instructed to read it aloud three times to all Nuns of Serene Perfection and servants residing in Cloud Abode Monastery? Well then, proceed!'

Yun Shu bowed her head in distress at such disrespect. Her eyelids fluttered.

'You read it,' she whispered.

Void nodded courteously and unrolled the letter.

'Assembled Servants of the Dao,' he intoned. 'On the 9th Day of the 9th Month in the Year of the Tortoise, let it be known that Divine Instructions have been sent to the Provincial Daoist Council of Hou-ming Province by the Blessed Queen Mother of the West! First, a message sent through spirit-writing. Then, a vision-journey experienced by the President of the Daoist Council in which he was summoned to the Queen Mother's throne room to receive divine commands.'

A few of the Nuns cried out in joy at such signs of divine favour. They did not doubt what everyone knew to be true: the Worthy Master was on the threshold of Immortality and conferred with the goddess on a regular basis.

'Ahem,' continued Void, 'there is more: "The Queen Mother instructs all loyal servants of the Dao to obey the following. Firstly, to give thanks for Her gracious condescension. Secondly, in order to heal the rift between Buddhist and Daoist in Hou-ming Province, Cloud Abode Monastery is to pass in perpetuity to the control of the Buddhist clergy at dusk on the 9th Day of the 9th Month in the Year of the Tortoise. Moreover, that the image of Chenghuang shall be likewise passed to them. Thirdly, any registered Nun, Priest, Monk or other sundry servants of the Dao questioning her Divine Edict shall be de-registered instantly and without appeal. Fourthly, the Nuns of Serene Perfection currently residing in Cloud Abode Monastery must gather their belongings and leave that place by dusk of the 9th Day, 9th Month, Year of the Tortoise or be de-registered instantly as Serene Ones.'

A shocked silence greeted this divine decree. No one dared speak lest all the protections offered by the law to a Serene One be confiscated: her license to preach and cast spells for a fee, to beg alms and sell amulets, let alone the food and shelter provided by the Daoist authorities. In short, she would be thrown upon her own resources in a city torn by war. A world where women were either wives, drudges or whores – often all three at once.

Yun Shu met the eye of her predecessor as Abbess, Lady Lu Si. Both women were pale. Perhaps they shared the same thought, for when Yun Shu replied, barely concealing her bitterness, Lady Lu Si nodded approvingly.

'Tell Worthy Master Jian we are obedience itself,' said the Abbess. 'Tell him that when the peace resumes and loyal followers of the Dao learn about his true motives in this matter, he shall have many questions to answer.' Trembling, she added, 'Tell him, I hope the Buddha's knucklebone makes him an Immortal very soon, for that is the only way he will escape those questions!'

Void bowed, smiling slightly. 'I think we can be quite sure of that,' he said. His face hardened. 'By dusk! You must be gone by dusk or I shall personally tear to shreds your certificates of registration!'

With that, he withdrew to a nearby chamber with his assistants. From this vantage point he could supervise the

Nuns' preparations for departure. It was significant the priest's entourage included a dozen guards armed with swords and thick, bamboo clubs.

天命

There was no need to call a conclave of the Serene Ones. All had been present in the Temple of Celestial Masters. Yun Shu ordered them to sit on the floor in a circle. Most were weeping. Only one, ancient Earth Peace, was saved by the bewilderment of old age from comprehending how the certainties of an entire lifetime had expired in an instant. Instead of joining the others, Yun Shu led her to a chair near the door where she sat patiently.

'I cannot believe the Queen Mother of the West wants this!' said Lady Lu Si. 'Yet the Worthy Master was quite clear he had spoken with the Goddess!'

Three Simplicities looked round to check whether they were overheard. Seeing two Daoist officials in the shadows she proclaimed loudly: 'I welcome this indication of Divine Favour! How blessed we are in our holy President!'

Yun Shu and Lady Lu Si shot contemptuous glances at their fellow *sanren*.

'I see Three Simplicities intends to profit from the destruction of an institution that has existed in this city for four hundred years,' said Lady Lu Si.

'Oh, I am obedient!' cried Three Simplicities. 'My dearest wish is that the authorities take note that *some* are loyal in this monastery!'

'We do not deserve this!' exclaimed Gold Immortal in her high, fluty voice. Realising what she had said, the old nun added hastily: 'Not that I am disobedient or questioning!'

A regretful smile crossed Three Simplicities' thin-lipped mouth. 'I have no choice but to report that,' she said. 'Why did you have to say that, Gold Immortal? I have no choice!'

Lady Lu Si cleared her throat. 'Three Simplicities can make any report she likes,' said the former abbess while Yun Shu continued to watch silently. 'As soon as the Worthy Master gets his inch of bone I'm sure he will lose interest in us. My own fear goes deeper.'

The other Nuns waited. Even Gold Immortal stopped sniffling miserably.

'I fear that Chenghuang is punishing us for not serving him with true zeal. Our conduct of the rites must have displeased him. This is his punishment.'

The circle of Nuns broke into fresh wails and tears. Yun Shu, however, clapped her hands for stillness. She had mastered the illusory anger within her soul – or most of it – and was now calm enough to speak.

'Though sincere in her suggestion, I believe Lady Lu Si is wrong. Chenghuang has been betrayed, but not by us. I have learned a terrible lesson from this. I must advise you that four centuries of devout practice in this holy place has been exchanged so one mortal man might gain Transcendence.'

Then Yun Shu explained the goings-on in Wild Goose Pagoda, concluding with the Worthy Master's unfortunate release of twenty years' worth of *jing*. There were shocked moans and exclamations from the other *sanren*. Nevertheless they required more detailed information concerning the 'accident'.

'Three Simplicities,' added Yun Shu, 'you have my full permission to report *that*. Now I must pack my possessions,' she said, rising. 'My final instruction as Abbess is that all, without exception, do likewise. We shall assemble in the hour before dusk to bid farewell to our beloved Chenghuang. Then we shall leave together, our dignity unblemished.'

The Nuns rose, some hugging, others finding a corner to weep alone. Most hurried to their own quarters, desperately speculating where they could go; not least, where they might sleep that night.

It took little time for Yun Shu to pack away her possessions. She recollected how the hoarded valuables of Cloud Abode Monastery had already been transferred to the Worthy Master's treasure rooms in Golden Bright Temple, leaving only a few chests of faded ritual robes and masses of worthless documents. This thought reminded her of the scroll given to her by Teng in the garden of Deng mansions, a lifetime ago, it seemed. She unrolled it curiously: it granted ownership of Wei Valley to the Yun clan forever. Yun Shu believed she was the last of that clan, unless some still survived in far off Nancheng. So perhaps there was a place she might flee, after all. Except that her choices seemed to lead, one way or other, back to her father's house and the dubious tutelage of Golden Lotus. Yet the moment she re-entered that household there would be no escape from discontent, misery, conflict and bitter reminiscences.

Yun Shu placed the scroll in her leather travelling satchel and went to inform an Honoured Guest that he must find new shelter.

天命

Ever since the destruction of his ancestral home, Deng Nan-shi had been staying in a chamber next to Bo-Bai's, part of a brick outbuilding at the rear of the monastery complex. Few visited that part of the ancient warren of buildings. Most of the narrow alleyways and flights of worn stone stairs were disused except by servants bringing the old scholar his meals or empty-ing his chamber pot. Occasionally, Bo-Bai helped Deng Nan-shi to the garden where he stared at clouds or hopping birds, meditating on matters he would only divulge through sighs. Yun Shu visited him as often as she could, finding the old man's tenacious hold on life remarkable. She sensed he was waiting for something – or someone – before allowing himself to be transformed.

487

When Yun Shu arrived at his door, she heard low voices within and wondered if Bo-Bai was explaining that Deng Nan-shi must find fresh quarters that very night. Despite her high position as Abbess, she possessed little in the way of *cash* to pay for an inn. Yet she was determined the venerable scholar would not spend a single hour beneath cold stars.

After a light knock, she opened the door. The man who was talking to Deng Nan-shi provoked a cry of surprise. She recoiled, looked around. Satisfied they were unobserved, she slipped into the small chamber, bolting the door behind her.

Teng had not stirred from the stool beside his father's bed. Now he rose and bowed very low to the Abbess. When he straightened she saw marks of pain and grief on his face. In a flash she sensed something new about him, something formidable, a wisdom acquired through suffering. Tears were in his eyes as he met her own. Both glanced aside.

She remembered the painting and poem. The promise implicit in the symbol of a blossoming plum, the colours of red and green. Could a man of honour retract so bold a statement? But she was nobody now with Cloud Abode Monastery gone. Why should he consider her worthy of notice?

'Yun Shu,' he said, 'Father has told me everything! I will do anything I can to repay you.' He laughed oddly. 'I have acquired by the strangest good fortune, well, let us say, I *can* repay you with far more than gratitude.'

Yun Shu looked wonderingly between father and son at this speech. Deng Nan-shi sat propped in bed, a fierce light in his eyes.

'My son means to say,' he croaked, 'he has returned . . .' A hoarse, gasping cough interrupted him. The younger people waited patiently. 'Returned through grave dangers,' continued Deng Nan-shi, 'to fulfil his filial duty as First Son of the Dengs.'

Teng nodded. 'Yun Shu, I have loyal retainers in my service. Men sworn to protect the descendents of Yueh Fei. We shall carry Deng Nan-shi away with us after dusk. Bo-Bai has told me all about Worthy Master Jian's treachery!'

He cast an uneasy glance at his father. 'But tell me: when you leave Cloud Abode Monastery, are you provided for?'

'I suppose not,' said Yun Shu, miserably, 'I am certain the Worthy Master will revoke my licence as a Nun. Then I must return to my father's house, though it is the last thing I want – with all respect to you, Honourable Deng Nan-shi, as a father yourself.'

The old scholar laughed. 'Not all fathers make considerate parents,' he conceded. 'In any case, you are female so it is natural for him to be less interested in you. You can hardly blame him for what is natural.'

'No doubt,' said Yun Shu.

'What of Lady Lu Si?' asked Teng. 'Will she, too, lose her licence?'

Yun Shu thought of Three Simplicities' promise to report disloyal opinions.

'Most probably,' she said.

'Then, Father, we must take her with us as an Honoured Companion,' said Teng. 'I have the means to support her and many more followers.' He turned back to Yun Shu. 'If there are spies, and I assume there will be, it is vital we do not stir their suspicion. When you leave Cloud Abode Monastery for the last time at dusk, go to the gardens of Deng Mansions. Ensure my Honoured Father is carried there. Perhaps you will think me presumptuous, yet I wish to make a proposal that may be of great interest. Above all, bring the scroll I once gave you concerning an estate far to the West.'

Yun Shu bowed. It felt pleasant to follow someone else's plans. In her heart she had no expectation of a happy release. Her thoughts were dragged to Prince Arslan's compound, where the Salt Minister's house must become her prison, her one remaining task in this life to breed grandsons for him to spoil and corrupt, as he had his own precious sons and heirs, her dead brothers.

天命

It was no coincidence that on the other side of the city another restless mind brooded upon the same topics as Yun Shu. It belonged to Golden Lotus.

The petite man's lotus feet were restless, too, as he shuffled through the front courtyard of the Salt Minister's residence to accost a female servant. As usual, Golden Lotus wore silks and make-up worthy of the finest lady. The effect – overwhelming to a certain taste when he was young – threatened comedy in his thirty-eighth year. Still he retained the mannerisms of a coy, beautiful girl as he greeted the family's faithful maid, Pink Rose.

'What have you discovered?' he asked in a loud, falsetto, fluttering a painted silk fan.

The maid bowed. She was trembling. 'The guards said the streets are full of people trying to leave the city. When I asked about Cloud Abode Monastery no one knew anything until . . .' She hesitated fearfully.

'Well! Speak up!'

'A sergeant told me all the Nuns would be sold as whores if the rebels got hold of them.'

Still Golden Lotus's fan fluttered.

'And the sergeant said the Buddhists have been given Cloud Abode Monastery. All the Nuns are to be forced out onto the streets.'

The fan stopped. 'Stupid woman! Tell no one of this!' He slapped Pink Rose across the face with surprising strength for one so slender.

The maid bowed and hurried off to inform the other servants that Master's daughter, Abbess Yun Shu, was being violated by bloodthirsty bandits along with every other Nun in the city.

Golden Lotus was left standing beside the gatehouse of the

Salt Minister's compound, aware that he must decide whether to act – and soon.

His troubles had started shortly after dawn with a hysterical letter from Yun Shu, begging the Salt Minister to collect her from Cloud Abode Monastery without delay. Golden Lotus's unstable feelings for her – sometimes angry, insulted, unforgiving, sometimes touched by reluctant respect – reached back to when he had been Gui's beautiful, precious new consort, twenty-five years earlier. Then Yun Shu had been an irrelevance. Now she could not be dismissed lightly.

Should he respond at once? The whole city was in chaos apart from where Prince Arslan's garrison controlled the Gates. If only he could pass the decision to dear Gui! Not that it would make much difference to poor, put upon Golden Lotus! Even if his husband-master hadn't been away from Hou-ming, helping Prince Jebe Khoja supply and provision the Mongol forces, it was doubtful the Salt Minister would have helped.

Since his sons' executions in far away Dadu, Gui had grown odder than ever. For the first time his uncanny ability to drill and parade numbers deserted him. There were rumours of mistakes. One or two involved many thousands of *cash*. A newly acquired habit of reckless drinking was partly to blame.

Poor Golden Lotus suffered the consequences: sullen moods for days, rages, ever longer episodes where Gui quivered in his chair, muttering as though possessed by a demon.

Golden Lotus grieved for the time when he had been the Salt Minister's most prized object – other than his sons' advancement to high office, of course. Once, long ago, Golden Lotus had even attracted Jebe Khoja's attention. A night better left unmentioned. In the intervening years Golden Lotus's dainty, exotic beauty, poised between so many opposites – he was once hailed by a drunken connoisseur as the sublime midpoint between *yin* and *yang* – had coarsened and greyed. To his horror, he had acquired the faintest trace of a paunch.

Now he must decide: fetch Yun Shu from Cloud Abode

Monastery as she requested, and thereby regain the possibility of installing some purpose into the Salt Minister's life, or hide in the dubious safety of Prince Arslan's palace.

He shuffled over to the entrance of the gatehouse and ordered the porter to open the doors. Beyond, Prince Arslan's huge parade ground was deserted. A smell of burning tainted the air. Golden Lotus felt the entire world he had fought to win for himself would burn, too, unless he acted. He turned to the porter and clicked his fingers.

'Fetch all the male servants! And both of Master's palanquins. Quick! Quick!'

The old man scurried off as swiftly as his bandy legs would carry him. The entire household knew better than to cross Golden Lotus.

It was long past noon when he departed, seated in a curtained palanquin carried by four men. A second followed, borne by the same number of human mules. Golden Lotus intended that it would return with Yun Shu.

A small crowd had gathered at the gatehouse of Prince Arslan's palace. Most were courtiers or servants alarmed by rumours of a rebel victory. At first the Captain of Guards refused to let them leave. But had not Prince Arslan himself allowed free passage to all who wished to depart from the city? Wearied of entreaties, the officer waved through the column of people clutching bags and precious possessions.

Soon Golden Lotus's small cavalcade hurried through the streets of Hou-ming. Many were deserted: districts long ago fallen into ruin, home to groves of bamboo and half-collapsed wooden houses. Other areas were lined with anxious faces, hysterical crowds on street-corners.

Still the curtained palanquins jogged towards Monkey Hat Hill. For Golden Lotus, a bumpy, fearful journey. He dared not part the drapes to look round. He had spent so long locked away in Salt Minister Gui's house, a treasure too precious to be sullied by the world's eyes, that he recognised no landmarks and was helplessly lost.

The palanquins halted and Golden Lotus found himself surrounded by a fog of chanting, droning voices, tinkling bells and triumphant, blaring Tibetan rams' horns. Parting the curtains a knuckle's width, he saw a river of orange-clad devotees of the Lord Buddha spreading out at the foot of Monkey Hat Hill.

He recollected Pink Rose's tale of Cloud Abode Monastery being handed from Daoist to Buddhist. Though his understanding of such matters was limited to buying amulets or spells, he comprehended the danger Yun Shu faced. This encouraged him. There would be no disobedience or backsliding from the ungrateful girl this time!

It was twenty years since Golden Lotus lived on Monkey Hat Hill with the youthful Gui. That broad-hipped creature, Gui's wife, so adept at bearing children, had been dead by then. Golden Lotus had revelled in his triumph. And well he might. When no one was listening, Yun Shu's mother often threatened to send him back to the Yellow Eel House for lotus-footed boys where Gui had discovered and bought him for the full asking price, enamoured by his feet and pretty, smiling face! Bought him as one might an exquisite hen partridge calling and cooing for a mate!

With a shock of clarity, Golden Lotus understood why he had offered to bind Yun Shu's feet all those years ago, though really the girl was too old for such an ordeal. He had wanted to punish Gui's dead wife for her taunts!

In a flurried motion, Golden Lotus pulled aside the curtain of the palanquin. He let out a screeched command and the palanquin halted. In the silence that followed he could hear the porters panting. It was late afternoon. The autumn light showed signs of thinning and a breeze set the trees of Monkey Hat Hill sighing. Golden Lotus looked round fearfully, as though the restless pines were warning him. After all, to restore

Yun Shu would revive her mother, so long neglected and for-gotten. For Gui needed the one thing Golden Lotus could never provide, the gift of heirs. A gift Yun Shu's mother would offer again through her daughter. It would mean Gui's hated First Wife had triumphed in the end.

Tears filled his eyes. How foolish he had been! How sentimental! He saw that Gui's growing weakness, rather than being something to cure, was in fact his best hope. How else could he continue to please the Salt Minister now that his beauty had decayed into grey hairs dyed black, acrid aromas doused with musk, wrinkles concealed beneath ever-thicker make-up.

Golden Lotus rapped on the roof. 'Turn round!' he commanded in his shrillest voice. 'Go back! Back to the Palace!'

For a moment the exhausted porters hesitated. Then they swung the palanquins round and headed straight back into the mob of exultant Buddhists claiming their prize of Cloud Abode Monastery.

天命

In the hour before dusk, the Nuns of Serene Perfection and their servants gathered outside the Temple of Celestial Teachers. The mournful tolling of the monastery gong summoned them. Today it spoke of grief. For over four centuries it had summoned generations of Serene Ones to rites beneficial to the city they served.

To many of those waiting in the courtyard, the familiar, low echo triggered hopeless tears. Two women, however, stood impassively on the steps leading up to Chenghuang's sanctuary in the Temple. They wore their finest robes decorated with symbols of magical power. Their carefully arranged 'whirlwind clouds' hair rose proudly, decorated with modest bone hair-pieces shaped like the primordial egg of *yin* and *yang*.

They were, of course, Abbess Yun Shu and her deputy, Lady Lu Si. Despite her relative youth, the Abbess seemed to have aged over the last year and acquired a stern dignity that would have surprised many who had known her younger incarnations.

She did not show the least expression as Void led a group of porters and soldiers out of the monastery, bearing everything of value that hadn't already been transferred to Golden Bright Temple. With them went a handful of Nuns, seeking to implore Worthy Master Jian for a renewed certificate of ordination. At their head walked Three Simplicities.

Those women who could not bend as nimbly to the times, trapped by loyalty to old ideals and modes, those who could not discard all they held dear to fit an unknown future demanded by strangers, were left to the gathering darkness. Yun Shu turned to Lady Lu Si.

'Let us bid farewell to Chenghuang together,' she said, 'on behalf of the Nuns of Serene Perfection. But let us do it joyfully, lest He think we are not glad to have served Him so long.'

Lady Lu Si bowed. 'With joy,' she muttered. 'I have meditated upon the matter and no longer believe He is angry with us.'

'How glad I am,' said Yun Shu, weeping silently. 'Let us say farewell with pride and gratitude.'

So the two Serene Ones offered a final supplication to Chenghuang, ensuring the candles were renewed and burning bright when His new protectors entered the Temple of Celestial Masters. A place they would no doubt rename and improve according to their own notions, until someone else came along to replace them in their turn. They were all, Yun Shu told herself, merely inhalations and breathings out of eternity.

Yun Shu left the Temple and took up her rightful position at the head of the Nuns and their servants, the most notable being Bo-Bai, with their handcarts and bags of clothes, cooking pots and sacks of winter grain.

Following Three Simplicities' example, Yun Shu did not look back as she stepped through the bronze doors of Cloud Abode Monastery for the last time and approached the Hundred Stairs. She found them lined with Buddhist monks chanting sutras. Many bore torches that countered the fading light. Though they might have been expected to crow and jeer, all watched in silence as the proud, handsome woman led her people down the steps through the bamboo woods, down Monkey Hat Hill and toward the City of Ghosts.

Another dark day had passed in Hou-ming if the ribbons of smoke were anything to go by. When she looked out across the lake, distant fires and stray flashes glowed.

'That is the battle,' murmured Bo-Bai. 'It still seems to be going on.'

Yun Shu felt a deep revulsion and cried out defiantly: 'The Dao that is bright seems dull! The great square has no corners! The Dao conceals itself in namelessness! The Dao breeds one; breeds two; breeds three; three breeds the Ten Thousand Creatures!'

Chanting and singing, the Nuns of Serene Perfection left the Hundred Stairs and halted at the entrance to the smoke-blackened remains of Deng Mansions.

'Those who wish to stay with me shall rest here,' said Yun Shu. 'In the morning light everything will be clearer to us.'

Only a few of the servants and Nuns with family in the city departed. The rest, twenty-five strong, entered the broken gate-house of Deng Mansions.

thirty-five

天命

9th Day, 9th Month, 1322

The Ninth Day of the Ninth Month ended in mourning and defeat for the Nuns of Serene Perfection. It began with a nightmare for Hsiung.

He was back in the Buddha's Caves, naked except for a sword. Behind him the looming image of the Buddha smiled down, at peace with the Infinite Breezes. But in Hsiung's bitter heart there could be no peace, no release. As the first of his enemies entered the cave – a giant bearing Hornets' Nest's grinning head on bull-like shoulders – Hsiung almost threw away his sword rather than sully the Holy Buddha's sanctuary with fresh blood, always more blood. The dream shifted and he was pounding the skull of a wild dog with a bamboo staff, its jaws fastened onto his leg. However hard he ground the bamboo into the bubbling gruel of its brain the creature would not die, would not release its hold . . .

'Sire! Sire! It is dawn!'

Hsiung leapt to his feet, expecting to find a bamboo sword in his hand. There was only air.

'Your Highness!'

It was his faithful ship's captain, bowing fearfully. Hsiung followed the older man's pointing finger across the placid waters of the lake.

'What is this?' demanded the Noble Count. 'I have ordered no dawn attack.'

Admiral Won-do was sailing swiftly away from the rectangle of anchored rebel ships, heading for the lines of enemy vessels in the distance. With him went twenty Yueh Fei warships, some of the best equipped in the fleet. The captain hovered beside him.

'Speak up, man! Do not be afraid!'

'The Admiral, Your Highness, is not attacking. He is joining the Mongols!'

For a while Hsiung's face did not twitch. Nor did his eye move from the treacherous Admiral's yellow-painted paddlewheel destroyer. In that interval he comprehended why his campaign lacked any trace of surprise; why hundreds of the Great Khan's ships had gathered to confront the Newly Adhered Navy. His empty stomach sickened at the thought of the forces poor, honest P'ao must confront before he could lead the land army to Hou-ming.

'So much the worse for Won-du when we meet again,' he said, quietly. 'Summon my officers. We will confer!'

It was a glum assembly. By now everyone in the fleet knew of the Admiral's defection. Many concluded their cause was lost. Hsiung surveyed them proudly, his helmet resting on a broad arm.

'Officers,' he began, 'we have been in worse situations than this. Think of Fourth Hell Mouth! The traps they laid for us in the Salt Pans! I tell you, Heaven favours our cause . . .'

He proclaimed his faith until one of the long-standing rebel commanders stirred uneasily. 'Your Highness! Shall we attack or simply wait here?'

Hsiung nodded. 'That is the decision I must make. Yet we cannot sail back to Chenglingji, however tempting that seems. Even now General P'ao may be approaching the city. We must stay near Hou-ming until we know his dispositions and whether he requires our assistance.'

The commander, an old carousing companion of General P'ao's, nodded.

'That does not mean,' continued Hsiung, 'we must be like stones worn away by water! Send out our fastest ships to skirmish. Instruct all crews to prepare for a fight!'

It was the best he could do. Many of the officers muttered among themselves and Hsiung decided to execute the first who showed the slightest sign of wavering or following Won-du's example.

He turned to survey the ranks of enemy ships manoeuvring into five distinct squadrons, a force at least twice as numerous as the Yueh Fei fleet. The rebels' one advantage lay in their floating castles, armed with dozens of large catapults and giant crossbows. With these they could rain thunderclap bombs and dragon tongues of flaming naphtha on any warship foolish enough to draw near.

Hsiung stared at distant Hou-ming, a dark jumble of silhouettes in the dawn light. When would P'ao arrive? News from P'ao could change everything.

天命

By nature, General P'ao was not a reckless man. When gambling at *mah-jong* or cards he always contrived to secure favourable odds, often through sleights of hand. Likewise in war, though capable of bold strokes that surprised even himself, he preferred to progress by degrees. The proverb, *he who takes big paces leaves big spaces*, was one he often deployed against junior officers with too grand an opinion of themselves. So it was no coincidence he avoided the trap prepared for his army.

They were south of Hou-ming, traversing an area of low, wooded hills, when scouts reported large formations of infantry hidden amidst the trees. Although the most direct route lay through the woods General P'ao saw no reason for haste. Let Hsiung cruise round the lake a day longer if need be! After all, autumn was a pleasant season and the weather mild. Few hostile vessels opposed them. Accordingly, he sent a decoy force forward and out-flanked the would-be ambushers so effectively that he surprised their rear, gathering hundreds of heads and scattering the main force like panicking geese.

That had been on the 8th Day. Now, as dawn rose on the 9th Day of the 9th Month – the same dawn that commenced with Admiral Won-du's defection – General P'ao surveyed the distant Southern Suburbs of Hou-ming with undisguised satisfaction.

It had been remarkably easy to fulfil his half of the rebel plan. Perhaps Hsiung's confidence was justified. Now P'ao's task was to lead an assault on the ramparts and distract whatever troops Prince Arslan still possessed. All reports suggested they didn't amount to much, the best of the Prince's warriors having perished in the Salt Pans. After that, Hsiung would sieze the harbour and that very evening they'd dine in Arslan's own banqueting hall! P'ao also intended to claim ownership of a certain floating oriole house he had frequented when billeted in Hou-ming; and, of course, its delightful occupants. He turned to his regimental commanders, lined up behind him.

'Well,' he said, affably, 'our scouts have returned. Nothing lies between us and Hou-ming. They also report a small uprising of fishermen against the Mongols in the Southern Suburbs. All of which bodes well.'

The officers nodded approvingly.

'We must persuade as many of the enemy as possible to attack us,' continued General P'ao. 'For that reason we shall tempt them with false prizes.'

An old strategy favoured by the ancient commentators. The commanders accordingly returned to their regiments, the drummers beat a thousand times, and three hours later the Yueh Fei army drew close to the Southern Suburbs.

*   *   *

By the time they arrived, 'the small uprising' mentioned by P'ao to his officers lay all across the muddy lanes and smouldering hovels of the fisher-folk's villages. Bodies were everywhere, all bearing signs of savage blows, and not just men of fighting age – women lay in dishevelled piles, their clothes torn. Flies buzzed round the corpses. Amongst them were many children, cut down as they clung to their mothers.

'It seems the rebellion here didn't last long,' remarked P'ao. He glowered at the city ramparts and Southern Gate a few *li* distant. Tantalisingly, the gates stood open, but he was not so foolish to forget they could close in an instant.

'Commander,' he said, turning to the leader of the Yueh Fei Guards, 'find out who massacred these people.'

The answer came from a pile of corpses that moved suddenly.

'Beware!' cried the Guards Commander, drawing his sword.

A face daubed with blood popped out between a limp arm and leg. The face grew a chest then rose. It belonged to a young man clutching a notched axe.

'Your worship!' cried the young man, rolling his covering of bodies aside. 'I heard you talking. I can tell you what happened here.'

'Let him speak,' ordered P'ao, before adding. 'Oh, and take his axe away, just in case.'

But the fisherman was in no way hostile; he had every reason to welcome the Yueh Fei army.

'We heard you were coming and rose after dawn, killing the officials, curse them! Then they sent a few companies of soldiers and we worsted them as well!'

'So how did this happen?' asked P'ao, glancing at the piles of corpses.

He listened while the fisherman told his tale, all the while casting uneasy glances at the city ramparts.

'Many thousands hiding in there, eh?' said P'ao, when the

fisherman was done. 'Led by Prince Khoja himself. And more in the hills west of the city? Are you certain?'

The scattered bodies lent credibility to the man's tale.

'Well, well,' said P'ao, going over to one of the few fallen government troops and rolling him over with his boot. The soldier wore armour. Dragging off his helmet, P'ao discovered the typical shaved head of an Imperial Guardsman. Since when had such elite troops fought for petty rulers like Prince Arslan? P'ao licked his lips, not liking the taste. Advancing up to the city walls was pointless if such men defended them; worse, should the enemy appear behind them, it would be easy to get trapped.

'Send scouts to circle the city,' he said, addressing his officers. 'In the meantime, order the regiments to draw up ready to repulse an attack from any direction.'

'What of the wounded, sir?' asked the Guards Commander.

P'ao looked at the bodies around them; a few showed signs of life.

'We can do nothing for them until the ground is safe. Into position!'

He was interrupted by braying trumpets from the ramparts and the echoing boom of huge Mongol naccara signal drums. Drums that only sounded to issue commands. But that was not possible, Prince Arslan was trying to frighten the Yueh Fei rebels with the prospect of facing the Great Khan's wild horsemen, warriors that had conquered half the world.

P'ao's foresight in ordering a defensive posture was rewarded by the immediate confirmation of his worst fears. A full *minghan* of Mongol cavalry, a thousand strong, galloped round the corner of the city ramparts and rode to take up position blocking the rebels' retreat. Still the naccara pounded and P'ao faced the ramparts. The gates had opened to pour forth heavily armoured foot soldiers. When he turned to face the eastern corner of the walls behind which the cavalry had appeared, he saw jogging lines of halberdiers and archers. One of the battalions bore the standards of the Imperial Guards.

'You fool!' he muttered under his breath. 'You fool!'

Whether he referred to himself or Hsiung no one lived to tell. But when, hours later, General P'ao took his last stand with a final ring of Yueh Fei loyalists, determined to perish sooner than surrender, he remembered the fearless little boy who had killed the red dog with nothing more than a bamboo sword and remembered his own pride and amazement at becoming first a captain then a general, even for just a few splendid years. No longer put upon, no longer bullied Sergeant P'ao in the ignoble service of the dubious Salt Minister Gui. That was his comfort as the last of his men were cut down. Oh, he had lived well enough! He even left sons behind bearing his family's name into the future. Perhaps that was why, in gratitude or wonder, General P'ao bellowed out the name of the brave little boy until a mace crushed his forehead and stopped his tongue. *Hsiung! Hsiung!*

天命

By mid-afternoon Hsiung abandoned all hope of capturing Hou-ming. The one prize he desired was safety for his fleet, the many thousands trapped in floating wooden walls, men who had trusted his judgement and mandate to rule. He would lay down his life sooner than betray that trust.

Hsiung paced the deck, aware that the surviving ships of the rebel fleet were being driven steadily into a packed circle like a shoal of fish harried by river dolphins. Nearly a third of the Newly Adhered Fleet had been destroyed. Every direction he looked revealed floating spars and planks, clouds of smoke from burning ships set alight by jets of naphtha or thunderclap bombs hurled from catapults. Never mind that many more of the government vessels had perished the same way. For every ship the rebels crippled or sank, two more lined up to take its place, some led by Admiral Won-du and his squadron of turncoats. It was these Hsiung hungered to encounter. He did see Won-du's yellow paddlewheel destroyer earlier in the battle and almost gave chase before recollecting he could not leave the fleet uncommanded for the sake of revenge.

How many hours until darkness? His seasoned old captain estimated five. Night's cover was their only chance. With darkness they would attempt a desperate drive through the squadrons surrounding them, ramming aside any who got in their way. Then Hsiung would order the Newly Adhered Fleet to become its opposite – no longer adhered but fragmented into a scattering of fleeing boats. Those lucky enough, at best a few dozen, might make it back to Chenglingli. Fortune was their only guarantor of survival. Yet five hours was a long time to defy a superior enemy and already he could see the morale of his men flagging. He needed to give them fresh heart, convince them survival was possible if they remained brave. At last it came.

A flotilla of ten paddlewheel destroyers and sail-driven junks – for the wind was freshening as evening approached – had been sent forward in a probing sortie against a corner of the massed rebel fleet. At once thunderclap bombs curled through the smoke-filled air. Drums beat on all sides. Hsiung rushed to the rail of his prow. The flotilla was led by the treacherous Admiral Won-du and consisted of ex-rebel ships. Instantly, Hsiung saw how he could restore morale.

'Captain!' he ordered. 'Attack that yellow ship!'

For a moment the captain hesitated. Though Hsiung's battleship was a formidable vessel, it would be outnumbered as soon as they left the safety of the rebel lines.

'Do it now!' roared Hsiung.

'Damn them! Why not!' roared back the Captain. 'Order the attack, drummer! Attack!'

Hsiung's ship surged from the rebel ranks, paddlewheels cranking furiously, stirring a wake of foam. Other rebel destroyers followed. The manoeuvre evidently surprised

Won-du, who had been sailing parallel to the Yueh Fei fleet as a way of impressing his new masters, firing every kind of missile he possessed but avoiding close contact. Now, though he tried to head for open water, there was no time. Hsiung's vessel was alongside him and a boarding party massing. A long wooden arm with a huge iron spike crashed down like a hammer, puncturing Won-du's deck and binding him tight to Hsiung's vessel. Hundreds of arrows and crossbow bolts poured into Won-du's ship from close range, as well as dozens of fire-lances.

'Yueh Fei!' roared the Noble Count, sword in hand. 'Maitreya!' With that, he charged over a plank bridge lowered between the vessels and landed in a mass of struggling men. His one aim was to find Won-du. Ying-ge's subtle taunts concerning her cousin's superior swordsmanship set him aflame. No one must intervene . . . he swept aside a sailor with a fierce blow, then another . . . it would be like his triumph over Hornets' Nest long ago, only incalculably sweeter.

Yet when Hsiung reached the bridge of the destroyer where Won-du might be expected to skulk, he found a pile of corpses. Suddenly flags cracked. The wind was picking up force as air currents flowed inland. Hsiung poked angrily among the bodies. Had someone got Won-du first? He glanced over the side and saw a swift rowing boat propelled by four oarsmen speeding away towards the government fleet. In the prow, waving courteously, sat Admiral Won-du, evidently contemplating a long and prosperous future. Hsiung's throat and chest tightened: he kicked the nearest corpse.

'Damn his soul!' he roared.

But men other than Admiral Won-du were damned that late afternoon. For as Hsiung looked to the south his eyes widened.

'Back!' he bellowed. 'Back! We must return to the fleet.'

He could see government squadrons widening the distance between themselves and the Yueh Fei rebels as over twenty fireships were heading swiftly towards the dense concentration of the Red Turban fleet, manned by shadowy figures barely visible through the heat haze: expendable crews whose families were guaranteed a whole year's rice if they perished – as was most probable.

'Order our ships to disperse!' he cried to his signallers. Flags fluttered, drums beat, but there was chaos on his battleship as they struggled to lift the spiked wooden boarding arm. Men rushed back and forth. 'Order them to send out small boats to pole away the fireships!' commanded Hsiung.

Methods approved by the ancient commentators and certainly effective if the rebel fleet had been capable of concerted action. Yet only those ships facing south had the slightest idea of the approaching threat. Hsiung watched helplessly as the first fireship rushed into a huge floating castle designed to attack the ramparts of Hou-ming. At once the suicide crews leapt into the water and began to swim away, clutching inflated leather bladders. A huge explosion followed as the fireship became an inferno of naphtha, straw and oil. Sure enough the rebel ship caught fire. Screams and cries of alarm filled the air, along with scents of burning oil and wood. Clouds of smoke billowed up, blinding the Red Turban vessels on either side. Elsewhere other ships were ablaze.

'The fleet must scatter *now*!' ordered Hsiung, aware no one was listening. 'Order the flags!'

To no avail. A better trained navy might have avoided the hell that followed. Flames danced and skipped from ship to ship, many chained together in obedience to Hsiung's orders to form floating defences. Burning men leaped into the water for relief. Thunderclap bombs exploded like roaring giants. A swirling haze of heat and smoke engulfed the rebel fleet.

'We're free now!' said the Captain, tugging Hsiung's arm as he stared at the growing inferno. Although they were over two *li* away he could feel the heat of the fires on the wind. 'We've got free of Admiral Won-du's ship,' repeated the Captain. 'There is still a chance to escape, Your Highness!'

Hsiung realised they had drifted apart from Won-du's stricken boat. He reached for his sword then let his arm fall.

'Noble Count! Let us try to escape in the smoke!'

Hsiung glared at the Captain. Would that not be an admission of defeat? He was never defeated, too lucky, too favoured by Heaven. For a long while he watched the horrors of burning men and listened to their death cries, their beseeching screams drowned out by roaring flames, powerless to offer assistance. Reluctantly, he turned to the Captain and nodded. Too late. Hsiung had hesitated too long. Even as they rushed towards a gap in the enemy squadrons it closed and they were forced to flee back towards Hou-ming through the smoke clouds and shrieks.

A dozen enemy vessels pursued him, hurling iron-cased bombs from catapults. Hsiung's ship was driven onto the gravel beach of a small island near Hou-ming itself. The battleship began to blaze. Half the crew, including the captain, had already perished, but Hsiung led the other half ashore and ordered those who wished to surrender to get out of his way. Anyone else was welcome to die by his side.

天命

The small island was Eye Rock, the same holy place Yun Shu and Worthy Master Jian had sacrificed to Goddess Tien-hou, Protectress of Waterfarers. It was a misshapen lump of granite when not festooned with banners and candles during the Goddess's winter festival. Hsiung sheathed his sword and snatched up a halberd with a long, wickedly curved blade, a bone-strengthened bamboo bow and a quiver of arrows. He crunched across the gravel beach, remorseless as a toppling boulder in his lamellar armour. The ship burned behind him. A dozen faithful men of his bodyguard armed themselves in imitation of the Noble Count, while he climbed stone steps cut into the rock to a flat altar stone.

Deng Nan-shi had once told him human beings were sacrificed long ago on this altar to prevent storms on the lake. Perhaps his death would do the fishermen good.

Several *li* to the north lay Hou-ming harbour, its ramparts secure. Just as familiar rose the cliffs of Monkey Hat Hill. He noticed lights where Deng Mansions had once stood, in gardens he had explored until they mapped his boyish soul. A dozen of the victorious fleet's ships were circling Eye Rock, each carrying enough marines to overwhelm his feeble retinue. The only question, he thought, was how many he dragged to Hell with him.

He glanced at the soldiers of his bodyguard, gathering to form a shield round the Noble Count of Lingling, bows and fire-lances ready, as well as bags of porcelain-cased naphtha grenades, as if courage, somehow, might yet bring victory.

'Listen,' said Hsiung, 'and closely. You do not have to die with me. Join those on the beach below who wish to surrender. I will not think less of you. Life is a precious thing.'

As he said it, Hsiung recollected the joy and comfort he had felt when entwined in Ying-ge's warm limbs, the scent of her soft skin and reflection of her eyes in candlelight. How like a dream those joys seemed. For all he knew she had betrayed him like her cowardly cousin, Won-du. Yet it did not seem important, a child's quarrel or a squabble of sparrows in the eaves. All that mattered now was leaving without shame and disgrace. Perhaps his bodyguard shared the same fear for none threw down their weapons.

Darkness was gathering over the Middle Kingdom. The burning battleship cast an eerie light.

'They are coming, Your Highness!' cried one of the soldiers.

So they were. At least fifty heavily-armoured men in small boats. Hsiung responded by seizing his bow and loosing an arrow. Then forty-nine were coming.

Half an hour later the last of the landing party fell to a blow from the Noble Count's sword. Dozens lay wounded on the beach and stone steps. Dozens more would never stir again, including his bodyguard. It amazed him that the Mongols had not loosed a rain of arrows or even a few thunderclap bombs and settled the matter in moments. Evidently they wished to take him alive. All his own arrows were gone, his halberd broken. Gashes lay across his chest and outer thigh. He struggled to remain upright, waiting for the last assault. At first he considered suicide, after all, it was an honourable end. But the sight of the young men who had sacrificed themselves so he could die fighting stayed his hand.

It was night now. In the distance Hsiung could still see what remained of the rebel fleet burning. No, he did not wish to live longer than it took for those flames to die down.

More rowing boats of soldiers landed on the shingle beach. Wearily, Hsiung gripped the hilt of his long sword and took up position on top of the stone altar so his blows would have the advantage of height. Unexpectedly his mind filled with another fight, long ago. A barking, angry red dog worrying at his wounded thigh while he pounded its skull and slavering jaws. Hsiung's heart filled with a peculiar intensity. He had become a *xia*, after all, Yun Shu's brave *xia*, while Teng was his Noble Chancellor, a model of wisdom and integrity! Pine, bamboo and plum! So it seemed no defeat at all to wait on the altar stone and cut the first man down like a wild, red dog, though scores more followed.

thirty-six

天命

9th Day, 9th Month, 1322

Twilight had long passed when Hsiung was dragged down from the altar on Eye Rock by a dozen grasping, frantic hands. Across the lake, up on the cliffs of Monkey Hat Hill, peace filled the overgrown lanes and houses. Or, at least, a quiet punctuated by owls and the cries of nocturnal creatures. Among them were the refugees from Cloud Abode Monastery, sheltering in the old gardens of Deng Mansions.

Yun Shu had tried to make the best of her people's situation. At least the night was mild, warm enough to ignore if swaddled in a blanket. Nevertheless, she ordered the servants to build fires and prepare rice, though their stock could only last a week or so. After that? She dared not think so far.

Nearby, revealed by the flickering light of the cooking fires, stood the earth mound raised in imitation of Holy Mount Chang. All that remained of the Deng clan's many-roomed mansion, apart from rectangles of ash already obscured by ferns and swift-growing bamboo. Yun Shu could not help remembering her triumph on the real Mount Chang. A half-forgotten dream.

Bo-Bai ordered the old scholar's stretcher to be laid beside the stairs winding round the miniature mountain. As he looked up at the wooden pavilion, Deng Nan-shi began to sob. Harsh, wrenching grunts that tore at Yun Shu's heart. She took the old man's hand. He regained control and stuttered an apology for inconveniencing her.

'You cannot know how this pavilion saved my life,' he said, 'and that of my dear wife. But really, we were saved by a brave infantry officer who sired a brave son. That is how it is with us Dengs. Heaven always sends someone to save us.'

He relapsed into one of the coughing fits that frequently convulsed his lungs until he whooped for desperate breath.

'Carry me there,' he whispered, when the cough became a rattle.

'Honoured Sir,' began Yun Shu, meaning to dissuade him. She glanced up to find a man beside her, wearing a traveller's rough clothes and strong leather boots. At his side hung a sword. From his belt, a leather bag of writing equipment.

'I shall do as my father requests,' said Teng. 'If you could arrange blankets for a comfortable bed I would be grateful. No more is needed.'

Deng Nan-shi's chuckle of satisfaction at his son's sudden appearance became another whooping fit. Teng knelt beside the old man, watching gravely.

'Are you ready now, Honoured Father?' he asked.

'Yes . . . Good boy . . . Help me there.'

Despite the concern of all around him, the venerable scholar struggled upright, aided by Teng. Together they climbed the short way to the top of the model mountain. Bo-Bai lit the way with a flickering lamp, Yun Shu following with a large armful of blankets. Lady Lu Si came next with a bowl of warm rice and another of coarse wine. While Teng propped his father upright, pillowing his back with a bag of old clothes, Bo-Bai made up a bed of blankets.

'No,' gasped Deng Nan-shi, waving away the food and drink, 'give it to someone more needy.'

'You are needy,' said Lady Lu Si, earnestly.

511

'Ah,' sighed Deng Nan-shi, 'I need nothing now that I know my son is alive. Except, perhaps . . .' He shot a glance at Yun Shu. But whatever he wanted from her was lost in more coughing and Teng asked to be left alone with his father.

Yun Shu busied herself below, going between huddled groups of nuns and servants, ensuring all were fed. Occasionally she glanced up at the mildew-eaten pavilion on its Holy Mountain. Teng remained in earnest conversation with his father, alternatively remonstrating and dabbing his eyes. She also noticed that two men with swords had taken up position at the foot of the stairs.

Out on the lake there was a pink and orange glow. In between lay Eye Rock, also lit by flames, though she could see no more than the tiny dots of men and the dark silhouettes of ships. Eye Rock, forever associated in her mind with her triumph as Spirit Bride in the Ceremony of the Goddess Tien-Hou, brought on a desolate confusion.

Was Worthy Master Jian already an Immortal, impervious to guilt? Yet he had betrayed so many people's trust! At least, Yun Shu told herself, she was wiser for it. Never again would she judge a man by his words alone, but by the balance of his actions over long years. There lay the true test of worthiness.

Now she, too, must face a test: whether she could save from ruin those who trusted her leadership.

It seemed the battle on the lake might be over. If so, she had no idea who was victor. Perhaps no one, in which case the madness would resume with the dawn. She was joined by Lady Lu Si; like Yun Shu, misfortune seemed to have fortified the senior nun's determination.

'Abbess,' said Lady Lu Si, bowing gravely, 'may I speak frankly?'

'You use a title I no longer possess,' said Yun Shu.

For a moment neither spoke, staring out at the flames on the lake.

Lady Lu Si frowned. 'I have received no word from the

Provincial Daoist Council that my licence is revoked. Neither have you. Therefore, we remain what we were.'

'For now,' conceded Yun Shu.

'One can live nowhere else,' remarked Lady Lu Si. 'Much suffering has taught me that.'

'You are wise.'

'So are you. You are also stronger than me and must take the remaining Nuns of Serene Perfection to a safe place, away from Worthy Master Jian's schemes. Mind you, now he has his divine knucklebone – if it is truly what the Tibetans claim and not stolen from a dead goat – he will be too busy with his elixirs and concoctions to seek us out. Leading us is your duty, owed to Xi-wang-nu, Queen Mother of the West.'

Yun Shu nodded. 'Perhaps . . . I sense Chenghuang's will behind your words. But where should we go? Where *can* we go?'

'That is for you to discover as our Abbess,' said Lady Lu Si.

With that, she went over to ancient Earth Peace, who had convinced herself they were on a holy pilgrimage to the Blessed Isles. 'Seventy years I spent in Cloud Abode Monastery!' she croaked to Lady Lu Si. 'Miserable old hole! You young people will be far happier in the Blessed Isles. And so shall I.'

Yun Shu listened to this exchange carefully. Were Earth Peace's words divinely inspired? Perhaps Lady Lu Si was right. Perhaps she would lead the Nuns of Serene Perfection to a new home.

She watched Teng descend the steps of the mound and confer with the armed men. Both saluted him with much reverence, fists pressed together and heads lowered. She wondered if they mistook him for someone else.

Yet there was a commanding air about Teng, a new confidence. Perhaps he, like Lady Lu Si, had learned one can live nowhere but the present. Seeing her, he came over.

'You will have to excuse their devotion,' said Teng, quietly. 'Ts'u and Ts'an are pledged to preserve the last surviving descendents of Yueh Fei with their last breath.'

513

'Given the scrapes you get into that must be a comfort,' she said. 'How are your wounds? Have they re-opened?'

He touched the bandage on his scalp. Checked for fresh blood. The wound from Hua's sword seemed to be binding.

'No,' he said, 'and the cut on my arm is well-bandaged.'

'Is it true,' she asked, unable to disguise astonishment, 'you killed your enemy? That horrible Hua who spied for Hornets' Nest at Mirror Lake? Shensi told me but I thought he was joking.'

'You are sceptical, Yun Shu. I don't blame you. After all, we Dengs usually let others settle our disputes. I just hope Hsiung's sword arm has preserved his life as well.'

They glanced out at the glow on the lake.

'Let us hope he escaped,' said Yun Shu.

He watched her face in the moonlight. 'You are very afraid, aren't you?' he said. 'And not just for Hsiung.'

'Oh, Teng!' she exclaimed. 'Of course I am! Where are we to go tomorrow? All these people . . .' She waved at the huddles around them, sleeping or warming their hands before camp-fires. 'Where are they to go?'

Teng nodded. 'Please indulge me, Yun Shu. Are those your bags?'

'Yes,' she said, frowning down at her leather shoulder bag and roll of clothes. 'Why do you . . .'

'Do you still have the scroll I gave you?'

'Of course, it is . . .'

'Show it to me.'

There was something in his manner, an inner certainty absent in all the years she had known him, that inclined her to do as he asked.

'Very well,' she said, rummaging in the bag. 'Here it is. But I can assure you it won't fill a single bowl.'

The scroll in the gilded ox bone case was duly handed over. He promptly unrolled it.

'Bo-Bai!' he called. 'Fetch a lamp, there's a good fellow.'

Wearily the old eunuch rose and did as he was commanded.

'Hold it up so we may all read it, including yourself. See how it was written by my noble ancestor, Yueh Fei, granting a sizable estate called Wei Valley to the Yun clan *in perpetuity* – mark that! – and it says this fiefdom cannot be reclaimed by his future descendents – meaning Father and myself – without the consent of the Yun clan. Well, perhaps that is where we should go. To Wei Valley. And a property there called Three-Step-House.'

Bo-Bai glanced at his young mistress. 'Abbess, that is all very well. What if, as only seems likely, someone else already owns this Three-Step-House? They'll hardly like a band of nuns turning up and demanding their home. Even if you do possess a scroll written by the illustrious Yueh Fei.'

Teng's expression stiffened slightly, yet his smile retained every sign of satisfaction. 'Exactly, Bo-Bai! But might not such owners, or perhaps the owners of another suitable estate, be tempted into selling?'

Yun Shu decided her decorum in allowing the males to speak had gone far enough. Besides, Bo-Bai was hardly male at all. 'Teng,' she said, 'you mean well, and we are grateful. But really, unworldly as I am, even I know that to *buy* entails *payment*.'

Deng Teng's indomitable smile grew strained. 'Will this do?' he asked, peevishly. Whereupon he showed Bo-Bai and Yun Shu the contents of a large leather sack. Their staring eyes and indrawn breaths provided his answer.

'Oh, I'm sure we'll end up somewhere or other,' he said, jauntily. 'As long as we escape Hou-ming, that is.'

天命

There lay the problem, escaping Hou-ming, a dilemma that leather bags stuffed with gold and jewels and silver could not resolve until one worked out who to bribe. Discovering such vital information in a city swarming with soldiers was perilous in itself.

Yun Shu wandered to the cliff edge defining the eastern limits of the garden, looking for the first signs of dawn. If only she could escape her burdens! Fly all the way up to the Jade Emperor's Cloud Terrace.

As she stared out, Yun Shu hugged her chest. How small her own chance of flying to the Heavenly Places had become! Her *ch'i* energy, sowed by devotion and reaped by ritual, had been stolen and squandered by a perfidious teacher. Somehow she could not grieve too deeply. Witnessing the contortions Jian had endured to gain Immortality diminished her desire for it. Instead she conceived of humbler callings. There were many ways of serving the Dao. Why shouldn't she strive to be happy?

'Do not stand so close to the edge,' advised a low, familiar voice, 'I'd hate to see you step the wrong way.'

Yun Shu glanced at Teng. He bowed slightly before standing beside her. As ever, the perfect gentleman. But once she had thought that of Worthy Master Jian. For a while they stood awkwardly. He seemed, for a change, to have nothing to say. Yun Shu rarely felt uncomfortable around silence; it was the noisiest of places if one listened carefully. Yet this time she wanted him to speak.

'Yun Shu,' he said, 'I wish to tell you what happened to me in the Salt Pans.'

He did, and at length, not sparing the details. Every so often she winced in sympathy. Finally he described how Salt Minister Gui had sent him, crushed by a block of salt, on a hellish march to his death.

'I wish you to know so you can decide whether to hate me,' he said, 'for I am your father's enemy. I would not blame you for hating me. It would be filial of you to do so.'

Yun Shu smiled bitterly. 'I have been accused of dreadful disloyalty before now,' she said, 'and every kind of unfilial conduct. No, I shall make up my own mind when it comes to hating people. My Honoured Father is a model I choose not to follow. No doubt you find that shocking and reprehensible.'

He smiled sadly. 'Perhaps it is. What of it? I've learned people are not paper characters in a morality play of my composition. I have learned that about myself, Yun Shu. Above all, I have learned to want happiness *before* not *after* I die.'

Yun Shu was startled. He had guessed her earlier thoughts. Yet on reflection it did not seem strange. Of all people on earth he understood her best.

'I sometimes wonder if my happiness is served by being Abbess,' she said. 'As I approach my thirtieth year I think – you will smile at this – not of position or titles, but a family. Children and grandchildren.'

'That is natural, you are a woman. I'm glad you think of children.'

She watched him from the corner of her eyes. 'Are you glad I'm a woman?'

'Yes, I am glad.'

Her eyes filled with tears. 'Oh, Teng, I must tell you. I fear the Worthy Master's elixirs have hurt my womb! Hurt it forever! What if I cannot bear children? Yet I meant to save Cloud Abode Monastery by obeying him. And look at me now!' She gestured at herself. 'Everything I won for myself has been poisoned, even the future. I tell you this so there is no deceit between us. No misunderstandings.' She looked into his eyes. 'Are you still glad I am a woman? Answer me honestly!'

He met her frank gaze. Did not look away. 'Oh, I am glad,' he said, 'and I shall tell you why.'

Teng described his final thoughts as he lay staring up at the sky like a beetle on its back, pinned down by the block of salt. 'Do you know who I thought of at that last moment?' he asked. 'The moment I expected to die?'

Yun Shu's heart quickened.

'Your father, of course,' she said. 'As a good, loyal son should.'

'No, not him.'

'Then your mother?'

'No, another lady entirely. I thought of you, Yun Shu! And of something wickedly indecorous. In fact . . .' He coughed, struggled on. 'Of kissing your face, your lips.'

Silence on the cliff edge. It was hard to say who was more surprised.

'Evidently the thought of it revolts you,' he said, hurriedly, 'forgive me.'

Her eyelids fluttered involuntarily as she examined the distant fires on the lake. She turned to him. 'Teng, do you really believe I am Lady Serenity, as you once called me? Lady Purity? I am neither. You see, Worthy Master Jian . . .'

He gestured for her to go no further. 'Forgive my rudeness,' he said, 'I don't wish to hear his name ever again. And as for the elixirs damaging your womb, it seems an outlandish notion.'

'How can you be sure?'

He gestured expansively. 'Because I don't want it to be true! That is enough for me.'

Her sideways glance returned, bolder now.

'Yun Shu,' he said, 'I have one more thing to say to you. I wonder if you will recognise it.' Then he recited a poem, one she had learned from the book of her ancestor's poems given to her by her poor mother and read a thousand times over. One of the famous West Lake poems by Yun Cai:

> *The lake ripples as four winds will.*
> *Fish rise, mouths gape like coins.*
> *West Lake might as well be an ocean.*
> *Heart's desire waits for shores to kiss,*
> *No balance until they touch.*

Yun Shu realised she was shaking. Oh, to hear a tender poem she had learned and filled with her own longings and desperate need for affection when she was a dismal wife in vile Chenglingji! To hear it from a handsome, brave, kindly scholar's lips as she imagined Yun Cai must have spoken it! What did he mean by uttering such a charm? Yet they had known each other so very long, nearly all their lives.

'Thank you, Teng, I . . . Now I must ensure my people are safe.'

He laid his hand on her arm. 'Let me help you, Yun Shu, and *we* shall ensure their safety. When that is accomplished, our own happiness should . . .'

Of all the moments to choose, Shensi selected that particular one to stick his head between them.

'Teng!' he cried, ignoring the Abbess completely. 'You won't believe what I learned in the city.'

The tomb-finder scowled as he realised neither Teng nor Yun Shu were listening. The lady had discovered something wrong with her hair, the straightness of her robes. Teng had an itchy eye.

'The North Gates are still open!' said Shensi, impatiently. 'I could not believe it! An oversight by the authorities. Hundreds are still passing through into the countryside. If we go now we might escape before Prince Arslan closes the gates!'

At this Yun Shu stirred eagerly. 'Shensi is right. Let us go, Teng!'

He was looking up at the tiny pavilion on the top of Holy Mount Chang.

'Go!' he said. 'The rest of you must go! Father says it is his wish to die in the Pavilion. I cannot leave him here alone. Yun Shu, I shall give you my bags of treasure to help you on your journey.'

'That is foolish!' said Shensi. 'Neither you nor Deng Nan-shi can stay here.'

'It is his command,' replied Teng. 'And he is my Father.'

Now Yun Shu laid her hand on Teng's arm. Despite surprise at her light touch, he did not pull away. If anything he leaned towards her.

'I have spent my whole life disobeying an Honoured Father's commands,' she said, significantly.

'He is too weak to walk,' countered Teng.

'Put him in a handcart,' suggested Shensi. 'I'll help you push. Only waste no more time!'

Thus the Deng clan's residence in Hou-ming City came to a hurried and inglorious end after six hundred years of power, wealth and renown. The procession of Nuns and servants were among the last to escape through the Gate of Ten Thousand Victories, hurrying into the overgrown ruins of the Northern Suburbs and along shadowy paths, before winding into hills obscured by bamboo groves.

thirty-seven

天命

Hou-ming City. Winter, 1323

Hsiung's cell occupied the topmost storey of a brick and stone pagoda erected during the previous dynasty for contemplation and moon gazing. Since then its many windows had been bricked-up, its elegant apartments turned into dismal lock-ups. If he stood upon the slatted wooden bench that served as his bed he could peer through a single gap in the wall providing clean air and light.

The afternoon was advanced when he struggled onto the bench to examine the world outside. From here he could see across the gabled, tiled roofs of Prince Arslan's palace compound, its many walls and buildings and shady corners. Beyond the compound lay the Prince's deer park, a large area of cleared ground planted with grass where, as recently as Hsiung's own boyhood, a dense lattice of streets had stood. Snow hid any remaining traces of the generations who formerly bloomed and withered there.

Hsiung watched a herd of deer led by an antlered stag trot across his line of vision. Craning his neck revealed the leather *yurts* of the Prince's Mongol kinsfolk and guests. Somewhere a dog barked furiously and another replied.

However hard Hsiung strained, he could not glimpse

Monkey Hat Hill: just the uneven wooden rooftops of the city flowing away like irregular waves – and, in the distance, the real waves of Six-hundred-*li* Lake, grey beneath a snow-laden sky.

Thick, feather-like flakes fluttered down and he held out his hand to catch a few. When he licked his palm the snow tasted metallic, earthy, pure.

Despite his natural strength, it was no easy feat to remain upright on the bench for long. The iron manacles and chains weighed a little more each day. Then there was the feebleness caused by hunger and running bowels, so that he shivered continuously. Yet the Salt Pans and years of war had accustomed Hsiung to physical privation. Desolate thoughts were harder to endure.

Hsiung stared at the dancing flurries of snow and recalled the trial – if so casual a hearing deserved such a title – that had confirmed his fate a few hours earlier. It was the culmination of a few interrogations organised by the Mongols since his capture on Eye Rock. All had followed the same pattern: jabbering accusations in their unpleasant tongue no one bothered to translate. All the while Prince Arslan, a barrel of a man with a golden wine cup constantly in his bejewelled hand, listened and occasionally roared out something incomprehensible. Only Jebe Khoja, who was not always present, remembered to arrange an interpreter. Then the ugly jabbering became a stream of denunciations detailing Hsiung's many crimes against the Great Khan of Khans.

Earlier, as he stood defiantly in unwashed clothes, weighed down by chains, he had noticed Admiral Won-du among the watching courtiers. Hitherto, Hsiung had refused to answer any questions or utter the slightest word lest he stumble and give them satisfaction. Today he had turned to the treacherous Won-du.

'Hey!' he called, ignoring the Mongol prosecutor. 'I have a question for you, Won-du.'

The court fell silent, amazed the bandit-chief had finally spoken.

'Tell me,' said Hsiung. 'Was Ying-ge a traitor all along or was it just you?'

There was murmuring as those fluent in Chinese translated Hsiung's words to neighbours. Won-du smiled slightly and bowed, glancing round to assess whether his new masters were listening.

'Of course!' he shouted. 'Except *you* are the real traitor! Thanks to you, *Lady* Ying-ge shall return here a wealthy woman!'

Hsiung showed no trace of emotion. 'So she has not returned yet?' he asked. Won-du glanced away. 'I see she has not. And that you are worried. Liu Shui will see to *her*.'

'Silence!' screamed the official who seemed in charge of the hearing. The prisoner was so obliging he could not be persuaded to speak again, even when informed he would be executed without delay.

Snowflakes swirling as the afternoon wore on. Hsiung heard booted feet ascending to his cell and climbed down reluctantly from the bench.

A wary procession entered, for Hsiung's last stand on Eye Rock was already a source of awed legend. First came two burly Mongol warriors armed with maces, then the gaoler. Finally, dressed in furs against the cold, Jebe Khoja. He examined Hsiung gravely.

'I must inform you,' he said, in heavily-accented Chinese, 'Prince Arslan has set your execution for tomorrow at noon.' When the prisoner did not reply or even look his way, Jebe Khoja chuckled. 'I must also inform you,' he said, 'Prince Arslan will hear pleas for mercy.'

Hsiung remained silent.

The Mongol prince nodded. 'That is what I expected of you.'

He turned to go then paused, glancing into Hsiung's expressionless face.

'Twice you could have killed me,' he said, 'yet each time you showed mercy. If the Buddhists are right you'll be rewarded for that.'

A tiny flicker in Hsiung's eyes encouraged Jebe Khoja to say more.

'I pleaded for Prince Arslan to spare your life.' The older man smiled thinly. 'But other voices have His Highness's ear and I could not prevail. Yet I did manage to persuade His Highness to grant you an honourable method of execution.'

If he expected gratitude none was forthcoming. Hsiung turned to face the wall.

'Quite so,' muttered Prince Jebe Khoja, and with that he left.

天命

As Jebe Khoja descended the winding staircase of the pagoda he was troubled by an unusual doubt. Should he have done more to save the brave bandit? But the precise reason his influence with Prince Arslan had declined was the series of victories won by the young rebel. Before those, he might have directed his drunken uncle. Not now.

Jebe Khoja's fine boots echoed on the stone stairs. Lower down the pagoda cell doors became more numerous and the faces of anxious captives appeared at tiny barred windows. Once the prince had been recognised and his name called out by one of the wretches, others took up the cry, pleading for mercy or simply a trial of any kind; others begged to be told what they had been accused of. Jebe Khoja ignored their pleas until he neared the ground floor. There, as he passed a low door, he was startled from his thoughts by a roar like a bull's.

'Prince! Hear me! I am Salt Minister Gui's spy! Listen! It is I who gave you the Noble Count of Lingling!'

The man's desperate plea held such conviction Jebe Khoja paused. The mention of Gui interested him. The Salt Minister had supplied vital information concerning the Yueh

Fei bandit's plans. It seemed odd this prisoner should know of it.

'Open this man's door!' he commanded, on a whim.

The gaoler was quick to obey and direct a lantern at the prisoner grovelling in his tiny cell. He was tall and well-built; broad at the shoulder and thick-armed.

'Your Highness!' blurted the man. 'My name is Chao! I am Gui's loyal spy and have been locked here by mistake . . .'

Prince Jebe Khoja yawned. Then he was struck by an odd coincidence.

'Stand up!' he ordered. 'I want to see him stood up.'

The guards dragged the prisoner to his feet. The man winced from a deep wound across his shoulder. Yes! Jebe Khoja had not been mistaken. Though the slave's face was quite different, his height and build were peculiarly like the doomed Noble Count of Lingling's. A ridiculous possibility crossed Jebe Khoja's mind. For a moment he stared at the prisoner, then turned to the gaoler.

'Make sure this one is not released or executed unless I say,' he commanded. 'I might find a use for him.'

The gaoler slammed the prisoner's door while Jebe Khoja swept out of the pagoda, braving gusts of snow and a buffeting wind. The odd possibility turned over and over in his mind like the snow, forming a solid drift of intention.

天命

The blizzard and gnawing wind fell away with the coming of darkness. A fat, waxy moon rose above Six-hundred-*li* Lake, casting an ivory sheen over rooftops and streets thick with ice. With it came profound silence. Since the rebels' campaign against Hou-ming the curfew was enforced rigorously. Only a few foxes, cats or wild dogs dared flit through the alleyways. Even the Entertainment District remained dark and heavily shuttered – though strains of clandestine music and laughter occasionally seeped into the night, confirming the old proverb *where bribes are paid, arrangements are made.*

In Prince Arslan's palace the only curfews were self-imposed. While courtiers revelled, drunk on looted wine and the power afforded by fine clothes and a full belly when most of the world lacked either, Prince Arslan's more restrained servants took to their beds. Among the latter was Salt Minister Gui, accompanied by his consort, Golden Lotus.

They lay side by side in a bed heavy with quilts and brocade coverlets. Antique bronze lamps burned on lacquered tables, flickering slightly when a draught found its way through the shuttered windows. Apart from the Salt Minister's regular, whistling snores the room was silent. Yet not all its occupants slept.

A mouse sniffed and twitched its nose before following a trail of crumbs. Up in the rafters a lizard opened one eye. In the bed beneath, breathing shallowly so as not to wake Salt Minister Gui and the fit of rage that would inevitably follow, Golden Lotus stared up at the ceiling. The slender man's brain was too busy for sleep. Perhaps it was his heart rather than brain, for Golden Lotus hoarded many unpleasant feelings.

Foremost among them was outrage, mingled with mourning and sheer hatred. But who did he hate most? Gui for betraying years of faithful devotion and service? Or the petite, smirking boy with shiny teeth like melon pips Gui had somehow acquired while accompanying Jebe Khoja in the campaign against the Yueh Fei bandits?

The exact circumstances of the boy's purchase were mysterious. Only one thing was certain: ever since his arrival Golden Lotus had been summoned less and less frequently to warm his dear master's bed.

How he regretted his folly in not collecting Yun Shu from Cloud Abode Monastery! If he hadn't succumbed to old resentments against her mother, Yun Shu would be here now. And that would change everything. Even Gui, hardened as he was to the world's disapproval, could hardly parade a new yellow eel boy before his daughter without a little shame.

Golden Lotus froze, afraid his anger had somehow woken the Salt Minister. But no, he was just snuffling and grunting in response to a dream, clutching Golden Lotus's hand so tightly it hurt. Perhaps the snoring had stopped for the night. Then a fresh, quavering whinny burst from Salt Minister Gui's hairy nostrils.

Golden Lotus allowed himself a sigh. It was no good regretting Yun Shu. The girl had vanished and even costly bribes had failed to uncover her whereabouts. All he knew was that the Nuns of Serene Perfection, and Yun Shu with them, had escaped from the city amidst a crowd of refugees, heading north. That was months ago.

Still the antique bronze lamps burned into the night. With them smouldered Golden Lotus's hurts and fears.

天命

Towards midnight fresh clouds rolled across Hou-ming, obscuring moon and stars. Then the snow fluttered softly again. Some settled on the topmost storey of Wild Goose Pagoda where lights showed behind the thick paper curtains of the windows. From within came a low, droning chant, interrupted by hoarse coughing and cries of alarm. Suddenly there was a grating noise and part of the sloping roof lifted, emitting noxious-smelling fumes and wisps of steam into the night.

Inside the pagoda, two gaunt and skeletal figures, heavily swathed in robes against the cold were bent over a small steel crucible in which a precious concoction bubbled as it cooled. Solemnly, Worthy Master Jian added three drops of mercury into the mixture, followed by grains of incorruptible gold. Meanwhile Void chanted a sutra adapted from the ancient book of bamboo strips, to connect the mixture to the Heavenly Immanence. Finally, and with great care, Worthy Master Jian added a few shavings of the Buddha's knucklebone to the crucible.

'Master,' urged Void, 'you must shape the pills with your own fingers and swallow them while they are still warm!'

Worthy Master Jian's eyes were bloodshot, his pupils dilated. He laughed triumphantly and picked out a pea-size scoop of the mixture between finger and thumb. The pill shone like a pearl in the candlelight and he felt a momentary confusion, remembering the Pearl of Dew he had harvested from Yun Shu and lost at the very moment of transformation. Her guileless, handsome face and earnest enthusiasm created a baffling picture in his mind.

'Repeat the sutra!' he ordered Void. 'My thoughts have become sullied.'

While Void chanted once again, Worthy Master Jian swallowed the foul pill as though it was the finest delicacy this world could offer. Waiting for the elixir to take effect, he gazed up at the gap in the roof through which stray snowflakes entered the chamber; waiting for Realisation; waiting to never feel pain or decay or loneliness or dismay; waiting to fly through the hatch in the roof of Wild Goose Pagoda, dancing round and round with joy like wind-driven snow . . .

天命

Five hundred *li* to the west in the limestone hill country around Holy Mount Chang, there was no snow. Just a fat, indifferent moon peering at the campfires of a large army preparing to attack Lingling Town, the last remaining Yueh Fei stronghold.

The streets of Lingling were a confusion of people loading carts with bundles and boxes. Only fools believed the Great Khan's soldiers would show restraint when they overwhelmed the town's few defenders. The rebellion that had lasted for nearly a decade was over. One could only hope for escape.

In what had once been the Noble Count's residence, servants

and officials rushed to and fro, claiming anything of value that might support them and their families through the harsh months ahead. One official, however, sat motionless upon a lacquered throne reserved for the Noble Count's First Chancellor. His fleshy hands were hidden by thick silk sleeves. The lamplight made his ruddy cheeks appear more flushed than usual – or perhaps they were red with anger. Certainly his small piggy eyes glinted as he examined the woman kneeling before him.

A dozen soldiers – the Chancellor's fanatical bodyguard – lined the walls of the audience chamber. They also examined the young woman on the floor with hostile interest.

'Well, Ying-ge,' said Chancellor Liu Shui, 'you have heard the evidence against you. Do you offer any defence?'

The actress had aged in the months since Hsiung sailed from Chenglingji. Her perfect oval face bore the first traces of crow's feet. Without make-up or fine clothes she resembled a trades-man's pretty young wife rather than a celebrated court beauty. Liu Shui's eyebrows rose fractionally.

'Then we may take it you have no defence,' he said.

Ying-ge looked up with a trace of her old defiance. 'Why do you keep me prisoner?' she demanded, shrilly. 'Ever since you forced me to travel here from Chenglingji I have begged and begged you to let me go!'

Liu Shui glanced at the captain of his bodyguards. 'Do your duty.'

'Please!' she cried, half-rising. The soldiers lining the walls stirred. 'The letters were forgeries . . . I do not know who put them in my papers! Yes, now I think of it, I *do* know! They were placed there by Chao and Hua!'

A deep sigh escaped from the fat man. 'Ying-ge,' he said, 'you have heard my verdict. Your treachery demands nothing less.' Ignoring her wail he carried on. 'After *that*, I shall leave Lingling with my followers for a monastery deep in the mountains. Rest assured I am known by a different name there, but due to my generosity over the years, we can be sure of a warm welcome. There I shall spend my time in meditation and calm. At least, that is my intention. Yet I fear I shall not gain the peace I have so richly deserved for my services to the people. Do you know why?'

Ying-ge stared up at him, for once without words.

'Because of my poor, dear boy,' he said, quietly. 'Oh, I am aware Hsiung will be executed by Prince Arslan. All because of *you*.'

Another wail escaped Ying-ge's lips. Liu Shui turned to the captain of his bodyguard.

'It is time,' he said, tonelessly. 'Be swift.'

The officer bowed and drew a long, heavy sword. 'A pleasure, Your Excellency,' he said, grabbing Ying-ge by the hair and pulling back her head to expose the neck.

'No!' shrieked Ying-ge. 'You cannot . . .'

'Carry on,' commanded Liu Shui.

'I'm carrying his child! I'm pregnant with Hsiung's child!'

'Halt!'

The officer's sword, tensed for the severing blow, froze. Yet his grip on her hair tightened so that she wept with pain.

'You are a confirmed liar,' pointed out Liu Shui, in a reasonable tone.

'No! Not this time!'

'Time is pressing, Your Excellency,' said the captain, 'we must be long gone before dawn.'

Still Liu Shui hesitated.

'Prove you are pregnant!' he said. Realising that was impossible, he added, 'Besides, even if you are with child, how do we know it is his? A whore like you, it could be anyone's.'

The captain raised his sword arm once more.

'It is his!' she sobbed. 'It is! A woman knows. You must believe me.'

For the first time since the Newly Adhered Fleet went down, Liu Shui's expression lightened a tiny shade. He grunted in wonder. 'Captain! Let her go, but bind her hands very tightly. She's coming with us. And let us hope, my dear,' he said, leaning towards her, 'that the child does resemble my dear, lost boy. Or your pretty little neck will be wrung out like a wet cloth by the good captain here.'

An hour later, a small group of horsemen cantered through the gates of Lingling, escorting a carriage with closed curtains. When, late the next day, government forces ransacked the Noble Count's palace they found no trace of his First Chancellor or even his concubine, Ying-ge, though special orders had been issued to protect her.

天命

An hour after midnight, Hsiung woke suddenly from a dream or memory of Monkey Hat Hill in the cool warmth of early summer, before sticky dog days brought discomfort and monsoon.

He had been leading Teng and Yun Shu through the bamboo groves towards their secret watchtower, all three squabbling over nothing as usual. Stiff branches and softer leaves brushed his bare calves. Sunbeams slanted through the trees. Parrots rose in a cloud of red and green, disturbed by the children's argument, so that Hsiung was tempted to order the others to be quiet. But he knew they would not listen. Although, even in his dream, he sensed a need to bend their wills to his own, Hsiung realised he didn't care. Let them quarrel! He was simply glad to walk along the sunny path, soft underfoot from yesterday's rain, its scents and textures and colours.

'This way!' exclaimed Hsiung as he opened his eyes. 'I'll go in front!'

But there was no one left to hear. He became aware of cold, iron manacles round his wrists, the unrelenting slats of the bench where he lay.

Hsiung rose hurriedly, kneading life back into his fingers.

He stamped his feet to warm them, flexing his aching spine as he paced the dark cell. Something up on the wall startled him: a soft, mysterious glow. Hsiung smiled at his own fancy, for it was just the moon's waxy, round face framed by the window. He stopped pacing and stared at the mother planet.

One by one his fears for the morning that was fast approaching, the day of his death, faded as he gazed up. The clear, pale light seeped from moon to eye to soul, its gentle illumination falling across the landscape of his spirit, tortured crags and swamps, dark forests and cave entrances so black it seemed light would never find a way in, never reach the shadows – and yet it did, a pale, calm light, merging with the dark lights that had so often danced demonically from vile corners in his soul to master him. Merging with the dark lights until they were dark no more.

Hsiung understood the moon was Liu Shui's patient face, so reasonable and moderate, that it always had been. A face that was firm and just when the need arose, always seeking to cast peace upon the world.

For a moment Hsiung recollected his own folly. How his misjudgements had betrayed the Yueh Fei cause. His breath became uneven as tears of silent anguish stung his cheeks. Only the steady, clean light of the moon offered peace; and, at last, he no longer despised himself as a failure. There was still one way to make amends.

Tomorrow he would die well for Liu Shui's sake. For the thousands who had trusted him. For old Deng Nan-shi, haughty yet generous. Perhaps, even, to prove himself a *xia* to two children long transformed by time. Hapless, well-meaning people like Teng and Yun Shu needed a strong *xia* to protect them. Dying well might bring them good fortune. It was the only sacrifice he retained.

Hsiung stared at the moon until it shifted across the sky and no longer blessed his cell. Suddenly tired, he lay on the slatted bench and slept thankfully, as exhausted children sleep, without nightmares.

天命

The condemned man was led from prison into a clear, frosty noon. Fresh snow glittered on the wooden walkways of Prince Arslan's palace. Despite chains and manacles he walked proudly, looking neither right nor left. The officials and soldiers accompanying him spoke in low mutters. A few palace servants and courtiers watched him pass. One or two shouted taunts, aware that the Noble Count of Lingling's strong hands were safely chained.

Soon he came to a large gatehouse in the palace walls. Here his escort halted. Standing in the doorway of a guardroom was Prince Jebe Khoja. The escort bowed low.

'Bring the prisoner in here!' ordered the Prince, pointing at the doorway behind him. 'We'll sew him into it here.'

The officials in charge of the execution whispered amongst themselves.

'Your Highness!' protested one. 'That is not customary!'

Prince Jebe Khoja's glance made the unfortunate man quake.

'Of course, Your Highness! Quickly, you fools! Did you not hear His Highness?'

The condemned man was prodded into the gatehouse, whereupon the door slammed in the officials' faces.

Time passed slowly for the men outside. Prince Arslan himself and many notable guests were waiting out in the Deer Park for the spectacle to begin. A special pavilion had been constructed for the occasion. The chief executioner was about to knock timidly on the guardroom door when it opened. Within, Prince Jebe Khoja sat on a low-backed chair. At his feet lay a thick sack stitched from animal hides and, from the groans and twitching, stuffed with someone alive. Again the chief official risked a protest.

'Your Highness!' he exclaimed. 'The prisoner should not be sewn into the sack until he has had a last chance to beg for clemency. That is the custom.'

'He does not want clemency,' said Jebe Khoja. 'And do not contradict me again.'

'Yes, Your Highness!'

'Carry him to where it is to be done and see it is done.'

'Yes, Your Highness!'

So the procession resumed its journey, emerging from the fortified gatehouse into an area of parkland before the palace. In the distance a herd of deer watched with raised heads, their tails ticking, then returned to scraping up roots beneath the snow. A path of churned slush and mud led from the gatehouse to a large pavilion with open sides. Here Prince Arslan sat upon a throne, swaddled in furs, awaiting the demise of the upstart bandit who had caused him such loss of face at the Great Khan's court.

Scents of meat and crackling drifted, attracting dozens of pacing crows. A whole pig roasted on one spit, the fire hissing when fat fell upon glowing charcoal. Other spits bore lambs, fowl of various kinds, even a freshly-skinned fawn. Such plenty tormented hungry bellies amongst the servants and soldiers.

'There he is!' exclaimed Prince Arslan, as the prisoner was carried out. 'Trussed up for the spit, eh!'

Friends and hangers-on laughed heartily. All were drunk.

'Let's see how he takes to having his meat softened up, eh!' declared His Highness, encouraged by the success of his earlier witticism.

The executioners bowed hurriedly and dragged the leather sack out into the snowy field. No cries emerged from the condemned man, just occasional grunts.

Once they were a respectable distance from the royal party, the executioners threw down their burden and hurried away, leaving the sack like a huge brown slug on the snow.

For a while nothing happened. The drunken on-lookers exchanged tales of similar executions they had witnessed, pointing out it was normally a privilege restricted to prisoners of royal blood. Several argued that trussing the prisoner in a rolled-up carpet, not a sack, was the proper way. Prince Arslan replied that they must tell his nephew, Jebe Khoja. It was he who had insisted upon this method of execution, citing a deep debt of honour. A clatter of hooves interrupted him.

Two horsemen in burnished lamellar armour rode abreast from the gatehouse.

'Why, the rogue!' roared Prince Arslan. 'He just wanted a little revenge of his own!'

At the cavalry's head cantered Prince Jebe Khoja on a large black charger with a braided mane and tail. Iron-shod hooves kicked up snow and frozen earth as the horsemen gathered speed, forming a single file that became an arrow cantering towards the leather sack.

'Hey-ah!' called Prince Arslan. 'Don't finish him off too quickly!'

Perhaps Jebe Khoja did not hear. Perhaps his need for revenge was too strong. Instead of riding his horse over the prisoner's legs, as might reasonably be expected, he galloped over where his head must surely be. There was a crump as a hoof struck the very edge of the sack. Then he was past and hauling at the reins to turn his mount. The next rider was more accurate, aiming his horse at the condemned wretch's lower half. Blows were struck and the sack jumped.

'Hey-ya!' bellowed Arslan. 'More wine, damn you! Hey-ya!'

But Jebe Khoja had wheeled his mount and was galloping over the sack. A loud crunching noise followed. The horse whinnied in fear, almost stumbled, for it had smelt brains and blood. Red was trickling through a small tear in the leather, staining the snow.

'Damn it, they know how to do these things better in Dadu!'

muttered one of the Prince's guests. 'What a hurry to finish the swine! Where's the sport?'

'Quite remarkable!' exclaimed another. 'The bandit did not cry out once. No wonder he caused you such trouble! Eh, Arslan? Ha! Ha!'

The Mongol Prince flushed angrily. For the whole world knew he had not managed to tame the Noble Count of Lingling without help from the Imperial Court, despite outnumbering the Yueh Fei rebels many times over. Prince Arslan watched Jebe Khoja's men drag the blood-stained sack away and wondered if it might be amusing to show his guests what remained of the bandit's face. Too late, the body had already disappeared into the Palace. Prince Arslan frowned at this unorthodox end to the execution, only brightening when servants arrived with platters of freshly roasted meat.

天命

Thus, one version of a death. There was another.

In this, an exhausted Hsiung was forced into the guardroom of the gatehouse, stumbling as the door slammed behind him. The stone-flagged room was gloomy except for feeble rays slanting through slit windows. In the centre sat Jebe Khoja on a low-backed chair, surrounded by warriors in lamellar armour and furs. At their feet lay a flat leather sack, long as a coffin.

Jebe Khoja stroked his beard and examined the prisoner. At first he seemed unsure what to say.

'Now then,' he said, finally, 'I did think of forcing another prisoner into that sack on the floor and pretending it was you. There is a fellow just your height and size in the prison.' He coughed apologetically. 'But I have my own sons to think of and letting you go would be an act of treason.'

Hsiung heard a voice protesting in a chamber behind them. It was oddly familiar, and somehow disturbing, though he could not hear the voice well enough to identify it.

'That could still be accomplished,' continued Jebe Khoja, 'I have the man nearby, as you've clearly heard. And the world would be better off without him. Only, you would have to promise to never trouble the Great Khan or his servants again. You would have to leave this province forever. I would require your firm oath, certain that, as you are a man of honour, I could rely on it.'

Hsiung looked at the Mongol in disbelief. Was this a vile trick? A cruel game to torment him? The Mongols were well known for prolonging the pain of those they conquered. They were also famed for a sense of obligation if one saved their own or a kinsman's life. One glance at Jebe Khoja's face revealed his sincerity. Hsiung could scarcely believe the risks the barbarian was taking.

'Is that all?' asked Hsiung. 'An oath to betray my cause? To abandon my former comrades?'

Jebe Khoja nodded solemnly. 'That is all. Then you shall live. In obscurity and far away, it is true. Yet you shall live.'

The prospect of freedom, so near and apparently immediate, almost mastered Hsiung. Then he recollected last night's moon and Liu Shui's pure face, how he had sworn an oath to die well. Without hesitation, he shook his head.

'Too many good men died because of my mistakes. I shall not survive to end my days drowning sorrow in a wine bowl. Our cause is proper and just! Soon the Mandate of Heaven will be stripped from you barbarians. I'd rather die than betray that.'

Jebe Khoja nodded. 'I am glad,' he said, 'for your honour's sake.' He pointed at the leather sack. 'You know what this is for?'

Hsiung stared haughtily at the wall.

'I see you know. I shall do you one good turn, whether you want it or not. Gag him!' he ordered.

Chained as he was, Hsiung could hardly resist as the warriors stuffed a silk cloth into his mouth.

'Now you cannot shame yourself by crying out,' said Jebe Khoja. 'Rest assured, Noble Count, I will send you to the next life as swiftly and painlessly as I can.'

Hsiung did not bother to struggle as he was stuffed head first into the sack. Its open end was sealed with coarse stitches of leather twine. He found himself enclosed in darkness, breathing a foul stench of animal hide through his nostrils, struggling with the panic of a drowning man. There was no air! How could there be air when only his nostrils were free to breathe? Hsiung fought for a mental image to quieten his terror. Last night's dream of the bamboo groves on Monkey Hat Hill returned to him, of leading Teng and Yun Shu to the safety of the ruined watchtower . . .

What came next followed quickly. Despite his intention to be contemptuously passive, Hsiung did panic and writhe. Yet as he heard the horses' iron-shod hooves pounding the earth, he closed his eyes and lay still, glad of the gag allowing him to die well. Even when a hoof shattered his thigh like a huge hammer crushing flesh and bone he could not scream. Soon a blow to the skull stopped the agony in his trampled legs with an explosion of light that flashed a great brilliance across the troubled landscape of his soul, so that sun and world and spirit scattered like stars fleeing the night sky and dissolved into darkness.

epilogue:

天命

How Clouds Float

Thus, one version of destiny for Hsiung. Many years later an old man in a scholar's blue robe watched a honking vee of plump geese fly east. And he remembered another destiny. A version he imagined for life not death.

Despairing of greed, misrule and war tormenting the Middle Kingdom, the Jade Emperor in Heaven sent an official to fly over the lands and discover who, if anyone, deserved the Mandate of Heaven.

'Be they low or high, humble or noble,' he declared, 'only their virtue matters. Any displaying *that* shall be rewarded with great fortune.'

The Heavenly Official bowed and departed.

Naturally, he was an Immortal with magical abilities peculiar to himself. Glittering blue eyes able to spot a gnat a thousand *li* away. A uniform of vermilion with the power to transform his appearance in a flash – and even render him invisible. Glossy, porcelain skin capable of illuminating the darkest places. The Jade Emperor also gave him an enormous white goose as his steed.

The wings of the goose beat rhythmically and lands passed below. He skimmed the topmost peaks of snow-capped mountains and silent bamboo forests. Deer leapt for shelter, disturbed by his shadow. Paddy fields of muddy water and untended rice reflected the clouds.

At last he chanced upon a long, winding valley in the midst of the mountains: Wei Valley, named after its principal river. His eye followed the silver ribbon of water to a large lake and marsh where the valley began. Directing his steed, the Heavenly Official headed for Mallow Flower Marsh, for he sensed it was a centre of flowing dragon lines.

On solid earth, he folded up his goose like a piece of paper, tucking it safely into his writing case. Motionless as a heron, he studied the muddy depths of the lake. Then noises other than hooting waterfowl and rustling reeds disturbed him.

Armed horsemen were approaching. They escorted mule-drawn wagons of various kinds on which servants perched. One of the carriages was fit for a wealthy merchant or gentleman, its carved wooden panels and roof preventing vulgar eyes from peering inside. Other wagons carried wooden crates branded with the seal: *Property of Salt Minister Gui*.

The Heavenly Official watched as the procession, led by a local guide, left the Western Highway at Mallow Flower Marsh and took a little-used dirt track into the mountains, a track leading nowhere but Wei Valley and its one settlement of note, Wei Village.

Intrigued by so strange a caravan in a remote corner of the Empire, he unpacked his magical goose, turned himself invisible, then flew over the marsh, taking the same route as the wagons.

The road climbed past hillsides clad with pine and bamboo. Early summer had inspired blossom; obliging insects flitted from bloom to bloom. A clan of silver-backed monkeys groomed one another in an ancient wild plum grove. As he flew by, the Heavenly Official became aware of people travelling in family groups toward Wei Village. Evidently a festival was gathering, for the peasants carried food baskets and wore their best clothes.

Circling a boulder-strewn peak, he spied dozens of buildings clustered round a river fed by glinting streams. Wei Village was neither small nor large. In its central square a busy festival-market had commenced – pyramids of vegetables and fruit; barrels of salt fish and pens for bleating, barking, clucking meat of every kind; a dozen wine-sellers and as many fortune tellers; a troupe of acrobats performing to an audience of gawping peasants and their children.

On one side of the valley, above the village, stood an ancient gentleman's residence. Three-Step-House ascended the hillside exactly as its name suggested – in three distinct stages. The lower buildings contained the servants' quarters, the middle an audience hall, and the topmost housed the Lord of Wei's family apartments.

On the opposite side of the valley, directly facing Three-Step-House, a group of new buildings rose. Labourers swarmed over ladders and scaffolds. Others pushed wheelbarrows. Remaining invisible, the Heavenly Official guided his goose to earth and packed it away. Then he transformed his appearance to resemble a travelling holy man.

Suitably disguised, he strode over to a group of Daoist and Buddhist priests, monks, geomancers and magicians who were inspecting the construction of a small gatehouse. Clearly a rite of benefit to the entire district was taking place. Proof, perhaps, that someone – on however small a scale – deserved the Mandate of Heaven. Chatting politely with a monk, the Heavenly Official learned the new building's name: Cloud Abode Monastery.

天命

The rite was scheduled for noon exactly, the central hour of the day. Abbess Lu Si was to lead the Nuns of Serene Perfection into their new home. Never mind that it lacked a roof. The wisest astrologers and geomancers in Chunming agreed any other day threatened misfortune. Given the disasters that had befallen the Nuns in Hou-ming Province, Abbess Lu Si and her confidante, Lady Yun Shu, were taking no chances.

At the prescribed hour, chimes sounded in the village and, stall by stall, the noisy market hushed into silence. The only sounds: wind in trees, wailing infants, birdsong, the bleat of sheep and goats.

Abbess Lu Si bowed low to the Provincial Daoist Officials from Chunming and received a scroll confirming Cloud Abode Monastery's status as a registered holy place. It had seemed sensible to alter the dates on the registration certificate so that, on paper at least, Cloud Abode Monastery had been officially inaugurated during the Tang Dynasty, five or more centuries earlier. Purchasing such a distinguished pedigree had involved many formal presents and negotiations carried out by Lady Yun Shu's husband, the Lord of Wei.

This latter gentleman, though blessed by a grand title, wore a scholar's modest blue robes in the style of the previous dynasty. He stood to one side as his wife followed the Abbess and her Serene Ones up a steep path that led towards Cloud Abode Monastery. Then he turned to thirty boys of various ages lined up in pairs behind him and gestured they should follow.

Chants drifted through the hushed valley. As the Lord of Wei hastened to catch up with his wife, he noticed she wept while reciting the familiar sutra: *The Dao that is bright seems dull . . . The great square has no corners . . . The Dao conceals itself in namelessness . . . The Dao breeds one; breeds two;*

breeds three; three breeds the Ten Thousand Creatures . . .

Rubbing impatiently at her tears, she glanced his way. Understanding passed between them. A joyful sorrow too layered for simple words. Stifling his own emotion, he led the long dragon of boys up the flinty path, all dressed in the dark blue of students preparing for the Imperial Examinations.

At the half-constructed gatehouse, the Nuns of Serene Perfection formed the shape of the Great Dipper constellation to please Xi-wang-nu, Queen Mother of the West. Nearby, a travelling holy man watched, sipping a bowl of 'green wine' that miraculously appeared in his hands when no one was watching. The rite and those conducting it interested him enough to ask how the Nuns came to set up a new holy place in this obscure valley.

天命

After fleeing Hou-ming the party led by Teng and Yun Shu had joined hundreds of refugees heading west. Despite the wealth they carried, Shensi advised a show of poverty on the road, in order to avoid being robbed. His wise counsel took them as far as a port on the Yangtze where it was easy to purchase passage on a large merchant vessel sailing upstream to the Western Provinces.

Yet here, at the borders of Hou-ming Province, tragedy occurred. The Honourable Deng Nan-shi passed from this life as he was pushed along the road in a wheelbarrow covered by blankets. It showed much character in Teng that he restricted his father's funeral to hiring an undertaker. This craftsman reduced the corpse to bones and ash in a large brick kiln. Afterwards the Nuns hurried west, concealing the venerable scholar's remains in a sealed jar amidst the baggage.

Day by day, Hou-ming Province fell behind until, after six months of intermittent travel and sojourns in humble shrines or temples, they neared their destination: Chunming. It was late spring and that ugly, ill-aligned city appeared at its best; blossom on the fruit trees and gaudy, bee-haunted flowers in every garden. Here the balance of the Dao asserted itself. After excessive misfortune came great luck – with a little help from the courteous, gentlemanly Teng.

Aware the outer defines most people's assessment of the inner, he had ordered an assembly of the entire party a day before their arrival in Chunming. At his insistence, the refugees reversed their whole policy of avoiding attention. Travel-stained clothes were packed away and fine garments donned. Deng Teng looked splendid in silks stolen from the short-lived Minister Chao, except they were far too large. The Nuns created a pious impression in their ritual robes, especially the Abbess Yun Shu. Even Shensi, Ts'u and Ts'an polished their weapons.

In this guise they entered Chunming and collected, as Teng had intended, a curious and admiring crowd. What could be more natural than leading such notable travellers to the fore-most Daoist shrine in the city, Golden Lotus Monastery? Its abbot, Wang Daguang, head of the Provincial Daoist Council, greeted the Serene Ones with garlands of flowers.

Well he might. The Daoist cause in Chunming had suffered under Mongol rule and the arrival of so many blessed Nuns stirred immediate excitement among respectable wives and ladies. Although women were unimportant in nearly every respect, the Abbot understood their power when it came to household devotion.

At last the Nuns of Serene Perfection were treated with honour, especially after it became known a descendent of Chunming Province's most famous son, the illustrious poet Yun Cai, led the Holy Ladies. Hundreds gathered to stare and make offerings at Golden Lotus Monastery, prompting Abbot Wang Daguang to establish an impromptu temple market.

All that summer Teng went back and forth between Chunming and Wei Valley, accompanied by Wang Daguang and the faithful Shensi. He found it an uncultivated place in every respect, its population halved by war, banditry and the incompetence of a Mongol lord – a descendent of a certain Khan Bayke, now thoroughly Chinese in outlook and as poor as those he ruled. Hence, Teng bought a large estate for a trifle. With it came a noble title that once belonged to his ancestor, Yueh Fei: *Lord of Wei.*

When he returned to Chunming expecting praise and gratitude, Yun Shu turned away, her eyelids fluttering dangerously.

'I see you are angry with me,' he said, taking her aside.

'Of course.'

'I do not understand.'

'Because Wei Valley belonged to the Yuns! It belonged to my family! Did not Yueh Fei state in the scroll you gave me that it should be ours forever? And now it is lost to us forever!'

He smiled. 'Forever is a long time,' he said, 'perhaps it need not be so long.'

'Oh, do not provoke me!'

Teng maintained his faint smile. 'I want to. I have always wanted to. Besides, *forever* could be as short as a week if . . . but I must do this properly.'

The next day Wang Daguang called upon Yun Shu with gifts and a proposal on behalf of his new friend, Deng Teng. The Abbot played the role of matchmaker with gusto, outlining the numerous advantages of such a match for one and all, not least the continuation of the noble line of Yun Cai. 'Think what a blessing *that* would be for our Province!' declared the Abbot.

Afterwards Yun Shu sought out Teng's company.

'It seems everyone thinks I should resign my position as Abbess and breed like the Ten Thousand Creatures,' she said. 'Is that why you asked for my hand?'

Both stared at different corners of the room.

'We do owe it to our ancestors to produce heirs,' conceded Teng, cautiously. 'You know that as well as I. It was Father's dearest hope. You were the daughter-in-law he always sought for me. His face lit up when you entered the room. But that is not why I ask. It is because I owe it to my heart. Perhaps you feel the same, dearest Yun Shu? Do you owe it to your heart?'

If she did, no immediate sign was given, for she bowed and left in evident agitation. Teng cursed himself for approaching such a delicate matter too bluntly. He feared Yun Shu believed he did not honour her. That she would never surrender her position as Abbess.

When Teng reported their conversation to Wang Daguang, the wily old priest smiled without revealing his teeth.

The refugees moved into Three-Step-House in autumn, nearly a year after leaving Hou-ming. They found it half ruined by neglect. Teng felt instantly at home amidst decaying roofs and walls, mildew and cobwebs, ghosts of former greatness.

During the bitter winter that followed Yun Shu agreed to become his wife, resigning her position as Abbess in favour of Lady Lu Si. A change widely anticipated, for people are neither fools nor easily fooled. Having fulfilled her duty to save the Nuns of Serene Perfection, it was clear Yun Shu felt no desire for the long, arduous task of re-building the holy order. And to be the Lord of Wei's wife offered great honour in a small world. Most importantly, she did owe her heart to Teng. To their longing for happiness in this world not the next.

Two miscarriages and a stillbirth demanded all the heart that the newlyweds could muster. Yun Shu grew certain Worthy Master Jian's elixirs had poisoned her womb. After each loss her husband found a hundred reasons why it could not be true. As someone who had returned from the dead he scorned obstacles.

Yet Yun Shu often stared bitterly into space or grew querulous and Teng laboured hard to distract her. They talked intimately at night, their chamber lit by glowing lamps, swapping poems and word games, reminiscing about Hou-ming and its characters, enjoying the simple pleasures of well-cooked food and strong wine. Or they would laugh over the trials of setting up home in this strange district with its even stranger accent. Later, when lamps were blown out, he marvelled at her knowledge of the bedroom arts. Some good had come of the bamboo books, after all.

Yun Shu pressed him to use Chao and Hua's looted fortune to build a new Cloud Abode Monastery, though it could be no more than a shadow of the Nuns' stolen glory. A boundary wall, a gatehouse, a shrine, a dormitory: they could afford no more. Even that hampered Teng's plans for Three-Step-House and the village's broken water wheels. Of course he agreed. He found it hard to deny his wife anything dear to her heart.

In one matter he did not consult anyone, other than the casket containing Deng Nan-shi's bones and spirit. A portion of Three-Step-House was set aside for a school, teaching any pupil who could pay a modest fee. There Teng led classes in the Five Classics required by the previous dynasty's Imperial Examinations, just as his father had taught the boys of Hou-ming. Teng never lost faith that the Emperor's Golden List would be restored as the proper means by which one gained high office, instead of wealth or birth or powerful friends.

Nearly three years after the Nuns of Serene Perfection fled Hou-ming Province, Cloud Abode Monastery was in a state of excited gestation prior to its rebirth. Yet Yun Shu still did not carry the child they craved.

天命

Gongs clanged and incense smouldered. Droning prayers continued into the afternoon. Twenty Buddhist monks from nearby Whale Rock Monastery arrived to offer a blessing. The new monastery's chief servant, Eunuch Bo-Bai, ensured the crowds were marshalled and that all priests, nuns and magicians were in their allotted places. He took a grave, dignified pleasure in his office and the crowd of country people viewed him with undisguised awe.

Eventually all but the most patient and pious among the well-wishers drifted down to the festival gathering pace in the village square. It was proper to leave the conduct of the rites to those best qualified – and generously paid – to enact them. People declared excitedly that a plentiful harvest could be expected with such a fine new monastery to bring the valley luck.

Teng also tired of chanting and prayers. Descending the new Hundred Stairs, he remembered how many times he had travelled their namesake in Hou-ming. Yun Shu remained at the inauguration, assisting Abbess Lu Si.

When Deng Teng reached the market place he sensed a changing mood. Everywhere people looked anxiously towards the road. A few stallholders discreetly packed away their wares.

He strode deeper into the market, glad to meet Shensi on the way accompanied by Ts'u and Ts'an, all wearing swords.

'Trouble,' said Shensi.

Teng nodded. Out of the corner of his eye he noticed a travelling holy man had appeared as if from nowhere. There came the sound of running feet. A dozen youths bearing halberds and other weapons gathered round their officers, Ts'u and Ts'an, for Teng had organised a militia in the village to deter brigands.

'Guests,' said Shensi.

'It is polite to greet one's guests,' said Teng. 'I shall do so before they take offence.'

Conspicuous in his scholar's robes, Teng walked through the subdued market until he encountered the source of the disturbance. Twenty armed men guarded wagons laden with boxes. Another carriage, its ornately carved doors closed, stood motionless. Horses snorted while grooms unpacked bags of grain. That small point set Teng more at ease.

'Lower your weapon,' he murmured to Shensi.

Teng walked over to the carriage with fancy doors. It looked oddly familiar, built in a style he remembered from Hou-ming Province. Then the door swung open and he stepped back in surprise. A round, Buddha-like man squeezed through the narrow entrance. Once upon the ground, he reached inside and helped down a boy – little more than three years old – who clutched the fat man's fleshy hand and stared fearlessly at the huge soldiers on their vast horses. Teng recognised a likeness in the child's face. He turned to the fat man and bowed low.

'Liu Shui,' he said, 'delighted to see you here!'

The old man returned the bow. 'Honourable Deng Teng, how I grieved to hear of your noble father's death!'

'I see you are as well-informed as ever,' said Teng, glancing at Ts'u and Ts'an, who avoided his eye. 'Honour us deeply by being our guest at Three-Step-House.'

Darkness had long fallen by the time the banquet celebrating the inauguration of Cloud Abode Monastery ended. Guests departed for chambers all over Three-Step-House or in the village below. Teng, however, lingered in an audience room beside the hall. He was not alone. Liu Shui, who had presented himself to the local worthies as a merchant-prince seeking good fortune by patronising the new monastery, sat with an untouched bowl of wine on the low, lacquered table beside him. At his request, Yun Shu was summoned from the women's quarters to join them. With her came the small boy who had stepped from the carriage. He lay asleep in a servant's arms, wrapped in blankets. The adults sat silently, examining the child.

'We are honoured by your presence,' said Teng. 'Does the noble cause of Yueh Fei still prosper?'

Liu Shui shook his head. 'We endure.'

'My ancestor will be glad even of that,' said Teng.

'I have not come to involve you in our struggles,' said the fat man. 'Quite the opposite. I have come with gifts.'

'You are kind,' said Teng.

'Perhaps. First, the boxes in the wagons bearing Salt Minister Gui's seal. Can you imagine what they contain?'

'No.' Teng turned to his silent wife with a smile to set her at ease. 'Can you?'

Yun Shu shook her head. She appeared distracted after her exertions during the rites. Teng easily imagined her contradictory feelings as Lady Lu Si led the ceremonies in the role of Abbess. Yet resigning that position, one of no practical importance in the world since the Nuns of Serene Perfection lost their ancient role as Chenghuang's guardians, had been entirely her own choice. Liu Shui's voice disturbed his thoughts.

'I have a pleasant surprise for you,' said the fat man, 'the wagons contain all that remains of Deng Library, which is to say, most of it. There are many relics of Yueh Fei. You would be surprised how I gained possession of them.' Liu Shui's smile grew wolfish. 'By the way, Lady Yun Shu,' he added, 'the last I heard, your father is well. He has been posted to supervise a new Salt Pans in the Yangtze Delta.'

Yun Shu nodded with every sign of gratitude for this information. Yet it was noticeable she made no further enquiries.

'Are you certain?' asked Teng, sceptically. He was referring to the restoration of Deng Library, not the Salt Minister's posting.

'Quite certain,' said Liu Shui, 'I have expended a great deal to be certain. The Salt Minister only agreed to surrender the library he stole from your father when I threatened to reveal that certain paintings he once sold for a large profit are forgeries. Paintings I believe you know rather too well.'

Teng bowed low. 'A fitting irony. If only my father were here to see this!'

Liu Shui cleared his throat. 'I have another gift, if you will accept it.' He glanced at the boy sleeping in the servant's arms. 'I suspect you have already guessed the child's father.'

Teng nodded. After all, the likeness was remarkable.

'What is the boy's name?' he asked.

'Hsiung,' said Liu Shui. 'What else?'

Yun Shu and Teng exchanged looks. She nodded fiercely and he relaxed, reaching out to take her hand though it was hardly decent in company. Liu Shui glanced away to spare them embarrassment, tears glistening in his eyes.

'What happened to Little Hsiung's mother?' asked Yun Shu.

The fat man's expression grew bland. 'She died suddenly.'

'How terrible,' murmured Yun Shu, looking at the child. 'I know all about lacking a mother. As does my husband.'

'Yes,' said Teng. 'Yet for Little Hsiung, we shall do our best to fill that lack.'

'Then I have every reason to sleep well tonight,' muttered Liu Shui. 'Every reason.'

天命

Not everyone slept. Many in Wei Valley had no wish for temporary oblivion unless it flowed from wine. The festival in the village below carried on into the night, punctuated by fireworks, raucous singing and countless draughts of 'green wine'. An impromptu circle dance between unmarried youths and maidens had to be dispersed by anxious parents. Even so, a few couples used the confusion to slip into the darkness.

It was a night when joy reigned in Wei Valley. Not only had a rightful Lord of Wei returned – and was not his wife a descendent of the poet Yun Cai! – but the new Lord was expending his own cash to build waterwheels, irrigation ditches, and clear ground left uncultivated by Khan Bayke's descendents. He had even established a school where none had existed since the last dynasty fell. To many, that seemed the greatest blessing of all in a land where sword, rather than brush, held sway. Little wonder they conceived dangerous hopes.

* * *

Up the hill, on the roof tiles of Three-Step-House, the Heavenly Official sat with knees pulled up to his chin. He was deciding where to fly next in search of flawless virtue. It seemed impossible to find anyone worthy of Heaven's Mandate.

Beneath the clay tiles he sensed Teng opening box after box and peering at the ancient scrolls and documents with growing excitement. Abruptly, the scholar stopped, touched his chin and smiled.

Laying down a dusty book, he made his way to a chamber where Yun Shu knelt beside a small boy's cot, stroking his hair to soothe him back to sleep. She glanced up. Her husband entered and she motioned him to be quiet as he knelt beside her. Reaching out, he took her free hand, entwining his fingers in hers so earnestly and lovingly she smiled at his foolishness. Continuing to stroke the child's head, she lifted Teng's ink-stained hand to her lips and held it there for a long moment.

On the roof, the Heavenly Official sighed. No sign of Heaven's Mandate here, just common affection. Unpromising material for a noble report to the Jade Emperor. Perhaps he should fly to the Great Khan's palace in Dadu and see whether anyone virtuous might be found among the grandees gathered in that splendid place. But ambitious minds, though promising when it came to gaining Heaven's Mandate, seemed narrow, dull and disagreeable after the pleasant day he had spent among the peasants of Wei Valley. Yet he was well aware that wickedness and bad faith were just as rife among them as in the Emperor's court. Only their scope for harm was smaller.

The Heavenly Official watched the Lord of Wei and his wife tiptoe, hand in hand, from the sleeping child's chamber to their bed. Suddenly he felt lonely. With a thoughtful nod he wrote three glimmering characters in the air with his forefinger. *Pine. Bamboo. Plum.* The characters glowed from gold to silver then faded. Later that night something quickened into life in Yun Shu's womb.

It was time to leave these mortals to whatever future they

might fashion together. A future cultivating the Dao's eternal cycles of growth and withering. One sown with goodwill, harvested by kindness . . . perhaps. No future is fixed where hearts float like clouds.

Reaching into his writing case, he unfolded the magical goose, hopped onto its back and rose into a heaven of space and peaks and stars – a thousand blessings of cloud.

Author's Note

As with the previous novels in this trilogy, *Taming Poison Dragons* and *Breaking Bamboo*, the characters and places are fictional. An exception is the hero-general Yueh Fei, whose memory is still venerated in China to this day.

The finally victory of the Mongols over the Song Dynasty in 1279 meant alien invaders now controlled the Middle Kingdom. Their Yuan Dynasty commenced with a semblance of good government under Khubilai Khan but by the time of his death their rule had deteriorated. Economic ruin set in: overtaxation by foreign tax collectors; inflation caused by printing worthless paper money (the Mongol version of 'quantitative easing'); costly wars; and extravagant wastefulness within the court.

The oppression and exploitation of native Chinese, who were literally fourth-class citizens in their own land, contributed to the people's troubles. Divisions between Chinese Daoists and Tibetan Buddhists imported by the invaders stirred religious discord. Khubilai Khan's successors proved increasingly inept and corrupt, provoking numerous rebellions of the kind led by Hsiung and his Yueh Fei Rebels.

Scholar-officials like Deng Nan-shi and Teng found themselves ejected from the upper strata of society, ranked lower than prostitutes. Crucially, the Imperial Examinations that once provided their gateway to high office had been abolished. Little wonder scholars detested the Mongols and mocked them as unwashed barbarians unfit to rule. Many literati were forced to gain an ignoble living as teachers and popular artists. Some, like Teng, wrote commercial dramas for the theatre. The scholars' fate demonstrates both the fragility of all culture and its ability to endure. In the end, writing brushes proved mightier than swords.

One or two commentators have suggested that in *Breaking Bamboo* the Mongols were presented in a far too negative way. Such critics will certainly be affronted by *The Mandate of Heaven*. The three viewpoint characters are all Chinese with little reason to love the 'barbarian' invaders. In reality, of course, there were as many 'good' Mongols as there were 'bad' Chinese – although contemporary notions of good and bad differed deeply from our own. The fact remains, however, that their government became emblematic in China of misused, incompetent power. Certainly that is what the Mongols represent to Teng, Hsiung and Yun Shu.

Although Yuan Dynasty China is a vanished world, I hope the concerns of the characters in this novel do not feel irrelevant to modern readers. Yun Shu's resistance to the odious practice of footbinding connects with struggles by generations of women to escape mental and physical confinements; as does, in a different way, her devotion to Daoism.

Above all, I hope Hsiung, Teng and Yun Shu – pine, bamboo and plum – affirm that the human spirit is a tree with generous and kindly roots, however tangled and diverse. If readers of this trilogy and its cast of characters find echoes of their own tangled lives, I shall count my labours more than repaid.

Acknowledgements

Many thanks to Ed Handyside for his continued faith in the trilogy and for making this book possible. His incisive editing also deserves a special mention. As ever, grateful appreciation for the help of Jane Gregory and everyone at Gregory and Company. A number of people were kind enough to read early versions of the novel and their comments were tremendously helpful: Alex Quigley's suggestions on the Worthy Master Jian clarified my thinking; Jane Collins went 'above and beyond' with her typo spotting; Dr Craig Smith's encouragement was appreciated deeply. I would also like to thank the numerous people who have supported this trilogy in diverse ways over the years, not least Dr Lily Chen and Miss Li Xiaoxi for their wonderful Chinese translations of *Taming Poison Dragons* and *Breaking Bamboo*. Finally, my biggest thank you is reserved for my wife, Ruth, without whom neither pine nor bamboo nor plum could have blossomed.

ALSO BY TIM MURGATROYD

Taming Poison Dragons

"A riveting story." John Green *The Morning Star*

Western China, 1196:
Yun Cai, a handsome and adored poet in his youth, is now an old
man, exiled to his family estates. But the 'poison dragons' of misfortune shatter his orderly existence.

First, his village is threatened with destruction in a vicious civil
war. His wayward second son, a brutal rebel officer seems determined to ruin his entire family. Meanwhile, Yun Cai struggles to
free an old friend, P'ei Ti, from a hellish prison.

Throughout these ordeals, Yun Cai draws from the glittering
memories of his youth, when he journeyed to the capital to study
poetry and join the upper ranks of the civil service: how he con-
tended with rivalry and secured the friendship of P'ei Ti. Above
all, he reflects on a great love for which he paid with his freedom
and almost his life.

Yun Cai must consider all that he is and all that he has ever been
before can summon the wit and courage to confront the warlord
General An-Shu and his beautiful but cruel consort, the Lady Ta-
Chi.

PAPERBACK £8.99   ISBN 978-1-905802-39-5

Breaking Bamboo

I, the great Khan Khubilai, order my armies to advance by sea, river, land and mountain. Those who serve us by persuading the treasonous to submit to our just rule shall be rewarded. . . those who persist in foolish opposition shall endure every woe imaginable. . .

Central China, 1264. . .

When Mongol armies storm into the Middle Kingdom, the descendents of the poet, Yun Cai, are trapped in a desperate siege that will determine the fate of the Empire. Guang and Shih are identical twins, one a heroic soldier idolised by the city he defends, the other a humble doctor.

In the midst of war, jealous conflicts over Shih's wife and concubine threaten to tear the brothers apart. Enemies close in on every side – some disturbingly close to home. Can the Yun family survive imprisonment, ruthless treachery and Kublai Khan's bloody hordes? Or will their own reckless passions destroy them first?

PAPERBACK £8.99   ISBN 978-1-905802-76-0